More praise for
Betrayed

BETRAYED

Bertrice Small

FAWCETT GOLD MEDAL • NEW YORK

A Fawcett Gold Medal Book
Published by The Ballantine Publishing Group
Copyright © 1998 by Bertrice Small

www.randomhouse.com/BB/

Library of Congress Catalog Card Number: 98-96287

ISBN 0-449-00182-2

Manufactured in the United States of America

First Hardcover Edition: February 1998
First Mass Market Edition: November 1998

10 9 8 7 6 5 4 3 2 1

To two dear friends, and fellow authors: Roberta Gellis, who always knows where to find it when I don't. And to Cynthia Wright, the little sister I always wanted.

PART I

SCOTLAND AND ENGLAND

Late Summer 1422-Spring 1424

Chapter 1

The silvery blue mists hung in streamers over the late summer field where the shaggy, large-horned cattle browsed placidly in the light of early dawn. The clansmen, hidden in the shadows of the tree line, watched as a lone figure moved carefully among the beasts, separating several of the creatures from the main herd and driving them off in the opposite direction.

"He's a cheeky devil," Jamie Gordon remarked softly, and not without some small admiration, to his eldest brother, the laird of Loch Brae.

Angus Gordon's eyes narrowed, a certain sign of his acute annoyance. Then he said in a cold, measured voice, "He'll be with his master in hell before the sun reaches the mid-heavens this day. *Loose the dogs!*"

Freed of their leads, the canines leapt forward, barking and baying frantically as they scattered the cattle in their desire to chase after the intruder violating their master's pasture. It was a mixed pack. Smooth-coated greyhounds, as gray as the skies above, and darker, wiry-coated deerhounds, bigger, bulkier dogs capable of bringing down a man on the run.

"After him, laddies," the laird called to his men. "We'll hang the thieving bastard from the nearest tree when we catch him!"

The Loch Brae clansmen moved from the shelter of the trees, running across the meadow after the now fleeing cattle thief, who was making for the forest on the far side of the fields. The clansmen knew their best chance of catching the thief was before he reached the safety of the woodlands, but their quarry knew it, too. That knowledge added speed to his desperate flight. He ran as if wings had been attached to his heels.

"God's boots!" the laird swore violently as the thief disappeared into the trees, the dogs close on his heels. "We've likely lost him."

"The dogs could still bring him down, Angus," his brother said hopefully. "Let's follow a bit further."

The laird shook his head as they ran. There was a stream not far into the woods, and if the thief was familiar with this territory, which he surely was, he'd head straight for it. The dogs would lose the track. Nonetheless he led his clansmen into the trees. Ahead of them the dogs continued to bay and then suddenly stopped. Almost immediately there was the sound of barking and whining.

"They've lost him," the laird said, irritated. "He has gone to water."

They came upon the dogs, milling about at the brook's edge. Jamie Gordon dashed across the stream, seeking to discover where the thief had exited the bank, but he was unable to find any tracks. Shaking his head, he crossed back over to his brother.

The laird was moving slowly along the bank, his eyes lowered. Surely the fleeing felon would have left some mark in the soft earth. Finally Angus smiled wryly. "Our thief is experienced at evading pursuit," he said thoughtfully. "Interesting." He signaled to his men. "Spread out upon both sides of the stream, and see if we can pick up the bastard's track. He canna have vanished into thin air."

For some time the Gordon clansmen moved carefully along the swiftly flowing water, but no trace could be found of their prey.

"Where could he have gone?" Jamie asked.

The laird shrugged. "We have saved the cattle," he said, "and while I should have liked to have hung the pilferer, I must be satisfied to have prevented their loss, Jamie-boy. Let's go home." Calling to his men, he turned and made his way out of the woodland, the clansmen following. When they had again reached the laird's pasture, however, Angus Gordon burst out swearing.

"Jesu! Mary!" he said angrily.

"Angus, what is it?" his brother asked.

"Look, Jamie-boy! The herd is short by eight head. God's boots! The son of a bitch doubled back!" Then comprehension dawned in his eyes. "No wonder we could not find a trace of him. He hid himself up in the trees. That great branch over the water! Of course! He went into the stream, throwing the dogs off, and swung himself up into the trees. That's why there was no trace of him, the clever devil. I have been a ruddy fool! We have been neatly diddled." He turned to his head herdsman. "How many does that make in the last twelve-month, Donal?"

"An even dozen, my lord," the herdsman answered. "Four last autumn, and now eight today. 'Tis bold, our thief is."

"Aye," the laird agreed grimly. "Bold as newly polished brass and a wee bit too clever for my taste, but mayhap not clever enough. The ground is yet damp from yesterday's rain. Not wet enough to betray our fleet-footed robber, but certainly damp enough for the heavy-footed beasties he'll be driving to make their mark in the earth. I'll wager we can track my cattle now. We'll give our thief a good bit of time to believe he has managed to outfox us; then we'll see if we can find his trail and follow it to his lair. I want him to have time to reach his destination. I don't want my cows stampeding among the trees and doing themselves an injury."

The laird, his brother, and their men settled themselves down to wait for a time. Pipes were lit. Oatcakes and flasks of cider were pulled forth and consumed. The talk was low. Finally Angus Gordon rose to his feet. He stretched his length in leisurely fashion.

" 'Tis time," he told the others, and they all got to their feet obediently, pipes knocked free of ash, flasks empty. "All right now, laddies, let's go!" the laird said. "A silver piece to the man who first finds the trail!" The clansmen spread out and shortly found the track of the laird's pilfered cattle. It led back into the forest at a different point, and across the same stream their earlier quarry had half forded. Then they began to climb a barely discernible path up the ben. The imprint of the cows' hooves was visible in the ground. A fine rain had begun to fall, but the trail clearly led to this path, and there was no other way but the way that they went. The woodlands were thick with the summer's green growth.

"Donal"—the laird turned to his chief herdsman— "where does this trail lead? Do ye know?"

"These be the lands of the Hays of the Ben, my lord," Donal replied, "but that old devil, Dugald Hay, and his wife, God assoil her good soul, are both long dead. I heard they had bairns at one time, but I don't know anyone who has ever seen them. I canna even be certain there is anyone left of that family."

"There is someone left, for they've taken my cattle," the laird replied grimly, "and when I catch the thief, we'll hang him as a lesson to all who would think to steal Gordon cattle."

Suddenly the pathway opened into a clearing on the edge of the mountain. Nestled against the top of the ben was a stone tower house. Beyond it was a barn built of the same material. *And there was a small meadow in which eight cattle were grazing placidly.* The laird of Loch Brae smiled, well pleased to have found his property, for he had no doubt it was his property. Now he had but to find the thief and punish him. Leading his clansmen, he walked boldly up to the sturdy oak door of the tower house and pounded upon it with his clenched fist. It opened almost immediately.

"My lord?" Before him stood a little old woman with sharp brown eyes. Her gown was clean, if well worn. Despite her size, she most successfully blocked his entry.

"I am the laird of Loch Brae," Angus Gordon said loftily. "I wish to see yer master."

"Well, ye canna see him unless yer willing to go to hell, and if ye did, 'tis unlikely from the look of ye that the devil would let ye come back," the old woman said sharply. "Dugald Hay be dead these past five years, my lord. Now I'll ask ye again, what is yer business here?"

"Who are ye?" the laird demanded, refusing to be intimidated by the old woman, especially in front of his clansmen, although he would wager that many were cowed by her.

"I am Flora Hay, the housekeeper here at Hay Tower. Whatever it is ye want, we don't have it!"

"How do ye know what I want?" the laird said, a slight smile lifting the corners of his mouth. He was curious as to who, or what, the old dragon was protecting as she stood so defiantly barring his way.

"I don't know what ye want," Flora told him, "but whatever it is, 'tis not here, my lord. As ye can surely see, there is little here of any value." She curtsied and attempted to close the door on him.

Angus Gordon swiftly placed his booted foot in the door, preventing her. " 'Tis a fine herd of cattle ye have in yon field," he said.

Flora nodded. "Aye."

"And just where did ye get such fine cattle?" he asked her.

"*Get?* We didn't get the cattle, my lord. We raised them. They are all we have, and are to be used to dower two of my young mistresses," Flora told him, looking straight at Angus Gordon without so much as a blink.

"These lasses are Dugald Hay's get?"

"Aye."

"And how many lasses did that devil's spawn beget?" the laird demanded.

"Flora! Flora! For shame! Don't keep the laird of Loch Brae standing on the doorstep. Ask him into the hall for a cup of cider." A young female had appeared behind the housekeeper. She was tall for a girl, and almost too slender. She wore a simple wool gown, dark in color, and draped across her chest was the red and green Hay plaid, which was fastened to her shoulder with a rather fine silver brooch. "I am Fiona Hay, my lord, the eldest child of Dugald Hay and his wife, Muire," she said quietly.

It was impossible not to stare. Fiona Hay was absolutely lovely. Her hair was the color of a raven's wing, with the faint hint of a blue sheen. She was very, very fair of skin. Her features were perfectly set in a heart-shaped face. She had small white teeth, a slim, elegant, straight nose, a lush mouth, and a pair of oval-shaped emerald-green eyes, fringed in thick dark lashes, that were looking directly at him.

"A-Angus Gordon, mistress," the laird finally managed to grate out, tearing his gaze from the girl.

"And yer business with the Hays of the Ben, my lord?" she asked him coolly, ushering him into the tower house.

"I want my cattle back, lady," he said bluntly.

She turned her emerald-green eyes on him, saying as she did, "I don't have yer cattle, my lord. Why would ye think I have yer cattle?" Her tone was deceptively innocent. She led him up the stairs into the hall. "Flora, cider for the laird."

"There are eight head of cattle in yer meadow, mistress," Angus Gordon said evenly as his brother and clansmen entered the hall behind them. "Eight head of cattle were stolen from my herd this very morning. The trail led up the ben to yer meadow, where eight head of cattle now graze. Ye don't have to be clever to solve such a puzzle."

"The cattle in the meadow belong to me, my lord," Fiona said calmly. "They are my twin sisters' dowry. I am sorry ye have lost yer beasts, but those in my meadow are not they."

How could anyone look so sweet and innocent and be so bold a creature, the laird wondered. He knew damned well that the cattle in the field beyond the tower house were his. She knew it, too, yet she could look directly at him and lie without a quiver. She was obviously her father's daughter. Of that he had no doubt, but it would shortly be settled. "My brother has just examined the cows for a specific marking that all my cattle bear. If the cattle bear that marking, then there can be no doubt that they are mine," Angus Gordon told her sternly.

"The cattle are mine," Fiona Hay said sweetly. "I

mark each of our beasts by nicking them on their left ear."

He was astounded. This was the sauciest wench he had ever met in all of his life! "What a most odd coincidence," he replied through gritted teeth. "My cattle are marked in the exact same way."

"Then it is simply my word against yers, Angus Gordon," she said in a dulcet tone.

"Ye know verra well that the cattle are mine, mistress," he responded angrily. "They are mine, and I mean to take them back!"

"*The cattle are mine,*" Fiona responded, but then her voice softened. "My younger sisters, Elsbeth and Margery, are to be wed tomorrow. Each brings her bridegroom four cattle apiece, my lord. Would ye ruin the only chance these poor lasses have to be respectably married?"

He had not yet gotten his cider, and he badly needed it, he decided. His own men were crowded about, listening avidly to the exchange between their chieftain and the lovely girl. He could see that their sympathies lay with the girl, not because they were disloyal but because Fiona Hay was fair, orphaned, and obviously doing her best by her family. *Or so it would appear.* He muttered a dark curse under his breath.

"Yer cider, my lord," Flora said, shoving a tarnished silver goblet into his hand while casting him a black and disapproving look.

"Jamie-boy, the cattle?" he asked his brother.

James Gordon nodded in the affirmative. "Left ears, all notched," he said cheerfully. "They *could* be ours, Angus."

"*Could?*" The laird shouted at his younger brother. "*Could?*"

"Well, Angus," Jamie replied, nonplussed by the

outburst, "if Mistress Hay notches her cattle on the left ear as we do, then who can tell whose cattle they are, unless, of course, the beasties could talk."

The clansmen in the hall chuckled, only to be silenced by a fierce glare from their master.

"Angus." James Gordon spoke low so that only his brother might hear him. "Don't be so stony-hearted. If the cattle are indeed ours, then the lassie was damned clever to have stolen them from beneath our very noses. Ye have more cattle than ye can count. Without them her sisters will not get their husbands. Ye canna take them back now. Besides, there is the chance they might be hers, and then ye would do a great injustice to the Hays."

"The cattle are mine," Angus said in a near whisper to James. "For God's sake, Jamie-boy, look about ye. 'Tis a poor excuse for a chieftain's house, this tumbling-down tower. And look to the girl. Beautiful, but as thin as a sapling, and the old woman, too. I will wager there is nothing in the stable even worth stealing. Did ye look?"

"An ancient plow horse and a pony, both as thin as their mistress."

"Then how, ask yerself, could they have a herd of eight fat cattle?" the laird said reasonably. "The cattle are mine. If I allow the lass to steal them and I don't punish her, or at least collect payment for them, every petty thief in the district will come to try and steal my cattle. I will forgo punishing her, for she is but a lassie, but she certainly canna give me their worth in any kind. So I have no choice but to take them back."

"At least give her the option of purchasing them," softhearted James said.

"Yer a kind lad, Jamie-boy," his elder brother said. Then he turned back to Fiona Hay. "The cattle are mine, Mistress Hay. We both know that is the truth of the matter. I will argue it with you no more. If, however, ye wish to purchase the beasts from me, I will gladly sell them to ye." He looked her directly in the eye.

She stared back. Tall with a hard-looking frame he was, Fiona Hay thought. Hair as black as hers, and green eyes, too, but a dark green, not the emerald of her own eyes. He couldn't take the cattle, she thought desperately. *He couldn't!* Not with Walter Innes and Colin Forbes coming on the morrow to wed her sisters. Why had she waited until the last minute to steal the damned beasts? If only she'd taken them two at a time over the last few months, but the truth was she hadn't the means to feed them. The cattle would have lost weight if they had been in her care for too long. She couldn't offer her prospective brothers-in-law scrawny cattle. She had attempted to take the creatures last week, but the cowherd's dog had set up a barking to wake the dead. She supposed that was what had alerted the laird of Loch Brae to watch his cattle more closely. What on earth was she to do?

"Well, Mistress Hay? Will ye buy my cattle, or will I drive them back down the ben to their own meadow?" Angus Gordon demanded.

A proposal, outrageous but possibly workable, entered Fiona's mind at that moment. He could not accept, but he would certainly be shamed by it and leave her in peace. "I have only one thing of value that I might give ye in exchange for the cattle, my lord," she told him, refusing to admit even now that they were his. "It is my most precious possession. Will ye have it?"

"Take it!" James hissed at his elder sibling. "Honor will be satisfied, and none will call ye weak, Angus."

"I would know what this valuable property is first, Jamie-boy," the laird told his brother. He looked again at Fiona. "What is this most precious possession that ye would offer me in exchange for my cattle, Mistress Hay? A dozen head of cattle don't come cheap, lass."

"Eight, my lord," Fiona replied softly.

"Twelve, including the ones you stole from me last autumn," he answered her as softly, his eyes meeting hers.

"Twenty head total. I'll need eight more head to dower my two youngest sisters, but they're only seven and ten years of age now, so I would not want them until Jean and Morag are old enough to wed. I canna feed them."

She was the most outrageous lass he had ever encountered, Angus Gordon thought again, amused in spite of himself. She audaciously stole his cattle, yet when caught, attempted to bargain with him for more of them. He was not as hard-hearted as Jamie thought, but if he allowed the girl to evade the consequences for her thievery, he'd have no end of trouble. He managed to keep the look on his handsome face severe, but it was not easy. His brother was right. Fiona Hay was a very clever wench. However, he was no fool. "Twenty head of cattle is a costly amount, Mistress Hay. Ye must be certain that what ye offer me in exchange for them has an equal or even greater value. Just what do ye propose to give me in exchange for my beasties?"

"My maidenhead," Fiona said quietly, her gaze never leaving his. She stood tall and proud and defiant.

"Jesu!"

The laird's amazement was evidenced only in a slight widening of his dark green eyes. It was the most brazen proposal he had ever heard. Then he realized that the girl did not expect him to accept her offer. He was obviously supposed to be so taken aback by her boldness that he would demur and depart, leaving her with his cattle. He smiled wolfishly at her. "I accept yer offer, Mistress Hay. *Yer maidenhead in exchange for twenty head of my cattle.* It seems a fair bargain, although I think ye may have gotten the better of me."

He had accepted her! Fiona grew very pale with shock. What kind of a man was he that he had accepted her? What kind of a fool had she been to have even made such an offer? The laird of Loch Brae spit into his palm and held it out to her. Her knees were suddenly threatening to give out on her. The Hays of the Ben might be poor, but they were honorable, or so her mam had always said, and Fiona had no choice now, lest she bring disgrace upon her family name. Spitting into her own palm, she reached out and shook his hand. "Done, my lord!" she told him, never once looking away, although her stomach was roiling with nervousness.

"Oh, no, Fi! Ye canna do it!" two young voices cried in unison.

The two girls pushed through the Gordon clansmen to where their elder sibling stood. They were auburn haired, amber eyed, and identical in features. Their distress was more than evident.

"The bargain is now struck, sisters," Fiona said.

"But if ye give him yer maidenhead, who will have ye to wife one day?" asked Elsbeth, tears in her bright eyes.

"If I don't give him my maidenhead, who will have *ye* to wife, Elsbeth? Or Margery either?" Fiona asked. "The Forbeses and the Inneses will have their dowries or they will not have ye, I fear. Besides, by the time I see Jeannie and Morag safely wed, I'll be much too old to marry. I won't mind growing old here upon the ben." She patted her sisters, comforting them as best she could.

"But what if he gives ye a child?" asked Margery.

"The Gordons take care of their own, Mistress Hay," the laird reassured her. "If yer sister bears my bairn, I will not desert either of them."

The twins began to weep simultaneously.

"Flora," their elder sibling said, "take my sisters to our chamber and stay with them until I call for ye."

The older woman shepherded the two girls off, alternately scolding and cooing at them as they went. "Now, hush, ye two. Up the stairs with ye! Embarrassing yer sister. And her so brave and only looking out for yer happiness."

"Tam, where are ye?" Fiona called out to Flora's husband.

"Here, mistress." An old man shoved through the clansmen.

"Have we cider enough to quench the thirsts of all these men?"

"Aye," he answered dourly.

"Down the stairs and outside with ye, laddies," the laird ordered his men. "Tam will bring ye cider. Refresh yerselves while Mistress Hay and I make final our arrangement. Ye, too, Jamie-boy." Angus didn't need James appealing to his conscience.

When the hall had emptied, Fiona invited the laird to sit by the fire. "I canna offer ye wine," she told him honestly. "I have but two barrels left in the cellar. The Forbeses and the Inneses are mighty drinkers."

He nodded and raised the goblet. "This cider will be fine. The weddings are tomorrow?" He settled himself by the hearth, but the blaze was small, offering little warmth.

"Aye, Colin Forbes is to wed Margery, and Walter Innes will wed Elsbeth. They'll be here with their clansmen and pipers early in the day. A priest is coming from the abbey at Glenkirk to perform the ceremony.

We don't have our own priest. My father didn't like priests, although my mother insisted on calling one each time she gave birth so we might be baptized, or buried. When she died giving birth to our Morag, he would not send for the priest. Morag is not baptized, nor was our mam shriven before she was buried. When our father died, I didn't call the priest for him, though he begged me to do so," she said with a fierce satisfaction. "I shall ask the priest to baptize wee Morag tomorrow after my sisters are wed. 'Tis not right she be a heathen."

"Ye'll come with me to Brae Castle after the weddings," the laird told her. "And yer two little sisters, and the old servants. They can't remain here, Fiona Hay. I'm amazed this tower has not fallen in by now. Ye'll all be safe with me." What on earth was he letting himself in for? Angus Gordon wondered. But of course he could not leave the two elderly servants alone to care for the two small girls in a dwelling about to tumble down about their ears.

"This is my home, my lord," Fiona said proudly. "It may not be as fine as yers, but I won't abandon it. Ye haven't the right to ask me. I have offered ye only my maidenhead. Though I know nothing about the business, ye can only take it once, I believe."

Angus Gordon had to laugh. She *was* as bold as brass, though he suspected she was afraid, even if she wouldn't show it. "Don't think for a moment, lassie, that I intend letting ye off for yer offenses, for I will not, but a maidenhead, even a royal one, is scarce worth twenty head of my cattle. Ye'll come back to Loch Brae with me and live there as my mistress until I deem that ye have worked off yer debt to me," he told her. "I'm a fair man, Fiona Hay. Yer sisters will live with ye, and yer servants, too. They will be well treated. I will care for them as if they were my own family. You will have regular meals, for if the bairns are as thin as ye and the two brides, then good food will not be amiss."

"We don't need yer charity!" Fiona cried.

"*Charity?* Nay, lassie, 'tis not charity. Ye'll pay me back for every penny, I promise ye." Reaching out, he took her hand, smiling slightly at her startled look when his fingers enclosed hers. "How old are ye, Fiona Hay?"

"Fifteen," she told him. Her hand trembled in his.

"When did yer mam die? I remember her long ago. She was to have been my father's second wife. The twins are her mirror image, but for their brown eyes."

"She died when Morag was born. I was but eight, but I became the woman of the house then," Fiona told him. "Our father died when I was ten."

He was astounded. Except for her two old retainers, she had been alone up here, raising her sisters since she was ten years old. "How did ye manage to make matches for yer sisters?"

"We went to the games last summer," she told him. "Anne met Duncan Keith there, and they were married last autumn. Margery and Elsbeth met Colin and Walter then, but they were too young until now to wed. Thirteen is a good age to marry, I think. Anne will not be here tomorrow, for her bairn is due to be born soon, and she has not been wed even a year. Duncan is verra pleased that she is such a good breeder."

He smiled at her. "Yer mother was, too."

"Aye, but Mam only birthed live daughters. Her three sons were born dead, or died soon after birth. 'Twas my grandmam's curse on our father, ye see," Fiona told him solemnly. " 'Tis why ye have the glen lands that belonged to my grandfather Hay. Did ye know him?"

"Aye. Ye didn't?"

"My father would not allow us to go into the glen, or our mam either, after he took her forcibly from her parents," Fiona explained. "He said our grandfather was a stubborn old man who would not see reason and would give away Hay lands rather than admit that he was wrong. He never forgave our grandfather and cursed him with his dying breath."

"Ewan Hay never forgave yer father for stealing his daughter away, but he was a fair man, proud and good. He would have liked ye, lassie, although I don't think he would have approved of yer bold ways."

"Would he approve of yer bold bargain with me, my lord?" Fiona asked him slyly. "I may be brazen, but I have done what I had to do in order to see to my sisters' futures. They have only me to look after them and protect them."

"Ye'll not shame me, Fiona Hay, with yer goodness," he teased her. "Ye must see, however, that I canna allow ye to go unpunished for yer crimes against me. If I did, I should open myself up to all sorts of difficulties from our neighbors, who would think me a weakling. I must help to keep this region peaceful for the time when the king returns to Scotland. I canna do that if I am thought ineffectual or craven. No, lassie, ye'll have to pay the piper."

"Do we have a king?" she asked, surprised. "I thought the Duke of Albany was our ruler."

"He was regent in the king's name, for King James has been held captive in England since before ye were born," he explained. "When the duke died two years ago, his son, Murdoch, took his place, but he is a weak fool. Negotiations are under way even now to bring the king home at last. I have spent time in England with the king. We are kin. Both our grandmothers were Drummonds."

Fiona managed to extract her hand from the laird's gentle but firm grasp. It was difficult to think, she found, when she could feel the heat of his skin. "Why has the king been in England instead of here in Scotland, my lord?" Her curiosity was overcoming her nervousness.

"Because he was captured by the English when he was but a wee lad. Ye see, his father, old King Robert, was not a strong king. He was past fifty when he came to the throne, neither sturdy of body nor majestic of presence, and he was given to deep black moods. He was truly unfit to govern, but he was a decent prince, and 'twas thought it better to proceed with the coronation. After he was crowned, however, his brother, the Earl of Fife, was made Governor of the Realm by the lords. There was much corruption, with lawlessness increasing daily. The king, a good man even if he was ineffectual, finally recommenced his responsibilities with much urging from the queen, Annabella Drummond, my grandmother's own sister. For the next few years he tried to rule, but 'twas not easy, for the high lords were used to having their own way.

"Then, two years before the queen died, she attempted a small coup. She saw the danger her brother-in-law posed. She wanted to be certain the oldest of her sons was secure in his position as heir to Scotland. The eldest of the royal sons, Prince David, was created Duke of Rothesay, and made Lieutenant of the Realm. The king's brother, however, objected so strenuously that the king felt he had to name him Duke of Albany. The queen died. Then David Stewart died mysteriously while he was with his uncle.

"The king feared for his only surviving son,

Prince James. He decided to send him to France for safety's sake. Unfortunately, the merchant ship upon which the prince traveled was captured by the English. The wee prince was sent to King Henry. The shock of learning of his son's capture killed old King Robert. His uncle, now Scotland's ruler, didn't try verra hard to regain the laddie's person, which was, perhaps, the best thing that could have happened. He surely would have killed the little king. The English, however, took good care of the lad."

"So now the king is coming home to Scotland?"

"Aye, he is. And Scotland will be the better for it, lassie. King James is a strong man. He'll keep a tight rein on his kingdom."

"He'll not be able to tell the clans what to do," Fiona said wisely. "The old chieftains don't like being told what to do. My father always said that those in the south never understood those of us here in the hills. And those in the highlands, he said, were even more independent. No king can rule all of Scotland in truth, I fear, my lord."

"King James will do his best," Angus Gordon said, allowing himself a small smile at her rather astute assessment of the political climate in their country. It seemed that as each year passed, the peoples in the south and those in the north grew further and further apart.

Old Tam came in, bringing a pitcher of cider. He refilled the laird's cup and poured one for his mistress, then disappeared again.

"You know the king," she mused.

"The English didn't mind the visits, for in a sense all of us who came to be with the young king were hostages for Scotland's good behavior. We came to keep company with our liege lord and to be certain he did not forget his own country, for the English captured him when he was verra young." He suddenly changed the subject. "Where am I to sleep tonight?"

"Surely ye don't mean to—" Fiona stopped, pale of cheek. *Not tonight!*

"Jesu, no, lassie!" Looking closely at her, he said, "Yer a sly wench, Fiona Hay. If I find yer not a virgin, I'll kill ye, I promise ye. Do ye swear to me that ye never have been with a man?"

"I am a virgin, my lord, and not dishonest, I promise ye. It's just that the house is small. My sisters and I sleep in the room above the hall, while Flora and Tam have their bed in the attic above us. Ye may sleep in the hall by the fire. There is no other place for ye but the stable. Yer men may rest there."

"When I take ye to my bed, Fiona Hay," he told her seriously, "it will be a pleasant experience for ye, I promise—and ye will not be afeared." He tipped her face up, looking intently at her with his dark green eyes. "Yer a pretty lass, but I see none of yer mam in ye."

"I look like my father, I am told," Fiona replied. "It is not surprising, for I was conceived, my mother told me, the day of her marriage to my father. She didn't love him, ye know, nor he her. He wanted her for the glen, but he didn't get it. He loved me, or so he said, for I was his firstborn, but then when my sisters kept coming and my brothers kept dying, he became impossibly cruel. The night our Morag was born, he took one look at her and howled his outrage. My mother lay dying, yet she somehow found the strength to laugh at him. He had taken her from the only man she always told me she loved, and only for the glen, but in the end she beat him, and he knew it. I believe my mam died a happy woman, my lord."

"My father never stopped loving her," he said, releasing her chin from his hold.

"I might have been yer sister," she said softly.

"But ye are not my sister, Fiona Hay. Yer a defiant little thief who will shortly be my mistress, though why I even accepted yer offer I'll never know. Ye will, I suspect, be more trouble than ye are worth. Still"—he chuckled—"ye'll not bore me, I'm thinking."

"No, my lord, I'll not bore ye."

He wasn't certain whether her words were a threat or a promise, and that in itself was intriguing. Standing, he stretched his long frame. "I must see to my men, Fiona Hay. May I take supper with ye?"

She nodded. "Ye may, and yer brother, too, my lord."

Finding Jamie, he proffered the invitation, but his brother refused.

"I want to return to Brae Castle and bring back our piper for the wedding," Jamie explained.

"Also bring back two casks of my best wine and two sheep ready for roasting, Jamie-boy. Mistress Hay will not be embarrassed by the scantness of her hospitality tomorrow. If I am to have the responsibility of the lass and her sisters, a poor reception would reflect badly on the Gordons of Loch Brae. Go now, and come right back in the morning, for the bridegrooms are due early."

Angus Gordon joined the Hay sisters for supper. It was a simple meal of rabbit stew, bread, and cheese, but it was served upon a polished high board on pewter plates with silver spoons. Fiona, very well mannered to his surprise, had introduced him formally to the two brides-to-be, Elsbeth and Margery. Then she had presented him to her two younger sisters, Jean, who was ten, and Morag, who was seven. Like the twins, Jean was auburn haired and amber eyed. She had a sprinkling of freckles across the bridge of her elegant little nose.

"Are ye *really* going to make my sister yer mistress?" she asked him bluntly.

"Aye," he drawled, amused. Turning to Fiona, he inquired, "Are all the Hay women as brazen as ye, lassie?" To his great amazement he saw that Fiona had blushed at her sister's inquiry.

"Jeannie, mind yer tongue!" she scolded her sibling.

"Well, Margery says ye are," Jean replied. "Didn't ye think we ought to know such a thing, Fi?"

Fiona ignored the query and introduced the youngest of the sisters. "This is our wee Morag, my lord."

Morag Hay was but a younger version of her eldest sister. Her emerald-green eyes surveyed the laird of Loch Brae. Then, following Jeannie's example, she curtsied carefully. "How do ye do, my lord," she lisped prettily.

"I do very well indeed, lassie," he answered her, enchanted.

Morag favored him with a brilliant smile, and when he grinned back at her she giggled. It was a wonderful sound, like water tripping over small rocks on a clear bright day.

"She does not usually take to strangers, particularly men," Fiona observed, surprised. "She isn't used to men. By the time she could distinguish between men and women, most of my father's clansmen had run off back to their relatives in the glen."

"I was raised with two sisters, and they have daughters, although not as old as Mistress Morag. I believe yer sisters will like Brae Castle," he told Fiona. "It is set upon a small island in the loch, and connected to the shore by a causeway. The lasses can learn to swim, and row their own boats."

"Ye speak as if we have some permanent arrangement," Fiona said to him, "and we don't, my lord."

"For now it is permanent. Afterwards, who knows? No matter, I don't believe yer grandfather, Ewan Hay, would approve of my leaving ye here upon the ben now that I've found ye. I think if he had but known ye, the lands in the glen would have been yers, and ye an heiress. Yer father was not just a cruel man; he was a foolish one as well, I fear. Ye could easily be in danger now that so many are aware of yer existence. Keiths, Innes, and Forbes all know ye live here upon the ben, alone and unprotected with but two elderly servants. Any of them could attack ye and steal yer lands, poor as they may be. Ye and yer sisters will be safer with me. Tomorrow I will make certain that yer brothers-in-law and their clansmen know that ye are under the protection of the laird of Loch Brae."

"I wonder, my lord, who is more dangerous? My brothers-in-law or ye?"

Angus laughed. Then, reaching out, he took her hand and raised it to his lips. "In due time, Fiona Hay, ye will learn the answer to yer question. For now I would but ask that ye trust me." He kissed the hand in his, turning it over to press his lips upon her upturned palm, his eyes never leaving hers.

Fiona felt as if she had been struck in the belly. She couldn't breathe, and she could feel her heart leap suddenly, then pound wildly in her ears. Startled, she pulled her hand away.

He gave her a slow smile. "Don't be afraid, lassie," he murmured so only she might hear him, and not be embarrassed. "I will not hurt ye. Harming ye is the furtherest thing from my mind." This morning, he thought to himself, suddenly bemused as to his softening in attitude, he had wanted to hang the thief who had stolen his cattle. Now all he wanted to do was cover her face with kisses. What sorcery was this wench practicing upon him? She had made a bold bargain with him that he fully intended she keep. She would pay in full for the cattle she had so daringly pilfered from his meadows. There would be no escape for Fiona Hay from Angus Gordon's bed.

Fiona arose quickly from the high board and shepherded her sisters up the stairs to their chamber. "We'll have to waken early so we can bathe. Ye'll not go to yer husbands dirty," she added, looking at the brides-to-be.

"He's verra bonnie," Elsbeth remarked as the door to their chamber closed behind them.

"Who?" Fiona asked.

Elsbeth laughed. "The laird, ye witless fool."

"He has the look of a rogue," Margery said primly.

"I like him," Morag said.

Jean looked thoughtful. "I wonder if he'll give us our own ponies? I'm going to like living at Brae Castle."

"How can ye be certain? Ye've never even seen it," Fiona said.

"It will be warm and dry, and we'll get to eat regularly," Jean said, thinking practically. *"I'll like it!"*

Fiona felt guilty at her sister's words but then wondered why she should. She had done her best for her siblings, especially in the years since their father had died. But it was true that Jeannie was always hungry and complaining about it, whereas the others, if they were also hungry, had not whined and fussed. "Wash yer faces and get out of yer clothes," she ordered the girls. "Morning will come before ye know it, and there'll be water to draw and heat for the baths. Elsbeth, Margery, are yer trunks packed for the morrow?"

"Aye," the twins chorused.

"Then see to the younger ones and get to yer beds. I must make certain the laird is settled and comfortable before I can sleep," Fiona told them, hurrying from the room before they might tease her further.

"She is giving up a great deal for us," Margery said slowly. "I wonder if it is right that we let her do it."

"And if we don't, what would happen to the rest of us?" Jean asked, with far more wisdom than her years allowed. "We'd all die old maids here upon the ben. No, tomorrow ye two will wed with yer laddies because that is the way Fi wants it to be. Then we shall go off to Brae Castle to live. If Fi pleases the laird, he will probably find fine husbands for our Morag and for me."

Fretting, Margery asked, "But what would our mother think of such an arrangement as Fi has made?"

Jean snorted. "Our mother did what she had to do to survive our father, and Fi will do the same to survive the laird."

"Ye don't know that," Elsbeth said. "Why, ye can't remember our mother, for she died when ye were barely three."

"No, I don't remember her," Jean admitted, "but Flora often says how like Mother in character Fi is, even if she looks like our father."

"Did I know our mother?" Morag wondered aloud as Margery wiped her face clean of the supper stew.

"Mam died when ye were born," Margery said.

"Why?" Morag said. She always asked why, though she knew the answer that she would be given.

"Because God wanted her in heaven, our Morag," Elsbeth replied in kindly tones. Margery drew off the child's gown, leaving Morag in her chemise to climb into the large bed she shared with the twins and settle herself in the middle, which was her usual place. "Now shut yer eyes, and go to sleep. Tomorrow is a big day for us all."

The three other girls finished their ablutions and, garbed only in their chemises, climbed into bed.

"I'll leave the candle burning for Fi to see by," Jean said, snuggling down into the feather bed she shared with Fiona.

In the hall below, Fiona found the high board cleared, but her two aged servants were nowhere in sight. She suspected they had already climbed to their attic and gone to bed. Folding back the wooden shutters on a sleeping space set in the wall near the fireplace, she hauled a feather bed from a storage chest and placed it in the space, adding a pillow and a coverlet. "When yer ready to sleep, my lord, ye'll find the sleeping space comfortable," she told the laird.

"Have ye slept in it, then?" he teased her.

"Aye," she said shortly. "Whenever our father wanted to use our mam, he sent us to the hall to sleep. Good night, my lord." Fiona hurried back up the stairs to her chamber.

Watching her go, he contemplated what a strange female she was. Saucy and bold she was without a doubt, yet loyal and protective of those she loved. She seemed to have little use for Dugald Hay, her sire, but then few had ever had use for the Hay of the Ben. He had not been a well-liked man, particularly after his rape of and forced marriage to Muire Hay, who had been betrothed to Angus Gordon's father, Robert. Dugald had kept to himself after that, siring child after child upon his unfortunate wife in his desperate attempt to gain his father-in-law's lands, for those lands would only be his if he sired a son on Muire. What had he been like in the years after Muire's death? How had it affected his daughters, particularly the fierce Fiona?

He smiled. She was really quite lovely. He would enjoy initiating her into the amatory arts. Even though he had earlier questioned her virtue, he knew without asking that she was absolutely ignorant about what transpired between a man and a woman. She had been too young for such things when her mother had died, and it was unlikely Dugald Hay had enlightened his daughter. *Unlikely?* Unthinkable!

Tomorrow night they would be safe at Brae Castle. Tomorrow night she would be his. Why did the thought excite him so? He had just met the lass. He hardly knew her. Yet he wanted to possess her, wanted to taste that ripe mouth, wanted to caress that fair white flesh, wanted to feel her lithe body beneath his. The laird of Loch Brae climbed into his bed space and, not without some difficulty, finally fell into a restless sleep.

He awakened slowly, realizing that it was still dark, although the skies outside the tower's window were graying. He heard soft sounds in the hall, saw shadows moving about. He reached for his sword and waited to see who the intruders were and what they could possibly want from this poor place. Then suddenly he heard a giggle, followed by an authoritative "shush," and he realized that there were no intruders. It was the Hay sisters.

He watched from his bed space as they struggled to maneuver a large oaken tub from its storage nook at the end of the hall, pushing and pulling it down the length of the room, setting it before the fire. The door to the hall was flung open then, allowing him to observe the girls as they carried bucket after bucket of water from the well outside, heating it in an iron cauldron over the fire, and pouring it into the tub until finally it was filled to Fiona's satisfaction. Two of the girls dragged a screen from another cranny, fitting it about the tub area.

"Elsbeth and Margery first," he heard Fiona say. There followed much whispering and giggling from behind the screen as each sister took her turn in the oaken tub.

Angus Gordon lay quietly, enjoying the sounds, his bed space quite cozy with the freshly built fire blazing away. He, too, came from a large family. Besides his youngest brother, Jamie, he had another brother, Robert, who was two years his junior, and two sisters, Janet and Meggie. His mother had been Margaret Leslie, the daughter of the laird of Glenkirk. She had borne her children over an eight-year period, dying as Muire Hay had in childbirth. How strange, he thought, that both he and Fiona Hay were the eldest of their siblings, and had each lost mothers when they were but eight years of age. At least his father had lived until he was grown, Angus thought gratefully. He had been a good man who grieved hard the wife he had loved and lost, as well as the lovely Muire Hay, whom he had also loved—and lost in an equally cruel manner.

"Upstairs, all of ye," he heard Fiona ordering her sisters. "I'll be with ye in a few moments' time. Flora, good, yer up! Is the bread baked yet? Give the lasses a loaf, some butter, *and* honey before they dress. I want to bathe, too."

"Oh Fi! Honey? This really is a grand day," the laird heard Jean say enthusiastically to her sister.

The hall grew silent. He could hear the sounds of splashing behind the screen. He could hear Fiona humming softly. Sliding from the bed space, he pulled on his boots and wrapped his kilt about his lean frame. He needed to pee, but first he would bid his hostess a good morning. It was simply too irresistible. Striding the hall, he moved around the screen.

"Good morrow, Mistress Hay," he said cheerily.

The emerald-green eyes looked up, slightly startled, but she made no great outcry. "Good morrow, my lord. I imagine we awakened ye, but 'twas time," she said calmly. Then she washed her face. Little else of her was available to his eyes but her shoulders and upper chest, for the tub was deep and well filled.

The most incredible urge overcame him. He wanted to lift her dripping from the tub, and kiss her cherry-red lips! He wanted to pull the pins that secured her black hair atop her head, and let it fall over her wet shoulders, where he might bury his face in the soft, fragrant mass of her tresses. Then he wanted to carry her to the dark security of the bed space he had only recently vacated, and make love to her until she cried with the pleasure he would give her.

Instead he bowed politely to her, saying, "Ye were a verra courteous hostess, Mistress Hay, and I thank ye for yer hospitality. I hope ye will not be offended, but I wanted to repay that hospitality. I sent my brother back to Brae for two whole sheep to be roasted and some casks of wine. By the time ye run out," he told her with a smile, "the Forbeses and the Inneses will be verra drunk, and fortunate to find their way back down the ben to their own lands."

" 'Tis most generous of ye, my lord," Fiona acknowledged as she vigorously scrubbed her neck. "I'll serve yer wine first, for it's certain to be better than the poor stuff my father had in his cellar. Would ye hand me my towel, please?" she requested sweetly.

Why the little vixen, he thought, half-amused, as he complied. He had sought to tease her, but she was giving him back as good as he had given her. Would she really arise from the dirty water in the tub while he was still with her? He decided to wait and find out.

Positioning the towel carefully before her so that he could view nothing of her charms, Fiona stood and wrapped the cloth tightly around her body. Then with the grace and dignity of a young queen she descended the narrow little steps from the tub to the hall floor. "Thank ye for yer help, my lord," she gently mocked him, turning and running up the stairs on slender white legs to the chamber she shared with her sisters. As she gained the landing, she looked down and stuck out her tongue at him.

The laird of Loch Brae burst out laughing. "Ye'll pay for that insult, Mistress Hay," he vowed, shaking his fist at her. He went out into the clearing before the tower house, where he found his men preparing themselves for the wedding.

James had obviously returned. Two shallow pits had been dug in the earth, and the sheep were already roasting slowly upon their spits over the hot fires. Angus Gordon walked into the woods near the tower and relieved himself, but even emptied of his waters, his manhood was still swollen and sensitive. He cursed softly beneath his breath. How could she be affecting him so strongly when he scarcely knew her? He had never known his lust to be so quickly engaged as it was now. He would have to slake that lust immediately, or she would drive him mad. He thanked God that she was too young and innocent to understand the effect she was having upon him.

By midmorning the priest had arrived from Glenkirk Abbey. His first order of business was to baptize Morag Hay. Then he went into the Hay burying ground and prayed over the graves of Muire and Dugald Hay. The skirl of pipes was heard coming up the ben from first one side, then the other. Elsbeth and Margery were almost sick with excitement. Which of the clans would reach the crest of the ben first? The Forbeses or the Inneses? A clan feud was averted, however, when by prearrangement the two families marched into the clearing before Hay Tower together. The Forbeses, in their blue-and-green tartan with its single white stripe, had come up one side of the ben. The Inneses, their tartan a more complicated plaid of red, black, and green with narrow stripes of yellow, white, and blue, had come up the other side. Each had a single piper with them and together with the Gordon piper brought back by James, the ben rang with wild and savage music such as it had never heard.

Fiona Hay, dressed in a fine green velvet skirt and white linen blouse, the red-and-green Hay tartan across her bosom, a small flat green velvet cap with an eagle's feather upon her dark head, stepped from the house. She wore the clan badge of a Hay chieftain on her shoulder, and her family's plant badge, a sprig of mistletoe, was pinned to her cap. "I bid those who are to become my kinsmen welcome," she said. "Have ye come in peace?"

"We have," the Forbeses and Inneses chorused.

"Come into the house, then, that we may celebrate the marriages between our families." She ushered them into the hall.

The hall had been swept clean. A roaring fire burned in the fireplace. The Gordon wine casks had been set up to one side of the hall. The high board glowed with candles. The clansmen crowded into the hall, Forbes, Gordon, and Innes plaids mingling. The two fathers of the bridegrooms immediately saw the laird of Loch Brae and hurried to pay their respects, for he was the most important chieftain in the near region.

They wondered why he was there. Then, simultaneously, each remembered that Angus Gordon had inherited the lands in the glen that had belonged to the Hay sisters' mother's family. Perhaps the laird felt some sort of responsibility because the lasses had been so unfairly disinherited, and had come to the wedding to smooth over any hard feelings.

Andrew Innes introduced his son, Walter, to the laird. Then Douglas Forbes presented his son, Colin. Angus Gordon was gracious, wishing both young men a long and happy life with their brides and, of course, a houseful of sons.

The Innes chief, bolder than his companions, asked, "What brings ye to Ben Hay, my lord? I was not aware ye knew Dugald Hay's lasses."

"Mistress Fiona purchased the cattle yer sons are receiving as dowry from me," Angus Gordon said pleasantly. "I have decided to take an interest in the welfare of the Hay sisters from now on, Andrew Innes. 'Tis not easy for them, although I will admit that Mistress Fiona has done well by her sisters so far. Still, when none knew they were living upon the ben 'twas safer. Now, however, I fear for them. I shall take Mistress Fiona, Jean, and Morag back to Brae with me today and set my own men upon the ben to watch over it for them."

"An excellent idea, my lord!" Douglas Forbes said jovially, with a smug grin at Andrew Innes. The Forbes chieftain knew that Innes, a recent widower, had planned to court Fiona Hay this very summer, with an eye to annexing the lands upon the ben for himself. *And he hadn't intended taking no for an answer.* Douglas Forbes chuckled softly to see Andrew Innes so neatly foiled. He had not been happy at the thought of an Innes taking over the ben, and its lands, but he had a wife, and all his sons were wed.

The priest from the Glenkirk Abbey announced
that he was ready to begin the ceremony. Fiona Hay led
her sisters down the stairs, putting Elsbeth's hand in
that of Walter Innes, and Margery's hand in that of
Colin Forbes. The twins were garbed as their elder sister, in green velvet skirts and linen blouses. Neither
wore a plaid, or a cap upon her head. Instead their hair
was loose and flowing to signify their innocence and
virtue. In their hands they carried posies of wildflowers
that Jean and Morag had gathered for them earlier. The
priest performed the ceremony for the two bridal couples together. When he finally pronounced them man
and wife, each of the bridegrooms carefully laid their
own clan tartans, in sash form, across the breasts of
their brides, afixing them to the girls' shoulders with
pretty pewter pins. Margery's was decorated with a
piece of green jasper; Elsbeth's was studded with black
agate. As the pipes began to play once more, the young
couples kissed each other, and congratulations rang
through the hall.

Fiona noted with gratitude several Gordon clansmen aiding her two aged servants in passing wine to
her guests. The wedding party settled itself about the
high board. There were trestles below for the others.
Plates were heaped high with lamb, fresh bread, butter, and cheese. The goblets never seemed to grow
empty. When everything had been eaten but there was
wine yet to be drunk, the trestles were pushed back to
the sides of the hall. Crossed swords were laid upon the
floor, and as the pipes began to play, the laird of Loch
Brae danced for the entertainment of the guests, nimbly
treading between the swords, slowly at first, and then
prancing more quickly until the dance reached its end-
ing. With a shout each bridegroom followed him. The
hall rang with merriment and goodwill.

"Yer most graceful, my lord," Fiona said. "Ye have made more than one contribution to this day, and I am grateful to ye for it. I don't believe this wedding would have been as fine without ye."

Angus Gordon nodded in acknowledgment of her appreciation, and then he said, "That silly fool, Andrew Innes, lusts after ye. Have ye noticed it, mistress?"

"It isn't me, my lord," Fiona laughed. " 'Tis the ben and its lands he wants. That's all."

"Then he's a fool, Fiona Hay, for yer far more valuable than the lands ye believe he covets, and tonight ye shall be mine!" His voice was ragged with his desire, and he silently cursed himself for being so open with her. She would learn soon enough her power over him.

She could hear the hunger in his voice, a hunger she could not understand. A hunger for what? The intensity of it, however, sent a ripple down her spine. For a brief moment she closed her eyes in order to regain her composure. It wasn't that he frightened her, because he didn't. Rather, he excited her with an unspoken promise of something wonderful to come. She should probably be very ashamed of herself, Fiona thought, but she wasn't. She had made an outrageous bargain with this man, but what else could she have done if these marriages were to be brought successfully to a favorable conclusion? She had done the right thing. What happened to her did not matter. Fiona would put a high price on herself, for if she was to be the laird of Loch Brae's mistress, Jeannie and Morag would get better husbands for themselves. Fiona promised her mother when she had died that she would look to her lasses, and Fiona had done so.

It was two hours past noon, and time for the brides to depart with their new husbands. Their chests with their clothing and linens were lifted up by their new clansmen. Outside the house, Fiona turned over four cattle apiece to each of her brothers-in-law. "The dowry, paid in full," she said, and they accepted them, nodding in agreement. With each clan's piper playing and leading the way, the Forbeses and the Inneses departed down their respective sides of the ben, driving the beasts before them. The brides hugged Fiona, Jean, and Morag but once, then were happily gone, arms linked with those of their new husbands. The remaining Hay sisters stood with Flora and Tam until the sound of the pipes had faded completely. It had been a gray day, but they had not noticed until now.

Flora sniffled, wiping her rheumy eyes with her apron. "God keep them safe, my bairns," she sobbed.

"Now, then, old woman," her husband said gruffly, but Flora cut him short.

"Don't ye scold me, Tam Hay!" she said fiercely. "Yer just as brokenhearted as I am, and don't ye attempt to deny it!"

The Gordon clansmen were beginning to regroup in the clearing before the tower house. "It is time for us to go, too," Angus Gordon said to Fiona Hay. He turned to the elderly servants. "I would have ye stay here tonight. Pack the lassies' belongings, and tomorrow my brother will return with the men to bring ye to Brae."

"Aye, my lord," they chorused, accepting his authority, and Flora curtsied to him.

"Can we walk to Brae by nightfall?" Fiona asked him.

"Jamie has left the horses at the foot of the ben," the laird told her. "Have ye ever ridden?"

"The pony, but not often," Fiona admitted. "I

would like to learn to really ride, my lord. Will ye teach me?"

"Aye, lassie," he promised her, taking her hand in his. "I will teach ye to ride all manner of beasties before much more time has passed. Come, now, and let us go home to Brae." He turned and called to the two younger girls. "Jeannie, Morag, we are ready to go. Follow closely now, and don't get lost in the trees."

"Will I ever come back here, my lord?" Fiona asked, suddenly unsure of herself for the first time. Had it been only yesterday when he had come into her life? Somehow it seemed much longer.

"The ben is yers, lassie, as Dugald Hay's eldest child," he reassured her. "I'll keep it safe for ye, and I'll keep ye and yer sisters safe, too, but first we have a wee matter of payment for the eight cattle that have gone off down the ben with the Forbeses and the Inneses, and the four that went with the Keiths last autumn. Are ye ready to meet yer obligations, lassie?"

"Aye," she said slowly, and her heart beat just a little faster as he squeezed her hand.

Chapter 2

Fiona Hay had never been farther from home than Glen Hay, a small valley separating the bens of Brae from her own mountain tower. They had walked down the treed slope to the glen, where the horses were waiting for them. The laird had casually ordered that two of his men take Jean and Morag up upon their mounts. Little Morag had gone, wide-eyed, with a big, red-bearded clansman, a man called Roddy, who lifted the little lass up and, giving her a kiss on the cheek, set her before him. Jean Hay, however, chose her own companion.

"Take me up with ye, Jamie-boy," she wheedled the laird's brother, giving him her most winning smile.

"And have all the lasses at Brae laughing at me for carrying a bairn like ye? I think not, Jeannie Hay." James Gordon was seventeen and thought himself quite a man.

"Then I must walk all the way to Brae, for I'll ride with no other, Jamie-boy," Jean answered him boldly, not in the least discouraged by his rude refusal, or the fact that she was only ten.

"Take her up with ye, Jamie-boy," Angus Gordon ordered his brother sternly. "We don't have time to stand here and argue." He bent, and lifted Fiona into the saddle before him. "Are ye comfortable?" he asked.

"Aye." She nodded as they moved off. She had never been in such close proximity to a man before. The hard arm, firmly clasped about her narrow waist, was disconcerting, but even more confounding was that the only way she could be truly comfortable was to lay her head against his shoulder. The leather of his jerkin was soft against her cheek, its coolness offsetting the heat she felt in her face.

"If ye don't breathe, Fiona Hay," he said to her as they rode, "ye'll soon swoon. There is nothing to be afeared of, lassie." He struggled with the urge to kiss the top of her head in its velvet chieftain's cap. What on earth was the matter with him?

"I'm not afraid of ye, Angus Gordon," she replied. "I am simply in awe of so many new places and experiences. I've never been farther than the glen in all my life, and we only just came to the glen last year for the games. Our father didn't want confrontations with our grandfather." She drew a deep breath, blew it out gustily, and then she laughed up into his face. "Aye, that's much better!" she said.

"Have ye any idea of what ye have really agreed to, Fiona Hay?" he asked, suddenly overwhelmed by a surprising wave of guilt. This was no simple peasant lass. This was a maid of good family. Despite her thievery, it had been as wrong of him to accept her brazen proposal as it had been for her to even make such a suggestion of payment to him. Yet had he not, he would have looked the fool before his men . . . before everyone. Now, however, he was having second thoughts.

"Tell me exactly what I have agreed to, Angus Gordon," Fiona asked. "In truth I have never known a man. I have never even kissed one. I know a maidenhead is the most valuable possession of any woman. I know when it is lost outside of marriage a lass is not considered pure. I realize that in giving myself to ye I will not be fit to become any man's wife, but I don't mind. I promised my mam on her deathbed that I would see my sisters safely wed. It is great good fortune that my sisters have fallen in love with the men they married. My mam insisted that they not be sent to loveless marriages." She took a deep breath. "Now, tell me what I face."

The simply spoken frankness of her words, said without any remorse, or even a touch of self-pity, impressed him. He realized that Fiona Hay was as proud as he was. She would insist upon keeping the bargain she had made with him. She would never admit to having stolen his cattle, he suspected, but her innocent willingness to meet her obligation to him stemmed from an innate honesty. Only Fiona's deep desire to keep her promise to the desperate, dying Muire Hay had driven the lassie to the pilferage of his herds. He should have looked to the welfare of Ewan Hay's young granddaughters before he had so casually annexed the glen to the Gordon holdings. Perhaps if he had, this situation would not have arisen.

"My lord?" She looked anxiously into his handsome face.

"Between yer legs," he began slowly, "is an opening into yer body. I will join my body with yers through that opening." He didn't know how else to explain it to her. He wasn't certain there was another way.

Fiona looked a trifle confused. "How?" she asked him. "How will ye join yer body to mine, Angus Gordon? Certainly there is something ye are not telling me." A small chuckle escaped her. "This is as hard for ye as it is for me, I expect. I don't imagine that ye have ever had to make such an explanation to a lass before."

He laughed, almost relieved by her practical approach to the whole matter. "No, sweetheart, I have never had to explain bedsport to a maid, and yer right. I have forgotten something. We will be joined by an appendage that all men are blessed with."

"I think I have heard of such a thing," Fiona said thoughtfully. "Is it called a manhood?"

"Aye," he answered. "Where did ye hear of one before?"

"When our sister, Anne, married Duncan Keith, she came after a few months to tell us that she would have a bairn by Lammas next. I asked her if she was still happy with her man. She said, aye, she was, that Duncan has a verra fine manhood, and kept her happy. I asked her what a manhood was, but Annie just laughed. She said 'twas not for a maiden to know such things and that when I wed would be time enough for me to learn about manhoods."

"I have told ye enough for now," Angus said. "Ye will learn by example, Fiona Hay, but I promise ye that I will not be rough with ye. There are certain men who enjoy being cruel, but I am not one."

When they had finally reached the shores of Loch Brae, Angus Gordon drew his horse to a stop so she might see the castle in all its beauty. He loved his home deeply and never grew weary of it, happy to remain there. "Brae Castle," he told her.

Fiona caught her breath in wonderment. She had never in all her life imagined such a beautiful place.

Brae Castle had been built in the year 1295, in the reign of John Balliol. This unfortunate king had sworn his fealty to the English king, Edward I, better known in Scotland as the Hammer of the Scots. The castle was situated on an island just off the north shore of an inland loch. The loch was considered small in comparison to the more famous lakes of Scotland, but it was big enough, being almost a mile and a half across at its widest point and four miles in length, for protection.

The island was connected to the shore by a wooden bridge. The builder of the castle had originally thought to construct the bridge of the same stone as the castle, but his wife, the legend went, had pointed out that in case of an attack, an enemy could march easily over a fine stone bridge right up to the doors of the castle, whereas a wooden bridge could be torched, making it difficult for an enemy to reach the island.

The area between the bridge and the castle itself was kept in field. There were no trees or large bushes behind which an intruder might hide. The shoreline had no sandy beach. It was very rocky, making it difficult to gain the land unless one came over the bridge itself, or via boat to the small landing on the south side of the castle, which was guarded round the clock.

The laird nudged his horse around a bend in the shore to the bridge that connected with the castle, and they crossed over. Grooms came to take the Gordon brothers' horses as they clattered into the stone courtyard. The laird dismounted, lifting Fiona down, setting her gently upon her feet. He then took Morag, who was already half-asleep, from Roddy. The little girl's head fell heavily against his shoulder. Angus Gordon handed her to a young maidservant, who hurried from the house, instructing her where the child was to be put to bed.

"Jean will share the chamber with her," he told Fiona, who looked about for her.

Jean still sat upon James Gordon's horse. "Will ye not help me down, Jamie-boy?" she cooed at him, her amber gaze soft and inviting.

The young man flushed beet-red, and with obviously gritted teeth he reached up and set her upon the pavement. "How old is this wench?" he demanded of Fiona.

"Ten," she replied. "Why do ye ask?"

"She is not ten," he muttered balefully. "And if she is, she is possessed by the demon of a well-versed courtesan. Ye would not believe the things she said to me as we rode down the ben."

"Jeannie!" her elder sister said, scandalized by the young man's words. "What have ye done? And what did ye say to James Gordon?"

"Only that when I was older I wanted to lay with him," Jean Hay replied sweetly. "He is verra bonnie, is he not, Fi?"

"Jean Hay, ye will remain chaste until I find a good husband for ye," her sister said in her most severe tones.

"Oh I don't mean to be his mistress like ye will be the laird's mistress," Jean said blandly. "I mean to marry Jamie-boy one day, Fi. I think he will make a grand husband!"

"I'd never wed a bold baggage like ye!" James Gordon declared.

"Aye, ye will," Jean told him calmly. "When I finally get my titties grown, ye'll not be able to resist me, Jamie Gordon. Just ye wait and see." She smiled sweetly at him.

"Jean Hay," the laird said sternly, "ye'll behave yerself, or I will personally paddle yer skinny little rump. I can see ye'll need to be kept busy while yer in my custody, and busy I shall see yer kept. Now, follow along after Giorsal, who will show ye yer chamber. If yer hungry tell her, and she will bring ye food."

"Thank ye, my lord," Jean said, not in the least put off by the scolding she had received. "Good night, Jamie darlin'," she said, and hurried after the maidservant carrying little Morag.

Rolling his eyes to the heavens, James Gordon disappeared toward the stables, and only when both of them were out of earshot did the laird burst out laughing. "He has not a chance against her." He chortled.

" 'Tis not a bad idea either, unless, of course, in the next four years either of them falls in love with another. Would ye accept James for yer sister Jean, Fiona?"

"If he learns to love her, aye. I've never known Jeannie to behave so boldly," she said apologetically.

"She knows what she wants," he told her with a smile, leading her into the house. "Still, she will have to obey me while she lives under my roof. How old was she when yer father died?"

"Five," Fiona said, "but she remembers little about him. Ye see, he was disappointed when I was born, but I was his first child, and he loved me in his strange way despite the fact that I was not the son he so desperately desired. I think he felt a wee bit of guilt for the manner in which I was said to have been conceived. I was born nine months to the day my parents were married. I think he always believed I was the result of his rape of my mother, and I may have well been."

"Ye know the *whole* story?" the laird asked, a trifle shocked.

"Aye," Fiona nodded. "Flora and Tam were my mother's personal servants since her childhood at Hay House. They hated Dugald Hay with all their hearts for what he did to my mother. Because he loved me, they made certain that I knew his sins, for they did not want me growing up estranged from my mam. But my father was not so loving of any of his other daughters. Each one was a reminder to him that unless he sired a son on my mam, he could not have the glen. We kept my sisters out of his sight as much as possible," Fiona told the laird. "If any of them came too close to him, he was just as apt to beat them for their mere existence as for any fault they might have. He slapped Anne so hard once that she lost a tooth, but she was young and another grew in its place, praise God! Jeannie and Morag, being the youngest, hardly knew him at all, and are not used to men in their lives. I think ye'll take some getting used to, Angus Gordon."

He laughed again, escorting her into the Great Hall.

A tall, austere-looking man hurried forth. "Welcome home, my lord!" His bright blue eyes fastened upon Fiona Hay. "I understand that ye have caught the thief who was pilfering yer cattle."

"Indeed I have, Aulay, and I have been offered payment in full for the cattle. The matter is closed. This is Mistress Fiona Hay. She and her sisters are now in my custody. They were all alone upon Ben Hay with only two old servants in attendance. She and her two little sisters are safer here at Brae. Her servants will arrive tomorrow. They are elderly. See they are made comfortable." He then turned to the girl by his side. "This is Aulay, my steward, Mistress Hay. He will assign a maid to ye."

"Nelly, I would think," the steward said, his blue eyes twinkling. "She is a young lass, too, but she has more sense, I'm thinking."

"Indeed?" Fiona said sharply. She would not be cowed by any man, but particularly not by a servant.

"Aye," Aulay responded calmly.

"Don't try to get the upper hand with Aulay," the laird warned Fiona. "He's been at Brae since the day of its creation, I think, and is the real power here, are ye not, old friend?"

"If my lord says so," the steward said with a small smile and a bow.

"Are ye hungry, lassie?" the laird asked, and Fiona nodded. "Come," he said, leading her to the high board and seating her.

Almost at once their goblets were filled with a fine

red wine such as Fiona had never tasted. It had a fragrant bouquet to it, and she drank half her portion before she even realized it. Platters were set before them. One held thinly sliced salmon on a bed of greens. Another contained a fat duck, and the third a haunch of venison. A loaf of hot bread was brought, along with a small tub of sweet butter and a half wheel of hard cheese. There was a bowl of small green peas. Fiona's eyes widened. She had never seen so much food and so much variety on a table in her life. Meals at Hay Tower had always been simple. One dish, bread, a vegetable if she could find one. She ate heartily and unabashedly, taking from each platter and dish, devouring half the loaf herself, and almost half of the sweet apple tartlet that was brought to conclude the meal. She downed two cups of wine without so much as a blink.

The laird watched her with a mixture of awe and amusement. He had never seen a woman of such good appetite. "Ye enjoyed yer meal?" he asked her with droll understatement.

Fiona smiled blissfully, her green eyes narrowing, catlike. "Aye! I've never had such a feast. Do ye eat this way every day, my lord?"

He nodded, and then said, laughing, "But ye canna, sweetheart, or ye'll grow as plump as the cattle ye stole from me."

She laughed with him. "No," she promised him. "The women in my family don't run to fat, my lord."

"I'll be watching ye closely, Fiona Hay," he teased her.

"How many servants do ye have?" she asked him.

"Ye met Aulay," he began. "His wife, Una, is my housekeeper. Beathag is the cook, and she has a helper, Alice. There are four maidservants, and when we need them several of my clansmen help within the castle.

There are stableboys, a gamekeeper, several herdsmen, and some others I canna remember, lassie."

"With all those mouths to feed," she wondered, "will there really be room for Flora and Tam, my lord?"

"Aye," he reassured her. "Aulay will be happy to have Tam to help him, and Flora must look after yer sisters as she has always done. I will give her Giorsal to help her, for I can see the old woman is a wee bit frail now, but I will not relinquish her duties out of loyalty to yer late mother, may God assoil the sweet soul of Muire Hay."

"Thank ye, Angus Gordon. Yer a good man," Fiona said quietly.

He flushed at her words. She almost made him feel in her debt instead of the other way around. "Ye will want to go to yer chamber now, lassie," he told her. He looked about for someone to show Fiona the way, and Una seemed to materialize out of a dark corner of the hall.

"I will show Mistress Hay, my lord," Una said. Like her husband, she was tall and spare. "Come, lassie. Ye'll want a bath, I've no doubt, to rid yerself of the stink of the horses and yer journey."

Fiona followed her obediently, asking, "Are my sisters settled, please? I don't want them to be afeared. They have never been away from home overnight before, and they will miss our Flora."

"They are fine, lassie," Una reassured Fiona. "The wee one has been fed and put to bed already. The other is eating down in the kitchen. I have never seen a child tuck away so much food as that bright-eyed girlie is now doing."

"Ye didn't leave Morag alone, did ye? She is fearful of the dark when there is no one with her," Fiona said worriedly.

"No, lassie. Giorsal is sitting by her cot, and there is a light burning as well. Don't fret. The bairn will outgrow her fear eventually. Yer mam was like that when she was a wee one, and she outgrew her fears by the time she was six."

Fiona was amazed. "Ye knew my mother?"

"Aye," Una said calmly. "I was born a Hay, lassie. I only became a Gordon when I wed with my Aulay." She led Fiona down a corridor and up a flight of stone stairs into another hallway. "Did ye really steal the laird's cattle?" she slyly asked the girl as she opened the door to a large chamber and ushered her inside.

"He believes I did," Fiona said, refusing to admit her guilt to anyone, even now.

"Yer grandfather, God assoil his good soul, would not approve the arrangement ye have made with the laird," Una said frankly.

"Then he should have made provision to dower his granddaughters," Fiona snapped. "Instead, he and my father continued their feud to their graves, leaving me with five little sisters to provide for, and not so much as a merk to my name to do it with, may God help me! Well, I have married off Annie, Elsbeth, and Margery to their sweethearts, and my arrangement with the laird will assure that Jeannie and Morag will have fine husbands. I do what I must, and I'll hear no more about it, Una Gordon!"

Una nodded, not in the least offended by the girl's outburst. She had learned what she wanted to learn. The lass was no adventuress out to take advantage of her master. She was her mother's daughter, for certain, accepting her fate for the sake of those she loved. "Ye'll be verra comfortable in this chamber," she told Fiona calmly. "The fireplace draws well and is large enough to heat water for yer bath, as ye can tell by the cauldron hanging there now. I see Nelly is already attending to her duties. She is my niece, and a good lass. I canna imagine where she has gotten to, however."

Her words had scarcely died when the door opened and a young girl hurried into the room, carrying a silver tray upon which was a carafe of red wine. Sticking out from the pockets of her apron were two silver goblets. She was a pretty creature with bright blue eyes and carrot-red braids. Placing her burden upon the table, she then curtsied to the two other women. "I have already begun warming the bath water, Mistress Una," she said politely.

"Aye," Una answered approvingly, "and ye have fetched wine. Good. Well, I can see ye have yer duties well in hand, Nelly. Greet yer new mistress, Fiona Hay, and I'll be on my way."

"God's greetings to ye, lady," Nelly said, curtsying prettily.

"God's greetings to ye, Nelly," Fiona returned. The girl looked to be about her own age.

"I'll bid ye good night then, Mistress Hay," the housekeeper said, and she departed the room.

"I'll get the tub," Nelly said briskly. "Whew! I can smell the horses on ye. Did ye ride far today, lady?"

"From the bottom of Ben Hay," Fiona replied, then looked about the chamber.

This was to be her new home, and it was far grander than anything she had ever had. She wondered if her sisters were as finely ensconced. It was, to her eye, a very elegant chamber. There were heavy draperies of crimson velvet drawn over the shutters that covered the windows. There was a fine big bed with curtains of scarlet and cream-colored brocatelle hanging from polished brass rings. But the ultimate luxury was indeed the fireplace. There had been but one at Hay

Tower, in the hall, but their bedchamber above the hall had been so cold on many a winter's morning that the contents of the night jar had frozen.

"Can I help ye?" she asked Nelly as the girl struggled to wrestle a round oaken tub from its storage space behind a small door.

"No, thank ye," Nelly said, rolling the tub before the fireplace. " 'Tis just getting it out 'tis tricky." She began emptying a line of buckets set up by the fireplace into the oaken tub. "The lads will be up with more hot water any minute now. It cools on the way from the kitchens, but that is why I have this big kettle over yer fire." No sooner had she spoken than there was a knock upon the door. At Nelly's bidding the door opened to admit a line of young clansmen bearing two buckets apiece, which each dutifully dumped into the tub.

It was a fine tub, Fiona thought. It stood about three and a half feet in height. The sturdy oak was made even stronger by several iron bands that had been wrapped about the tub. The outside of the tub was polished smooth and clean, and she suspected the inside would be as well. Despite her early morning bath she was beginning to look forward to a lovely long soak in the tub, for her muscles were starting to tell her that riding was a sore business. The last of the water bearers disappeared out the chamber door, Nelly closing it firmly behind them.

Fiona pulled off her cap and laid it aside.

"I'll help ye, mistress," Nelly told her. " 'Tis me duty." She quickly undressed Fiona, then said, "Pin yer hair up, lady, while I add the boiling water. Do ye like it good and hot?"

"Aye," Fiona said, a trifle embarrassed to find herself totally naked before a stranger, but Nelly didn't seem to take any notice as she cheerfully went about her task of swinging the iron arm holding the black kettle of boiling water out from over the fire, lifting it up using a cloth to shield her hands, and pouring it gingerly into the oaken bathtub.

"There now, and we're ready," Nelly said briskly as she helped her new mistress mount the two steps up so she could enter the tub.

Fiona sank down into the hot water with a gusty sigh. "Ahhh, Nelly lass, nothing ever felt so good to me as this does now," she said.

Nelly chuckled. "Ye've never been on a horse before?"

Fiona shook her dark head. "They're hard creatures, and I've a soft behind, I fear."

Nelly laughed. "I prefer me own feet, thank ye," she replied.

Suddenly there was the sound of a door opening, and a tapestry hanging upon the wall by the bed was lifted up as the laird stepped into the room. "Good evening, my dearie," he said to Fiona. "Ye may continue in yer duties, Nelly." Then he sat down upon the bed.

"My lord!" Fiona had finally managed to find her voice.

"Aye, lassie?"

" 'Tis most unseemly that ye be here in my chamber while I bathe," Fiona protested heatedly. "Please leave at once!"

"Lassie," he explained in an amused voice, "watching one's mistress bathe is a pleasure, and I'll not be denied it. Besides, I see little more of ye than I already have seen. Nelly lass, bring me a goblet of wine before ye begin washing yer mistress." He stretched his length out upon the bed, the pillows at his back, accepting the silver goblet the wide-eyed Nelly handed him. "Thank ye, Nelly."

Blushing, Nelly curtsied and hurried back across the chamber to the tub where Fiona sat glaring angrily at the laird. "The soap has a nice fragrance of heather," the girl said softly as she set to work to wash her mistress. Lathering her cloth, she gently scrubbed the creamy back and shoulders, the slender neck and arms, quickly rinsing them. "Ye'll have to raise yer legs, one at a time, lady, or I canna do them," she whispered. Grimly Fiona followed the girl's soft instructions. "Oh lady, how are we to do the rest if ye canna stand up, and ye canna with *him* here."

Fiona's eyes met the wicked glance of the laird as he sprawled lazily upon her bed. With a small mocking gesture he raised his goblet to her. Not a word passed between them, but Fiona was aware of the silent challenge. Taking a deep breath, she stood up, saying as she did, "Hurry, Nelly, 'tis chilly. When ye've finished, I'll want to soak a bit. While I do, please warm my night attire."

Nelly swallowed hard but went swiftly about the task of finishing her mistress's bath. She heard the laird's deep chuckle, yet did not see him once again raise his goblet to Fiona in appreciation of not simply her charms but her defiance. As for Fiona, she kept her glance impassive, although she was frankly mortified at having to display herself. She knew she was too damned slender, and her breasts were no bigger than young apples in early autumn. They would never really be big, she feared.

Angus Gordon drank his wine, but he hardly felt the heat of the liquid as it slid down his gut. He viewed Fiona's nakedness, astounded by the sensuousness of her form. Everything was in perfect proportion, even her pretty little breasts. They would grow a bit fuller in time, he suspected, but he hoped they would never lose their curvaceous charms or the pert sauciness of their pink nipples. He could not see much else, for the height of the tub precluded it, and Nelly was discreetly attempting to shield Fiona from his curious gaze. After draining his cup, he set it aside and stood up, even as Fiona sat quickly back down in the tub.

"Ye've done yer duty nicely, Nelly," he complimented her. "Now go to bed. Yer mistress won't need ye until the morning." Firmly, a hand beneath the startled girl's elbow, he ushered her from the room. Closing the door behind Nelly, he made a great show of turning the key in the lock. Then he came to perch upon the edge of the tub. Reaching out, he twirled a damp tendril of Fiona's hair between his fingers, noting with admiration the creaminess of her neck and shoulders.

"Yer as bold as ye accuse me of being, my lord," Fiona said softly, surprised to find that her voice was in working order.

"A man should be bold, but a woman should not be," he answered her quietly. Her emerald eyes were really quite spectacular, he thought.

"Are ye just going to sit there while I soak?" she demanded.

"Aye," he said calmly. "Ye canna soak forever, lassie."

Silence descended, a silence so heavy it felt oppressive. Fiona hunched down as far as she dared without being cowardly. For a time the water was warm, but then it began to feel cool. She sneezed. Angus Gordon said nothing. Then he stood up and lifted her dripping form from the water, wrapping her in a towel. She was so surprised by his action, she had no time to protest it.

"Don't be witless, wench, and catch yer death. Ye have yer sisters to consider. They're better here with me than with one of yer brothers-in-law's families." He began to rub her down.

"Take yer hands from me," she snapped, her

composure returning. "I'm completely capable of drying myself off."

"But I am enjoying doing it," he said, continuing. "Since ye are to be my mistress, Fiona Hay, 'tis time ye began learning what is expected of ye. For the present, until I tire of ye, I own ye, lassie, body and soul. Whatever I desire of ye, ye will do."

"Why, ye pompous lout!" Fiona returned, snatching the towel from him. "I promised ye my maidenhead for those damned cattle, and no more. 'Tis ye who have changed the bargain, *and after we shook on it!*"

"The maidenhead of the Blessed Virgin would not be worth twenty head of cattle," he shouted back at her. "A lass's virtue is worth so much and no more, Fiona Hay. Do ye think me a fool?" Grasping the towel, he yanked it from her and stared hard. She was outrageously lovely with her dainty breasts, slim waist, and long shapely legs. "Jesu!" he muttered.

Frozen, Fiona couldn't move for a moment. There was something in the tone of his voice that bespoke danger, but she would not flee him.

Angus drew her slowly into his embrace. He touched her face, and her cheek was hot. She stared at him, wide-eyed, but there was absolutely no fear in her. He felt the gentle pressure of her bosom against the linen of his shirt. "Unlace me," he growled at her, his voice fierce and commanding. Her fingers trembled slightly as she obeyed him. "Push my shirt off, lassie!" Her hands on his chest were soft as she removed the garment. He pulled her back against him, reveling in the sensation as skin touched skin. He ran his fingertips down the soft swell of her buttocks.

Her heart was pounding in her ears. Her vision was becoming blurry. She couldn't breathe. With a soft cry Fiona did what she had never thought to do. *She fainted.*

Angus Gordon shook his head as he carried her to her bed, where he gently laid her down. If her brazen demeanor had ever led him to question her virtue, he now knew for certain that she was indeed a virgin. The look upon her face just before she swooned had been more than enough to convince him. It had been a mixture of slow sensual awakening and absolute terror. He didn't know if he was up to this. Cudgeling his brain, he tried to remember the last time he had deflowered a virgin. Then it dawned upon him. *He never had.* In fact, he had carefully steered clear of such lasses, for virgins were a capricious lot, forever falling in love with you and wanting to marry. Or so his late father had warned him. "Couple with the ones who enjoy it, laddie, but avoid the others, especially virgins, unless ye plan to wed one," Robert Gordon counseled his son, going on to explain why.

He should have listened more closely to his father's advice, Angus Gordon thought ruefully. Still, the lass owed him a debt, and he'd not be made a laughing-stock before all the world. Pouring a bit of wine into his goblet, he cradled the girl with one arm while forcing a bit of the liquid down her throat with his other hand upon the cup. Fiona Hay was going to meet her liability to him, but perhaps he could go a bit more slowly with her. She coughed, pushing his hand away, and some of the ruby liquid spilled onto her chest. He had the worst urge to lick it off, but restrained himself lest she swoon again. If a hand upon her shapely bottom could cause her to faint, surely his tongue between her untutored breasts would send her into fits.

"Are ye all right now, lassie?" he asked solicitiously.

Fiona nodded slowly, her head beginning to clear. "I don't know what happened," she said. "I am not craven," she defended herself.

"I know," he said, "but yer a virgin, and don't know what to expect. I was clumsy in my approach, for if the truth were to be known, Fiona Hay, yer a lovely lass, and ye have aroused me."

"Aroused ye to what?" she demanded suspiciously.

"Ye've aroused my lust," he said, honestly answering what he realized was an honest question. "I want to couple with ye, lassie." Gently he cupped one of her breasts, caressing it lightly.

Eyes wide, Fiona stared at his hand, amazed as his long fingers brushed over her skin, sending tiny tingles throughout her whole body. It was certainly not an unpleasant sensation, she mused, wondering at the same time what he expected of her. Their eyes met as she looked into his face. It was a strong face. Long in shape with a cleft in his chin and an aquiline nose. His cheekbones were high, his eyelids heavy, his mouth a narrow elongation.

His hand moved up from her breast to take her chin between his thumb and his forefinger. He brushed his lips across hers, and she caught her breath softly. Angus Gordon smiled, and the smile extended to his dark green eyes. "Yer not afraid, are ye, lassie?"

"I never imagined . . ." Fiona carefully considered her words. "I don't know what to expect, my lord, but it would seem that if I please ye, then ye will please me."

He couldn't help but grin at her. This was hardly the sort of conversation he had expected to have with the brazen hussy in the midst of his seduction. "Ye talk too much, lassie," he said even as his mouth took firm possession of hers. He kissed her hard, wanting her to understand that he would not be deterred in his purpose to have her maidenhead. Holding the naked little witch in his arms, he could hardly resist her as it was. She smelled delicious, and her skin was silken and sweetly resilient beneath his touch. He pulled the pins from her hair, then let it tumble around his hands.

It was her first real kiss, and it was wonderful, Fiona thought as she let herself drift within the security of his strong arms. Her belly kept knotting and unknotting. She was being assailed by a hundred different sensations. The kiss was harsh, yet it was sweet. Her mouth softened beneath his instinctively, her lips parting, their breaths mingling. She sighed as the pleasure deepened. Whatever had caused her to faint earlier had been dispelled in the magic of his kiss. Finally he broke off the ardent embrace, for he knew she had much to learn.

Fiona stared into his face. " 'Twas verra nice, my lord. I like this kissing. Did I do it well? I haven't done it before, but it seems to come naturally to a body."

His breeks had never seemed so tight. Laying her back upon the bed, he stood and began to divest himself of the remainder of his garments. "Aye," he agreed, his eyes never leaving her face, "kissing is a most natural thing, and ye do it well, lassie." He pulled his boots, hose, and breeks off. He kept his face impassive as his drawers fell to the floor. He kicked them aside as her eyes widened, although she said nothing.

Could a man be called beautiful, Fiona wondered? His limbs were long and straight, and pleasingly curved where they should be. He had nicely shaped buttocks, round yet firm. He turned back to her, slipping again onto the bed. Fiona glimpsed his male appendage, pale and bobbing from a nest of curls as dark as her own. He saw where her glance had fastened itself.

"Are ye afeared again, lassie?" he asked her in a quiet voice. "Ye don't have to be afraid of it, ye know. He's a braw fellow, my Gordie is, and will give ye much pleasure once he's become acquainted with ye."

To his utter amazement Fiona reached out and

touched his manhood, her face thoughtful as well as curious. He flinched with surprise, and she said in a serious voice, "Does it hurt when I touch it?"

"No."

"Then why did ye start?"

"I would not have thought a virgin so curious."

"Do virgins usually quail at the sight of yer Gordie, then?"

Her fingers slid along his length, and he swallowed hard.

"I don't recall," he muttered.

He felt as hard as iron and near to bursting beneath her gentle yet bestirring touch. Her boldness was confusing to him. It wasn't that he wanted her shrieking and swooning with fear, but should not a virgin be more respectful of his male member? Just a few moments ago she had fainted at his touch, and now here she was, boldly stroking him with fingers as skilled as any whore's. He would have remonstrated with her but that he could see her actions were actually born of curiosity, and the fact that she truly did not know how a respectable lass should behave in such a situation.

His fingers closed tightly about her wrist. "Enough, lassie. Yer touch sets me afire with lust." He pushed her back into the pillows, kissing her hard again.

Fiona pulled her head away. "Show me where it goes," she demanded of him.

"Jesu Christus!" Angus exploded. "Is there not any delicacy in ye, lassie? What kind of thing is that to ask a man?"

"I don't like the uncertainty," Fiona told him. "Ye kiss me and ye caress me till I can bear it no longer! Will ye not take my maidenhead and be done with it, my lord?"

She was afraid! He realized it in that brief moment,

but of course she would deny it and claim once again that she was not craven. He moved his body so that it was partly covering hers. His hand gently touched her cheek. "When a man makes love with a woman, lassie," he began, "it should not be a quick coupling. There is little pleasure in quick coupling. Particularly the first time. It should be slow, and hot, and verra sweet between them." His lips brushed her lips and then her purpled eyelids. His hand plunged into the mass of her dark hair, taking a fistful of it up, inhaling the clean fragrance of it against his nose.

Fiona shifted nervously like a mare newly brought to the harness. Why did his voice sound so intense? Why did her breasts ache and her nipples feel so irritated against his smooth chest? His presence was suddenly very overwhelming. She bit her lip in her effort not to cry out. Her eyes closed as if in doing so she could shut this all out, but the very scent of his masculinity assailed her nostrils. It was a powerful and exciting fragrance that seemed to call out to something equally primitive within her. Her hands smoothed slowly over his shoulders.

He kissed her again, but this time he gently forced her lips open and pushed his tongue past her teeth to find her tongue. Fiona shivered violently as their tongues touched, sleeking back and forth, intertwining in an amorous first mating. She sighed and arched her body, pressing it more tightly into his.

"Ummm, 'tis nice," she murmured against his mouth. "Ah!" she sighed as he broke off the kiss, his lips spreading kisses across her smooth chest and down to cover her breasts. Her belly contracted almost painfully as his mouth fastened itself over a nipple, tongue teasing tenderly, lips drawing gently upon her flesh. "Oh!" she half moaned. *"Oh!"* His fingers were teas-

ing the curls on her Venus mons, pushing between her
nether lips.

"This is where it will go, lassie," he told her, raising his head from her sweet young breasts. Gently a single digit invaded her now trembling body, pushing itself
carefully into a place she had not until just a moment
ago even known existed. Reaching the barrier of her
maidenhead, he stopped, withdrawing the finger slowly.

Fiona's eyes were wide with a mixture of shock,
surprise, and a budding desire. "Yer Gordie is too braw
a fellow to go where ye just went with yer wicked finger," she told him.

"Nay, lassie," he reassured her. "Yer wee slit will
open herself wide so my Gordie may forage in yer honey-
pot for its sweetness." His dark head moved down her
torso, spreading kisses as it went. Once again his finger
slipped through her nether lips, this time touching her
in another place she hadn't before known. " 'Tis yer
sugar button," he told her, teasing at the small fleshy nub.

Fiona's head whirled with shock as a wave of delight spread over her entire body, rendering it weak
with her pleasure. How was a finger capable of giving
her such enjoyment?

"Don't stop!" she begged him, a burst of stars ex-
ploding behind her eyelids. "Oh. Ah. *Ah!*" She was suddenly weak with gratification.

"So ye like that, do ye?" he murmured low as he
swung himself over her slender frame. He spread her
thighs with firm hands, and then, while she was still in
the throes of dawning awareness, he grasped his manhood, positioned it, and leaning forward over her,
pushed firmly into her body. She opened for him like a
fragrant flower, encasing him inch by inch within her
velvet sheath. Angus Gordon groaned with anticipation.

She felt *it. It* pressed relentlessly into her, thick and

hot, driving deep. Fiona had never imagined such an invasion of herself. Instinctively, she stiffened.

"No, no lassie," he whispered hotly in her ear. "Don't fight me now. Ah, yer sweet! Sweet!"

He pushed onward, finally meeting with the barrier between Fiona Hay's girlhood and womanhood. Swiftly, he crossed it, thrusting as far as he could, then resting.

She felt a sharp sting of pain that spread down into her thighs and up into her chest, rendering her breathless for a long moment—and then the burning melted away. Fiona gasped, drawing a great draught of air into her lungs, which she almost immediately expelled. "Does it hurt all the time?" she managed to ask, finding it impossible to understand why *anyone* would enjoy *this* if it did.

There was an almost pained expression in his eyes. "No, lassie," he whispered against her lips, kissing her softly. He began to move upon her, pinioning her lightly, his big hands pressing down upon her wrists on either side of her head. With an almost primitive instinct she began to move in rhythm with him. He stared down into her face, amazed at the savage beauty of it as she began to experience passion. He was surprised that despite her inexperience he was finding great pleasure in coupling with this girl. The tightness in his groin was building and building.

The pain gone, Fiona closed her eyes again. The deed was done, and her virginity shattered. There really had been nothing to be afraid of, and she began to relax, joining him in the erotic cadence he created. She broke his light grip and put her arms about him, drawing him closer to her. The stars were beginning to sparkle behind her eyelids again, and a feeling of growing exhilaration began to fill her entire being. She cried out, and his mouth descended fiercely upon hers, intensifying her euphoria. She could feel him, hard and demanding within her. Her nails dug into his shoulders. "Ah! Ah! *Ah!*" she sobbed, and then she sensed the impending burst of his lust, and his juices flooded her, mingling with her virgin's blood. In that instant Fiona soared, her heart beating wildly, clinging to him. *It was wonderful!* She drifted mindlessly for what seemed several minutes, aware of their ragged breathing, aware that their bodies felt hot and wet, and were still intertwined. Finally he withdrew from her, lifting himself off her body, his big hand tenderly smoothing the tangle of hair from her face. Fiona opened her eyes and looked up into his face.

"Ye were verra braw, lassie," he told her with a small smile.

She smiled back. "Yer satisfied, then, that I was indeed a virgin, and my debt is paid to ye, my lord?" Fiona said mischievously.

"Ye were a virgin, lassie," he agreed, "but ye have just begun to pay yer debt to me. Have I not warned ye that twenty head of cattle are verra expensive? Yer a brazen little thief, Fiona Hay, and I'll have my full measure of ye. I'll give ye and yer sisters yer living free, for I owe that to yer grandsire Hay, but the cattle are another matter."

"Yer a hard man," Fiona said softly.

"Jesu!" he swore as softly. "Is there no end to yer wiles, lassie? Yer flirting with me."

"I don't have any knowledge about being a man's mistress," she answered him pertly. "Is a mistress not permitted to flirt with her lord? At least in the privacy of their chamber?" Her dark eyelashes fluttered at him wickedly, and her mouth was suddenly pouty.

"I don't know the rules of this game we play myself, lassie," he responded with a chuckle. "I've never kept a mistress."

"I suppose 'tis no different than keeping a wife," Fiona said, "except, of course, 'tis not respectable to be a man's mistress."

"It is not respectable to steal a man's cattle either," he reminded her with a grin, then ducked as Fiona whacked him with a pillow. Angus Gordon climbed from the bed. " 'Tis time ye got some sleep, lassie," he told her, and drew the coverlet over her.

"Do ye not sleep here with me, my lord?" she asked, puzzled.

"No, lassie, this is yer private chamber. Mine is through the door beneath the tapestry where I entered."

"But I've never slept alone before!" Fiona wailed. "I have always slept with my sisters. Stay with me, my lord!"

"Until ye fall asleep," he agreed. "In a few days ye'll be used to having yer own chamber, and ye'll like yer privacy."

Dubious, Fiona nestled against him tightly when he climbed back into the bed. He smiled to himself. On one hand she was fearless, and on the other she was like a small child, afraid to be alone. He was silent, his arm about her, and gradually he felt her relax. When she was sleeping peacefully, he slipped carefully from her bed. He saw the bloody stains upon her slender thighs and upon the sheets beneath her. He almost felt guilty as he drew the coverlet back over her. Bending to blow out the candle by the bed, he had second thoughts and left it burning. Then, going to the fireplace, he added more peat. At least if she awoke it would not be in total cold darkness in this unfamiliar chamber. He gazed down on her a final time before stealing through the door that connected their two chambers.

Chapter 3

"Fi! Fi! *Wake up!*"

Fiona Hay dimly heard the voices of her two younger sisters. Her arm was tugged quite rudely. She turned over, grumbling.

"*Oh,* our Jeannie!" Morag's voice piped, shocked. "She isn't wearing any shift! 'Tis not nice to be naked."

Fiona opened catlike eyes and glared at her smallest sister. She felt somewhat stiff, and the place between her legs was slightly sore. She needed more sleep, and yet here were these two troublesome wenches demanding her attention. "What do ye want?" she growled at the pair.

Morag stepped back at her elder's tone, but Jeannie wasn't in the least intimidated.

"The laird's elder sister, Lady Stewart," Jean said, "is down in the hall, and she's demanding to see himself. Jamie-boy says it's because of ye. We'll not learn anything if we canna listen. Get up, Fi, and put some clothes on this minute! Black Angus is dressing. They say he respects Lady Stewart greatly."

Fiona was puzzled. "*Black Angus?*"

" 'Tis what he is called for his black, black hair," Morag volunteered.

"Take Morag and wait outside," Fiona instructed Jeannie. She didn't want either girl to see the stains upon her legs or the bedclothes. They would only ask for explanations they were too young to hear. She waited until the two girls had departed the chamber, and then threw back the coverlet and leapt from the bed.

There was a kettle of water warming over the fire. Obviously Nelly had already been into the chamber. Fiona poured some of the water into a small polished brass basin, and taking up a cloth set next to it, she first washed her face, then scrubbed the dried blood from her person. There was a clean soft cotton shift laid out next to her skirts, which had obviously been well brushed, and her blouse was freshly laundered. A pair of sewn stockings, the first Fiona had ever owned, were laid across her boots. They fit to above her knees and had plain ribbon garters. She pulled them on, affixing the garters tightly, imagining her embarrassment should the stockings droop or fall. Janet Stewart would think her a little savage. She had finished dressing when Nelly entered the room.

"Oh, lady, yer up, and ye've dressed yerself! Don't let me aunt Una know, or she'll scold me for not doing my duty," the girl begged.

"I'm only awake because my sisters came to tell me the laird's sister is below," Fiona answered.

"Aye," Nelly said. "The laird is a wee bit afeared of her. She's just two years younger than he is. My aunt says they fought like cat and dog when they were growing up. 'Tis fortunate, my aunt says, she wasn't a lad, or they might have killed each other." Nelly chuckled.

"I want to listen," Fiona said in conspiratorial tones to her new servant. "Has the laird gone down yet?"

"Just now," Nelly replied, her eyes twinkling. "Come on, and I'll show ye where ye may hear them." She beckoned Fiona, and hurried from the chamber.

Jeannie and Morag were still outside, and at a signal from their elder sister they followed wordlessly as

Nelly led them quickly down the stairs, through the corridor, and toward the hall. When they had almost reached the hall, Nelly turned down a narrow passageway, drawing them into a small room. Finger to her lips, she crossed the chamber and cracked open a small sliding panel.

" 'Tis how we know when to serve and what is needed without being told," she said. "Come, lady, ye can hear everything."

Fiona peered into the hall. She could see Angus Gordon pouring a goblet of wine for a tall attractive woman.

"There ye are, Janet," he said, and Fiona heard him quite clearly. "What brings ye to Brae, sister? I hope Hamish and the children are well."

"I was at Glenkirk visiting our uncle, the laird," she replied. "Did ye really think that the priest would not gossip, Angus?"

"What priest?" he asked her, sipping from his goblet.

"The one that came from the abbey to oversee the marriages of the two little Hay girls to the Innes and the Forbes lads. Ye've caused a fine scandal, Angus Gordon! Where are Mistress Fiona Hay and her sisters? Oh, how could ye? What an infamous arrangement ye made with that poor innocent lassie. Ye'll have to wed her now—and perhaps something good will come of yer conduct, for 'tis certainly past time ye were married. Oh, Robert sends his regards to ye, and says he'll pray to the Blessed Virgin that ye'll turn from yer wicked ways."

"Who is Robert?" Fiona whispered to Nelly.

"The second brother," Nelly replied. "He's four years younger than the laird. He went to the abbey when he was ten and became a priest three years ago. Isn't Lady Stewart lovely?"

Fiona nodded. Angus Gordon's sister had shining black-brown hair in a braided arrangement. She was very fair, and her bright blue eyes snapped as she berated her elder brother for his outrageous behavior.

"Marry the wench?" the laird said, surprised. "Why would I marry the wench? She stole my cattle, and we made an arrangement that she pay for them in the only way she could. I don't want to marry anyone, Jan. I'm quite happy as I am, and besides, I'm too young."

"Yer twenty-five, Angus Gordon," his sister said sternly. "I'm but two years yer junior, and I've been wed nine years, and have five bairns."

"The wife should be younger," the laird said with some good humor, and sliced himself a piece of cheese to nibble.

"Fiona Hay can be no more than fifteen. She's almost past her prime. Another year, and she will be," Janet Stewart said firmly. "Ye've taken her honor, Angus. No other will have her now. Ye must wed her. This lass isn't some cottar's daughter. Her family is respectable."

"She's a brazen little cattle thief, my dear sister," the laird replied. "She has already stolen a dozen head of my cows, and had the gall to bargain for eight more for her younger sisters' dowers. Don't waste yer outrage on Fiona Hay."

"Did ye breach her?" Janet Stewart demanded of him.

The laird flushed. "What kind of a question is that for a respectable matron to ask a man?" he countered.

"Ye have! Dammit, Angus! Ye were ever greedy with a new toy! Now ye have absolutely no choice but to wed the lass."

Fiona had heard enough. Pushing past the startled

Nelly and her two younger sisters, she found her way into the hall. "I'll not wed with him, madam," she said loudly as she entered the room. "I'll not be shackled to a man I don't love, like my poor mam." She glared defiantly at the pair of siblings.

"Ye'll marry me if I say so!" Angus Gordon shouted.

"Go to hell, ye pompous jackass!" Fiona shouted back.

Janet Stewart burst into a peal of laughter. "Why, bless my soul, Angus, yer lassie has more spirit than I think ye can handle."

"I am not his lassie!" Fiona said fiercely.

"Come here to me, Fiona Hay," Janet Stewart said quietly. Reaching out her hand, she drew the girl closer to her, looking into one of the fairest faces she had ever encountered. "If ye will not have my brother for yer husband, then no other will have ye, lassie. 'Tis a good marriage for ye both, and Angus already has a dowry in yer grandfather's lands." She gently caressed the girl's cheek. "Yer mother, may God assoil her good and sweet soul, loved my father. Having to wed with Dugald Hay must have been hell on earth for her. Nonetheless, we canna all wed just for love. Love usually comes afterward, lassie."

"Did ye not love yer man when ye wed him?" Fiona asked.

"Hamish? No." Janet Stewart laughed. "His family wanted a suitable bride. The match was made when I was in the cradle. He's almost twenty years my senior, and I didn't see him until a month before we were to wed, for he was a soldier for the French in France. But he's a good man, my Hamish, and I have grown to love him as the years passed. We have made two sons, and three daughters."

"He's besotted over her, and ever was," the laird of Loch Brae muttered in response to his sister's words.

"Meg didn't know her David well either," Janet Stewart continued, "yet she's happy." Then she explained, "Meg is our younger sister, and she's wed to David Hamilton. They have two of the dearest little twin laddies. Ye see, Fiona, marriage must be worked at as ye would work a fertile field. Little will grow if ye don't plow it, seed it, and water it. Love comes with time, with respect, with knowing a man day by day. It all takes time. Ye and Angus, for all yer rough start, are, I believe, an ideal match." Her smile encompassed them both.

"I'll not wed him, nor any man I don't love," Fiona said stubbornly.

"Nor will I wed a thief and besmirch the honor of the Gordons of Loch Brae," the laird said in equally stubborn tones.

Janet Gordon Stewart looked discomfited by her brother's attitude. Why did Angus always have to be so damned difficult? Fiona's mood she discounted. The lass was obviously proud and idealistic. She could be gotten around in time, but Angus was a different matter. Perhaps, she decided, if left alone for the winter, love would actually bloom between the adamant pair. Then the matter would be solved.

"Where are your little sisters, my dear?" Janet Stewart asked Fiona.

"Jeannie, Morag," Fiona called, and the two younger girls came into the hall. "Make your curtsies to Lady Stewart."

"How adorable they are!" Janet Stewart cooed. "The wee one is yer spit, Fiona Hay." She cocked her head, and stooping down said, "Are ye Jeannie or Morag, my pet?"

"Morag, lady," came the lisping answer.

Janet stood again. "Then ye must be Jeannie. Do ye like ponies, Jeannie Hay?"

"Aye, lady." Jeannie nodded slowly, wondering what this was all about. She suspected from the lady's dulcet tones she wouldn't like it.

Janet Stewart turned to Fiona and her brother. "These two bairns must come to Greymoor to live with me," she said. When Fiona opened her mouth to protest, Janet continued, "Ye have made yer decision, Fiona Hay, but that decision when spread far and wide, will make ye known as a high-priced whore."

Fiona blanched, but her lips were tightly compressed as she listened to Janet Stewart's further explanation.

"If ye expect to find respectable husbands for Jeannie and Morag one day, then they canna remain here at Brae else they eventually be considered fair game for yer fate. Ye do understand, don't ye?"

Fiona nodded slowly, but there were tears in her eyes.

"For God's sake, Jan, don't speak so harshly to her," the laird protested. "Jeannie and Morag are but bairns. No one will think ill of them. Fiona's mothered her sisters admirably. Yer being unnecessarily cruel."

"No," Fiona spoke, surprising them, "she is not cruel, my lord. She speaks the truth. I wanted to leave my sisters up upon the ben with old Flora and Tam," she explained, turning to Janet Stewart, "but yer brother said 'twould not be safe now. I did think of them, lady!"

"Of course ye did," Janet said. "I can see yer mettle, Fiona Hay. Angus was right, however, about leaving two little lasses unprotected but for two servants. Still, they canna remain with ye and be respectable. They must come home with me."

"I'll not leave my Jamie-boy," Jeannie said firmly.

Fiona ignored her. "Will ye let me send our Flora and Tam with my sisters, lady? They were my mother's servants, and have cared for us our whole lives. There is nothing they can do for me, as my lord has kindly supplied me with a servant of my own. They will feel useful looking after my sisters as they have always done. They are obedient and will give ye no trouble, my lady."

"Of course they must come."

"I'll not leave my Jamie-boy!" Jeannie repeated, and this time she stamped her foot for emphasis.

"My little brother comes most frequently to Greymoor," Lady Stewart said, immediately understanding Jeannie's concern. "I have a daughter just a wee bit younger than ye, too, Jeannie Hay. Ye'll have someone to be yer friend. Have ye ever had a friend before?"

Jeannie shook her head in the negative.

"Have ye a little girl my age, lady?" Morag demanded, tugging upon Janet Stewart's skirts. "I've never had a friend either."

"I do!" Lady Stewart said, smiling, "and I have two little boys as well, but they play with each other."

"Fiona!" Jean Hay looked to her sister.

"Lady Stewart is correct, Jeannie. If ye stay with me, ye will be thought no better than I am. Ye must remember that ye are Hays, not common folk. If ye are raised in Lady Stewart's household, ye'll retain yer respectability. Ye'll be considered for fine husbands one day." She spoke carefully as if she were struggling to maintain her composure, which indeed she was.

Janet wanted to smack her brother. This was all Angus's fault. If he were not so unreasonable, so bloody unyielding, this whole situation might have been avoided. All he had had to do was pretend to believe Fiona Hay when she said the cattle were hers, but no! Angus would be ruled by his pride. No one must believe for a single moment that the laird of Loch Brae had a kind heart. When she considered what the Hays of the Glen had done for her brother! Janet swallowed back her outrage. "I'll take good care of yer sisters, Fiona Hay," she said. "Ye have my word on it."

"Then it's settled!" the laird said jovially, secretly relieved to be rid of the two younger Hay sisters. He hadn't been quite certain what he would do with them, and Jeannie, he could see, was going to prove quite a handful.

"I'll not take the lassies today," his sister said sweetly. "Ye'll need a week or two to see they are properly outfitted for my household, and their servants as well, brother dear. And ye'll pay me an ounce of gold each year for their keep, *and* I'll expect a declaration in writing from ye regarding the size of their dowers." She turned to Fiona. "Four cattle was it? Each?"

Fiona nodded, slightly astounded by Janet Stewart's manner.

"Four cattle or the equivalent in silver coin, plus linens, clothing, *and* a piece of jewelry," Janet concluded.

"Ye ask a great deal for two little lasses from the ben," the laird said.

"Ye got a great deal from their grandsire that by rights should have been theirs, and let us not forget what ye've taken from their eldest sister," Janet responded sharply.

"Agreed," he replied grudgingly.

"Oh, thank ye, my lady!" Fiona said, catching up Janet Stewart's hand and kissing it fervently. "I shall ever be in yer debt."

"Fall in love with him, lassie," Janet said softly,

"and make the arrogant devil love ye so much he suffers when out of the sight of yer splendid green eyes." She winked at Fiona, then said to no one in particular, "Fetch my cloak! I must be off to Greymoor to tell Mary and Annabella that they will soon have two new friends to play with."

"Yer visit, sister," said the laird, "has, as always, been interesting. Let me know when ye would fetch Jeannie and Morag to Greymoor."

"Don't be paltry in their accoutrements, Angus," his sister said sharply as she departed.

Fiona couldn't help but laugh. "She is like the wind. Blowing in, sweeping clean, and then blowing out again."

"She is more like a plague," the laird grumbled. "Ever since we were children she has been telling me what to do—and what not to do. Yet her husband thinks the world of her, and her children adore her. I don't understand it, lassie." Then, forgetting that the two younger Hays were with them, his glance softened briefly, and he said, "How do ye feel this morning?" His big hand reached out to tilt her face up to his, and leaning down, he brushed her lips gently.

Fiona stared back nervously, admonishing him with a shake of her head and a glance toward Jeannie and Morag. *"My lord!"*

Angus Gordon laughed softly. "I think I shall outfit those two as quickly as possible so I am able to kiss ye whenever I choose, lassie. Last night but whetted my appetite for ye."

Fiona blushed, a fact that irritated her, for she did not think of herself as some milk-and-water wench.

The laird did not visit Fiona's bed for the next few days, and she was grateful, as she was much too busy preparing her sisters for their entry into the household of Hamish and Janet Stewart. Hamish Stewart, the master of Greymoor, was a distant cousin of the king's. While there was no real court under the protector, the noble families did visit back and forth. The Hay sisters would need at least two fine gowns with matching surcoats. Their everyday gowns were rather tight-fitting and had long waists. The fine gowns were made of velvet, and the surcoats were embroidered with colored beads and tiny pearls.

" 'Tis verra pretty," Jeannie noted. "Do ye think Jamie-boy will like me in it?" She pirouetted for her sisters. "Do I look older?"

"Don't be in such a hurry to grow up," Fiona admonished the girl.

"Why?" Jeannie asked. "Do ye not like being a woman? They say the laird is a bonnie lover." She carefully removed the gown.

"Don't speak of things ye don't understand," Fiona said.

"But I do understand," Jeannie replied. "I know all about how a man and a woman make love. Did ye not know that Margery and Elsbeth were sneaking out to meet their laddies in the weeks before their wedding? Margery is already with child. She was terrified that ye would learn of it before she wed her Colly. They told me everything I wanted to know about men and women so I would not tell you or Flora about their mischief," Jeannie concluded smugly.

"They are only lucky I was able to procure their dowries," Fiona said grimly, "else Margery's bairn be a bastard."

"What is a bastard?" Morag asked innocently.

Jeannie giggled, and even Fiona was unable to keep from laughing. "Don't fret yerself, our Morag,"

Fiona told her baby sister. " 'Tis not a word a proper young lady would use."

"Are ye not proper, Fi?" Morag asked.

"No, I am not proper anymore, sweeting. That is why ye and Jeannie are to go and live with Lady Stewart. Look at all the fine clothes the laird has provided for ye. Yer a verra fortunate lass."

And indeed the women brought in from the laird's cottages had worked hard to produce new wardrobes for Jean and Morag Hay. Besides their fine gowns, surcoats, and everyday gowns, there were sleeved camisias for sleeping, shertes, sewn stockings, and garters. Each had, too, a sturdy wool cape lined in rabbit's fur. The cobbler had come, measured their feet, and produced fine leather ankle boots. There were gauze head veils, and the laird presented each girl with a ribbon sewn with pearls for her hair. Neither would be embarrassed by her garments in the household of Hamish and Janet Stewart.

Flora and Tam had arrived from Hay Tower, and to Fiona's surprise Flora fully approved of Janet Stewart's decision to take the two younger Hay sisters into her keeping. She never asked Fiona about her relationship with the laird, and she slept with her husband in a room next to the two littler girls.

The night before they were to depart for Greymoor, Fiona sat with her old servant by the fire in the hall, her head against the old lady's knee.

"Do ye not love me anymore, Flora Hay? In the week since ye came down from the ben ye have not scolded me once, and tomorrow ye will be gone."

Flora caressed the raven-black hair on her young mistress's head. "What is there to say, lambkin? Ye set yer path that day on the ben when ye made yer infamous bargain with this laird."

"Ye know I had no other choice. He would have taken the cattle without a moment's thought. Jeannie tells me Margery and Elsbeth met secretly with their laddies all the summer long, and that Margery was with child on her wedding day. 'Tis true I didn't know all that, but what else could I do, Flora?"

"There was nothing ye could do, my lamb. Ye remembered yer promise to yer own sweet mam to care for her lasses. She knew ye would have to sacrifice to keep yer promise."

"Would she be proud of me, Flora?"

"Aye," the old lady said, "but I canna help but think she would have hoped that ye wed with the laird. He has a good heart, my lamb."

"The laird doesn't want a wife, and he doesn't want me in particular. He said I would besmirch the honor of the Gordons of Loch Brae. As if I wanted to wed the arrogant fellow!"

"Ye *must* make him wed ye, lambkin," the old servant said. "No other will have ye now that he has robbed ye of yer virginity."

"Is that all a woman's worth is valued at, Flora? Her virginity and her ability to bear bairns? I want a man who will love me for more than those qualities, and Black Angus doesn't love me at all. To him I am no more than a thief. A thief who is now his mistress. When he is done with me, I shall return to the ben, but Anne, Elsbeth, and Margery are properly wed, and Jeannie and Morag will have fine husbands one day."

"And ye have provided for my Tam and me as well," Flora said quietly. "I am happy to be off the ben. I never liked it, but yer mam was our lady, and then when she died, we could not leave her bairns."

"I know," Fiona said, "but now yer old bones will

have warm fires for ye to sit by while ye watch my sisters grow up. I would not have left ye on the ben."

"There are things I must tell ye before I leave," Flora said to her mistress. "There are certain precautions that ye can take to prevent yerself from having a bairn if ye don't want one. The seeds from the wild carrot, the plant with the lacy white flowers, will keep ye from mischief. Take a spoonful of the seeds, followed by a goblet of warm water. Or chew the seeds if ye will. A dose of pennyroyal can help, too. Don't bear the man a bastard if ye can prevent it, lambkin."

"Greymoor isn't far," Fiona said. "I'll come to see ye for advice as I have always done. I'm learning to ride a horse."

Flora nodded. "Still," she said, "I should have told ye before the laird bedded ye. If ye find yerself with a bairn, come to me, and I will help ye to rid yerself of it."

Fiona was surprised by Flora's knowledge, but she was grateful for it. "How often do I take the seeds?"

"Once daily, and I'll give yer Nelly a bag of them to tide ye over until next summer when the plants bloom again. Yer mother used them when she wanted to defeat yer father of a son, though 'twas not often enough. She feared he would learn of her deception, for he scattered his bastards far and wide."

"Aye," Fiona agreed. "He would have been suspicious, for he so wanted to regain the lands in the glen." Arising from her seat upon the floor, she shook her skirts out, then offered Flora a hand, pulling her from her bench. " 'Tis past time we were in bed, old woman."

Hamish Stewart came for the two Hay sisters. "Yer sister, clever lass she is," he said to Angus with a pleased grin, "seems to be breeding again. I hope it is another lad, for we surely have a houseful of lassies, and here we are adding more." He chuckled. Brown eyes twinkling, he glanced from his brother-in-law to the two girls. "Are these the little Hay girls, Angus?"

Amazed, Jeannie and Morag looked at Hamish Stewart. He was the largest man that they had ever seen. He stood at least six inches over six feet, and his big round head with its mop of hair was as red as fire, as was his bushy beard. "Be he a giant, Fi?" little Morag said, eyes wide.

Hamish Stewart's laughter rumbled forth. Lifting the little girl up into his arms, he grinned at her. "No, no, lassie. My mam and my father just grew me big." A thick finger tickled her, and she giggled. "Be ye Mistress Morag Hay?" he asked her.

"Aye, sir," Morag said, and then, surprising everyone, she demanded of Hamish Stewart, "Will ye be my father?"

"Morag, what a thing to ask," Fiona gently admonished her littlest sister. "Lord Stewart will be yer guardian."

"I want a father!" Morag said adamantly. "I have never had one!"

"She was only a wee bairn when our father died," Fiona explained.

Lord Stewart's eyes were warm and sympathetic. "I'll be happy to be yer father, lassie," he replied. He set the little girl down again.

Fiona pushed Jeannie forward, and the girl made her curtsy to the big man. "I am Jean Hay, my lord," she said.

"Ye don't look old enough to be a shameless wench, but my young brother-in-law seems to think ye are," Lord Stewart said with a chuckle. "Are ye, Jeannie Hay?"

Jeannie grinned. "Only where my Jamie-boy is concerned, my lord. I promise to comport myself in most ladylike fashion otherwise."

Hamish Stewart roared with laughter and, turning to the laird, said, "I can see that my household will be all the more exciting for the addition of these two lassies, Angus." Then, taking up Fiona's hand, he kissed it. "Ye will be Mistress Fiona Hay," he said quietly. "Let me assure ye, Mistress Hay, that I will take care of yer sisters as if they were my own bairns, and yer two servants will be well treated. Ye are always welcome at Greymoor, lassie."

"Thank ye, my lord," Fiona said. Tears pricked her eyes, but she fought them back. She did not need her sisters weeping at their departure. "Please send my felicitations to your good lady upon the expectation of your next child. I am grateful to ye both for your thoughtful kindness of my sisters." She curtsied prettily.

There was approval in Hamish Stewart's eyes at her words. His wife had been correct. Fiona Hay would make Angus a fine wife, if the bloody fool could only see past his overweening pride.

The girls' baggage was loaded into a mule-drawn cart along with old Flora and Tam.

"I have given Nelly the bag," Flora whispered as Fiona kissed her worn cheek.

"I have brought ye mounts I thought ye would like to have for yer own," the master of Greymoor told his new charges. Helping Jeannie onto a small dappled gray mare, he then lifted Morag onto a fat black pony. "Yer mare is called Misty," he told Jeannie, "and the pony, my bonnie Morag, is Blackie."

"Oh," Fiona said enthusiastically to her sisters, "how fortunate ye both are to have such beautiful beasties for yer very own!" She kissed Morag on her rosy cheek and squeezed Jeannie's slender hand. "God bless ye both, sisters. I will come and see ye soon."

Hamish Stewart signaled their departure, for he knew if he waited much longer there would be weeping. Fiona walked with the slow-moving party to the bridge. Then with a cheerful wave she turned back to the castle, listening to the steady *clop-clop* of the horses' hooves as they clattered over the wooden span. Although Jeannie had been uncharacteristically silent as they parted, Fiona could hear Morag chattering away to Hamish Stewart. She smiled weakly. It was the right thing for both girls. *It was!*

She was saddened by her loss, and the rest of the day she wandered about the laird's small island aimlessly. She found a large boulder by the shore with a smooth indentation partway up the rock facing the loch. Seating herself within the surprisingly comfortable notch, she gazed out upon the blue water. It had a soothing effect and helped allay her fears for having rearranged her siblings' lives so quickly. She now wondered about her own. What was she to do with her life? Although she didn't think the laird was particularly taken with her, he seemed to want to retain her company, although why, she didn't know. He hadn't come near her since the night they had arrived at Brae Castle. Was her maidenhead really all he had wanted of her, despite his words to the contrary?

She stared out at the waters, becoming familiar with the rhythm of the small waves, spying a ripple of current. The shore beyond the island was treed right down to the craggy bluffs along the waterline. Here and there was a small patch of sandy beach. The trees were already beginning to show their autumn colors. The aspens and the rowan trees were turning a bright gold. The rowans would be heavily hung with orange berries. The oaks would show russet and red, mixing among the tall stately dark green pines. Fiona sighed deeply. She dearly loved the autumn, but this year her autumn was tinged with sadness. For the first time in her life she was alone, without her family.

Above the treed bens the clouds began to mass, leaving torn patches of bright blue. The late afternoon sunlight turned the castle golden, reflecting brightly into the loch. It was so beautiful. She had never been in such a lovely place. Her father had taken so much from them in his cruel quest for Glen Hay, and in the end he had not even possessed a handful of ashes. Perhaps if he had made his peace with her grandfather, none of this would have happened. Perhaps she might have even been honorably betrothed to the laird of Loch Brae. Fiona shook her head, laughing softly at herself for being a fool. Dugald Hay had gone to his grave cursing his father-in-law and the unkind fate that had denied him what he believed was rightfully his. He had left his daughters poverty-stricken. And she, the daughter of a proud clan, had sold herself for the good of her sisters. She slipped from her niche and walked slowly back to the castle.

In her chamber Nelly greeted her worriedly. "Where were ye, lady? Black Angus could not find ye, and has been in a terrible state!"

"I am used to being out-of-doors, not confined within the walls of a castle," Fiona said. "I didn't leave the island. There is a large rock by the shore with a notch in it. It makes a fine seat upon which to sit and think while watching the water."

"Ye miss yer sisters," Nelly said wisely.

Fiona nodded. "I have never been alone before. I don't know what to do with myself."

"I have yer bath ready," Nelly replied. "After a

good soak ye'll feel better. The piper is to play tonight in the hall."

When Fiona had bathed and dressed herself in a clean skirt and blouse, she followed Nelly down to the hall where Angus Gordon was already at the high board.

"Where have ye been?" he demanded, his dark green gaze fastening on her. "I thought ye had run off and that I would have to send the hounds after ye, lassie." He shoved a platter with a roasted joint upon it down the table at her while signaling with his other hand that her goblet be filled with wine.

Fiona tore off a piece of the joint, taking a bite from it. "Because I am yer mistress, my lord, does not mean I lack honor. We have made a bargain, and I intend to keep it." She chewed the venison, washing it down with the wine, then reached for the bread and cut herself a chunk. After smearing butter across it with her thumb, she bit off half of it. Her look was intractable. She would not be bullied by the likes of Angus Gordon.

He said nothing more, nor did she. When the food had finally been cleared from the board, a piper came forward, stood before them, and began to play. A faint smile touched Fiona's lips. The music made by the pipes was a raucous sound, yet it touched her heart to its core, understanding her sadness, sympathizing with it, soothing it. She sighed deeply as the piper finally ceased and walked away into the shadows of the hall. Without another word Fiona arose and went to her chamber, Nelly on her heels. Angus watched her go, his look, for the briefest moment, thoughtful.

Nelly helped her mistress to disrobe, handing her lady a soft linen camisia with flowing sleeves. Fiona tied the two halves of the garment closed at the neckline. After bathing her hands and face, then carefully cleaning her teeth with pumice, she was ready for bed. Nelly busied herself with folding the discarded garments and laying them aside.

Fiona went to the window and pushed the shutters open. The night air was cool, autumnal. "Go to bed, Nelly," she said. "I'm not yet ready to sleep. Too much has happened today."

"God give ye sweet repose then, lady," Nelly said, closing the door behind her.

There was a quarter moon tonight. It glowed brightly down on the waters of the loch, silvering the little wave tops. The wind was light, but definite in its course. Fiona smiled as it caught a tendril of her hair before she began to braid it. Fastening the single thick plait with a bit of ribbon, she sighed and, placing her hands on the sill, gazed deeply into the night. *She was alone.* For the first time in her entire life she was truly alone. Her sisters were all scattered. Old Tam and Flora were gone from her. It was an odd sensation, almost like having no body or floating free and not knowing where she was going. What was to become of her, she wondered, but Fiona was neither sad nor frightened by her silent question. She was simply curious as to what life held in store for her. She could not remember a time when she was not responsible for her siblings. What on earth was she going to do now that they were all settled?

The arm that slid about her waist was not unexpected. She had sensed that he would come tonight. It had been more than a week since he had lain with her, and she was shy all over again, but at least this time she knew what to expect.

"What are ye thinking?" he asked, surprising her.

"Of my sisters," she said, wondering if he would really understand.

"Ye miss them?"

"Aye, and I wonder what my life is to be now I no longer have them to care for, Angus Gordon," she told him honestly.

"Ye are my mistress," he replied, bending to place a warm kiss in the place where her round neckline revealed her skin.

Fiona laughed in spite of herself. "What does a mistress do, my lord?" she queried mischievously.

"Why she . . . she—" He stopped, confused by her question.

"Exactly," Fiona told him. "If I were yer wife, I would have the care of this castle and its people, but I am not yer wife. What is it that I am, then? I am not a toy to be put in the corner when ye don't want me, my lord."

The laird was astounded. By Fiona, by their very conversation. What did she want of him? "Una and Aulay have charge of the castle," he began, but he realized that had he a wife, they would defer to her.

"Una and Aulay have their proper place, as do all those here at Brae. They know what is expected of them each day. I do not." Fiona's backbone seemed to stiffen as she spoke. Why on earth had she even begun this conversation? He would think she wanted to be his wife.

"Yer place is in my arms, in my bed," he told her. "That is the duty of a man's mistress, lassie."

"I canna spend all my time in yer arms, in yer bed," Fiona said desperately. "I need something to do. I am not used to being idle!"

His mother had died when he was relatively young. He scarcely could remember what she did with her days, if he'd ever known. He'd been out and about as much as possible from the earliest age, a male absorbed in male pursuits. As far back as he could recall, Una and Aulay had run the castle. "What do ye want to do?"

Fiona thought a moment. "I want to learn to read and write," she said. "Can ye read and write, my lord? My father could not, although my mother said she could write her name. Nothing more, mind. Just her name. I never saw her do it, though."

"I learned to read and write when I was a boy in England with the king," the laird said slowly. "My brother, Robert, has learned these skills at Glenkirk Abbey, but neither Jamie-boy nor my sisters nor Hamish Stewart, for that matter, can read or write. If it is what ye want, lassie, I shall teach ye," he promised her.

Fiona nodded, satisfied.

"The moon is bright tonight, is it not?" he said finally.

"Aye."

His fingers began to undo the ribbon tie at her neck. Her camisia opened to the navel. His hand slipped inside to capture a breast. It nestled like a small round apple, just filling his palm. Her skin was very soft and warm with pulsing life. He began to rub the nipple with his thumb, his lips again finding the almost invisible hollow where her shoulder met her neck. His mouth lingered for a long moment.

"I left ye alone these past days not because I don't desire ye, but so ye might have time with Jeannie and Morag," he murmured against her ear. His tongue delicately explored the pink whorl of it.

"I know, and I am grateful," Fiona replied, shivering at the warm wetness in her ear. This love play of his was exciting, but at the same time it was a little frightening. She shifted nervously, trying to fix her attention upon a bright star just above the bens on the other side of the dark loch, but it was impossible. She wanted to snatch his hands away. Instead her arms lay by her sides, her fingers clenching and unclenching nervously.

Angus Gordon could feel the tenseness in the lassie, and it was no wonder. An enthusiastic student when her initial fears were overcome, she was still greatly inexperienced. Gently he drew her camisia off her shoulders. It slid down her torso to puddle about her ankles. Slipping his hands beneath her arms, he reached up to cup both her breasts in his hands. He fondled the delicate flesh.

Fiona's breath caught achingly in her throat. Unable to help herself, she shuddered hard.

"No, no, hinny lamb," his voice caressed her. "Don't be afeared. Do ye not remember how sweet it was between us the last time?"

"Aye!" She forced the word out. It had been sweet between them that only time he had made love to her, taking her virginity in a blaze of hot passion.

"It will be sweeter this time, lassie, I swear it!" He turned her about to brush her lips with his.

She was surprised to find he was naked. She had been so concerned with herself that she hadn't even noticed the feel of his skin against hers. She could feel the heat in her cheeks. His big hands enclosed her buttocks and pulled her close against him. Fiona could feel the hard length of the rampant manhood against her thigh, and her cheeks burned again.

"My Gordie has missed ye, lassie," he murmured suggestively.

"He's a bold fellow," she said softly, and reaching down with a hand, she stroked him softly. "Ah, yer so hard, my lord!"

"I want to be inside of ye, Fiona Hay," he told her

harshly. "Ye canna know how I burn for ye, lassie. 'Twas not easy to resist grabbing ye every time I saw ye these past few days, but I kept to the proprieties for the sake of yer sisters." His mouth took hers again, but this time the kiss was fierce and demanding.

Fiona responded, sliding her arms about his neck, her breasts pressed hard against his chest, her fear melting away in a rush of desire. He lifted her, palms beneath her bottom, sheathing himself within her, and instinctively her legs wrapped about him. She was astounded by what he had done, by what they were doing. He pressed her back, and she felt the sill against her spine as he groaned into her mouth, his lower torso pushing and thrusting against her. She matched his rhythm, amazing herself, but finally she pulled her head from his, gasping. "Ye'll cripple me, Angus Gordon, if ye dinna stop pushing me into the stone of the window!"

He replied by ceasing the action of his loins. His arms tightly about her, he walked across the chamber, then placed her on the edge of the bed. Standing over her, he continued the savage meter once again, driving himself hard and deep within her ripe body.

Fiona raked her nails down his back, her passion burning so brightly, she was surprised it did not light up the whole room. She felt as if he were devouring her whole, yet at no time was she afraid, even when he grasped her wrists and, pinioning her to the mattress, growled, "Don't claw me, lassie," just as he ground into her as far as he could. Ecstasy washed over her, catching her up in a rapture so intense that she felt as if she were being transported to the heavens and back. Then the great throbbing within her burst. With a cry he fell across her breasts, half sobbing. Fiona stroked his dark hair, well satisfied with his efforts. There had been no pain this time. Indeed, there had been nothing but utter pleasure. Did all women feel this way after such a bout of passion? Did wives? Or was it only a man's mistress who enjoyed this special delight?

Angus Gordon breathed slowly and deeply, working to recover his equilibrium. He was somewhat surprised at himself. He hadn't realized his lust was so great that he would take her in such a primitive fashion, but Fiona had not seemed to mind, except for reminding him that he was bruising her back against the windowsill. Her legs fell away from him, and she sighed deeply. Raising himself up on his elbows, he stared into her face. "I'm pleased to see yer every bit as brazen as ever, lassie," he said by way of a compliment.

"Get off me, ye great oaf," she replied, and when he had raised himself just a bit more, she rolled away from him, getting off the bed and hurrying across the chamber to gather up the basin, which she filled with water. She then cleansed herself and looking to him, she said, "Come and let me wash yer Gordie, my lord. Ye'll not want to sleep with him dirty."

He complied, coming across to her, asking, "Where did ye ever learn such a thing, lassie?"

"My old Flora said I was to do it. She says a manhood can become diseased if it is not kept clean." Pushing back his foreskin, she washed him most competently, dried him, and then, drawing the flesh down back over the knob, she smiled up at him even as she gave it a pat. "There now, 'tis done, and ye'll be all the better for it."

He laughed, charmed by her ingenuousness, but then he teased her, "Yer tender ministrations will but encourage my Gordie, lassie."

Her eyes widened. "Ye don't mean we could do it again tonight, do ye, my lord?" To his amusement her look was very hopeful.

"When I was yer age, Fiona Hay, I could do *it*

a dozen times a night. Now, alas, I can but manage three or four. Get into bed," he ordered her, his look suddenly menacing.

She caught her lower lip with her teeth, and to his surprise she giggled. "How many times do ye think ye can do it tonight?" she demanded wickedly. "I like it when ye take me, Angus Gordon."

"So I've noticed," he said. "Get into bed, lassie."

Her tongue slid seductively over her lips. "Three times or *four*, my lord?"

He grinned at her. "Ye'll not know, lassie, until we get back into yer bed." He chuckled. "I think, however, I can manage four."

She pulled him eagerly by the hand, and when they lay sated a second time, Fiona thought to herself that being the laird's mistress was not such a bad fate after all. She was still of the same mind when she awoke in the morning, sore, but certainly more than well satisfied.

Chapter 4

Robert, Duke of Albany, brother of the late king, Robert III, uncle to the young captive king, James I, and regent of Scotland, had not been the most popular man in the land, but his rule was a strong one.

The moment he'd assumed the regency for his captive nephew, the Duke of Albany had renewed the peace with England, then grandly declared that during his tenure as Scotland's temporary ruler no burden should be placed upon the poor by his administration. It was an extremely clever move, for the differences between the highland Celtic population and the more civilized Scots of the lowlands were becoming more and more pronounced. There was utter anarchy and lawlessness throughout Scotland, which while more manageable in the lowland regions, was impossible to control in the highlands. There each powerful chieftain renewed his independence in the ways that the clans had been independent prior to the rule of Robert the Bruce. The Duke of Albany sought to overlook what he could, which was much.

The lords of the Isles were the worst offenders, possessing a fleet of their own with which they harassed the rest of the coastal regions of Scotland at their convenience. The MacDonald, the most powerful of the chiefs, had made his own peace with England. He considered himself their ally. The regent, a man far more interested in adding to his family's wealth and power, pointedly ignored The MacDonald.

The English held two hostages of interest to the regent: his nephew, the young king, who was technically his overlord; and his own son, Murdoch, Earl of Fife. While Albany's first duty was to negotiate the release of the king, his aims in that direction were lukewarm. It was his own son for whom he had interceded with all the passion in his ambitious soul. It was greatly to his advantage that his nephew remain in England, but in a calculated and tender show of familial concern, he had sent the young sons of the Scots nobility south on a regular basis to keep their boy-king company. Angus Gordon had spent two years with his king, during which time he had learned to read and write. It hadn't been easy, but young James Stewart had insisted.

"When I come into my own again, Angus, I'll need men of intellect, as well as those who are good with a sword," he had cajoled his youthful companion.

"Ye'll need men who are *loyal* to ye, my liege," the boy Angus had replied. "Remember that yer uncle murdered yer brother to keep him from the throne. He'd just as soon ye remained in England. He has ambitions for yer throne, and this English king who holds ye has gotten his crown by usurpation as well. He understands the regent's desires, for they are his own."

"There is more to it than that," the king replied to his friend. "There is a rumor that the last English king, Richard II, was not murdered at Pontefract Castle, but escaped to the isles where he was captured by Lord Montgomery, and given to my father as a hostage. It is said my father maintained him, that now he lives in royal state, cared for by my uncle, Albany. I saw the man once. He indeed looks like a portrait of that king that I have seen here in my captivity in England. King

Henry keeps me here so that the regent will not send his rival back to England to dispute his claim to the throne. They counterbalance each other, Angus Gordon. Only when this man dies will I be able to return home again, I fear."

And so the fragile peace had continued between Scotland and England. The death of Henry IV changed little but that Albany was able to finally regain custody of his own son, Murdoch, Earl of Fife, in exchange for the young Earl of Northumberland, son of the famed Percy lord known as Hotspur. Henry V went to France to fight for its throne. He took with him the young king of the Scots, for the wily regent was allowing Scotsmen to fight for the French. Having the Scots king fight by the side of the English king was a psychological victory, and many Scots withdrew from the French army, feeling torn between their national loyalty and their desire to earn their keep, for many were younger sons. The regent died at the age of eighty, to be succeeded by his eldest son, Murdoch, for whose release he had struggled so hard.

The new Duke of Albany unfortunately lacked his father's political astuteness. He was neither crafty nor ambitious, although he certainly didn't wish to give up all the material gains that his father had garnered. He was a basically lazy man of easy character, unable to wield much authority over the land, let alone his own family. He was quickly bored with trying to manage an administration that was in fact unmanageable. The country slipped deeper into anarchy.

To add to Duke Murdoch's troubles, there came a contagious malaise, with fever and dysentery, that afflicted the entire country from highlands to lowlands. The murmurings began that God was displeased because Scotland had denied its rightful master. The dukes of Albany had held power for too long, while the poor young king languished in the custody of their mortal enemies, the English. The illness was God's judgment on Scotland.

The nobility laughed scornfully. Most were content with things the way they were, yet the more responsible among them realized that the violence and disorder would only lead to more of the same.

In an odd turn of events, Walter, the Earl of Atholl, suddenly decided he would have to involve himself personally in a negotiation to bring home his nephew, the rightful king of Scotland. Yes, James Stewart was a man full-grown, and it was past time for him to return. Further, the Protector of England was said to be inclined to be reasonable because he was at war with France and needed to have peace on the northern border. The time was propitious. Walter formed a delegation to go to England and negotiate for the release of James Stewart.

It was a small delegation, the most important members of it being, of course, Walter himself; John, the Red Stewart of Dundonald; and the bishop of St. Andrews. Arriving in England, the Scots discovered first that James Stewart was no weakling, as his father had been, and fully intended to rule Scotland with an iron hand. Their second surprise came when they learned the king had chosen a bride, Lady Joan Beaufort, the infant English king's older cousin, and a granddaughter of the formidable John of Gaunt. James Stewart expected his delegation to arrange not only his release but his marriage contract as well.

It took almost a year and a half to bring the negotiations to complete fruition. The king of Scotland would return home; his people would pay sixty thousand merks over a period of six years to the English as remuneration for James Stewart's keep while he had lived in England. Further, the Scots promised to cease giving aid to the French against the English; Lady Joan Beaufort would become Scotland's queen, her dowry to be a quarter of the sum due the English from the Scots.

The marriage was celebrated at St. Mary Overy in Southwark on the thirteenth of February in the year of our lord fourteen hundred and twenty-four. On the twenty-eighth day of March the royal Scots train set off northward, crossing over the border on the ninth day of April. To everyone's surprise the rugged road was lined upon both sides with men, women, and children, all eager for a glimpse of their long-lost king and his pretty new queen. They cheered James Stewart until they were hoarse. Here and there one of the border bonnet lairds would step forward to shout out his fealty as the king rode by.

At Melrose Abbey James Stewart met up with his cousin Murdoch, Duke of Albany, who had come with his sons, Robert, Alexander, James, and the other Walter Stewart. With them were as many of Scotland's noble families as could reach Melrose in time for the king's coming. Here the English departed, leaving James Stewart safely on his own territory for the first time in eighteen years.

Duke Murdoch came forward and knelt before the king, who sat upon his horse. "Let me be the first to swear ye fealty, cousin," he said.

The king looked down. His amber eyes were unreadable. "Ye are tardy with yer allegiance, *cousin*," he said coldly. "The delegation ye sent swore me fealty before the negotiations for my release even began."

Rebuked, the Duke of Albany flushed, then pulled himself to his feet. "I am happy to see ye home, my liege," he said, knowing even as he spoke that he and his family would not find favor with this king.

James Stewart turned away from his cousin. He would never forgive the dukes of Albany for the irreparable harm they had done his branch of the family, and he could not forget that they had let him languish in England for almost twenty years while they usurped his authority.

"I have brought home my own executioner," the Duke of Albany said quietly.

" 'Tis bad, I will admit," his father-in-law, the Earl of Lennox, said, "but yer family. He has much to do. His anger will surely cool. In the meantime, be as much help to him as ye can be."

Duke Murdoch nodded, watching the king, who had not bothered to wait to be introduced to his four sons, moving on instead to the others who had come to greet him. Some were impressed by James Stewart's air of strength and determination. Others were not at all pleased, especially when he said, "If God grant me life, though it be but the life of a dog, there shall be no place in my realm where the key shall not keep the castle, and the bracken bush the cow through all Scotland." In that short sentence he told the Scots nobility that he intended reigning as a king should reign.

As the king moved among the nobility, his eyes suddenly met those of Angus Gordon. A wide smile split James Stewart's face, and he pushed aside those bodies separating him from the laird of Loch Brae. "Angus! Angus Gordon!" He embraced his old friend warmly. " 'Tis good to see you again, and come down from your beloved Brae to greet me."

Angus knelt and kissed the king's hand, only to be pulled to his feet again by his liege lord. "I am flattered that you remembered me, my lord," he said modestly.

"It has been many years since we last saw each other, but no one could keep me from coming to greet you. Home at last, thank God!"

"You will stay in Perth with me," the king said. "I will need one man near me who is truthful."

The laird flushed slightly. "I have brought my mistress with me, my lord," he said low.

"She is welcome, too," the king replied. "Both Ramsey and Ben Duff brought theirs to keep them company in England. Grey even wed his lady just before I married my Joan. Is your lass with you?"

Angus drew Fiona forward, and she curtsied low to James Stewart. "This is Mistress Fiona Hay, chieftain of the Hays of the Ben, my neighbors, sire."

"Mistress Hay, I greet you," the king said, raising Fiona to her feet.

"And I you, my liege lord," Fiona said quietly, her heart hammering with excitement. "I hope you will allow me to pledge you my loyalty."

"And that of your clan, too, I hope," the king replied.

Fiona chuckled. "I fear, my liege, that I have few clansmen."

"How many?" His amber eyes were amused.

"There are but five of us, my liege. Myself, my two little sisters, and our two servants," Fiona told him.

"Five loyal Scots is as good a start as any king can have," James Stewart said gravely, and then he bowed gallantly to her.

"You have pleased him," Angus Gordon told her when the king had left them to greet the others.

The royal party moved on past Edinburgh to the capital, Perth. The young queen was charmed by the raw beauty of the land. As they moved farther north, the terrain became more mountainous. They crossed many swift-running streams and traveled by and around a number of lakes.

They came to the town of Perth on the twentieth of April. The king and his queen would stay at Scone Palace on the grounds of the abbey.

"I love ye, my liege," Angus Gordon said when the king asked him to join his court, "but I canna do so, for there are matters at Loch Brae to which I must attend."

"Stay with us for the coronation, Black Angus," the king said, "and afterward I will ask ye to but bide with me a little while. In the autumn ye will go home, and I will come with ye to hunt the red deer."

It was a request, but it was also a command. The laird of Loch Brae bowed his head in submission to the king's will.

" 'Tis not for very long," Fiona comforted her lover that evening as they lay abed. She stroked his dark head resting upon her naked breasts. " 'Twill be verra exciting to see a king crowned, Angus. We're not likely to have such an opportunity again."

"Ye'll need a new gown."

"Nay," she said, "the gowns I have are barely worn, and my surcoats are in good condition."

"A white undergown," he said, "and the gold-and-white brocade surcoat must be trimmed in white fur."

"As you wish, but I will not wear one of those silly headdresses," Fiona said. "Imagine putting horns upon a woman's head. It makes a female look like a cow with a veil." She sighed as he began to caress her.

"I can understand yer aversion to cattle these days, lassie," he teased her, raising his head just enough so he might kiss her now plump breasts. "Why, ye've become almost respectable."

She gave the dark hair a severe yank, and he swore softly, half laughing. "Yer a villain, Black Angus," she said, "despite yer close association to our king. Will I never be free of this debt to ye?"

"Never!" he said fiercely, pulling her into his arms and kissing her hard. "I will not let ye go, Fiona Hay. Ye are mine!"

Hamish Stewart and his wife, Janet, came down from the hills to attend the king's coronation. They brought with them young James Gordon and Jean Hay. The sisters embraced warmly; then Fiona stepped back to look at Jeannie, who was now twelve. Her sister had grown taller and had the beginnings of breasts, but in one thing she had not changed. She was still determined to marry James Gordon.

"Why, Jeannie lass, ye've grown quite fair," the laird complimented the girl. "Ye'll soon be a woman, I can see."

"Then match me with my Jamie-boy," Jean Hay said boldly.

The object of her affections groaned and rolled his eyes, driving the others to laughter.

"It would be a good match for ye both," Angus Gordon said. "I have always thought it, brother. Perhaps the time has come to arrange it before some other swain sweeps Jeannie off her feet and takes her away from ye." He smiled.

"She's too young to bed," James Gordon grumbled. "I want a wife I can bed. Besides, she has no lands of her own, and I want a wife with property, Angus. Surely ye can understand that."

Janet Gordon Stewart looked to her elder brother but was uncharacteristically silent.

"I'll give ye some of the lands in the glen," the laird said.

"For Jeannie Hay?" was the surprised response.

"They were her grandfather's lands, Jamie-boy," the laird replied. " 'Tis only right she have some of them as a dower portion."

"She's still too young to bed," James Gordon said.

"She will not be in two years, brother," Angus Gordon said. "Ye can wait that long, for yer but a lad yerself. Where else will ye get such a good offer? Yer the youngest son, and have little to offer a lass of greater property but yer pretty face, Jamie. No father would want a lad with so little to offer, despite his pretty face."

Jean Hay held her breath, not daring even to move.

"Well," James Gordon allowed, "I suppose I could wait to bed a wife. How much land in the glen, Angus?"

"We'll discuss it when we are back in Loch Brae, Jamie," the laird said quietly, "but 'tis agreed between us that ye will take Jean Hay to be yer wife in two years' time."

"Aye," James Gordon agreed, and the two men shook hands.

"Ye may kiss me, Jamie-boy," Jeannie Hay said grandly, her heart pounding with excitement that she would finally have the man she wanted for a husband.

James Gordon looked at the young girl. Bending, he bussed her on her rosy cheek. "Yer too young, lass, for the lips," he told her sternly, seeing the mutinous look in her amber eyes.

Then to everyone's surprise Jeannie Hay answered meekly, "Aye, Jamie. Whatever ye say."

"Ye could take a lesson from yer little sister, Fiona Hay," the laird said, a twinkle in his eyes.

Fiona looked outraged, but Janet Gordon Stewart laughed aloud, and her big husband chuckled, the deep sound rumbling about the room.

"The day I become a fool over a *man*," Fiona sputtered, "ye'll know I have lost my wits!" Then she stormed from the chamber.

"Take yer betrothed and go," Angus Gordon said to his youngest brother, waiting until Jamie had departed with Jean Hay to look to his sister and brother-in-law. "Say yer piece, Jan, for I know ye will anyway," the laird told her with a small chuckle.

"Yer foolishness has gone on long enough, Angus," Janet Stewart said sternly. "When are ye going to set the day and wed with Fiona?"

"When she tells me that she loves me, sister, for to my surprise and my amazement, I seem to be in love with her, but I will not wed with a lass who does not love me," he finished implacably.

"Nor would Fiona, with her unfortunate parents as an example, wed with a man who did not love her," his sister answered him. "A woman needs to know her man loves her, Angus. Only then will she dare to admit to her own feelings. Remember that we women are the weaker vessels."

"*Hah!*" her brother responded, and even the patient, kindly Hamish Stewart had a difficult time remaining silent. "Most women have stronger wills than any man I have ever met," the laird said. "When my lass tells me that she loves me, only then will I admit to her that my heart is filled with love for her."

Janet Gordon Stewart shook her head. "God help us all, then, for both ye and Fiona are so stubborn that ye may go to yer graves without ever being wed."

PART II

SCOTLAND
Spring-Autumn 1424

Chapter 5

The coronation of James I and his queen, Joan Beaufort, was set for the fourteenth day of May. In that same week the king stood before his parliament, declaring firmly, "If any man presume to make war against another, he shall suffer the full penalties of the law." The pronouncement was greeted with a deep, respectful silence. In the month since the king had returned to Scotland, his nobility were learning to their great dismay that he was not at all his father's son. Rather he was his great-great-grandfather, Robert the Bruce, reborn, but, intrigued by the management of his government, a stronger king. The bonnet lairds and the general population were well pleased with this prince. The mighty were not, but it was too late. James Stewart had taken up the reins of his power most firmly. He would not be dislodged.

To Angus and Fiona's great surprise they were housed with their royal master and mistress in Perth. They had been given a small apartment with a bedchamber that had its own fireplace, a day room with a second fireplace, and two smaller rooms off the day room, one for their clothing and the other for Nelly. The windows of their apartment looked out over the river and to the bens beyond the town.

"I don't know if we are deserving of such luxury," Fiona said, "but I canna say I dislike it." She plucked a strawberry from a dish at her elbow and plopped it in her mouth. "Anything we desire at our beck and call, Angus. 'Tis not a bad life, is it?"

He laughed. "Don't get used to it, lassie," he advised her. "I promised the king to bide with him but a short while. We'll be back at Loch Brae by autumn, I promise ye. I do not intend venturing far from home again unless the king truly needs me, but once I am well out of his sight, he will forget us, I am certain, for we are really of no import to him, Fiona Hay. Remember that, and don't be lulled into a sense of false importance because ye now serve the queen at this moment. She, too, will forget."

"I know," Fiona admitted, "and I also will be glad to be back at Loch Brae, Angus. However, I canna help but have a wee bit of fun, since we are forced to remain at court for the next few months. What stories I'll have to tell our Morag!"

The coronation was celebrated at Scone Abbey with all the pomp and circumstance the Scots could muster. The king and the queen in their ermine-trimmed robes were both attractive in their youth, yet most dignified. There was something very assuring about the pair. And afterward when they rode, crowned, through the city, the crowds cheered mightily at the sight of their sovereigns, men tossing their caps in the air in celebration, women wiping joyful tears from their eyes. *A good king. A fair queen. And peace with England.*

" 'Tis a pity we could not have the stone to crown ye on, my liege," the Earl of Atholl told his nephew.

"I was long ago crowned upon the stone," the king said with a smile, and then went on to explain how Angus Gordon had *crowned* his prince when they had been children together in England.

"This bonnet laird is too clever to my mind,"

Atholl told his eldest son, who would shortly depart for England as a hostage. "I will not be sorry to see the back of him and his equally canny mistress. She is too close to the queen, this wench of no importance."

Now truly king, James Stewart began to rule as Scotland had never been ruled. Immediately he forced through the parliament several new laws. Next James set about reclaiming crown properties that had been usurped or badly managed by his unfaithful vassals during the regency and the reign of the two previous weak monarchs. This was a highly unpopular move. The king complicated matters further by insisting that every nobleman and woman, every laird of the realm, bring the patent for his or her lands to be examined by the king's justices that their validity might be attested to and reconfirmed. Those who could not prove their rightful ownership of their lands and titles were carefully examined as to their loyalties over the past years. They were either reissued their rights by the king's court or had their properties confiscated. The appropriated lands were then given to James Stewart, and he, in turn, set those men loyal to him upon the seized properties to oversee them for him.

So many changes, and so quickly come. Now the king sought to better the justice system in Scotland, both civil and criminal.

"What think ye of my plan, Angus?" James Stewart asked his friend one afternoon as they practiced their skill at the archery butts.

"If yer chancellor and the men chosen for this court cannot be bribed, my liege, then the poor will at last have an honest champion," the laird replied. "If, however, these men can be corrupted, the verdict will go to the highest bidder." He loosed an arrow into the center of the target.

"I shall personally oversee this court myself," the king replied. "I know men's weaknesses when it comes to riches and power." He let fly his own arrow, which buried itself into the laird's arrow, splitting it in twain. Then, turning, he looked to his companion.

The laird was astounded, but suddenly a great grin split his face. "What a grand shot, my liege!" he said enthusiastically. "Ye must teach me how ye did it so I may equally astonish my own men."

James Stewart laughed. " 'Tis easy," he vowed. "I'll be pleased to teach ye the trick of it. I owe ye for yer company, Angus, for it helps take the weight of my duties from my shoulders. 'Tis not easy to be a king, I am finding. There is so much to be done, and so many who oppose me, whether they say it or not."

"Scotland has lived for too long without a master," Angus Gordon said quietly. "It is like a horse gone wild that must be reconditioned to the bridle and the bit. Ye have done much already this summer, my liege. Perhaps if ye would go a bit easier, ye would have time to win more men to yer cause. There are many who are faithful, and others who would be, I know, if they were but given the chance to know ye better so they might see how worthy ye are."

"I know that ye speak the truth, Angus," James Stewart said, "but there is far more to do to improve life in our land than I can possibly accomplish in an entire lifetime, even were I to live to be a very old man."

"May God see that ye do!" the laird replied enthusiastically.

"Ah, Angus, if half the men at this court were as loyal to me as ye are, I should have no fear for Scotland's future," the king answered, his tone almost sad, "but, alas, too many are ingrained in their bad ways. Soon I must act to make an example within the bosom of my own family if I am to put the fear of God into the others."

While the laird kept his king company, Fiona Hay was with the queen. Joan of England had become genuinely fond of the highland girl, but the noblewomen who surrounded her were less tolerant of the laird's mistress. For one thing, she was much too beautiful—and hardly respectable. She was not from a powerful family, yet she carried herself proudly. She deferred only to the queen and the king.

"She is much too proud for a lass in her position," Lady Stewart of Dundonald said sourly. "She should not be allowed to serve the queen. The wench is no better than a common whore."

"Much the same was said of my grandmother, Catherine Swynford," said the queen, who had overheard Lady Stewart's remarks. "My grandmother, like Mistress Hay, was in the lowest rank of the nobility. She had, thanks to her sister who served Queen Philippa, been given a place in the household of Lady Blanche of Lancaster. She served my grandfather's first wife. My grandfather fell in love with Catherine Swynford, but only after his wife died would she admit her affections for him.

"King Edward III, however, married his son off to a second politically expedient wife, Constance of Castile. He was forced to live in Castile for a time. He had to leave my grandmother and their children behind. His second marriage was of a short duration, for the lady of Castile died. My grandfather returned home to England to wed with Catherine Swynford.

"He spent much time in the assizes, and with the church hierarchy, making certain that his three sons and his little daughter were legitimized. He was successful. My grandmother defied convention for the man she loved. In the end God smiled upon her, for she was a good woman at heart. Mistress Hay has sacrificed herself and her good name to provide for her orphaned sisters. I will not condemn her, nor should any of ye. I am ashamed ye would be so mean-spirited." Having rebuked them, the queen turned her attentions to her needlework.

"Alas," Maggie MacLeod, now Lady Grey of Ben Duff, said to Fiona, "ye are a clever lass, but ye don't have the wit to take advantage of the queen's good nature to bring yer Black Angus to the bridle." The two women had easily become friends over the past few weeks.

"What makes ye think I want to wed with a man who doesn't love me?"

"Yer in love with him." Maggie MacLeod laughed knowingly. "And can ye not see that the man is mad in love with ye? God's boots! He positively glowers at any man foolish enough to give ye a passing glance, Fiona lass. Have ye no eyes in yer head, then, that ye canna see it?"

"He has not said it," Fiona replied stubbornly.

Maggie MacLeod snorted with impatience. "Surely ye are not waiting for Angus Gordon to declare himself, Fiona Hay? Ye cannot be that silly! Men are children; they never grow up. A man needs to be reassured that his suit will not be denied before he can muster up the courage to tell a woman that he truly loves her."

"But I thought I should wait for him to say it first, and the queen agrees."

"*Blessed Mother!*" Maggie MacLeod swore. "Listen to me, Fiona Hay. I have no doubts that the king loves the queen, but the first thing that crossed his canny

Stewart mind when he decided to choose a bride was her suitability. Do ye understand me?" Lady Grey's eyes bored into Fiona's.

"Joan Beaufort was certainly the most eligible maid in all of England. James Stewart swept her off her innocent little feet with his charm and his attentions. And she, encouraged, no doubt, by her powerful Beaufort relations and by daydreams of a queen's crown blurring her vision, probably whispered shyly to our liege lord that *she loved him*. Only then, I promise ye, did he say that *he loved her*.

"That is how it always is in the battle between men and women, and how it is always likely to be. If the women of this world did not take matters into their own hands, not a man would take a woman to wife." She laughed. "How do ye think I caught Ben Duff? A more sly widower there never was, but I was a canny lass, and when my Andrew learned I was carrying his heir, there was no holding him back. He couldn't get me to the priest fast enough!" She laughed again, her bright blue eyes sparkling with mischief.

"What yer saying to me, Lady Grey, is that I have been a damned simpering little fool," Fiona replied. "Is that not so?"

"Aye," Maggie drawled. "Yer a highland woman, Fiona Hay, and we highlanders take what we want. We don't wait to be invited. Did ye not steal yer laird's cattle?"

"I have never admitted to it," Fiona quickly replied, but Maggie MacLeod only laughed louder.

"Ye had better get Black Angus to the altar, lassie, before some bold baggage here at the court decides she wants him, or the king decides to give him a nice English heiress in return for his loyalty." Then she lowered her voice to a deep whisper. "Have ye been taking something to prevent conception?"

Silently Fiona nodded.

"Don't take any more, Fiona Hay. Let yer man put his bairn in yer belly, and for sweet Jesu's sake, tell him that ye love him before it's too late. Happiness is not an easy commodity to find in this world. Ye must hold tight to it when ye do find it." Maggie MacLeod took Fiona's hand in hers and gave it an encouraging little squeeze.

"Now I have two friends at court," Fiona said softly.

"I'm in good company." The older woman chuckled.

The queen's page announced that it was time for them all to adjourn to the Great Hall, where a new group of noblemen and lairds would be coming to pledge their loyalty and have the patents for their lands examined for approval. The queen, accompanied by her women, hurried to join the rest of the court.

"God's boots," Maggie MacLeod murmured, her eye scanning the hall and lighting upon a man. " 'Tis my cousin of Nairn, Colin MacDonald. What brings him here, I wonder, for he is as independent a highlander as was his sire."

"Who was that?" Fiona asked.

"Donald MacDonald, late Lord of the Isles," Maggie said softly. "Nairn is a bastard half-brother to Alexander, the third Lord of the Isles, but Colin MacDonald's first loyalty is to his brother and his clan. Their interests would be unlikely to coincide with the king's. What can he be doing here? The king will go to Inverness eventually to take oaths from the northern lords. Why has The MacDonald of Nairn come all the way to Perth?"

"Why not ask him?" Fiona suggested in practical tones.

Maggie MacLeod laughed. "I don't know if he would tell me the truth. Colin can tell a lie better than any man I have ever known." Her fingers worried her blue brocade surcoat as she considered Fiona's pragmatic suggestion. "It's been at least five years since I last saw him. He may not even know me now."

"Ye knew him," Fiona said dryly.

"Colin is not a man a woman forgets."

"Ye dinna mean—" Fiona didn't know whether to be shocked or not.

Maggie chuckled. "He had his hands up my skirts when I was twelve. We mature earlier in the northwest." She shrugged. "He was always a wild one, Colin MacDonald."

Across the hall the subject of their discussion watched the two women covertly. A small smile briefly touched the corners of his big mouth. Cousin Maggie had grown into a very pretty woman, but the girl by her side was a rare beauty. He was about to make his way across the chamber to greet his relation and be introduced to her companion when a tall, dark-haired man came up to them. He smiled, a few words were exchanged, and then the man escorted the beauty off. Before Maggie MacLeod might turn away, Colin Mac-Donald crossed the room in several large steps and was at her side.

"Maggie! And prettier than ever, I see," he said jovially, kissing her on the cheek. "How nice to see a friendly face among all these damned Sassanachs." He spoke to her in the Gaelic of the north.

"Mind yer mouth, Colly," Maggie warned him softly. "Enough of the court speaks the Gael to have ye hung. What are ye doing here?"

He answered her question with one of his own. "Who was the exquisite creature with ye a moment back?"

"Answer me first, cousin," she said firmly.

"Alex wants the lay of the land," Colin MacDonald said frankly.

"Why?"

The MacDonald of Nairn snorted. "Maggie, ye know that as well as I do. My brother does not know if he will swear fealty to this Stewart king. We may be better off as we are in the north allied to the English."

"James Stewart is allied to England now. This king will not let the highlands run wild," Maggie warned him. "He will, I suspect, destroy ye all first, Colly. I know ye love Alex and are his man, but look to Nairn and its future before ye decide yer own course." She eyed him appreciatively. "God's boots, I had forgotten how handsome ye are, cousin of mine." She chuckled at his suddenly cocked eyebrow. "Don't get any wicked ideas in yer head, Colin MacDonald, for I'm a respectably married woman now."

"And who is the fortunate man?"

"Andrew Grey of Ben Duff," she said, "and, aye, he's the borderer I left the north with because I was sick of all the killing and clan warfare. I wanted a quiet man who would love me and give me bairns. I'll have my first wee laddie or lass in the coming winter."

The MacDonald of Nairn took his cousin's hand in his, raised it to his lips, and kissed it. "If yer happy, Maggie MacLeod, then who am I to say no to ye? I'll want to meet yer husband, of course, but now tell me who that beautiful lassie ye were with is."

"Fiona Hay, the laird of Loch Brae's mistress, but don't even consider a seduction. Angus Gordon would kill ye, for he is fearfully jealous of any man who even looks at his Fiona. Besides he intends to wed her, I am certain. The queen wants it, and his family wants it."

"Does she want it?"

"Aye, verra much," Maggie said. Then she laughed softly. "Have ye any idea of how those long legs of yers poking from beneath yer kilt are affecting the ladies here? Why even Atholl's wife has a lustful look in her eye, and I thought her dried up long ago."

"Present me to Mistress Hay," The MacDonald of Nairn said, ignoring her teasing remarks.

"Colly, she will have none of ye, I swear it!" He hadn't changed at all from the heedless boy she had known as a child, Maggie thought. He saw something, he wanted it, and nothing would satisfy him until he had it. "Did ye hear nothing I said to ye? Angus Gordon is mad for her! And jealous. *Verra, verra jealous.*"

He grinned. "I don't blame him, for Mistress Fiona Hay is the bonniest lass I have ever seen, but I will meet her, Maggie, even if ye will not present me in a proper manner."

"Not now," Maggie MacLeod said, knowing that she was beaten.

"When?"

Damn him, he was so stubborn! "In a more casual setting than the Great Hall at Scone," Maggie said. "I promise."

"Good. Now, Maggie, let us find yer good lord so we may be introduced, eh?"

As he escorted her across the hall to where Andrew Grey of Ben Duff stood, the eyes of many of the women in the hall followed admiringly, their heads swiveling shamelessly. Colin MacDonald was a striking man who stood six feet four inches tall. Everything about him was long. His arms. His legs. His face with its high cheekbones and squared chin with its deep dimple. His eyes were, like Maggie's, sparkling bright blue. But it was his shoulder-length hair, a flaming red-gold, that attracted almost as much attention as his great height. He wore the ancient hunting tartan of the MacDonalds. The green, gray, and white wool was wrapped about his loins in a kilt; a second length of it was slung across his broad chest and shoulder and affixed with a clan badge.

"Who is that?" the king asked his uncle, the Earl of Atholl.

"I don't know," Walter Stewart said, "but I will find out."

Amused, the king watched the open interest of the women in his hall and, turning to his queen, said, "I think, my Joan, that ye and Fiona Hay are the only two women in the chamber not yearning after yon fiery-headed giant. He looks to be a highlander by his dress."

"Why would I long for another when I am wed to the best man in all of Scotland?" the queen replied with a sweet smile.

Walter Stewart's son, Alan, came onto the dais and whispered into his father's ear. The Earl of Atholl turned and said to the king, "The big highlander is Colin MacDonald, known as The MacDonald of Nairn, nephew. He's a bastard of Donald of Harlaw and half-brother to the current Lord of the Isles. I cannot help but wonder why he is in here at yer court."

The king caught the laird of Loch Brae's eye, and when Angus Gordon had come over to him the king said, "Angus, the big highlander with the flaming pate speaking with Lady Grey and her good husband is The MacDonald of Nairn. Bring him to me."

The laird nodded and turned away, silently approving Fiona's actions, for she had come to stand by the queen's side when he had answered the king's summons. Hurrying across the hall, he approached Andrew Grey, his wife, and their companion. Bowing to them, he said, "The king would speak with The MacDonald of Nairn."

Maggie MacLeod paled. "What does he want of my cousin, Angus?"

"Yer cousin, is he?" The laird looked The MacDonald of Nairn directly in the eye although there was a difference in their heights. "I think the king is but curious. 'Tis not often we are treated to the sight of red-haired giants in kilts in the Great Hall of Scone." His tone was slightly mocking, for there was something about The MacDonald of Nairn that annoyed him, although he could not put his finger on the source of the irritation. "Will ye come with me, then, man?" he asked brusquely.

"Aye, I'll come," Colin MacDonald drawled, "although I am not a man used to following another, but for my brother."

"Oh, Colly, do mind yer manners," Maggie fussed at him.

Colin MacDonald laughed, his long finger touching her cheek. "Don't fret, sweet coz, I'll not offend the king, for in doing so I would offend Alex, who has yet to make up his mind in the matter." He turned and walked away with the laird.

"A dangerous man," Andrew Grey murmured softly. "Is he really yer cousin, Maggie? And just how well did ye know him?"

"Our mothers were cousins," Maggie answered her husband, "and I know Colly as well as any cousin knows another cousin. He is at least eight years my senior, and I was hardly of interest to him except as a relation, Andrew." She clutched suddenly at his arm. "Ah!

I think I felt the bairn move, my lord, or perhaps it was my belly rumbling, for I am ferociously hungry these days."

Grey of Ben Duff put a protective arm about his wife and led her off to where she might sit and be more comfortable, not in the least aware of how neatly his wife had turned him away from the subject of Colin MacDonald of Nairn. The less said about her cousin, the better, Maggie MacLeod thought. While she was delighted to see the charming rogue, she was also made uneasy by his presence. She had striven hard to distance herself from her northern roots—and all they entailed. She glanced across the room to where her MacDonald relation was now bowing politely to the king.

"What brings ye to court, my lord?" James Stewart said.

"Did ye not put forth an order that the nobility bring their patents of titles and lands to ye to be reconfirmed, my lord?" Colin MacDonald said boldly. "Well, I have come at yer command and for no other reason. I should just as soon be hunting the red deer in my forests right now as crowding myself into a hall full of people, most of whom have not bathed in weeks, if at all this year."

The Earl of Atholl leapt to his feet, his hand on his dirk. "Ye'll speak to the king with more respect than that, MacDonald, or I'll slit yer bold gullet for ye," he said angrily.

"I meant no offense, my lord," Colin MacDonald said, ignoring Atholl, "but we highlanders are used to speaking our minds. We don't couch our words in pretty phrases that only hide their meaning."

The king nodded. "I prefer plain speaking myself," he said. "Tell me, how came ye by yer lands in Nairn, for I am given to understand that yer father was Donald of Harlaw, late Lord of the Isles."

"My mother, Moire Rose, was the heiress of Nairn. She was my father's mistress for a time. My father made it known to my grandfather that he wanted me to have my mother's inheritance. My grandfather made me his heir. I came into my own several years ago." Reaching into a space between his shirt and the swath of plaid across his chest, he drew out a silk pouch and handed it to the king.

After carefully taking papers from the pouch, James Stewart spent the next several minutes perusing them. "These are all quite in order, my lord, the line of descent clear." He folded the sheets of parchment, put them back into the pouch, and handed it to Colin MacDonald. "See my secretary in the morning, and he will affix the proper seals to yer documents. Ye are reconfirmed in yer titles, lands, and rights."

"I thank ye, my lord."

"And will ye swear yer fealty to me now?"

"No, lord, I cannot, for I am vassal to my brother, Alexander, Lord of the Isles. 'Twould not be right for me to swear my fealty to ye before my brother swears his. Indeed, my brother would be verra angry at me for such a presumption. I know that ye understand."

"I will expect ye at Inverness when I come, Colin MacDonald," the king said quietly, but there was a hint of a smile about the corners of his lips. "Ye will swear me yer fealty directly after yer brother."

The MacDonald of Nairn nodded his head in apparent agreement. "Aye, and I will. First to ye, James Stewart, and then to yer fair queen, may God make her fruitful." He bowed to them both.

"A wicked rogue if I ever saw one," Fiona Hay said when Colin MacDonald had taken his leave of the throne and moved back into the hall. "Ye had best beware of him, my liege. No MacDonald ever had Scotland's interests at heart, I fear."

"But he has great charm." The queen laughed softly, watching the big highlander make his way out of the hall.

"A dangerous man," the king said knowingly. "Aye, Mistress Hay, ye are wise to not be fooled by an easy smile and manner."

"I don't like the bold way he looked at ye," Angus Gordon said darkly.

"Did he look at me?" Fiona said, surprised. "I didn't notice. Have ye told me that ye are the only man for me, my Black Angus?" Fiona teased him wickedly, and the royal couple laughed.

"Yer a brazen baggage," Angus Gordon pretended to grumble. "I don't know why I even put up with ye." His eyes were twinkling.

"He'll wed her soon, before the year's end," the queen said wisely to her husband when the laird and Fiona had taken their leave and moved away from the dais.

"I thought to give him a nice English wife like I have," the king teased his bride. "Do ye not think he would like one, Joan?"

"If he were not so deeply in love with Fiona Hay, and she with him," the queen replied, "I would want him for my cousin, Elizabeth Williams. He is a good man, James, but then ye know that."

"Ye miss Beth," James Stewart said. It was a statement.

"Aye," the young queen replied, "I do. In the autumn Mistress Hay will return to Loch Brae with the laird. They are so desperate to get home, James. We cannot in fairness keep them here much longer, but then I shall have no confidant of my own age. Beth was always my confidant."

"In a few more weeks," James Stewart told his wife, "I will send down into England for your cousin. One little English girl can hardly offend the Scots, and ye will have yer dearest companion again."

"I'm glad," the queen said, and then, leaning over, she whispered into her husband's ear. He grinned, but Joan put her finger to her lips, pledging him to silence for now.

June passed, then July. Though the king worked hard at the business of restoring order and justice to Scotland, he also made time for pleasure. There were more young people at the court than there had been in many years. They hunted deer in the hills about Scone and waterfowl near the river Tay, and they fished for trout and salmon in the swiftly moving streams. The king enjoyed the game of golf. As it happened, the two best players at court were Angus Gordon and The Mac-Donald of Nairn, who fell into an immediate and fierce competition.

"Ye shouldn't grip yer club like that," Angus Gordon scoffed one afternoon as they played with the king and the Earl of Atholl. "Ye cannot gain any distance with yer ball if ye have such a grip."

Colin MacDonald drew himself up to his full six feet four inches and sneered down at the six-foot-two laird, "I managed to beat ye last time quite handily, Gordon, with just such a grip."

"Ye won at the end by only a stroke—and only because the wind blew a wee bit of grit into my eye," the laird snapped.

"But I won. I always win when I choose to win, Gordon. Be advised of that. By the way, how is yer pretty little mistress? She is surely the bonniest lass in all of Scotland." He grinned wickedly, and his bright blue eyes silently challenged the laird.

The laird of Loch Brae clenched his teeth and, concentrating with all his might, hit his ball a tremendous length down the green. Then he turned, grinning his own challenge to The MacDonald of Nairn. "Ye'll be going north again soon, I imagine," he said pleasantly.

"Those two are worse than a pair of lads," groused the Earl of Atholl. "Squabbling over a damned game of golf."

" 'Tis not golf they squabble over," the king said.

"Eh?" his uncle asked, confused.

The king watched the two younger men as they walked ahead of Atholl and himself. "I think it has something to do with Mistress Hay, although I have not yet figured out exactly what. If she is not with the queen, she is in Angus's company, yet I have seen Nairn eyeing her most covetously. I don't know if he has even spoken to her."

"Little escapes ye, laddie, does it?" the earl asked thoughtfully.

The king smiled cryptically. Then he said to his uncle, "I plan to execute Albany and his sons for treason. It will all be done under the law, of course. Albany will die for his presumption, and his offspring because they have the misfortune to be born his sons. I will not be threatened by my own kin."

Atholl nodded, fully understanding the unspoken warning his nephew had just given him. He was shrewd, and the moment he had met James Stewart, he had realized the mettle of the man and wisely chosen to be loyal. "When?" was all he said to the king.

"Soon. Ye are not sentimental, Uncle, are ye? There is no place for sentiment if a man is to be king."

"I have no sentiment where Albany and his whelps are concerned, Nephew," the earl assured the king. Then he drove his own ball down the long length of the green, pleased at his skill.

While the king played golf, the queen and her ladies were tossing a ball among themselves, laughing as Mistress Hay and Lady Grey got into a contest to see who could toss the wooden ball the highest. Finally the two women collapsed upon the grass, wheezing, while their companions took up the game. The queen, however, chose to sit demurely watching as her ladies raced back and forth, their hair becoming loose and blowing in the afternoon breeze.

"Ye have not met my cousin of Nairn yet, and he will soon be returning north," Maggie MacLeod said, her breath finally restored.

"I don't think it wise," Fiona said, breathing deeply. "Angus says he looks at me like a wolf eyeing a lambkin." She laughed. "I don't want to make him jealous, Maggie."

"Why would ye say that?" her companion asked. "Of course ye want to make him jealous, ye silly little fool! Ye'll get him to the altar a whole lot quicker if he thinks another man wants ye. They're all like that. Men are such donkeys! Besides, ye don't have to encourage Nairn. Personally I advise that ye don't, but it canna hurt to be presented to him. He's been dying to meet ye. I canna discourage him, but mayhap ye can. Actually I think the only reason he is hanging about the court is in hopes of meeting ye. So let him, and then ye can send him packing, for I certainly have no influence with him, and Ben Duff is beginning to get suspicious, for Nairn will tease him by making all sorts of suggestive remarks with reference to our childhood. Ye would be doing me a great favor, Fiona Hay, and I will not forget ye for it."

Fiona laughed again. "Oh, verra well, Maggie, for ye have been a good friend, but I warn ye I shall not be sweet."

"Don't be sweet!" Maggie MacLeod chuckled. "He would take it as a sign of encouragement, and ye don't want that!"

The king and his golfing partners returned to find the queen and her ladies still playing upon the grass. Colin MacDonald's eyes went immediately to Fiona Hay. She was wearing a yellow silk gown called a houppelande. Its short waist was set beneath her small round breasts, the long skirts flowing down into the green of the lawn. She was flushed, and her hair was loose about her face. He had never wanted a woman more in his life than he wanted Fiona Hay at that moment. Then he felt hard eyes upon him, and turned to meet Angus Gordon's gaze. Colin MacDonald smiled insolently but said nothing.

The laird of Loch Brae's heart and mind were filled with dark thoughts of murder and mayhem in that brief moment. He wanted to gouge those bold blue eyes from The MacDonald of Nairn's head so that they would never look with lust upon Fiona Hay again. *They had to go home!* They could no longer delay their departure. He wanted to be back at Loch Brae. He walked across the green lawn and slipped his arm about Fiona. "Did ye miss me, lassie?"

She smiled radiantly. "Aye, Black Angus, I did. Do ye think that means I love ye?" she teased him.

His heart soared at her words. "Do ye love me,

lassie? Truly?" Before he could get his answer, the king called out.

"Angus, come to me, man!"

Angus Gordon brushed Fiona's lips lightly, his eyes warm. Then, turning about, he answered the royal summons. "My lord?"

"I know ye want to return to yer beloved Loch Brae, Angus, but will ye do me but one favor before ye go?"

"Anything, my liege," the laird said enthusiastically.

"Will ye go down into England and fetch back the queen's cousin, Mistress Elizabeth Williams, for us, Angus? Ye need go no farther than York. She will be awaiting ye there. It is a long and perhaps even a frightening journey for a lass who has been as sheltered as Beth. 'Twill not take ye long, and 'tis not as if I were sending ye all the way to London."

The laird nodded his head in agreement. "I will go, my liege," he said, but he was perhaps just a trifle annoyed by the request. Was the king taking a wee bit of advantage of his good nature and his unswerving loyalty? He had been away from his home too long.

"A boon, my liege," he said, and when the king waved his hand, Angus Gordon continued, "When I go, will ye have my lass escorted home to Loch Brae? I shall want to join her as soon as I have brought Mistress Williams to ye. The autumn is upon us."

"Of course, Angus," the king agreed expansively, relieved to have the problem of Beth's journey taken care of so easily. "Ye need not leave for several days. The English messenger has only come this day saying that Mistress Williams has left the queen's mother and is en route. Her train, small though it may be, will move slowly." Such a simple request, the king thought, and yet his wife had wept with joy when he had told her that Beth was on the way.

Maggie MacLeod had seen her opening and, dragging her cousin of Nairn quickly across the lawn, she had greeted Fiona Hay. "Ye have not met my cousin, Colin MacDonald of Nairn," she said brightly. "He'll soon be going back north, and he has admired ye all this summer long."

Fiona turned her head up to meet the startling blue gaze of the man before her. "I have not seen a man so big before," she said bluntly.

"I have not seen a lass so bonnie, Mistress Hay," he responded.

"Yer bold," she snapped.

"Ye encourage it," he rejoined, his eyes dancing.

"Ye are mistaken, my lord," Fiona said coldly. "I don't encourage ye at all. I am not a woman to encourage a stranger, even out of kindness."

"Ye have a mouth that begs to be kissed."

"And ye a cheek that deserves a smack," Fiona retorted, furious to feel the flush warming her face. Quickly she turned her attention to Maggie. "I have said *it*," she told her friend. Then without another word Fiona hurried off to join the laird, who welcomed her with a warm smile.

"I must have her," Colin MacDonald said softly.

"Are ye mad?" his cousin whispered nervously.

"He will never have her as a wife, but I will," The MacDonald of Nairn said firmly. Then he laughed. "Don't fret, Maggie, but don't doubt my word either. Fiona Hay will be mine even if I have to kill Angus Gordon to have her. What sons I can breed upon that fiery wench!"

Maggie MacLeod felt a sinking feeling in the pit of her belly where even now her unborn child slumbered.

Fiona had made it very plain that she wanted nothing to do with him. More than likely Angus Gordon would complain to the king if Colin MacDonald accosted Fiona. The king's justice would certainly be severe against a highlander who had not sworn fealty to James Stewart and who threatened the happiness of the king's good friend. *No!* It was absolutely impossible.

"Why do ye fret, Maggie?" her husband asked, coming to stand by her side. When she had told him, Lord Grey said soothingly, "Do not worry yer pretty head about it, Maggie, my love. There is little chance of yer wild cousin carrying off Mistress Hay. She is safe here at court. He would not dare antagonize James Stewart, for not only would the king want his head, but his brother, the Lord of the Isles, would, too. Colin MacDonald does not strike me as a fool. Don't get yerself in a stew."

Chapter 6

The king sent for Lady Grey of Ben Duff to come to him in secret. She was to tell no one of the summons, not even her husband. Maggie MacLeod came fearfully, wondering what it was that James Stewart could possibly want of her. Her husband was but a simple border lord. Nervously she followed along after the royal page, her hands plucking at the fabric of her gown of rose-colored silk. It was a color she loved, and it flattered her auburn hair. The lad ahead of her stopped suddenly and put his hand on the wall. A hidden door sprang open and light spilled out into the dim corridor. The boy pointed. Swallowing hard, Maggie stepped through the small doorway into the king's privy chamber.

It was a small room with paneled walls and a coffered ceiling. There was a stone fireplace, flanked with stone greyhounds, within which burned a bright fire. Beyond the single window the rain poured down, graying the day. A table with a silver tray, a carafe of ruby-colored wine, and two silver goblets stood before the window. The only other furniture in the room were two chairs that faced each other on either side of the hearth.

"Come in, Lady Grey," the king said. His hand motioned to her from one of the chairs.

The doors closed behind her as she slowly made her way to stand before James Stewart. Maggie curtsied low, amazed her legs could still function so capably. "My liege," she said softly.

"Sit down, Lady Grey, and I shall tell ye why I have asked ye to come visit with me in private." Then, seeing her pale visage, he arose, saying, "Ye'll have a wee bit of wine, of course. 'Tis a wickedly dank day." He poured two goblets of wine, handed her one, and returned to his place by the fire, then sat facing his visitor.

Maggie tried hard not to gulp or spill her wine, but until she knew what the king wanted of her, it was difficult to control her nervousness. Had she somehow offended the monarch or his queen? Why was she here?

The king observed his companion furtively. Would she tell him the truth? Would he know it if she did? "Lady Grey," he began, focusing his eyes directly upon her pretty face, "I would have ye tell me why yer cousin of Nairn has come to court."

"Because his half-brother, the Lord of the Isles, would know the sort of man ye are, my liege. He has not decided whether he will swear fealty to ye." Maggie felt a wave of relief sweeping over her. She hadn't offended the king or his wife. She was in no difficulty, nor was she a danger to her husband.

The king had recognized immediately that Maggie MacLeod was being truthful with him. It was as he had suspected. Colin MacDonald had come to reconnoiter for his elder brother. "Why did ye leave the north, Lady Grey?" he suddenly asked her.

"Because I was tired of all the fighting. I didn't want to spend my life burying my men and living in fear of rapists and looters." She sighed deeply. " 'Tis so beautiful, my liege, but the beauty of the countryside canna make up for the constant danger."

"I don't suppose ye would consider a short visit to

yer relations to introduce yer husband to them," the king ventured.

"I am with child, my lord," Maggie replied softly. "Besides, my relations would not accept Ben Duff, for to them he is a Sassanach, a southerner, and not even worthy of their scorn."

"The Lord of the Isles has sent his agent to spy upon me," the king said. "I need someone to spy upon him. I had thought if ye went north with yer husband, I would have a better idea when ye returned of what Alexander MacDonald plans."

"My liege," Maggie said, placing her hand protectively over her belly, "I would help ye if I could. I have no loyalty to the Lord of the Isles, despite the fact that my father is his vassal. When I departed the north, I left it and its chaos behind. I am loyal to ye, but I could not possibly travel so far over such rough terrain in my condition. Ben Duff is forty and has no legitimate heir but the bairn I now carry in my belly. Please understand."

The king nodded. "I do, Lady Grey," he said in kindly tones, "and ye need have no fear of offending me. Nevertheless, I have the problem of placing someone I can trust, whom The MacDonald will not suspect, in the north. I can gain certain information from peddlers and those dissatisfied with the power of the MacDonalds, but it is not enough." He grew silent for a long few minutes while Maggie sat nervously. Then the king pierced her again with a look. "Nairn is quite taken with Mistress Hay, is he not?"

Maggie nodded slowly, her look now a fearful one. Kings could do whatever they pleased. Their subjects had to obey or be guilty of treason. Margaret MacLeod Grey was not a stupid woman. She now divined the direction that James Stewart's thoughts were taking. It was plain to her he had never intended for her to go north. That had been but a ruse to frighten her and extract her cooperation.

"Now," the king said, considering, "if Mistress Hay were in the north with yer cousin, I should have in her a perfect agent." His thumb rubbed his chin thoughtfully. His amber eyes glittered in the firelight. "She is a verra bonnie lass, Fiona Hay, and clever, too."

"Oh, my liege! She is in love with Angus Gordon," Maggie said desperately. "They surely will marry. It is Fiona's dearest wish. Besides, my liege, she detests Colin MacDonald!"

"Scotland's future, Lady Grey, is far more important than any future Angus Gordon and Fiona Hay may have together," the king said coldly. "If he intended to wed with her, he would have already done so."

"Each waits for the other to admit their love!" Maggie cried. *"Please, my liege"*—she fell awkwardly to her knees—"don't do this terrible thing, I beg ye!"

James Stewart lifted Maggie up gently and set her back in her chair. "Ye cry yer loyalty to me, Lady Grey, yet ye would try to turn me from the only means I have of getting information from the north, of knowing just what Alexander MacDonald is planning. Perhaps yer clan loyalty is greater than yer loyalty to me."

It was as if an icy hand had touched her. Maggie shuddered, looking at the king with hopelessness in her eyes. "I am yer vassal, sire," she said, beaten.

The king smiled a slow smile. "I would have ye taunt yer cousin of Nairn as only a woman can torture a man's pride. Tease him into stealing Mistress Hay for himself and taking her back to the north. The perfect time would be when she is returning to Brae. I will send a small troupe of men-at-arms with her. Their orders will be to desert her at the first sign of Nairn's attack, leaving her helpless."

"But how will ye get Fiona to agree to this, my liege?" Maggie asked him. "She dislikes my cousin verra much. Besides, her heart is with Black Angus. She may die before she allows herself to be taken. Then ye have lost yer advantage, sire."

"Fiona Hay is a patriotic young woman," the king said smoothly, "but even I would not depend on her patriotism in view of her passion for her laird. But what if she believed he was to be wed to another at my command, Lady Grey? What would be left for her then? Of course I would not force my friend, Angus Gordon, to the altar, but if Mistress Hay believed it so"—he chuckled, and Maggie shivered at the sound—"then I believe she would turn her heartbreak to a more useful purpose. I don't want a woman who will fall in love with The MacDonald of Nairn. I want a woman filled with anger and hate who will seek a means of easing her broken heart by helping me to destroy the power held by the Lord of the Isles and his ilk. *I need Fiona Hay!* She is clever and will not falter even under the worst pressure."

Maggie began to weep. The thought of Fiona being deceived into doing the king's bidding, of her friend believing that Angus Gordon was faithless and would wed another on royal command, was acutely painful. Maggie knew what love was. She had met her own husband when he had come north several years ago on a mission for the old Duke of Albany, and had fallen deep in love with him.

The king was a very cruel man, Maggie thought, sniffling. He had his beloved Joan. Would he sacrifice their love as easily as he was sacrificing Angus Gordon and Fiona Hay? Somehow, looking at him beneath her wet lashes, Maggie thought he would. His greatest passion was Scotland. Unlike his predecessors he was not satisfied with just part of it. He wanted firm control over it all. He would do whatever he had to do to gain that control.

The king let her cry until finally her soft sobs faded away. Then he said, "Angus Gordon leaves for England in just a few days. By the time he has departed, I want to know that yer cousin's lust has been stoked, that knowing Mistress Hay's route back to Brae, he will be waiting somewhere along that road to steal her for his own. Do not fail me, Maggie MacLeod. From what I can see with my own eyes, it will take little to encourage Colin MacDonald to commit such an outrageous act."

Maggie looked up at him, her eyes still wet with sorrow. "What will ye tell Black Angus when he returns from England, sire? What will ye say to the most loyal subject ye have? What would he think if he knew what ye had done to him and to his Fiona?" Maggie's voice was shaking with her audacity. Although she would be forced to obey the king, she did not have to like what he was planning—or the part she must play in his plans. She was not even certain that she liked him any longer. She wondered if the queen knew what sort of man he really was. Or would she, having been raised surrounded by ambition and power, even care? What was Fiona Hay to the mighty but a convenience, a pawn to be used in the greater scheme of things for Scotland. Damn Scotland, Maggie MacLeod thought savagely. Why could men not leave women in peace?

"Angus will be told the *truth*, Lady Grey. He will be told that Mistress Hay's little train was attacked by persons unknown. That she and her servant were carried off. That a search was made, but no trace could be found of either of the two women. Tragic, aye. Later I shall offer him the queen's cousin as a wife.

"And ye, of course, will remain silent, will ye not? After all, Lady Grey, if I find it necessary to question yer loyalty, I may have to question yer husband's loyalty as well. I know ye would not want that. And should ye doubt my sincerity in the matter, I will entrust another wee secret to ye. I shortly intend executing several of my relations. I'm certain ye can guess who. I will allow no one to interfere with my plans to unite Scotland and make her strong. Ye do understand that, do ye not?" James Stewart's voice was low and pleasantly modulated, but the threat was there nonetheless. He would have her complete loyalty even if that loyalty meant betraying her best friend into hell.

Maggie MacLeod nodded. "I understand, my liege," she said. "I understand that Scotland must come before all else."

"Aye, madam, it must. I will be merciless, even ruthless, to attain that goal," the king said grimly. Then he reached out and patted her hand comfortingly. "Though I arrange matters like someone arranging a chessboard, Lady Grey, I am not entirely heartless. If Fiona Hay eventually returns from the north, I will reward her lavishly for her sacrifice and her patriotism. I will even find her a good husband to care for her for the rest of her life."

Maggie said nothing. She could not, for her mouth was too full of terrible words she dared not utter to the king. She swallowed them back, almost choking with the effort it cost her.

The king arose and drew her to her feet, taking her now empty goblet from her cramped fingers. She hadn't even realized that she had drunk all her wine. He led her to the same door through which she had entered, pressing a hidden catch so that it swung open. "Thank ye for coming, Lady Grey, and my especial thanks for yer cooperation in this delicate matter. Young Douglas will see ye back to yer own chamber. I will speak to ye again in a few days to assess yer progress." The door closed behind her, and the page was at her elbow.

She couldn't tell Ben Duff of this meeting. She couldn't tell anyone. Their very lives, and the life of their unborn child, were at stake. She must not dwell upon what had to be lest she endanger the bairn, but half-grown, nesting in her womb. No matter how she felt about the dreadful thing she must do now, it must be done. She couldn't save Fiona Hay or prevent Angus Gordon's broken heart, Maggie MacLeod thought, but when this treachery was over and done with, she would go home with her husband and never return to court again. The memory of what she had done would remain with her wherever she might be, and damn James Stewart for it. *Damn him!*

Before they reached the chamber that Maggie shared with her husband, however, The MacDonald of Nairn stepped into her path, greeting her. She dismissed the page, saying, "I will walk out of doors with my cousin." Maggie put her hand through Colin MacDonald's arm. "I think we will soon go home to Ben Duff," she said. "Shortly I shall not be able to travel with my belly. Will ye return north, Colly?"

"Aye," he replied. "I have learned what I came to learn."

They strolled outside. The rain had finally let up, and the sun was peeping through the gray clouds, giving tantalizing little glimpses of blue sky. There was a light fresh breeze with the scent of September heather upon it. Autumn was definitely here.

"What a pity ye canna make progress with Mistress Hay," Maggie said innocently. "Ye must be losing

yer charm, Colly. I've never known a pretty girl to turn
ye away before." She laughed mischievously, but her
heart felt like a stone.

"I canna get near the lass," her cousin grumbled.
"That damned bonnet laird of hers is always hovering
about her like a dark cloud."

"He'll be off to England in a few days on a wee
mission for the king. He is to fetch the queen's cousin,
Mistress Williams, back to court, for the queen misses
her verra much."

"Ah."

"But Fiona is to return to Loch Brae while Angus
is gone. Ye'll lose yer chance entirely to seduce her." She
giggled. " 'Tis fortunate that none of our relations are
here to see ye made a fool of, cousin," Maggie said.

That evening Colin MacDonald kept his cousin
and her husband company in the Great Hall. His eyes
strayed constantly to Fiona Hay, and Maggie MacLeod
marked his interest well.

"Scarlet is a color that suits Mistress Hay well," she
said innocently. "It makes her skin even fairer by comparison, do ye not think, Colly? She really is a beautiful
lass. I'll miss her, but 'tis time we both go our separate
ways. I'll probably not see her again, for her laird will
not leave his lands except for a royal emergency, and he
will not bring Fiona under dangerous conditions. She'll
probably have a bairn within a year of their wedding,
when he finally decides to marry her, and several others
afterward. Her mam was a verra good breeder, she tells
me. Ye should find yerself a wife, Colly. 'Tis past time,
I'm thinking."

The MacDonald of Nairn said nothing, but he
never took his eyes from Fiona Hay. He felt a stab of
jealousy as she looked meltingly up into the face of the
laird of Loch Brae. He knew he had no right to this girl,

but he wanted her nonetheless. Her bonnet laird had treated her shamefully, but Colin MacDonald would not treat her that way. Given the chance, he knew that he could make her love him. *But how?* He could never get her alone to speak to her, and she would soon be gone from court.

Across the hall Fiona Hay was not even aware of The MacDonald of Nairn. For her he did not exist. Only Angus Gordon existed, and he would shortly be off to England while she went home to Loch Brae. *Home.* Aye, Loch Brae was her home, and its laird was her man. She was close to weeping with the happiness that was even now filling her. *I love ye!*

He turned to look down into her face. "Did ye speak, lassie?" he asked, his glance warm.

"Only with my heart, Angus," she told him softly.

The smile that creased his face lit up his eyes. He squeezed her hand. "I think we might escape, and no one be the wiser," he said.

The smile that touched her lips was as conspiratorial as his. Hand in hand, they slipped from the hall. The king, watching them go, had not even the slightest twinge of conscience. A woman agent, *his agent,* in the midst of the MacDonalds, would give him a great advantage over the highland lords. Had there been any other woman he might have chosen, had there been any other way, he would not have betrayed his loyal friend. *But there was no other woman. There was no other way.* Fiona Hay must be sacrificed for the good of Scotland.

Unaware of her fate, Fiona Hay could only revel in the kisses being rained upon her face and throat by her lover. They had practically run from the hall and through the stone corridors of the palace to the little sanctuary the king had given them for their own. One look at them, and Nelly curtsied, saying that if her mistress didn't need her any longer this evening, she would go to bed. They scarcely heard her, but Angus Gordon had the presence of mind to turn the key in the lock behind him even as his other hand was fumbling with the laces on Fiona's dress. Laughing softly, she helped him, and her garments fell away until she was naked before him.

"Brazen." He groaned, his hands caressing her.

Her hands darted about him, undoing, pulling, tugging until he was naked, too. "Yer beautiful," she said softly. "I thought it the first time I saw ye without yer clothing, and I still think so."

His big hands fastened about her waist, and he slowly lifted her up, drawing her closer to him as he did so, his lips kissing her sensitive flesh, and she felt as if he were branding her with his mouth. Then, after what seemed an eternity, he slowly lowered her, their lips met, and they sighed in unison with the delicious contact of lips and naked flesh. As he had lowered her, her arms slid about his neck, and she stood on tiptoes, their mouths welded together, drinking in each other's essence as if they were parched. Finally, when breathing again became a necessity, they drew apart briefly, reluctantly.

"What sorcery is this that ye weave about me, lassie?" he said, bemused, for the passion between them this night was greater than it had ever been before. But why? He touched her cheek with a fingertip.

"Ye've worked the magic yerself, my Black Angus," she told him, her hand caressing the back of his neck. Her nipples teased him.

"How?" he demanded, his hands cupping the halves of her bottom, drawing her hard against him, against his raging member.

"Do ye not love me, Angus Gordon?" she asked softly.

"Ye brazen, thieving wench, was it not enough for ye that ye stole my cattle?" he teased her, his dark green eyes warm. "Must ye have my heart as well, lassie?"

"Aye!" she responded. Damn him! Why would he not admit he loved her? She knew he did. Why else had he kept her?

His fingers delicately kneaded her flesh. His lips brushed her brow. He took her face between his hands, his thumbs softly brushing along the sides of her mouth. Then his lips took hers in a warm kiss, once, twice, a third time. Lifting her into his arms, he walked slowly across the chamber to place her gently upon their bed. He lay on his side, propped upon an elbow. His fingers trailed down her throat and across her chest. Bending his head, he rubbed his cheek against the swell of her right breast.

Fiona sighed deeply. He had never been a rough lover, but neither had he ever been so tender with her. There was something exceptionally exciting and alluring about him this night. She twined her fingers through his black hair, trying to draw him back to taste her lips, for his kisses were intoxicating. She felt his mouth opening, then closing over her nipple. He sucked strongly, and Fiona felt as if lightning were tearing through her. Never had her breasts been as sensitive to his loving as they were this night. An arm about her shoulder pinioned her lightly. His other hand slipped slowly, seductively down her torso, insinuating its long, slender digits between her soft nether lips.

"Ah," she let her breath out in a long hiss. "Ah!"

His fingers teased at her only long enough to stoke her rising excitement; then they caressed the velvety insides of her rounded thighs. He moved to take her left nipple into his mouth, his tongue encircling the hardened little nub. Her breasts felt hard, and ached with his attentions. She felt his tongue begin to lick at her skin, and Fiona shivered with delight. Pulling the hand on her thigh up to her mouth, she began to suck his fingers, each in its turn, and he shuddered at her voluptuous and carnal act. She had the most incredible instincts for the sensual. "Witch!" He groaned, knowing that if he did not soon plunge himself into her willing body, he would shatter into a thousand bits.

Fiona sensed the sudden urgency of his need. "Come into me, my love," she whispered, releasing his hand and spreading herself for him.

He covered her, struggling futilely to maintain his superiority but unable to resist the warmth of her and the sweet yielding of her flesh as he plunged his manhood deep inside her. "Ah, lassie." He thrust over and over again within the silken heat of her love passage. But rather than weakening him, her compliance seemed to strengthen him. Once more he became master of the situation and, realizing it, used her with renewed vigor.

Beneath him Fiona released her control, arching her body to meet his every downward thrust. She was mindless and yet totally aware. She burned with a fire that he strove mightily to quench. She could feel his hardness, pushing, pushing, pushing into her. It throbbed and burned with a life all its own until she thought she would surely die with the arrant pleasure he was bestowing upon her. Fiona ascended and aspired to the pinnacle of complete passion. Reaching it, she hovered for a long, delicious moment before hurtling down into a warm darkness. Then she heard him cry with his own satisfaction, an almost animal sound.

And afterward she wept with the magnificence of what had just transpired between them, but there was no sadness in the sound. It was pure and simple joy.

The laird spoke with the king. "Ye'll see that my lass gets safely home to Loch Brae, my liege?"

"Don't fear, Angus," the king said. "Everything will be exactly as it should be by the time ye return with Mistress Elizabeth. I canna tell ye how grateful the queen and I are for this last kindness before ye disappear into yer highland lair again."

" 'Tis little enough to do for ye, my liege," the laird answered. "I can understand yer wanting Mistress Williams to see a friendly face in York rather than one of yer less cultured subjects," he finished, laughing.

"Aye, exactly!" James Stewart agreed. "Scotland will be a revelation to the queen's gentle relative."

Fiona saw her lord off, offering him a stirrup cup before he departed on the rainy September morning.

"Try to be a good lass," he teased her. "Go straight home, and don't get into any mischief, Fiona Hay." Lifting her up onto his saddle, he captured her mouth in a long and sweetly lingering kiss, then set her down again.

She struggled to keep the tears from falling. He wasn't going to war. He was simply going to fetch the queen's cousin. She was being foolish, she thought irritably, as the laird of Loch Brae rode off into the gray morning. Then, after hurrying back to their apartment, she burst into fulsome tears and could not be calmed for a good half hour by the faithful Nelly.

"Ye'll feel better when we quit the court, lady," the little maidservant said. "In a few more days we'll be off to Loch Brae, and ye'll feel ever so much better."

"Aye," Fiona agreed, sniffling noisily. "I want to go home, Nelly, but I want my lord back with me."

"Och," Nelly replied, " 'twill be no time at all before we see the laird again. York is no distance. He'll be back in two weeks' time, and then 'tis just a few days to Loch Brae. When are we to leave?"

"I suppose we can go any time," Fiona said. "The queen has already dismissed me from her service. Will three days be enough time for us to pack, Nelly? I will help ye, and we don't have to wait for an escort from Loch Brae. The king has promised my lord that he will have his own men escort us."

"We had best get to work," Nelly said, "if ye want to go in three more days, lady. It's time enough, but only if we work hard."

Maggie MacLeod came to help the two women fill their trunks for transport. And afterward she deliberately sought out her cousin of Nairn to taunt him, for her time was growing short to succeed in the task given her by the king.

"Let us find some wine, Colly," she said. "I am fair exhausted from helping Mistress Hay and her servant pack up all their belongings. She sets out in three days' time for Loch Brae. Now that Black Angus is gone, ye have a chance with her, or are ye afraid that she will reject ye again? Ye must be growing old, Nairn, for I can remember a time when the lasses would not say no to ye." She laughed lightly, noting the muscle in his jaw that twitched as he handed her a goblet of wine. He was annoyed, and that was to the good. "Fifty years ago a man in yer position would have stolen the bride away if he desired her for his own," Maggie continued, "but we are more civilized now in Scotland, are we not?" She sipped her wine, sighing with satisfaction.

"Bride-stealing," said The MacDonald of Nairn,

"is still practiced in the highlands." His look was thoughtful.

"Ye would not dare!" Maggie said, subtly taunting him, her blue eyes wide with feigned shock. "This is not the highlands, cousin."

He smiled at her wickedly, and her heart contracted, for Maggie MacLeod remembered a time when Colin MacDonald's smile would have made her do anything he desired. "I shall not approach her before she leaves lest those who look for her consider I might have her. What road does she take to travel to Loch Brae, and how big an escort will she have, cousin?" he demanded, his finger gently caressing Maggie's flushed cheek.

"Colly, ye dare to do such a thing? Ye must not! If they catch ye, ye'll be killed. Angus Gordon will go mad with fury. He'll search high and low for her—I know it! Don't be such a fool! Are ye not past the time when ye would risk yer life just to have a pretty girl?" Maggie sounded genuinely distressed, and in fact she was. Her conscience was plaguing her mightily over her part in the king's plot. If she did her best, and Colin MacDonald did not steal Fiona Hay, could she be blamed? Aye! The king would indeed blame her. "Are ye so desperate for the wench then that ye would risk yer life? Oh, verra well! I'll get ye the information ye desire, but don't blame me if yer killed. Men! Why are ye such fools when it comes to a pretty woman?" She shrugged.

"Ye would betray yer friend?" he said softly. "For me?"

"When did ye ask something of me that I did not do it for ye, Colly?" Maggie replied, her gaze melting. "Are we not family, cousin? Doesn't our blood tie bind us to aid one another? I may think ye a fool, but I would not break a blood tie with ye."

"Yer Sassenach is a lucky man," The MacDonald of Nairn replied, kissing his cousin lightly upon the tip of her nose. "I leave for Nairn tomorrow with my men."

"Tomorrow," Maggie said, moving away from him. "I will have the information ye need tomorrow, cousin." She was not surprised in the least when the young Douglas came to her shortly afterward saying the king wished to speak with her, and she was to follow him. Maggie smoothed the dark green velvet of her gown and proceeded to the king's privy chamber, where James Stewart awaited her.

"Ye were deep in conversation with yer cousin," the king said by way of greeting her. "What news have ye for me?"

"He will, I believe, waylay her on the road to Loch Brae," Maggie replied. "I am to obtain the route and the size of her escort for him by tomorrow. If he takes his leave of ye on the morrow, then ye can be certain he means to kidnap her, for he will want to reconnoiter the road to find the best spot for his ambush. It canna be too close to the Gordon lands, and it must be in a place where he may quickly make his escape to the northwest."

"Ye have done well, Lady Grey," the king said. Then he dismissed her: "Ye can find yer way back to the hall, I am certain. I have a small mission for young Douglas, so he canna escort ye."

Maggie curtsied and departed the king's presence. She knew what his page was about. He would find Fiona Hay—whose nightmare would then begin. Maggie blanched and the child stirred in her womb. She rushed to find her husband.

"I want to go home, Ben Duff," she said vehemently. "Court is no place for a woman with a belly."

Andrew Grey put a comforting arm about his wife. He knew that something was disturbing her, for she had recently gained a haunted look, and she was not sleeping well at night. Whatever it was, Maggie chose not to confide in him, which hurt him on the one hand, but on the other he knew that she would eventually entrust him with her thoughts. One had to be patient with Maggie. She was a highlander, and they were a moodier, different people than the Scots living in the south.

"When do ye want to leave, my dear?" he asked her.

"By week's end," she responded. "We can be packed by then, if I tell the servants now. Send a messenger to Ben Duff to say we're coming home to stay. I canna abide the hubbub of Perth any longer."

"Aye," Fiona said when she saw her friend in the hall later on and learned their news. " 'Tis better ye go home now, Maggie. First bairns are tricky, I'm told. They don't always come when ye think they will. Ye want to give yer man his heir in yer own home. I'll be glad to get back to Loch Brae with my Black Angus. I'll tell ye a secret. I may already be with a bairn, Maggie. Before my Black Angus left, he was more passionate than I have ever known him to be. Somehow I think I may have conceived, but of course, it may just be wishful thinking on my part. Still, we will have a lovely long winter ahead of us to make a bairn if my hopes are dashed this time." Then Fiona's face filled with concern. "Maggie, are ye all right? Ye look pale. Shall I get ye some wine? Shall I get Andrew?"

"No, no! I will be all right," Maggie managed to gasp, swallowing back the bile that had risen in her throat. She had to change the subject, and then she saw her cousin of Nairn. "Look, Fiona, my cousin is staring at ye again. He is so taken with ye. I have never seen him behave this way with a lass. Admit it. Do ye not think him handsome?"

"His features are pretty enough," Fiona said, glancing briefly at Colin MacDonald, "but he has a hard look about those blue eyes of his. Yer eyes are the same color, Maggie, and yet yer eyes are filled with warmth and compassion. I see little kindness in The MacDonald of Nairn's eyes. And look at his mouth. It is much too sensual. I would not want to be his woman. 'Twould be a hard life with a hard man."

"Yet the lasses all adore him," Maggie said. "I know that I did when we were younger. He has quite a reputation with the lassies."

"So you've told me, and I have no doubt that he wields his weapon well," Fiona said, "or he would not have gained such a reputation, but ye know there is more to a man than just the bedsport, Maggie. Ye didn't wed with Ben Duff for only that. Not at his age."

"I only remember Colly from when we were younger," Maggie said finally.

"I'm certain he was utterly fascinating to a lass with no experience," Fiona said, not wanting to insult her friend, but she didn't think she would have ever been enamored of The MacDonald of Nairn. There was a wildness about him that did not appeal to her.

Colin MacDonald watched Fiona Hay furtively. The mere sight of her set his heart racing. He had never seen a more beautiful woman, nor one who carried herself so proudly despite the shame inflicted upon her by the laird of Loch Brae. Black Angus Gordon would not have her for a wife, Colin thought, pleased. No. He had had his chance, and had she been his lawful wife,

Colin never would have resorted to stealing her, but Fiona was not the laird's wife, nor even his betrothed. There was no legal or moral impediment to Colin MacDonald's kidnapping Fiona Hay and making her his wife, for his wife was what he intended that she be. He had never wanted a wife before he had seen Fiona, but now he knew she was what had been missing in his life. *He would have her!*

It would be difficult at first, he knew. She would hate him for taking her from the man she believed she loved. She would hate him for possessing her body. He would woo her despite it all—and he would teach Fiona Hay to love him as she had never loved Angus Gordon. No. It would not be easy, but once the children came, he was certain she would come to the realization that her life with him was the fate she was meant to have.

Chapter 7

Fiona Hay looked about the bedchamber she had shared with her laird for the past few months. The fireplace had been cleaned. The bed hangings, feather bed, coverlet, and linens were gone, and all the trunks packed. It had been an exciting time, but she was relieved and happy to be going home, as was Nelly.

"We must make our good-byes now," Fiona said as they departed the apartment. "I'll not be long, for 'tis early and we have the whole day before us. The earlier the start, the sooner we're there."

She had already bid Maggie and the queen farewell the previous evening, but the king had said she was to come to him just before she left. It was to his privy chamber she now made her way. James Stewart was an early riser, a man who slept little. Bidding Nelly wait for her outside of the royal chamber, she entered.

"Good morrow, Mistress Hay," the king said, taking her hand and leading her to one of the two chairs by the fire. To her surprise he pressed a goblet of fragrant wine into her hand and seated himself opposite her. "I will come immediately to the point, Mistress Hay," he began. "Do ye love Scotland and want peace throughout the land?"

"Aye, my liege," she said fervently.

"There will be no peace in Scotland until the northern clansmen honestly offer me their fealty, forswear their damned independent thoughts, stop warring among themselves, and cease their general mayhem. Would ye agree with me, Mistress Hay?" The king's amber eyes pierced her.

"Aye, my liege, I would certainly agree with ye," Fiona said, wondering what this could possibly be about.

"I have agents in the north watching and sending me word as to the activities of the Lord of the Isles and his allies," the king said, "but I need someone to observe them from a closer range. I need ye, Mistress Hay."

"Me?" Fiona was astounded. "How on earth could I possibly help ye in the north, my liege?"

"The MacDonald of Nairn is verra taken with ye, Mistress Hay. He is, as ye know, Alexander MacDonald's bastard half-brother. Nairn is devoted to him, and the Lord of the Isles to his brother as well. If ye were with Nairn, ye would be privy to what was happening, and could share yer information with me. Yer verra fair, Mistress Hay. Were I not a happily married man meself, I should be tempted by ye."

Fiona was dumbfounded by the king's words, but she was also suddenly afraid. "I hope to wed with my Black Angus one day," she tried to explain calmly to the king. "What ye are asking me is impossible. Surely ye see that?" Her heart was hammering, for James Stewart didn't look at all as if he was sympathetic to her view.

"Do ye know why I sent the laird to England?" the king asked her.

"Why, to fetch the queen's cousin," Fiona replied. Everyone knew that.

The king nodded. "The queen is verra fond of her cousin, Elizabeth. She would like her to remain in Scotland, which means Mistress Williams must have a Scots husband." He let his words sink into Fiona's consciousness before continuing. "The lady has a small but respectable dower. A wee bit of plate, some gold coins, and a nice flock of sheep. As an orphan she must depend upon her relations to find her a good husband. She is a tender virgin of just the right age for matrimony. Do ye understand what I am saying, Mistress Hay?"

Fiona swallowed a gulp of wine to calm herself.

"Mistress Williams has put herself in the loving care of myself and the queen, and trusts us to settle this matter of a husband for her. She will accept our decision in the matter. Angus Gordon is my friend, and a good man. We would bind him closer to us."

For a long moment Fiona could not speak, she was so shocked. At last she was able to utter, although her throat felt constricted with her effort, "Are ye saying that ye will not allow me to wed with my Black Angus, my liege?" She could hear her heart in her ears now.

"Mistress Hay," James Stewart answered her, "ye are a woman who always puts the good of others ahead of yer own desires. Ye risked yer life to dower yer sisters when ye dared to steal Angus Gordon's cattle. When ye were finally caught, ye paid yer debt with the most precious possession a lass has, yer maidenhead. Ye have seen also to the welfare of yer two youngest sisters. Jean, I am told, is to marry the laird's brother, and the littlest girl—Morag, is it?—has a fine dowry and will be well matched when she is old enough.

"Yer a woman who understands the realities of life. I need a united Scotland. I canna have it unless the northern clans are loyal, and they will not be loyal until The MacDonald of the Isles is faithful to me, or I destroy him. I don't know yet what I must do to bring this chieftain to heel, but having an agent near him will give me a greater advantage than he can possibly have over me." The king paused a moment to give her time to absorb all of his words. Then he continued.

"Ye are my advantage over the Lord of the Isles, Fiona Hay. Nairn's desire for ye is heaven-sent. Help me! Were ye not one of my first adherents even before we met? I cannot prevent ye from returning to Brae, but what would yer place be there now? Only think of the lives that could be saved by my knowing in advance what tack the Lord of the Isles will take. The agents I have planted in the north canna gain information like that. They can but sift the gossip for me. Only someone like you can learn what I need to know. A man's pillow talk is oft times valuable. Will ye not sacrifice yerself for Scotland? Think of yer sisters, Mistress Hay."

Those four words were innocent enough, Fiona thought, but she heard the menace in them. She thought of Anne and Elsbeth and Margery with their proud but powerless highland husbands, more apt than not to side with the Lord of the Isles in any dispute with James Stewart. She thought of Jean's joy over her betrothal to James Gordon, and little Morag, who would one day want her share of happiness, too. This king, so capable of forfeiting Fiona's future for his country's good, was capable of *anything*. Why had she not seen it before? Then she thought of Angus Gordon, the only man she would ever love. He deserved better than a Hay of the Ben for a wife. Worse, she had brought him nothing but responsibilities.

Elizabeth Williams would bring a dowry worthy of Angus Gordon. And when she saw how loving and gentle he could be, she would surely fall in love with him. And Angus? In time, and with the love of Mistress Williams, he would forget the Hay of the Ben, the brazen daughter of Dugald Hay. The king said she might make the choice, but he also made it impossible for her to do anything but obey his will. She could feel her heart breaking.

"Mistress Hay?" The king wanted her obedient attention.

"It is not necessary for ye to couch yer wishes in pretty terms, my liege," Fiona said sharply. "Ye need a spy who can gain the information ye need by whoring for ye. I am not a whore, and ye know it, yet ye would still betray yer best friend to gain yer own ends, James Stewart.

"Verra well. Ye give me no real choice in the matter, but if it salves yer conscience to believe ye do, I canna prevent ye, can I? Since I am not skilled in such matters as spying and whoring, ye will have to give me careful instructions, for I eventually intend returning alive from The MacDonald's lair. *And, of course, there is the matter of payment.* If ye would destroy my future, ye must pay verra dearly for it, *my liege*." She looked directly at him.

Her eyes were like green ice. They made James Stewart exceedingly uncomfortable. But if she was hard, he was yet harder. "Yer to have an escort of a dozen of my men-at-arms," he began, and she nodded. "Somewhere along yer route, and I suspect it will be today or early tomorrow, Nairn and his men will attack yer wee train. The men-at-arms have been ordered to flee as quickly as possible, leaving ye and yer maid helpless. Nairn will, of course, carry ye off into the highlands."

"Ye are certain of this?" Fiona said softly. "Perhaps all he wants to do is have a quick coupling. Will he not be suspicious if my escort flees so quickly? And how can ye be certain Nairn will kidnap me, *my liege*? If ye have not arranged this, too, then yer plan may well be futile."

"Nairn has been carefully goaded into rashness over the last few days," the king said. "His desire for ye has not been abated one whit. He will abduct ye. He would, I am told, make ye his wife. Bride-stealing is an old Scots custom, as ye well know, Fiona Hay. Did not yer father steal yer mother?"

"Aye, and she spent the rest of her life in misery because of it," Fiona said angrily. "She hated Dugald Hay as I shall hate The MacDonald of Nairn, but unlike my mam, I shall not spend my life in suffering. I will whore for ye, James Stewart, and I will spy for ye, but I will not marry a man I don't love!"

"That, Fiona Hay, is up to ye," the king said dryly. "It makes no difference to me if ye wed him or not."

"Now," she said briskly, "what am I to be paid for this great sacrifice I am making for Scotland, *my liege*?"

"What do ye want?"

What did she want? She wanted this conversation to have never taken place, she thought bitterly. She wanted to be on the road to Brae. *What did she want?* What was her happiness worth? She drew a deep breath. "I want a thousand gold merks."

"Five hundred silver," he countered, and she nodded.

"And two dozen head of cattle, and a virile bull," she continued.

"A dozen," the king said.

Fiona shook her head. "No! Two dozen and a virile bull, *my liege*. And, without Angus Gordon's knowledge, I want my tower house on Ben Hay repaired, put in habitable condition again for when I return, *for I will return*. I will have no other home then."

"Do ye mean to live alone up on yer ben again?" he asked in surprise.

"Until Black Angus brought me to Brae, the tower

house on Ben Hay was where I lived. No one knew we were there. Now my sisters are wed or have plans to wed. I must have some place to lie my head. I certainly canna go back to Brae and ask for shelter, nor do I desire to live with my sisters and their husbands. As chieftain of the Hays of the Ben, that house is mine. See it is made ready for my return. I will send ye a message when I am there. It is then ye will deliver my two dozen cattle and the virile bull. The five hundred merks is to be deposited in my name this day with Martin the Goldsmith on the High Street in Perth."

"What if ye don't return, Mistress Hay?"

"Then ye are saved the cattle and the bull, my lord, but the merks are to be divided equally among my five sisters, and my serving wench, Nelly, if she survives me. I will trust ye, my lord, to see to it. Now, how am I to get any information to ye that I gather?"

The king carefully explained to Fiona that he had a small network of male spies: a priest named Ninian; a cloth and ribbon merchant in Inverness, Master Malcolm; an Irish minstrel, Borra O'Neil, who earned his keep wandering from hall to hall in the highlands entertaining the clansmen; a tinker, Drysdale, who with his wife and blind son meandered about the north repairing the goodwives' pots and other tin utensils while gathering information. Giving detailed descriptions along with the names, the king said, "These four will be your contacts, Fiona Hay. They will be told of your coming. The merchant will be nearest to ye. The priest you are likely to meet on Islay, should ye go there, but the tinker and the minstrel will probably come to Nairn to seek ye out from time to time. Make them show ye this coin." He proffered a small silver piece, which she took. "Only six of these were struck when I was crowned this summer past. Ye now have one, I have

one, and the other four are in the highlands with my
agents."

"How did ye set up a network of spies so quickly?"
she asked him, suspicious.

"My uncle always had a wee group of agents
working for him," James Stewart said. "He didn't trust
his brother, the Wolf of Badenoch. I simply picked
these four from among the others, who are still useful
to me, but the four I have named are invaluable. Can ye
write?"

"Aye, I can," she answered him. "Black Angus
taught me."

There was that twinge of guilt again, but the king
pushed it aside. "Commit nothing to parchment unless
absolutely necessary," he warned her. "Neither the merchant nor the minstrel ever forget anything told them,
and the tinker has a unique memory in that he can repeat exactly what is uttered in his presence six months
later. It is an interesting talent, for unlike the others
whose business it is to remember, the tinker is a simple
man, I have been told."

Fiona nodded. "Is there anything else I should
know?"

"No," he said.

"How long must I remain with Nairn?" A minute
will be too long, she thought, forcing back the panic beginning to overwhelm her.

"Until I tell ye that ye may return, Fiona Hay," the
king said.

"A year?" she asked him. Dear Holy Mother, not
a year!

"Possibly more," he said honestly, noting how pale
she had become, and hoping that she would not swoon.
Suddenly he wondered if she was strong enough to do

this, but there was no turning back now. He needed her in The MacDonald of Nairn's heart—and bed.

There was a long silence while Fiona calmed herself and gathered her strength again. "I must tell my servant, my liege. She should not have to suffer my fate if she does not want to. I canna allow it. She is a faithful, good girl, and does not deserve unkindness. May I tell her here, sire? You will want me to be discreet, I know."

"Where is she?" the king demanded.

"Waiting for me outside, my liege," Fiona replied.

"Get her."

Fiona went to the door of the king's privy chamber, opened it, and called to Nelly to come in. Wide-eyed, the girl stumbled over her feet as she curtsied to the king, awestruck to be in such close proximity with James Stewart. He graciously invited her to sit, giving up his own seat to stand above the two women. Slowly, carefully, Fiona explained the situation. When she had finished, Nelly burst into tears. Understanding the girl's grief, Fiona remained silent until Nelly's tears finally abated. The king looked decidedly uncomfortable.

"Ye don't have to come with me, Nelly," Fiona said. "But if ye return to Brae, ye must keep this secret from the laird."

"Not come with ye?" Nelly's tear-stained look was indignant. "Of course I'll go with ye, Mistress Fiona! I would not be doing my duty if I deserted ye. I dare not go back to Brae without ye. Me aunt would have me hide; then she would weasel yer secret from me. Ye know she would!"

"Ye could stay behind in the queen's service, Nelly. The king could arrange such an appointment for ye, could ye not, my liege?" He nodded, and Fiona continued, "Yer aunt would not be able to get to ye then. Besides, she would be so proud that ye were serving the queen. She would suspect nothing and consider ye fortunate to have escaped being kidnapped along with me. I love ye, and I know ye love me, but I would not think badly of ye if ye decided to stay behind."

Nelly's eyes filled with tears again. "Mistress Fiona, ye'll need me, and I will not leave ye," she said, *"even for a queen."*

"Then it is settled," the king said briskly. "The sun is already up, Fiona Hay. Ye had best be on yer way. Scotland will be all the better for yer sacrifice. The merks will be deposited today, and the rest of our arrangement will be put into effect as well. May God and his Blessed Mother watch over ye, lady."

"How do ye dare to invoke God and his Mother under these circumstances?" Fiona's voice had a hard edge to it. Picking up her cloak, she nodded to Nelly, and the two women left the king's privy chamber.

"Are ye afraid, my lady?" Nelly asked her mistress as they hurried through the palace corridors toward the courtyard where their escort would be awaiting them. Her own visage was pale, the freckles across the bridge very prominent.

"Aye, I am afraid," Fiona said, "but that is to the good. As long as I am fearful, I will be careful, Nelly. I don't want to die. Ye must be cautious, too, lassie. Our lives depend on it. Are ye certain ye would go with me? There is still time to change yer mind."

"Nay," Nelly said stoutly. "I will not leave ye, my lady."

They met their escort in the courtyard. Nelly would ride in the baggage cart behind which Fiona's mare was tied. Fiona would ride the laird's gray gelding. The animal had a black mane and tail and was very handsome. Angus would be irritated with its loss, she knew, but there was no help for it. She had no excuse to leave the beast behind, and frankly preferred it to her own horse. It was surefooted and of a stronger disposition than the little mare.

It was a perfect September day. Fiona rode at the head of the small train with the captain. He remarked on her riding astride, and she laughed. "Have ye ever tried to sit atop a bouncing beastie sideways?" she asked him, and he chuckled. The truth was her long woolen skirts modestly shielded her legs, and what little showed was sheathed by boots. A length of red-and-green Hay plaid was slung about her shoulders. Her black hair was plaited in a single braid, and her head was topped with her chieftain's cap, its eagle feather set at a jaunty angle. Court garb was hardly suited to a ride into the highlands.

They rode the entire morning, stopping at midday to rest the horses, eat, and empty their bladders. The men broke their fast with oatcakes and whatever spirits were in their flasks; Fiona and Nelly opened a basket from the castle kitchens that held a fresh loaf of bread, a small cheese, a roasted chicken, two apples, and two pears. There was also a flask of sweet wine.

"Eat as much as ye can," Fiona said softly to her servant. "I am not certain when we will eat again. Nairn will strike today. Of that I feel certain. We have traveled north all morning, but we will turn northeast late today. 'Tis to his advantage to take us before then. By evening tomorrow we will be much too close to Brae."

"I wish we were there now," Nelly said low, and her eyes met those of her mistress, who nodded in agreement. "I am so afraid, my lady," she admitted.

"Nairn is just a man," Fiona replied, trying to put a more practical light upon their situation. "It is the unknown that makes us fearful right now, Nelly lass. I'm glad yer with me. An extra pair of eyes and ears will not hurt. And eventually we'll come home again; I promise ye that. Ye to Brae, and me to my wee tower on the ben."

"I'll pray every night for it, my lady," Nelly said fervently.

Prayer, Fiona thought as they continued along their way that afternoon. Prayer alone wasn't the answer. She was going to have to keep her wits about her. She could never let her guard down. Angus always claimed that she was brazen, but she wasn't. She was simply a woman with an instinct for survival. Could she really be of help to the king, or did he merely want to get her out of the way so he might marry Angus off to the queen's cousin?

Nay. James Stewart simply could have ordered Angus to do his bidding, and he would have had to obey. Fiona sighed. Why had she been so stubborn? Janet Gordon Stewart had wanted her to become Angus's wife ages ago. If only Fiona had let her arrange it, she thought regretfully, she would not be riding north now, waiting to be carried off by The MacDonald of Nairn.

The shadows were beginning to lengthen as the autumn afternoon deepened. The road ran alongside a small blue loch and into a misty glen. Fiona could feel the hair on the back of her neck beginning to rise like the hackles on a dog. *This would be where it would happen.* She could sense it, smell it! The glen was alive with other presences. She wanted to turn her horse back and gallop away from it, but she knew she couldn't. It was like waiting for a blow to fall. Her chest felt tight, and she could scarcely draw a breath.

Suddenly the captain of her escort hissed, "Lady, halt!" He pointed to the far end of the glen, where in the purple haze a troupe of horsemen stood silently. *"Ghosts!"* the captain whispered, sounding afraid, and indeed the mounted figures did have a spectral look to them. The men behind them murmured nervously, their horses growing skittish.

"They are highlanders," Fiona snapped back at the captain. "Can ye make out their plaids or badges? I canna tell, for the light is wrong."

The horsemen began to move toward them. Slowly at first, then more swiftly. Kicking their mounts into a gallop, they waved their claymores over their heads, shouting ferociously as they thundered down the glen toward Fiona and her little train.

Next to her the captain seemed to panic. *"Flee!"* he shouted to his men. Turning his horse about, he led a headlong retreat from the hazy glen.

Fiona turned to look to Nelly's safety, watching amazed as the driver of the baggage cart leapt from his seat and ran alongside his companions until one was decent enough to slow his horse so that the man could scramble up behind the rider. "Cowards!" Fiona shouted after them. "Come back, ye bloody cravens! Don't leave us!"

Their attackers dashed past them, chasing after the king's escort, but shortly they turned and reentered the glen to surround the two women. The moment was almost anticlimactic. Nelly had clambered to the cart's seat and now held the frightened mule in check. Fiona, still mounted, was by the vehicle's side, her gelding dancing nervously but under her firm control. Fiona recognized the gray, green, and white tartan that Nairn preferred to the Lord of the Isles' green-and-blue colors.

Colin MacDonald pushed his gray stallion through the press of his men. Mounted he seemed even bigger than she remembered. "Mistress Hay," he said solemnly, reaching for her horse's bridle.

Fiona yanked the gelding away from his grasp. "Are ye mad, my lord?" she hissed at him. "Ye have deliberately frightened away my escort. How are we to get home to Brae? Or do ye propose to escort us there yerself?" She glared furiously at him, watching out of the corner of her eye as a lad with the men climbed up upon the wagon next to Nelly, giving her a saucy grin and pinching her cheek.

Nelly slapped the boy, saying loudly, "I'll thank ye to keep yer paws to yerself, ye little highland savage!"

The men about them guffawed loudly, amused by both Nelly's actions and the lad's acute red-faced embarrassment.

"Tell yer men to leave my servant alone," Fiona said coldly to Colin MacDonald. "She is a good lass. I will not have her tampered with by force. I'll kill any man who harms her! Do ye savages understand?" Her gloved hand moved menacingly to her dirk. "Now get out of our way! We have several miles to go yet before we reach the convent of Saint Margaret, where we will spend the night. Hopefully our *brave* escort will have recovered their courage, and will meet us there," she finished boldly.

The MacDonald of Nairn moved his stallion next to Fiona's gelding again and reached once more for her bridle. She slapped his hands away angrily, but this time he caught her wrist in a hard grip. "Mistress Hay," he said, "ye are not going to Brae. Yer coming with me." His bright blue eyes bored into her.

"My lord, this is outrageous! Those poor fools ye frightened were the king's men. Surely ye knew that?" Fiona said.

Releasing her wrist, Colin MacDonald surprised

Fiona by leaning from his horse, wrapping an arm about her waist, and lifting her from her saddle onto his, seating her before him. "It will soon be dark," he said over her sputtered protests. "It is a ways to the place we will shelter tonight." He turned away from her, calling, "Roderick Dhu, see to the wench, the wagon, and my lady's horse. The wench is not to be touched by anyone." Then, kicking his mount, he moved forward.

"My lord!" Fiona protested as they rode. "I find your conduct most outrageous. Ye have no feud with the Gordons of Brae. Why do ye wish to start one? Give me back my horse at once!" She squirmed against him in an apparent effort to escape him.

"Do ye never shut yer mouth, woman?"

"I will not be treated in such a despicable fashion, my lord!" Fiona declared spiritedly. She attempted to slide from his grasp. "Let me go, ye uncouth heathen! Let me go this minute!"

"Woman," Colin MacDonald said grimly, "don't make me regret my actions this day in stealing ye away from the laird of Loch Brae."

"*Stealing me?* I will not be stolen!" she insisted. "Why would ye steal me from my Black Angus, my lord?"

"Because, Fiona Hay," he answered her, "I want ye for my own wife. Yer laird has had many a long month to make an honest woman of ye, but he would not do it. Well, I will! The moment I first saw ye I wanted ye, and by the blessed rood, I will have ye, woman!"

"Well, I will not have ye!" Fiona said angrily.

"Ye have no choice in the matter."

"Ye canna wed me if I'll not have ye," she insisted.

He laughed suddenly. She talked too much. She was opinionated, but by God, she made him laugh. He needed a woman who could do that. She was beautiful, and he had wanted her not even knowing the sort of woman she was. He had thought it wouldn't matter because he desired her. He hadn't even cared, but now that he could see some of her many aspects, he was becoming more intrigued, more fascinated by her.

"I wanted ye. I have taken ye, and there is an end to it, Fiona Hay," he told her firmly. "Now be quiet, for I must concentrate upon the track in this fading light if we are to reach the safety of our shelter tonight. Remember, there is not an early moon to guide us."

Fiona grew silent. It had gone well, she thought. The king would be quite pleased. Now she must follow her instincts in order to keep Colin MacDonald interested in her without boring him. If he was learning about the woman he desired, she, too, must learn about the man he was. She snuck a peek at him. His handsome long face was deep in concentration as he carefully moved his mount along the barely discernible trail, leading the men behind him. Once they had exited the glen, there was a bit more light, but not for very long. They had turned northwest, Fiona noted, for the sunset was almost directly ahead of them. Nairn was more north. Where were they going?

They rode for close to another hour, and then in the last fading vestiges of the twilight Fiona saw stone walls and buildings ahead of them. Was it St. Margaret's? It couldn't be. Shortly she discovered that their destination was the ruins of some small castle. Their party entered the courtyard and dismounted. The horses were carefully tethered in a wooden shed that had a roof. A fire was started in the courtyard's center. Water was drawn from the castle's well and given to the animals.

Fiona and Nelly sat silently in the cart, watching as the clansmen skinned and gutted the rabbits they had hunted along their way, then put them on spits over the fire.

"At least we'll not starve," Nelly said quietly to her mistress. "We have some bread, fruit, and cheese left in our basket, too."

Soon they were brought a joint of the hot, freshly cooked rabbit to share. When they had finished their meal, Nelly hurried across the courtyard beneath the hot eyes of the men to fetch some water from the well so they might wash the grease from their hands and faces. Then the two women sat quietly together, wondering where they were to sleep. Finally The MacDonald of Nairn, in the company of Roderick Dhu, joined them.

"Yer servant will sleep in the cart," he said. "The men have been warned again that she is not to be touched. Roderick will watch over her."

"Thank ye, my lord," Fiona said quietly. "Nelly is dear to me. I should be most angry if anything were to happen to her."

"I'll guard her with my life, lady," Roderick Dhu said.

Fiona nodded at him.

Colin MacDonald took her hand in a firm grasp. "Come with me," he said, and before she might demur, he pulled her from the cart, half dragging her away from the fire and into the darkness of the night.

"Where are we going?" she demanded of him, her heart beginning to pound quickly. It was too soon! She wasn't ready for this!

He said nothing, leading her instead from the courtyard 'and around behind the castle, away from the others. Finally he stopped. The moon was just beginning to rise over the eastern hills, and in its dim light

Fiona watched as he spread a cloak upon the grassy embankment.

"*No!*" she said, backing away from him.

He caught her hand. "Come now, Fiona mine."

"I am not yers," she said softly.

"Aye, sweeting, ye are," he answered. "From the first moment I laid eyes upon ye, ye were mine, though ye knew it not." Inexorably he drew her into his embrace. Fiona turned from his passionate gaze, but Colin MacDonald caught her chin between his thumb and forefinger, his mouth taking possession of hers.

The touch of his lips on hers was strange, for she had never kissed any man but Angus Gordon. His lips were warm, firm, demanding. She had only begun to explore the sensation of his proximity when he kicked her legs out from beneath her, lowering her to the cloak upon the grassy knoll. Fiona gasped with her surprise to find herself upon her back, and Colin MacDonald straddling her. " 'Twas not fair!" she cried at him.

He laughed softly at her. "I mean to have my way with ye, Fiona sweeting," he told her bluntly. He pinioned her between his legs, resting himself upon his heels so that his great size would not crush her.

" 'Twas unfairly done," she said indignantly.

In response to her protest he reached out, drawing her plaid aside, and began to unlace her blouse. She caught at his hands, but Colin MacDonald shook his head admonishingly at her and, grasping her wrists in one of his big hands, imprisoned them above her head. "No, no, Fiona sweeting, don't hinder me. Those sweet breasts of yers have tantalized me for weeks. I must see them!" His large fingers were surprisingly supple and skilled. Swiftly they unlaced the garment, then the chemise. Pushing aside the soft fabric, he gazed upon her bared bosom. "Ah, Fiona," he finally said, "how perfect ye are."

She flushed beneath his hot gaze, biting her lip to hold back her cry. She didn't understand what was the matter with her. To her shame she found his hungry look exciting. Her breasts had matured in the last two years, becoming fuller and almost perfectly round in shape. The skin was milky white and very soft to the touch.

Colin MacDonald reached out to caress the two sweet globes of flesh. His fingertips touched her tenderly, brushing across the fullness lightly, stirring up feelings she had not believed any but Angus Gordon could awaken.

"No more," she pleaded with him. "Don't touch me, I beg ye, my lord. Why must ye shame me like this?" There were tears in her emerald-green eyes that glittered in the light of the quarter moon. She had known this morning what the king expected of her, but faced with the reality of it, she did not know if she could bear it.

His expression serious, he bent in answer to her plea, kissing the flesh of her bosom. "Yer mad, Fiona sweeting, if ye think I can stop now," he told her. "What is between us is as unquenchable as a roaring fire. Ye canna stanch it any more than ye can stem the rising tide."

"I will never yield my heart to ye, Colin Mac-Donald," Fiona said honestly to him. To her despair a large tear rolled down her face.

"Aye, sweeting, ye will, given time," he responded, a single finger reaching out to catch her tear, lifting it from her cheek to his lips. "I will honor ye as Angus Gordon never did. He took ye for his whore and paraded ye before all of Scotland, but I will wed ye, Fiona

Hay. Ye will be my wife, and I will be proud of it," he said.

For a moment Fiona saw the vulnerability in his bright blue eyes, and her heart contracted. Did James Stewart in his righteous quest for a united Scotland have any idea of the terrible betrayal he had put into effect? He had forced her from the man she loved in order to betray a man who loved her. It was monstrous, but she had no choice in the matter else she, too, be destroyed. And there were others also to be considered. Her sisters. Nelly. And—oh, what did any of it matter any more! She would do her duty, and spend the rest of her life ashamed of her part in this secret deception that would destroy them all. And for what? Scotland? *Damn Scotland! Damn James Stewart and all his kind!* They knew only power and more power.

Suddenly and to her utter amazement Colin Mac-Donald began to lace up her blouse again. When he had finished, he raised himself from her body and lay next to her. Fiona was completely puzzled. What was the matter? Why was he not ravishing her as she assumed he meant to do? Had he suddenly found her distasteful?

He smiled gently at her confusion. "I will not take you until we are man and wife, sweeting. We highlanders honor our women, particularly those we intend to wed." He took her hand, raising it to his lips to kiss her fingertips. "I will sleep by your side to protect you and so that my men understand the seriousness of my commitment toward you." Then he drew his cloak about them, and pulling her closer so that she faced him, he closed his eyes.

Fiona stared at the sandy lashes brushing against his tanned cheek. For several minutes she couldn't bring herself to move as he appeared to slide easily into a deep sleep. Finally she shifted herself into a more comfortable position, resting her dark head against his broad chest. His heart beat rhythmically beneath her ear. Her nostrils twitched at the mixture of scents emanating from him. Horse. Sweat. Soap? Aye, 'twas soap she smelled beneath the other traces of male fragrance. A tiny smile touched her lips. So he was eager to please her, she thought. Considering his behavior, she found that interesting. She was surprised by his tenderness, for his reputation was that of a fierce, hard man, but then had not Maggie said all the lasses were mad for him? If he treated them all with such sweetness, it was no surprise. Her instinct was to reach out and caress his red-gold hair, but she restrained herself. It was such an outrageous color of hair for a man, and yet it suited him admirably.

She lay in his arms now, drained by all that had happened this day. She had awakened at Scone, ready to return to Brae. Now this night she lay upon a grassy knoll in the arms of The MacDonald of Nairn, her hoped-for future despoiled. She had a new future. She was the king's secret weapon against the MacDonalds. She would do her duty, even if her heart was broken into a thousand pieces.

Chapter 8

She awoke, surprised that she had slept at all. It was still dark, although the sky was giving evidence of the new day in the fading of the stars above her and a glow along the edges of the horizon. Colin MacDonald's face came into her view. He kissed her mouth slowly, and she did not resist him. What was the point now?

"We had best get up," he told her. "We canna tarry long here. Can I trust ye if I let ye ride yer horse today?"

"I don't know if ye should ever trust me, Colin MacDonald," she said bluntly, "but if ye are asking me if I will run away from ye, where would I go? I canna return to Brae." She stood up, drawing close about her the cloak upon which they had lain. "Send Nelly to me with some hot water," she told him. "I will not ride this day with the scent of ye upon me."

"Hot water, eh? Have ye always been such a fine lady, Fiona mine, or did Angus Gordon make ye such?" His look was both curious and amused.

"Do ye not bathe regularly, then?" she demanded of him. "I do. I always have done so, my lord. A vessel of water over the fire will be enough for my ablutions this morn."

He was dismissed, and he knew it. What a firebrand this woman was. She could obviously hold her own with him, but it amused him more than angered him. Such a strong woman would breed up strong sons for Nairn. Colin MacDonald found Nelly wide awake and looking as if she had not slept a great deal.

"Good morning, lass," he greeted her. "Are ye all right?"

Nelly nodded at him. "I'm not used to sleeping in the open, my lord," she told him honestly. "I was a wee bit frightened."

"We'll not let anything harm ye," he promised her. "Now, fetch some hot water to yer mistress. Ye'll find her around on the eastern side of the castle's ruins." He pointed to show the direction.

The fire had not been allowed to die completely away in the night. Nelly saw a small metal pot sitting upon the coals that was already filled with water. Sticking a finger in it, she determined the water was warm enough to wash in, and picking the pot up with the edge of her skirt so as not to burn her hands, she hurried to take it to Fiona, finding her mistress easily.

"Ye were safe in the night?" Fiona asked.

"Aye," Nelly replied. "Just a wee bit cold and frightened, but none of the men came near me after his lordship's warning. I slept up in the cart atop our bedding with that Roderick Dhu fellow dozing right at the foot of the wagon, my lady."

"I am grateful for yer safety. Do not even think of flirting with any of these savages, Nelly, unless ye seek to lose yer virginity. They will take the slightest thing as encouragement. Put the water down here."

"I brought ye a scrubbing cloth," Nelly said. "I was able to retrieve it from the luggage, my lady." Handing it to her mistress, the girl then turned away to give Fiona her privacy. "I'll fetch you some food," she said, hurrying off.

Returning in only a few minutes, she gave her mistress, who was now finished washing, a tin plate.

"There was a bit of cheese, bread, and some fruit remaining from our basket. Let me take yer cup, and I'll get ye some water from the stream which is nearby."

Grateful for Nelly's thoughtfulness, Fiona sat down and began to nibble the food her servant had brought. Moments later Nelly rejoined her. Together they ate, sharing the cup of clear water the girl had fetched for them. They did not speak. There was nothing to say, and if there had been, there was the danger of being overheard. Everything was as the women had expected it would be at this moment.

Colin MacDonald came to them as they were finishing their meal. "Come and pick the clothing ye want to take with ye," he said. "I'm sending the cart, and most of my men, home to Nairn."

"Where are we going?" Fiona asked him, surprised.

"To Islay, to my brother, the Lord of the Isles," Nairn said. "He'll want to know all about this king of the Scots, *and* he'll want to meet the lass who's finally turned my thoughts to marriage." He grinned at her.

Fiona climbed to her feet and cocked an eyebrow at him. "I don't know if it is just yer person or yer foolish boasting that repels me the most, Colin MacDonald."

"Did Gordon ever beat ye, sweeting?" he asked her. "Ye obviously need to have a hand taken to yer bottom."

"If ye value that hand, my lord," Fiona warned him darkly, "don't ever raise it to me. I will cut it off the first chance I get." She smiled sweetly at him then and moved back to the encampment.

"Would she?" he asked Nelly.

"She'd try," Nelly replied, "and if she failed, she'd try again."

Nairn looked thoughtful, then laughed. "I don't

know her at all, do I?" he said. Motioning to the serving girl to follow him, he turned back toward their campsite, where his men were making ready their departure.

Fiona had gotten into the luggage. She pulled out some undergarments, two pairs of knit stockings, a clean shirt, and a comb for her hair. Seating herself on a nearby rock, she began to undo her plait to comb out her raven-black hair. She then sat quietly while Nelly rebraided her tresses. The girl handed her mistress her chieftain's cap with its eagle feather, and her clan badge, wrapping a warm cloak about her afterward.

"These few things are all I'll need," Fiona said. "My court clothing would be out of place on Islay."

"I'll pack them," Nelly said. She went to gather her own things as well.

The MacDonald of Nairn had overheard Fiona. Following after Nelly, he caught her arm and drew her aside. "I will not argue with yer mistress, for she is filled with anger now and verra stubborn. Pack at least one fine gown for her and some jewelry. My brother's hall is every bit as fine as the king's. I don't want her embarrassed when she sees it."

"A houppelande would be simplest, my lord. The green velvet is her finest, but I think the violet damask will pack better in a small space," Nelly told him politely. "Are ye certain we canna keep the baggage cart? My mistress has some lovely things."

He chuckled. "Ye love her, do ye not, lassie? Aye. I can see yer loyalty, and 'tis good. The cart will slow us, Nelly. We are closer to Nairn than we are to my brother's castle on Islay. Without the cart it will take us a week to reach there. Ye don't want to be on the road forever, do ye? Besides, we will not stay with Alexander. I have my own lands to look after, and I have been away long enough in my brother's service. The cart must go to Nairns Craig. Once we have finished our business on Islay, we'll go home. Then yer mistress can show me all her finery." He patted Nelly's cheek. "Quickly now, lassie. The sun is already rising, and we must be on our way as soon as possible. Ye understand?"

"Are ye afraid the king's men will come after ye and rescue my mistress?" Nelly asked him slyly.

He grinned at her. "Aye, and that, too."

Nairn chose six men to accompany them, including the trusty Roderick Dhu. They would travel west and just slightly south across Scotland. The countryside they journeyed through was mountainous, forested, and lake-filled. They rode from sunrise to sunset, stopping briefly only twice. Their dainty food from Scone Palace's kitchens gone, Fiona and Nelly subsisted on what the men ate: oatcakes, whatever small game could be caught and cooked, and water. The second night of their journey they camped by a small, nameless loch.

"Why do we not stop at a religious guest house or at the home of one of yer brother's allies?" Fiona asked her captor.

"Because there are few religious houses in this area," he told her, "and besides, I don't want ye seen by anyone. Those poor frightened men-at-arms who fled, leaving ye to my tender care, didn't know who we were. Therefore it will not be known who has taken ye or where ye have been taken. I don't want yer former lover coming after us simply to kill me because his pretty mistress is now to be my wee wifie. Besides, what good would it do ye? Did ye not say he wouldn't take ye back after thinking I'd had ye?"

She felt the tears beneath her eyelids and quickly blinked them away. She had said it, and it was true. Angus would never want her again. Anger overwhelmed her once more. Throwing herself at him, she scratched his handsome face, hissing at him, "I hate ye! I hate ye! Ye have ruined my life!" To Fiona's great shock he picked her up, and tossed her, fully clothed, into the loch. She screeched curses at him in the Celtic tongue, and his men howled with laughter. Fiona was not certain if it was her colorful expletives that amused them, or the sight of her flailing about in the shallows.

Colin MacDonald put his hand to his cheek and then, taking it away, gazed at the blood on his fingers. There would be a slight scar. She was an absolute little wildcat. He was beginning to wonder if he hadn't taken on more than he could, or wanted to, handle, but it was too late now. He had her.

Fiona struggled from the water, furious. "These are the only clothes I have, ye fiery-headed oaf!" she shouted at him. "How the hell am I supposed to get them dry by morning?"

"Then ye'll ride wet," he shouted back, "and next time don't use yer claws on me, Fiona mine! I'll not be marked again by ye!"

Nelly was appalled. "Ye have to get out of these things, my lady. Ye'll catch yer death if ye don't. Ye've another chemise, and we'll dry the rest by the fire. Ye'll not travel damp, I promise."

Fiona's glare of fury silenced the chortling clansmen. "Since I'm soaked through," she said to Nelly, "I might as well bathe. I stink of the horses."

"Thank God ye didn't have yer cloak on," Nelly said. "The skirt will be hard enough to dry, and yer wool stockings as well. Come along then, my lady. Just down the shore we may have a wee bit of privacy." She turned to the men about the fire. "And don't any of ye skulk along after us!"

They grinned, and Roderick Dhu said blandly to

his master, "They be two strong wenches with blazing tongues, my lord."

The MacDonald of Nairn grinned back at his companions. "Aye, and ye'll all treat them with respect. The raven-haired lady is to be my wife, lads, and wee Nelly, as her servant, must be esteemed, too."

The two women could feel the men's eyes upon them as they moved down the shore, but shortly a large clump of greenery obscured them. The ground beneath their feet was sandy. They stopped, and Nelly helped Fiona out of her wet clothing. She spread the garments over the bushes and emptied the water from her lady's boots. Then she laid her mistress's cloak upon the ground and seated herself upon it, watching as Fiona entered the water.

"Yer braver than I am, my lady," she said with a small giggle.

" 'Tis cold," Fiona admitted, "but I'm beginning to smell the horses less and less." She paddled about. The water in the loch was so clear that she could see her legs and feet just above the sandy bottom. "What will I dry myself with, Nelly? We have no toweling."

"We'll use yer wet chemise, my lady. I've wrung it out. 'Twill do no more than take the droplets away, but wrapped in yer cloak, ye'll soon be warm and dry again. When ye are, I have yer other chemise for ye to put on."

Fiona stepped from the water. As she did, Colin MacDonald came upon the two women. Fiona grit her teeth in annoyance, saying to Nelly, "Pay him no heed, lassie, the oversize oaf!"

"I came to see what was keeping ye," he said. "Ye haven't been swimming, have ye?" His eyes swept over her naked body. *Jesu! Mary!* he swore to himself. She was absolutely magnificent! He hadn't realized it until now, for his passion had been for the woman herself, but by the rood she had a wonderful body!

"I told ye I am accustomed to bathing daily," Fiona said loftily, finishing her drying and wrapping her cloak about her lush form. "Since we carry no tub for me to bathe properly, I have made my ablutions in the loch. Nelly, lass, run back and fetch my dry chemise for me, please." She looked critically at the man before her. " 'Twould not hurt if ye would wash yerself. Ye, too, reek of the horses."

"Wash? Every day?" He sounded slightly horrified.

" 'Twill not harm ye, my lord," she told him sharply.

"Yer a verra high-handed wench, I'm thinking, Fiona Hay." He stood before her, back to the water, hands upon his hips, legs spread wide in a show of authority.

Fiona met his gaze, thinking at the same time it was just too delicious an opportunity not to take. She let her cloak fall open and walked toward him. He tried valiantly to maintain eye contact with her, but the temptation to look upon her luscious breasts and white, white body was too strong. He succumbed, and in the moment his eyes left hers to fasten hungrily upon her bosom, Fiona shoved him hard backward into the waters of the loch, laughing so hard that she almost collapsed as he scrambled to his feet in the knee-deep water, sputtering with outrage. "How the hell am I supposed to get a wool kilt dry by the morrow?" he roared at her.

"Ye'll simply have to ride wet, my lord," she mocked him, disappearing into the greenery to come face-to-face with the startled Nelly. "Quick!" she said, "Give me my chemise, lass!" She flung off her cloak, slipped on the chemise, and drew the cloak back about her shoulders.

"What have ye done to him?" Nelly asked, hearing a string of colorful oaths from the beach behind them. "He sounds as if he would kill ye if he could but get his hands about yer neck, my lady."

"I just gave the bastard a taste of his own medicine." Fiona laughed. "I pushed him in the loch, and he's verra wet, I fear. Offer to dry his kilt for him, will ye, Nelly? I don't want to kill him—at least not yet." She smiled. She might not like the task the king had set her to, but there was no reason she couldn't have a little fun while she was about it.

Reaching the comfort of the fire, she gratefully accepted a plate of oatcakes from Roderick Dhu. When he handed her a steaming cup, she looked surprised. "What is it?"

"A wee bit of wine mixed with water and heated in the fire, my lady. Ye must be chilled after yer swim," he told her, the ghost of a smile hovering about his lips.

"Ye had better fix a similar draught for yer master," Fiona said sweetly. "I fear he, too, fell in the loch." She turned away, sipping the heated drink thankfully, for it was strong, and set her blood to warming beneath her cloak.

She sat herself on a small outcropping of rock, daintily eating the oatcakes and sipping her wine, Nelly beside her. Colin MacDonald came grimly into the clearing, taking the cup of hot wine from Roderick Dhu. He was soaking wet, his hair hanging lankly about his shoulders, the droplets sluicing off his kilt. He drank the wine down in several gulps, accepted his portion of oatcakes, and ate. He was stonily silent, speaking to no one.

Finally, when he had finished eating, Nelly dared to approach him. "If ye like, my lord, I'll dry yer garments by the fire with my mistress's."

"Aye," Nairn answered her, standing up. He beckoned to the two women. "Follow me," he said shortly. "Roderick Dhu, ye have the responsibility of Nelly's virtue until we reach Nairn."

"Aye, my lord," the clansman answered, looking menacingly at his companions.

Fiona and Nelly followed Nairn back to the little beach, where he stripped his garments off, heedless of Nelly's gasps and blushes. Handing them to the serving girl, he said, "Your mistress and I will sleep here tonight, lassie. Lay yourself next to Roderick Dhu. He will protect you."

Dismissed, Nelly hurried back to the campfire.

"We'll sleep wrapped in your cloak," The MacDonald told Fiona.

Mesmerized, she stared at his big, naked body. Everything was large, arms, legs, torso. His back and shoulders were very broad. His buttocks were rounded and tight. She was unable to prevent her gaze from dropping to the fiery red bush between his thighs from where his male member hung, a thick, pendulous length of pale flesh. Even chilled from the water of the loch, it was a formidable and impressive sight.

He pulled her chemise-clad form against his nudity, nuzzling her ear. "Fiona mine," he murmured, "do you know how very much I desire you? How difficult it is for me not to possess you?" His teeth gently worried her earlobe.

She could feel the maleness of him against her; she could tell how much he strained to curb his fierce lust. She swallowed hard, saying, "It really makes no difference to me when you effect your rape of my person."

"When we finally couple," he told her evenly, "you will be my wife."

"I will be unwilling nonetheless," she hissed at him.

"Truly?" he whispered, pulling her down to lie with him upon the sandy beach. "How old are you, Fiona Hay?"

"Seventeen this Lammastide past," she told him. "How old are ye, Colin MacDonald of Nairn?"

"Twenty-seven," he said. "Jesu, yer sweet," he said thickly, holding her ever so tightly against him. His hand smoothed slowly down her back. It swept over the curve of her buttocks again and again while he nuzzled into the tender curve of her back, murmuring unintelligibly. Then, suddenly, he sat up, drawing Fiona with him.

"Loosen yer hair, sweeting," he said low.

Fiona drew the pins from her tresses, unplaiting the braid and combing the dark locks with her slender fingers. "Does that suit ye, my lord of Nairn?" she queried him.

"Aye," he said, drawing her back down, taking a bit of her hair in his fingers and sniffing it. "Ye wash yer hair with heather soap," he noted. "When we return to Nairn, I shall take ye to Inverness one day and buy ye a silver comb, sweeting. Then ye shall sit by the fire in our hall on a winter's night and comb yer raven tresses. Ye must never cut yer hair, for it is beautiful. I watched the sun shining off it yesterday as we rode." Then, pressing her lightly back, he kissed her, softly at first, but with growing ardor that did nothing to mask his lust for her.

Fiona, curious, allowed herself to taste and savor him. He was not at all unpleasant, she discovered. She found herself unable to keep from yielding to those kisses, from kissing him back just a little before a wave of guilt overwhelmed her, and she tried to draw away from him.

He immediately sensed the first breach in her defenses, and pressed forward eagerly. The tip of his
tongue ran along her lips. Fiona turned her head, but
he instantly drew it back and repeated the gesture. She
shivered, but whether from cold or her rising excitement, he was not certain, but her lips softened beneath
his. He was able to push his tongue into the dark cavity
of her mouth. Their tongues began to touch, and it was
as if she had been struck by lightning. Fiona wanted to
flee him but suddenly realized she could not.

His lips left hers and began to wander across her
face. They sought her throat, feeling the pulse in the
base of her neck beating a wild tattoo. He moved on to
her chest, whispering to her, "Ye want this, sweeting. I
can tell that yer own lust has been engaged."

"Nay! Nay!" she denied.

He laughed softly, his lips brushing the hillocks of
her breasts. They were swollen with their longing, and
as firm as two round apples. *"No?"* he mocked her, and
his tongue licked teasingly at a nipple through the fine
lawn of her chemise.

"Ohhh, don't do that!" she moaned, squirming
nervously.

His mouth closed over the nipple, and he began to
suckle upon her. Fiona's body arched up. Cradling her
with one arm, he let his other hand caress her torso.
Her skin was fiery to his touch. His mouth drew
fiercely upon her flesh until her belly felt cramped and
knotted. He moved to her other breast, and it was torture. Aching, sweet torture, and to think she had believed only Angus Gordon capable of such power over
her. His long fingers slipped beneath the chemise, moving up between her nether lips. Finding her little jewel,
he worried it and worried it until she was gasping with
her own desire. How, she managed to think in a clear

moment, could she work effectively for the king if she was filled with all this passion? She needed release, and this man offered her that release. Letting go of all her common sense, Fiona soared.

The sudden knowledge that she was yielding to him drove him onward. *"Fiona mine!"* He groaned into the softness of her perfumed hair.

The moon was risen now, lighting the waters of the loch, making dark shadows from their fair bodies lying upon the sandy beach. He reached for her hand. It felt small in his, but not helpless. He was proud that she was a strong woman. He drew her cloak over her and said only one word, "Sleep."

Colin MacDonald awoke to find Fiona swimming in the cold silver waters of the loch. He joined her, but neither spoke to the other. Nelly came along the beach with their garments. They dressed, returning to the campsite to eat the oatcakes and drink hot, watered-down wine again.

For the next few days they rode across the wilderness of Scotland, avoiding settlements. Finally they reached the west coast and crossed to the island of Jura. Here the land was very mountainous, and covered with deer forest. The island was bisected by Loch Tarbert. Finally they reached the far side of Jura facing upon Islay Sound, a narrow stretch of water. A small cockle was drawn up upon the shore.

Colin MacDonald directed two of his men to cross over and inform the Lord of the Isles that his brother of Nairn was waiting to pass over the water to Islay. The men were eagerly off, for this end of their journey meant hot food, good ale, and willing wenches.

"How will we cross?" Fiona asked.

"A barge will be sent for us and the horses," he

told her. "Ye must ask permission, however, to enter my brother's domain. Islay has never been taken by strangers or our enemies, or even the Irish."

"Yer brother behaves as if he were king."

Colin MacDonald laughed. "He is a king, Fiona mine. The Lords of the Isles have always been kings. That is why James Stewart is so eager to have their fealty. The northern clans will not pledge to him without the approval of the Lord of the Isles."

"Scotland can only have one king," she wisely told him.

"This is not Scotland. These are the Isles," he explained patiently. "It has always been this way. It was only in the time of The Bruce that the Isles became of interest to the Scots kings. We prefer being left to our independence."

"But ye don't even live in the Isles."

"True, I live near Inverness on the opposite side of Scotland, but I am a MacDonald, sweeting," Nairn said proudly. "And from the time I was six I lived here on Islay with my father and my siblings. I visited my mother only once a year until I was sixteen. Then my father sent me back to Nairn so my grandsire might teach me to govern my own lands, small as they are." He smiled. "I was already a seasoned warrior, having earned my spurs at Harlaw fighting with my father and brothers. My father knew I was competent at sixteen to rule Nairn, though I did not inherit it until I was twenty, and my grandsire died."

She was amazed. He had been a mere lad of fourteen when he fought in one of the bloodiest battles in Scotland's history. *And he had survived!* "Ye loved yer father, didn't ye?" she asked softly.

"Aye, I did," he admitted to her. "I was fortunate to be here last year when he died. Almost all of his children were here. Donald MacDonald had a great heart. He loved all his offspring no matter which side of the blanket they were born on. His own mother was Princess Margaret, a daughter of King Robert II. She taught him kindness and duty to family, he always told me."

They walked along the beach, and the air from the sea was fresh and invigorating. Above them the gulls swooped and mewled raucously, scanning the waters below for food. As they gazed out to Islay, they could see a large flat-bottomed vessel making its way toward them.

"Fraoch Eilean!" They heard the cry.

Nairn grinned, and stamping down to the sea's edge, he cupped his big hands about his mouth and called out, "Fraoch Eilean!"

"What is it?" Fiona asked him, puzzled.

"What?"

"Fraoch Eilean. I know the words. It means 'the heathery isle,' but what does it signify?"

"It's the war cry of the MacDonalds of the Isles. My brother himself is coming to meet us!"

The barge was finally anchored in the shallows off Jura, and a ramp was lowered. A man leapt forth into the waves, wading ashore to join them. He was every bit as tall as Colin MacDonald, but his hair was a dark brown to match his eyes. He embraced Nairn warmly.

"So yer safely back," he said, sounding faintly relieved.

"Aye, and I've much to tell ye, my lord," Nairn replied.

"Let us to Islay, then, brother," Alexander MacDonald said, pausing when Fiona caught his eye. He smiled winningly at her, the look identical to Nairn's. "What have we here, Colly? Have ye brought me a wee giftie from Perth?" His look was both admiring and lustful as he took in the girl, who gazed boldly back at him.

"No, Alex, 'tis not a gift for ye that I have brought to Islay, but the lass I am to wed with. This is Fiona Hay. Sweeting, my brother, Alexander MacDonald, Lord of the Isles."

Fiona curtsied politely but said nothing.

"Ye can tell me of this on the way," The MacDonald of the Isles said, surprised.

The horses were led into the surf and up the ramp onto the barge. As the winds were light, the sea was relatively calm, and the journey was a gentle one. Nairn had warned her that it could also be rough, with waves crashing over the barge and soaking them. Fiona was thankful it was not that sort of day, since her wardrobe was scant and could take no more damage.

"So ye've finally found a woman who satisfies ye enough to wed," Alexander MacDonald said, sounding pleased. " 'Tis past time ye were married. I am three sons up on ye already, Colly."

"I stole her," Colin MacDonald said quietly.

"*Ye stole her?*" Alexander MacDonald laughed in delight. "I'm glad to see yer heart is all MacDonald, brother. 'Tis rare in these days that we steal our wives. Why was it necessary for ye to do so? Has she a hard-hearted guardian who could not see that young lovers will not be denied, and attempted to keep her from ye so he might wed her to some rich old lord? If that is the case, ye were wise to steal her."

"He stole me from the man I love," Fiona said suddenly. "Even if Black Angus knew where I was, he would not have me now that yer brother has had his hands all over me, my lord. I can only hope Angus Gordon thinks me dead."

"*Colly?*" The Lord of the Isles was serious now. He

listened to his brother's explanation, nodding in satisfaction when it was concluded.

"No one can connect Mistress Hay's kidnapping with me, my lord," Nairn said. "I left court several days before she did. Although I did attempt once to gain her favor there, she would have none of me. No one will suspect that I took her. There is no danger to ye or to the Isles over this matter. I would not bring trouble to ye, Alexander."

"So there is little or no harm done, then," the Lord of the Isles said. He looked again at Fiona. "I canna blame ye, Colly. She is verra bonnie. I'm sorry this is one we canna share."

"No harm done?" Fiona was outraged. "I have been taken from the man I love, and mistreated, and ye say no harm is done, my lord?"

"Ye have but exchanged one husband for another, my bonnie," the Lord of the Isles said reasonably.

"Angus Gordon is the king's good friend."

"Then surely he will find his friend another bride," Alexander MacDonald answered her with perfect logic. "Even if it were known where ye were, there is little likelihood they would come after ye, unless, of course, ye are a great heiress. Are ye?"

"I am a chieftain in my own right," Fiona said proudly. "I am the Hay of the Ben, my lord."

"A steep hillock with a tumbled-down towerhouse," Colin MacDonald said matter-of-factly, "and don't deny it, sweeting. Maggie told me."

"Maggie MacLeod is a wretched gossip!" Fiona muttered balefully.

"Ye saw Margaret MacLeod, brother?"

"Aye. She has wed with her bonnet laird, and is with bairn," he answered. "She is happy, Alexander," he finished meaningfully.

"So be it, then," the Lord of the Isles replied. "Besides, the old lord they were to wed her with has died. They wouldna want her back, considering the shame she brought on her family by running off as she did. She cost them a dowry they could ill afford, though, for the old man would not give it back to them. He considered it damages for the insult done his fine old name. She was always a wild lass, our cousin Maggie MacLeod was." He laughed at his memories.

Fiona was fascinated. Maggie had never spoken about exactly why she had fled her home on Lewis. And in learning her friend's story, her own anger cooled. Fiona chided herself for appearing to be eager to escape Nairn. What if the Lord of the Isles had believed her and sent her back? She would be no use to the king then. She had to learn to better temper her apparent outrage with her actual purpose in being here. She moved to the far end of the barge and watched as the shore came closer.

"When will ye wed her?" the lord asked Nairn.

"I'll handfast her in yer hall tonight."

"Not with a priest, Colly? Why will ye not wed her properly?" Alexander MacDonald asked him, disturbed.

"She is still angry at having been taken from Angus Gordon," Nairn replied. "I have spared her my attentions each night that we have traveled for I swore to myself I would not have her without a wedding. The term of a handfast marriage is a year. I will have brought her around in that time, and I will then wed her before a priest."

"Will she agree to a handfast union?" the Lord of the Isles wondered. "She appears a hot-tempered lassie."

"Aye," Nairn grinned, "she is, but she will, for she has no choice. Within a year she will declare her love for me, brother."

The Lord of the Isles looked his younger sibling in the eye. "I can see yer already in love with her, Colin. Love is a dangerous condition for a man. Ye know it to be true. A man in love does not think clearly. Are ye certain ye will not wed her before a priest? I have one temporarily in residence. Father Ninian. He could do the deed."

Nairn shook his head. "I would have to coerce her before a priest, and I will not do that." He chuckled ruefully. "I am not certain I could force her. When we stand before a priest it will be because she wants to do so. No, a handfast marriage will have to do us now. Under a handfast any child we produce will be legitimate, brother."

The barge bumped onto the island of Islay. Leaping out, the men-at-arms drew it up onto the shore. The ramp was lowered, and the horses and riders made their way off the vessel. Fiona looked about her. Whereas Jura had been mountainous, Islay was a fertile, green pastureland of softly rolling earth. In the distance she could see a castle, obviously their destination. She moved her horse forward and found herself between the two brothers.

"Welcome to Islay, sister," the Lord of the Isles said graciously. "I hope yer stay with us, short though my brother says it is to be, will nonetheless be a pleasant one for ye."

"I thank you, my lord," Fiona responded politely.

As they rode toward their destination, Fiona could not help but be impressed by the large herds of fat cattle grazing in The MacDonald's green meadows. When she commented upon it, Nairn laughed mischievously.

"Fiona has been a cattle thief, though not a successful one, in her time," he told his elder brother.

"I never admitted to such a thing!" Fiona said indignantly. "Why do ye all assume that the charges Black Angus made against me were true? Why does no one believe me?" she demanded.

He chuckled. "Because ye were a brazen little liar. Ye could not feed yer sisters, let alone the fat cattle that Gordon found grazing in yer pastures," he told her. "Maggie said—"

"Maggie MacLeod again?" Fiona snapped. "If I ever see her again, I'll have to pull her wagging tongue out, the gossip!"

Donald MacDonald was now laughing. "Tell me the story, brother," he said, "and don't fret yerself over it, Fiona Hay. Cattle-stealing is an old and honorable custom, as ye know. The trick is to not get caught, as ye obviously did, but I admire yer spunk, my bonnie. Yer going to breed up fine MacDonald sons for my brother."

Pretending irritation, Fiona fell back to ride with Nelly, who, though reluctant, had been mounted upon Fiona's mare since the departure of the cart. "Men are mad," she said to her servant.

"These MacDonalds are certainly big handsome fellows, are they not?" Nelly commented. "The lord looks like his brother of Nairn, I'm thinking, despite their different coloring."

"Ummmm," Fiona answered her absently. She was far more interested in the castle that they were now approaching, for it appeared even from a distance to be larger and grander than she would have expected. Everyone always said that the MacDonalds were savages, but the Lord of the Isles had hardly appeared that, and his castle looked very impressive. It stood upon the highest point on Islay, a low rocky hill slightly larger than the other few hills on the island. There were four square towers, one at each compass point of the dark stone walls, which were unmarked by any opening. Its entry, with walls half as high as the main walls, had two small rounded towers halfway up the stone. There were massive oaken doors over which was drawn an iron yett, or grille, each night.

As they drew closer, Nelly remarked, "It looks a fearsome place, my lady. I think I am glad we will be here but a short while."

"It may be paradise compared to Nairns Craig," Fiona said in reply. "It is surely not Brae." There was a wistfulness in her tone.

They rode through the gates into a small courtyard. After dismounting, the women followed the Mac-Donald brothers through another heavy gate into a larger courtyard. It was like going from night into day. Here there was a camomile lawn beneath their feet, and a garden blooming with late roses, Mary's gold, and fragrant herbs. A slope-roofed house was built into two sides of the wall. They mounted the steps and entered the house.

"I'm sorry my wife is not here to greet ye, my bonnie," The MacDonald apologized, "but she is off with my lady mother to their estates in Ross. I fear ye will be gone before they return, but perhaps when ye bring yer first son to Islay ye will meet them." Then he swiftly directed the servants who came at his entrance to take Fiona and Nelly to their apartment and give them whatever they desired. "Come with me, Nairn," he said to his brother. "I would hear what ye have to tell me before ye take yer ease. I would know all about James Stewart."

"If ye would know *all* about him," Fiona interjected, "then ye should speak to me, too, my lord. I know the king well, as he was Black Angus's best friend. I was also in the service of the queen, and count myself among her friends. Women speak of more than gowns and household matters." She smiled prettily at him.

"Ye are obviously loyal to James Stewart, madam," The MacDonald said. "Why would ye help me?"

"My lord," Fiona said with perfect logic, "I would help ye better understand the king so that ye will swear yer fealty to him. Nairn can give you but impressions of what he saw and thinks. I lived within the royal enclosure. I was with the king and queen for several months. Yer brother has stolen me from the laird of Loch Brae. Since I canna go back, I must make my peace with what I have. Tonight I will handfast myself to Colin Mac-Donald. Aye, I heard you tell your plan, my lord of Nairn." She looked from Colin to his brother. "I will one day bear his bairns. *MacDonald bairns,* my lord. I don't want to see my lord, his family, and my own offspring sacrificed in the unending warfare that has wracked Scotland these many years. If I can help ye to make yer peace with the king, I would do so for the sake of Nairn and for our unborn children."

"She's clever as well as bonnie," The MacDonald said to his brother. Then he beckoned Fiona. "Verra well, lass, come with us. I'm a fair-minded man and will listen to what ye have to say."

"Go and unpack what little we have," Fiona instructed Nelly, and then she followed after the two men.

In the Lord of the Isles' privy chamber, a small stone room with a fireplace flanked by stone griffins, a fine tapestry hung from the wall opposite a window with a view of the garden. They ensconced themselves—the lord in a high-backed chair with a tapestry seat, and his companions on an oak settle facing him. A servant brought them each a silver goblet of pungent wine, then discreetly withdrew.

"First," Alexander MacDonald said, "tell me what he looks like, Nairn. I heard he is a wee man."

"He is of medium height but strongly built."

"He is a skilled warrior who fought in France with Henry V," Fiona said. "That king personally trained James Stewart in the arts of warfare. He is proficient with weapons of all kinds, including a crossbow."

"The crossbow?" The lord cocked a dark eyebrow.

"Aye, my lord, and the king has made it law that all young men must learn to use such a weapon so that Scotland quickly will have an armed force like the English," Fiona said.

" 'Tis cleverly done," the lord noted, "and not a bad idea at all. What kind of a man do ye ascertain him to be, Nairn?"

"A verra determined one, brother. He is not a feeble-minded weakling like his father before him was. He is strong-willed, and bound to rule Scotland as it has never before been ruled."

"Is he like old Albany, then?"

"Many compare him to The Bruce," Fiona said quietly. "A great soldier but a better governor in that he already knows how to rule."

Colin MacDonald nodded in agreement with her.

"Can he be bought like old Albany?" the lord wondered.

"No, brother, I don't believe he can. He is an honorable man, if a stubborn one, with a keen sense of justice."

"How stubborn, I wonder."

"He is so resolved to rule Scotland, to bring peace and real prosperity," Fiona said, "that he has decided to execute the most troublesome of his relations. The year will not end before Duke Murdoch and his ilk have gone to whatever fate awaits them on the other side of the door."

"How do ye know such a thing?" the lord asked her, fascinated to hear so intimate a disclosure.

"My lord," Fiona said, "I told ye that I lived within the royal residence. Neither the king nor the queen were shy about speaking their minds within the privacy of their own apartments. We all heard the king planning."

"Would none warn Duke Murdoch?" the Lord of the Isles asked.

Fiona laughed. "No, my lord. None would dare betray this king for fear of the civil unrest that would follow, *and* in far greater fear of what the king would do to the tattler. Besides, those of us who served their majesties love him."

"Would ye swear yer fealty to this king, Fiona Hay?"

"I already have done so, my lord," she told him honestly. "As chieftain of my family it was my duty to do so. My lands, poor as they are, have been reconfirmed mine by the king. The laird of Loch Brae holds my grandfather's lands in the glen, but the ben is mine."

"Do ye think I should pledge my loyalty to this James Stewart?" Alexander MacDonald asked her craftily.

"I think, my lord, that ye will come to yer own decision, and do what ye believe right for yer own clan."

The Lord of the Isles burst out laughing. "Nairn," he said to his brother, "ye had best beware this lass ye are so determined to take as a wife. She is far cleverer than ye are. I believe I am content to see ye in such competent hands. She will bear yer bairns, control yer mam, manage yer household, and keep ye from yer own folly so ye may continue to be of use to me. Ye have chosen well, although ye chose her with yer randy prick, and not yer head."

"I chose her with my heart," Colin MacDonald said quietly. He was pleased that Fiona met with his brother's strong approval, and prouder yet that she would be so candid about the Stewart king with Alex.

"Take her to yer apartment, brother," the lord said, "and prepare for the handfasting in the hall tonight."

They departed the lord's privy chamber. Nairn led her with unerring familiarity through the castle to a comfortable apartment that had been prepared for them. To Fiona's delight a large oaken tub stood in the bedchamber before a roaring fire. Nelly was grinning.

"I asked, and they brought it, my lady," she said, pleased.

"Ye'll have to brush my skirt well, though I doubt we'll ever get all the dust from it," Fiona said. She turned to Nairn. "If I had the cart, I would have a respectable gown to wear into yer brother's hall this night." She sighed. "Praise God yer sister-in-law is not here, or ye should be truly shamed."

"Ye have a decent gown, my lady!" Nelly crowed. "The lord Colin suggested I pack one gown for ye along with yer jewelry. The violet damask was the one I thought would pack best. I've already hung it out, and it has hardly a wrinkle in it."

Fiona turned to Nairn. " 'Twas clever of ye," she said by way of thanks. "I would not embarrass ye, my lord. Not in public."

He nodded, saying gruffly, "Have yer bath, sweeting. I can wash when ye are through. I'll fetch a clean shirt from my brother."

"Ye could bathe with me," she said softly. Her smile was enticing.

"We'd not reach the hall this night if I did," he told her, his look smoldering. Then he left her, closing the chamber door firmly behind him.

"He truly loves ye," Nelly said to her mistress.

"Don't say it," Fiona told her. "If I can but do what the king requires of me without betraying him or his family, I will count myself fortunate. Do ye think I don't see the way he looks at me? Ah, Nelly, if I had not been so stubborn, I should be at Brae with my own Black Angus now."

"Don't take all the blame upon yerself, mistress," Nelly said in practical tones. "The laird was just as stubborn as ye. He has always been a difficult man, my aunt Una said. 'Tis mostly his fault." As she spoke, she helped Fiona divest herself of her clothing, then settled her in the large oaken tub. "Soak yerself a moment," she told her lady. "I want to go brush this skirt for ye and fetch yer clean chemise."

Fiona nodded and closed her eyes. The water in the tub was actually hot, and it felt wonderful. How many days had she washed herself in the cold waters of highland lochs or icy running mountain streams? This was absolute heaven. She sighed with bliss and let the heat penetrate her body. It seemed a hundred years since she had been really warm, and she believed she could remain there in the hot water forever. Finally, however, she opened her eyes, taking up the little scrubbing cloth and tiny cake of soap Nelly had left her. Fiona washed her face, appalled at the dirt that came off it.

Nelly returned, laying the clean chemise across the bed, then washed her mistress's long black hair and scrubbed her back. She pinned the wet hair upon Fiona's head and urged her to finish her bath. When Fiona stepped from the tub, Nelly dried her off briskly, wrapped her in the toweling, and began to dry her lady's dark hair, rubbing and brushing the water from it near the heat of the fire. Satisfied at last, she helped Fiona into her clean chemise and tucked her into the bed.

"Now ye rest a bit," she counseled. "I'll dry the toweling before the fire for his lordship when he comes to bathe."

Fiona never heard her, for she had fallen fast asleep. The lord's fine wine, the hot water of the bath, the heat of the fire had conspired to lull her. She awoke to the sounds of splashing, and Nelly's giggles.

"Oh, my lord, yer a wicked laddie, and that's for certain!" Nelly said. "Now cease yer teasing, and let me get that fiery head of yers clean. I vow ye have enough soil in it to grow cabbages."

" 'Tis true," Fiona heard Colin MacDonald say. "Ye have stolen Roderick Dhu's flinty heart, little Nelly. He'll be wanting yer hand in marriage, mark my words. I can only hope yer not toying with him."

"I'm not toying with the big dour ox at all, my lord," Nelly protested vehemently. "Why, the man doesn't know me!"

"He knows ye have a sweet smile and pretty titties," Nairn teased.

"My lord!" Nelly's indignant voice was enough to wake the dead. " 'Tis a shameful thing to say, and I'd not have any man who didn't walk out with me, and court me proper-like. I'm not some kiss-me-quick and under-the-hedge-with-ye kind of lass, ye know!"

Nairn roared with laughter, suddenly cut off when Nelly dumped a small bucket of clean water over his head to rinse it. From her bed Fiona listened to them and chuckled softly. Her conscience was beginning to plague her again. If only The MacDonald of Nairn were not such a charming man . . . but he was. In a short while she would handfast herself to him in marriage only because she could not bear to contract an honest union with him, for whatever her fate, and despite the fact that Angus Gordon would marry Elizabeth Williams to please the king and queen, Fiona Hay loved the laird of Loch Brae.

She would never be his again, and it would have been so easy to draw the warmth of Colin MacDonald's love about her, but she would not. She hated the lie that James Stewart was forcing her to live, but she could not compound it by marrying this man in God's name when one day she might have to betray him. The handfast marriage was to please Nairn. To allay his suspicions. *To give a name, and legitimacy, to Angus Gordon's child, who was even now growing beneath her heart*—and whom she would pass off as The MacDonald of Nairn's bairn when she eventually announced her delicate condition.

Chapter 9

The Great Hall at Islay Castle was larger than Brae but not as large as Scone. It was, nonetheless, a fine hall with two great baronial fireplaces, beautifully woven tapestries upon its gray stone walls, and silken battle flags hanging from its carved rafters. The floor was swept clean, for, as the Lord of the Isles explained to Fiona, his wife did not like rushes. It only encouraged peeing in the corners and the disposal of unwanted food, which the hounds sometimes ate. The high board was laid with a fine white cloth and held a silver candelabra with beeswax candles. The rest of the castle's inhabitants ate at the trestles below.

There were but five places set at the high board. Fiona was seated next to the Lord of the Isles himself in the place of honor. Nairn was to his brother's left. To his left his brother's captain, another of the half-brothers, Owen MacDonald, sat. To Fiona's right was a priest, whom the Lord of the Isles introduced to her as Father Ninian.

"He travels the highlands ministering to those in far-flung regions," Alexander MacDonald said. "We are fortunate to see him twice a year, sometimes three."

The priest greeted Fiona. "God be with ye, my lady."

"I thank ye, Father," she replied. "Will ye hear my confession?"

"Of course, my child," he answered her, "but I should far rather perform yer marriage this night."

Fiona shook her head. "Nairn has stolen me," she said low. "I will handfast him for my reputation's sake, but I must find peace within my own soul before I can stand beside him in the church before a priest. Please understand, Father."

The priest nodded. "I will pray for ye both."

Fiona turned to her host. "And where are yer sons, my lord?"

"They have gone with their mother," he replied. "Their company pleases her."

"My lord"—Father Ninian interrupted their conversation—"I would hear this lady's confession before the handfast, not after." He smiled briefly at them to lessen the rebuke in his tone.

"Aye," Alexander MacDonald agreed with a grin. " 'Tis better she unburden herself now, for later her sins could be worse!" He winked at his brother. "Eh, Nairn?"

The priest arose, and Fiona followed him from the hall. He led her to the chapel and into a small privy chamber. "Now, my child," he said, "if ye would like to unburden yerself to me . . ."

Fiona looked carefully about her. Shutting the door softly, she pulled the king's coin from her pocket and handed it to the priest.

His face betrayed nothing as he carefully examined it, matching it against his own identical coin. Then he said softly, "Where did ye obtain this, my child?"

"From James Stewart himself," Fiona said in even lower tones.

"Tell me yer story," Father Ninian responded, listening as the beautiful young woman before him spoke quickly yet succinctly of her history. When her narrative had come to an end, the priest said, "Now I understand why ye would not take Nairn in the sacrament of marriage, but ye know, do ye not, that the handfast is just as binding under law, both civil and church? And ye'll surely conceive a bairn, for the MacDonalds are prolific breeders. What of any child?"

"I am already with child," Fiona told him, holding up her hand for his silence while she explained. "The bairn is not Nairn's, although I will lead him to believe it is for the safety of my infant. Had I been certain before I left Scone, I would not have let the king force me to this, but I was not certain. I feared that if I bled after telling the king I was with child, he would have believed me lying to have my own way and deceive him. I have learned, good Father, that ye canna trust the words of the mighty. Unable to punish me, he might have punished my Black Angus." A tear rolled down her cheek. "I could not let Angus Gordon suffer for me."

The priest nodded, his heart sad. So much suffering for their blessed Scotland, but one day with sacrifices such as those Fiona Hay was making, the land would surely know peace. He handed her back her coin. "Do ye need something passed on, my child?"

"Tell the king that the Lord of the Isles will bide his time for now until he decides just how determined James Stewart is to rule *all* of Scotland. For the present, Alexander MacDonald will remain at peace in the highlands, but while some of the northern and western clans may swear fealty, most of the clans will wait to see what he is going to do. That I have from his own mouth."

"The king will have yer message verra soon, I promise ye. I had planned to spend some time here on Islay, but I will shortly take my own departure. Drysdale, our tinker friend, will soon be heading south for the winter months. 'Tis he who will carry yer message. Now, so we may not be accused of deception, ye will make yer confession to me."

"I thought I already had," Fiona said softly.

The priest considered, and then he said, "Why, so ye have, my child, so ye have. Kneel and receive my blessing."

"What is my penance?" Fiona asked him.

"In honor of yer marriage," Father Ninian said, "I will absolve ye of any penance, Fiona Hay. Ye have been given a verra hard road to take." He raised his hand in blessing over the penitent.

They returned to the Great Hall of Islay Castle. The clansmen, respectful, made clear that they thought the bride very beautiful. She wore her violet damask gown. It had a short waist that was fitted just below her breasts, a simple rounded neck, a full flowing skirt, and long flaring sleeves that were lined in a reddish-purple gauze shot through with silver stripes. Her hair was parted in the center and held by a silver caul. She had chosen to wear no jewelry except her clan badge despite Nelly's insistence. Save for that badge, it was all Angus Gordon's jewelry. Though she possessed it, she would never wear it again. One day she would tell her child the truth and pass it on to the bairn, but Fiona did not think she had any right to the jewelry now. Nairn agreed with her decision not to wear it. He would give her her own gems, he promised.

Now Colin MacDonald stood before the high board in his eldest brother's hall, and before the Lord of the Isles he swore to take Fiona Hay to wife, in handfast. When Fiona then declared her intentions to take him as a husband in handfast, they were considered legally wed for the period of one year. If at the end of that time, either decided not to formalize the union within the church, they were free to go their own way. Any children born of a handfast marriage were considered legitimate despite the parents' future decision to continue or discontinue the union. The handfast must be sworn to before witnesses, which all the men in the hall constituted.

The meal was served. Roast boar, roe deer, game pies in red wine gravy, stewed eels, raw oysters taken from the beaches and waters surrounding Islay, a single capon in lemon and ginger as a courtesy to Fiona, several large sea trout upon beds of cress, cod in cream and sweet wine. There were fresh-baked bread, tubs of sweet butter, and several wheels of cheese, along with ale and wine.

"Where are the greens?" Fiona asked, slightly taken aback by the heavy bounty. "There is not a pea or a beet, an onion or a carrot to be seen. Have ye no lettuces?"

"The men don't like them," the Lord of the Isles said. "The kitchen will prepare them for my lady, who wishes them. I didn't think to ask the cook tonight, but ye shall have them as long as ye are with us, my bonnie."

Fiona nibbled on breast of capon and buttered bread, sipping on a fine wine as she did so. She watched, not certain whether to be amazed or appalled, as the men about her devoured all the food laid out for them. Her own belly rolled slightly at the sight and smells. It was much too rich. Only the wine seemed to calm her.

When they had finished eating, the Lord of the Isles's piper took up his pipes and played for them. After a time four crossed swords were placed upon the stone floor of the hall. The Lord of the Isles and The MacDonald of Nairn leapt down from the high board to dance amid the weapons. As the music became more fierce and wild, Fiona realized that the two men were in a serious competition. Their dancing was furious, almost frenzied. She gazed, fascinated, her green eyes glittering with excitement as she leaned forward to watch the two brothers.

"It has always been this way between them," Owen MacDonald said to her. "They are equally matched in the dance."

"Who will win?" she wondered aloud.

"Sometimes my lord wins, and at other times yer husband outdances our elder sibling. There is no bitterness. It is all for amusement."

Her husband. The two words were very startling, for to her the handfast had been nothing more than a means to protect her child. Had she refused the ceremony, she knew that Nairn would have kept her tightly by his side. Their temporary marriage, however, gave her a great freedom. She was now considered one of the MacDonalds. She hated James Stewart for putting her in this position, but he had been right. The priest and the other agents would not have the advantage of intimacy that she would have. She smiled absently, thinking of how she had said she would not marry Nairn, and of the king's response: that it was up to her what she did as long as she passed along what she learned.

"Look, lady," Owen MacDonald said. "My lord is tiring. Yer husband will take the competition this night."

And sure enough the Lord of the Isles gave way to his brother of Nairn, grabbing up his swords and laying them aside with a bow. Bounding up onto the high board, he held out his hand to Fiona. "Come, Fiona MacDonald, and dance with yer bridegroom." He led her down to the hall floor, handing her off to his brother of Nairn.

A shout arose from the men in the hall as the newlyweds danced together, Fiona lifting her skirts to prance daintily in the familiar steps of the wedding dance that every highland girl learned at an early age. She had never thought to dance it with anyone but Angus Gordon. Then again, her own mother had never danced it at all. How strange, she thought, that both she and her mother loved Gordons but were forced into marriage with other men.

His arm clamped about her waist, and he lifted her up, swinging her about, then back down again. Unable to help herself, Fiona laughed up into his handsome face while the men about them cheered wildly, some leaping onto the floor to join the couple, so that Fiona found herself with several partners. She danced until she could dance no longer, and retired, panting, back to the high board, where a well-trained servant placed a cup of chilled wine into her hand. Her head was spinning.

The atmosphere in the hall was becoming raucous and boisterous.

"Take yer wife to bed," the Lord of the Isles ordered his brother. "The men are rowdy and will become more strident as the night passes."

Nairn took his wife's hand, and they quietly slipped from the hall to find their way back to their apartment. There Nelly was already awaiting them. "Help yer mistress, and then be quickly gone," he told her firmly. "Do not come until ye are sent for in the morning."

Nelly nodded, and he disappeared into his own chamber while she helped Fiona remove her gown and chemise. Fiona sat as Nelly pulled the shoes off her feet and rolled the stockings down her legs and off her. Standing, Nelly drew the silver caul from Fiona's hair. "There's a basin with warm water to wash yerself, lady. God grant ye good rest," she said, and hurried from the chamber.

Fiona walked slowly to the basin and, taking up the cloth, bathed her face and hands. Then she scrubbed her teeth with a bit of pumice and ground mint Nelly had left her, rinsing her mouth afterward with wine and water. Taking up her comb, she drew it slowly through her tresses, smoothing the knots out, making it shine in the firelight. Finally satisfied, she peed in the chamber pot, then made her way to the bed, climbing in and drawing the coverlet over herself. She wore no chemise, for she knew he would simply remove it.

Her heart was beginning to beat a little faster as she waited for her *husband*. What was the matter with her? She was no virgin to fear coupling with a man. Her idyll with Angus Gordon had been just that, and James Stewart had taken any future she might have had with him out of their hands—and into those of The MacDonald of Nairn.

He was a handsome man, Fiona admitted to herself. He had no end of charm, which he had persisted in working on her. That night by the loch when he had caressed her, touching her so intimately—and she had responded—burned in her memory. How could she claim to love Angus Gordon when she felt the passion in another man's touch? She must not feel any emotions for Colin MacDonald. How could she serve the king if she fell in love with her husband?

He entered her bedchamber saying, "I bathed for ye, sweeting. With soap, too," he told her proudly. "I smell like a damned flower."

"I'll prefer the flower to the stink of the horses," she said, and quickly added, "I didn't know ye were such a fine dancer, my lord. I did not see ye dance at court. The ladies would have loved ye."

"The ladies loved me despite my seeming lack of social graces," he taunted her. "The ladies have always loved me, Fiona mine."

"And they may continue to do so, for I care not a whit," she said wickedly.

He chuckled. She was so prickly, and he liked her that way. He was never certain where he stood with her, and he found it exciting. She did not cling and weep with love over him, although one day he would make her love him, but it would be on Fiona Hay's terms, he knew, not his. She was not a weak woman, and that was to the good. "Come here to me, sweeting," he said. "I have something to show ye." He opened the doors of a cabinet that was set on a side of the room.

Slipping from the bed, Fiona approached him, watching as he swung the two doors open wide. Then she gasped, catching her breath. *"What is it?"* she whispered, amazed.

" 'Tis called a mirror," he said.

"Nay, 'tis no such thing!" Fiona declared. "Do ye think me a dimwit, my lord? I have seen a mirror before. The queen has one that she held in her hand, and 'twas set in a silver frame. This is not like that! This is big, and surely magic."

He stood before the mirror. "What do ye see, sweeting?" he asked her. "Is it not Colin MacDonald reflected in this glass ye see?"

Fiona peered hard. It was indeed he. "Aye," she said slowly, "but how can this be? The king doesn't have so fine a thing as this surely is."

He laughed heartily. "The king is not a MacDonald," he boasted.

"Is it truly a mirror? It must certainly be the biggest mirror ever." She was awestruck. "Where did it come from?"

"A MacDonald son served a king in a place called Byzantium. When his term of service was over, he told his master that if he would safely transport two of these mirrors home to Scotland for him, the mercenary MacDonald would take them in lieu of coin for his ten years of service. The other of the mirrors is in the lord's apartments." He held out his hand to her. "Come, sweeting, and see how beautiful ye are. The glass will not lie to ye."

Slowly Fiona came to stand before it. For the first time in her entire life she saw all of herself as others saw her. She stared hard at the reflection in the mirror. The warm light from the fire in the hearth and the flickering candles gave her milky skin a pale golden glow. Fascinated, she gazed upon her body, shivering slightly as Colin stepped behind her, his big hands sliding around to cup the globes of her breasts. They nestled in his palms like two doves. She watched, spellbound, as the thumb and forefinger of each hand played with her nipples, pinching them slightly, pulling them out so that they stood hard and pointed. Her head spun slightly, and she realized that she was not breathing. Fiona slowly drew in a deep draught of air to clear her brain. What was happening to her?

"This is our wedding night," he murmured in her ear, "and I would have it be a night ye will not forget." His breath was hot in her ear as his tongue tickled the shell of it.

He turned her about so that their bodies touched. Instinctively Fiona pressed her palms flat against his chest in an effort to hold him off. The heat from the pressure of her hands made him almost dizzy with desire. The contact between their two bodies was heady. He groaned with the pure pleasure.

"Ah!" The sound escaped her before she might

stop it. Dear Holy Mother! She must surely have the heart of a whore to be so aroused by this man. Suddenly she wanted to weep, but she forced back her tears. Tears were a luxury she couldn't afford. Then all the anger she had been bottling up these past weeks overcame her, and she began to beat him on his chest and shoulders with her small fists.

"Nah, han, hinny lamb," he murmured, catching those little hands, kissing them, and then pinioning them behind her back with one great paw. With his other hand he began to caress her, stroking her like a pet cat, knowing he could have gone on all night simply touching her, but realizing that until he possessed her completely, she would continue to fight him. "Don't struggle against me, Fiona mine, for you know I mean to have you. You are my wife, sweeting, and I love you."

Damn him! How easily he said those words to her, and he did not have to simply to take her. *Damn him!* Why couldn't Angus Gordon have said those words to her? She struggled against Colin MacDonald, swearing at him most colorfully in their native Gaelic tongue, a language that made her maledictions even more threatening.

Another man might have hit her, but The MacDonald of Nairn put a gentle hand over her mouth, admonishing her, "Do you want the entire castle to hear ye, sweeting?"

Fiona bit the hand that covered her mouth. Now it was he who swore, slapping her lightly, his blue eyes finally darkening with anger, and seeing it, she grew still at last. This big man could kill her if he chose, and then where would she be? Certainly no help to the king.

"Hush now, Fiona mine," he said softly, his anger easing. "Listen to me, sweeting, for I don't want to harm you. You see I am a big man in every aspect. I do not

want to injure you. You must be still. Let me love you.
You will find that I can give you great pleasure, even
as you will give me pleasure."

He turned her about again, wrapping a single arm
about her torso, drawing her back against his hard
body. His hands pushed the mass of her hair aside so
he might place kisses upon her neck. The fragrant scent
of her newly washed hair excited him further. His hand
wandered the length of her, caressing and fondling the
soft skin. A single finger insinuated itself between her
nether lips, finding with unerring aim the tiny jewel of
her sex.

Fiona couldn't look away from the great mirror.
She was mesmerized by the sight of this man making
love to her. Unable to help herself, she let her head fall
back against his shoulder. She sighed as he elicited
sweet pleasure from her. She could feel his manhood
raging against the flesh of her buttocks, but she could
not contain the grinding of her hips into his hot loins.

"You belong to me now, sweeting," he murmured
thickly in her ear.

"I belong to no man," she managed to gasp. "I
will be owned by neither you nor Angus Gordon. I will
not be owned by *any man*!"

Laughing softly, he kissed her angry mouth.

"I hate you!" she raged.

"Hush, lambkin," he said low.

He turned her once again to face him, and cupping her buttocks in his palms, he lifted her up to im-
pale her upon his throbbing love rod. Then to her
amazement he turned them both about so she might see
as he pistoned her.

The sensation of him within her was overwhelming, almost too much for her to bear. He filled her so
full that her body felt stretched beyond all bearing.

Completely sheathed, he leaned forward to kiss her lips, to brush kisses across her face and throat, to whisper of how much he adored her. Then her body seemed to widen to accommodate him.

Colin Macdonald knew how to give a woman pleasure, and he gave her extreme delight despite her resistance to him. The subtlety of his movement reached out to Fiona, cajoling her to cease her opposition to his tender blandishments; in spite of herself her body responded to his. His big manhood delved deeper and deeper within her softness. She felt as if she were melting layer by layer. The hard thrusts of his loins grew sharper and quicker. Her eyelids felt heavy and threatened to close. She let her gaze stray to the large mirror in which they were reflected. Had it not been so intriguing, she would have swooned at this sight of their bodies locked together in amorous combat.

Fiona clung to him, her legs wrapped about his waist, her hands clutching his thick neck as he brought her to a pleasure peak. He withdrew from her, still hard, still eager, and dragged a small table before the mirror. He had her bend, her palms flat upon the oaken surface of the table. Then, grasping her hips to steady them, he slowly slid into her sheath again. She was unable to look away as he thrust back and forth within her; she felt bewitched and almost detached from her body as she watched the alluring tableau they made in the mellifluous glass. Honeyed fire was pouring through her, over her, and then she shuddered as his pulsing manhood saluted her with its love juices.

Her body was wet with perspiration. Her heart was pounding wildly. Enchanted, she watched as his manhood retired from the field of battle. Drawing her into his arms, he kissed her passionately over and over again until finally her knees gave way, and he lifted her

up to lay her on their bed. He pulled the table away
from the cabinet and closed the doors, hiding the mirror from their view.

" 'Tis a wicked thing, that glass," Fiona managed
to say as the bed sagged with his weight. "I could not
take my eyes from it."

She was half-stunned, half-shocked, not simply by
the erotic tableau she had just observed, but by the fact
she had actually felt pleasure, keen pleasure, with this
man. He was her kidnapper. A virtual stranger, despite
the fact he was now her handfasted husband. Angus
had been right. She was brazen. She wanted to cry, but
she didn't. She would show Colin MacDonald no
weakness.

He looked at her with curious eyes. "Did ye enjoy
what ye saw, sweeting? Did ye like seeing our bodies
locked together in a tender bout of passion?"

"Aye," she told him, realizing that it had but added
excitement to their lustful combat. "To see us was . . .
was . . . intoxicating, like a rich wine. I don't think I
should want to drink such wine all the time, would ye,
my lord stallion?"

"Ye were quite drunk with yer lust," he teased her,
bending to kiss her lips. "Ye were like a bitch in heat,
sweeting, and I really felt ye were mine, for ye held
back nothing."

She was shocked by his words, but she quickly
realized that he was right. She had been so fascinated
by the sight of them coupling, reflected in the mirror,
that she had not resisted him even subtly. "I was not
aware I resisted ye, my lord. How could I possibly resist
ye, for ye are bigger and stronger than I am," she said,
feigning innocence.

He laughed. "I have known too many women,

sweeting, not to know when one withdraws into herself while I'm laboring over her."

She sat up, glaring at him. "Did ye expect me to declare undying love to a man who kidnapped me from my love? When the year is up, Colin MacDonald, don't expect me to stand before the priest with ye! I'll not do it!"

"In a year ye'll love me," he mocked her. "Ye'll cry for love of me, Fiona mine. I swear it!" Then he began to kiss her again, and she fought him angrily as she had that first night when she thought he meant to rape her. Her fists were flying, her nails raking at his back in her fury, but Nairn only laughed at her. He pinioned her beneath him, brushing off her attempts to do him a mischief. Within moments her anger had turned, despite her best efforts, to a steamy passion again. They were well and truly mated several times before the dawn broke over Islay Island.

They remained for several days on the island. Each night the mirror reflected their unchecked desires before Nairn closed it. He had it turned toward the bed so she might watch them as they shared their lust among the tangled sheets. Fiona remained as enthralled by the big glass as she had been when she first saw it. Colin MacDonald had told his brother how much Fiona enjoyed the mirror, much to her embarrassment. She had never been a woman to discuss such things, even with an intimate.

She had been with him for over a month. Her appetite was growing peakish, and he noticed it immediately. "My seed has taken root in yer womb, sweeting," he said, well pleased. "Ye have not had any show of blood since I took ye. Do ye not realize yer with bairn?"

"I was not certain," she told him, "since I've never been with child."

Nelly gasped, her face white with shock, and Fiona went to her. *"Mistress?"* was all the girl could say.

"Leave us," Fiona ordered her husband. "I must calm poor Nelly, for she has obviously sustained a shock by this news."

When Nairn had departed and Fiona had made certain he was gone from their apartment, she led Nelly into the tiny inside chamber where the girl slept. Her voice was low as she spoke. " 'Tis not his bairn, Nelly! Do ye understand me? Had I been certain, I would have refused the king, but I was not certain. I dared not spurn a royal request only to learn I was not with bairn. What if he had revenged himself on my Black Angus? I could not take the chance. Do ye understand?"

"What if the lord Nairn finds out?" Nelly asked, her voice quavering.

"How?" Fiona said scornfully. "If the bairn is born with dark hair, he will think the lass or laddie favors me, that is all. Nairn thinks because Black Angus had two years with me and did not put a bairn in my belly that his seed is feeble. Ye must keep the secret, Nelly."

Nelly was recovering. "I know," she said. "But what of the other bairns he will get on ye, my lady?"

"Hopefully by the time I have this bairn, we will be free to escape Nairn and return to our own home. The king said a year," Fiona murmured, almost to herself. "Are ye all right now?"

"Aye," Nelly said, "but ye gave me quite a turn, my lady. Why did ye not tell me before now?"

"Because I wanted that great oaf of Nairn to come to the conclusion before I said anything," Fiona answered. "Ye see how pleased he was. Undoubtedly he has gone off to his brother to crow over his prowess."

"They're all like that, these MacDonald men. Roderick Dhu is forever telling me what a fine upstanding cock he has, and 'tis meant just for me if I would but say the word." She giggled, and her carrot-colored braids bobbed up and down with her mirth. "I've told the great gawk I'm a good lass, and will not give my cherry to any man but the man who weds me. That sends him off, I can tell ye. Oh, they like a good time with the lasses, my lady, but mention marriage and they flee. All but yer lord. He said from the first he would wed ye, and he did."

" 'Tis only handfast, Nelly. In a year it will be over," Fiona said. "If I canna have my Black Angus, I want no husband."

They departed Islay on a gray morning, crossing over to Jura on a choppy sea. Alexander MacDonald accompanied them, for he intended to hunt deer upon Jura. He bid his new sister-in-law a fond farewell.

"I am glad," Fiona told him, "that ye will keep the peace, my lord brother. It comforts me now that I know I am to bear my lord an heir. War, I think, is as hard on the women and bairns as it is on the men who fight the battles." She kissed his cheek.

"I have said I will but bide my time, my bonnie," the Lord of the Isles reminded her. "We will see what the spring brings."

"I have heard the king say he would call the northern clans to Inverness next year," she reminded him. "Can ye not bide yer time until then, my lord brother? If James Stewart does not challenge ye, why would ye challenge him?" Men, she thought! They were such children even in their maturity. This unspoken warring between the king and The MacDonald of the Isles reminded her of nothing so much as two lads attempting to see who could piss the farthest. It was ridiculous.

"If yer king will keep the peace until we meet in Inverness, then I will try to keep my peace; but remember, my bonnie, one of the clans could swear fealty to James Stewart before Inverness and then make war on me. If that happens, I canna stand by merely because that clan is yer king's ally. I will strike with all the power at my command."

"As well ye should," Fiona said. "Such craven behavior would merit the severest penalty, my lord brother."

"Take good care of yer bride, Nairn. She is a clever lass, and ye would not be foolish to seek her counsel in times of trouble, and on other matters." Then he bid farewell to Father Ninian, who would travel with Colin MacDonald part of the way north before turning south. "Godspeed, good Father, until we meet again," the Lord of the Isles said.

"May God's love shine favorably upon ye and yers, my lord," the priest responded. "God willing, I shall see ye in the spring."

Fiona rode with the priest a ways, which her husband looked upon with approval, for it showed a deference to the churchman. "Ye heard?" she murmured low to him, and he nodded pleasantly.

"I shall see it is known to *him*," he responded softly. Then he said to her, "Has yer husband spoken of his mother, lady?"

Fiona shook her head. "No. Is she alive, then?"

"Sustained by her own venom," the priest said tartly. "She has both a wicked tongue and an evil mind. She will not welcome yer coming to Nairn. She considers it hers and has lived there all of her life. Ask yer man about her, my lady," the priest advised.

Fiona nodded, moving her gelding forward so she might ride with Colin MacDonald. He smiled when she reached his side. Fiona could not help but smile back at him, for despite it all, she liked him. "Ye have spoken of yer father to me, my lord, but what of yer mother?"

His handsome visage darkened a moment. "She is a hard woman, sweeting, with no kindness in her," he said candidly. "My father was taken by what he believed was her wild spirit. She was a challenge, to be tamed by him, but alas, he miscalculated."

Fiona raised a quizzical eyebrow at Nairn. "Like father, like son?" she teased him, and he laughed.

"Yer not like my mother," he hastened to assure her. "My mother was, so my grandfather said, always mean-spirited. She is one of those poor souls who is jealous of everyone else. No matter what she has, it is not enough. Envy eats at her. She was betrothed to a cousin, for with her brother dead, she became Nairn's heiress. Then my father passed through the district, stopping to accept my grandfather's hospitality. My mother, I am told, flirted with him until he felt he could not resist the obvious invitation. He remained there the summer and into the autumn to hunt grouse with my grandfather.

"The old man knew what was transpiring, but he could not control his daughter. My grandfather also knew that in the end The MacDonald would leave her to return to Islay, which is precisely what happened. By then my mother's belly was growing big. Her cousin repudiated his promise to wed her, but she sent him away laughing, for she thought my father so enamored of her that he would take her with him to Islay. Of course he did not take her. He would not shame his wife with such an open liaison. No woman of breeding objects to her husband's wee distractions provided that he does not bring them into her view or within her hearing.

"When I was born she would not look at me. I have her coloring, as ye may have guessed, but other than that I am all MacDonald. She would not give me suck, and my grandfather was forced to find a cottar's wife with extra milk so I would not die. He sent word to my father, and The MacDonald sent back a gift of six silver cups with his crest, and a dozen gold merks. There was also a parchment, witnessed by a priest and signed with my father's hand, acknowledging his paternity. As my mother would not name me, he did."

"She would not name ye?" Fiona was shocked.

"Each morning I was brought to her chamber by my nurse and presented to her. She would not look upon me or say a word to me. Finally one day when I was past two and walking, I was brought to her in the morning, and as usual she turned her face from me. I was desperate for her attention, and so I kicked her in the shin. Only then did she look upon me for the first time. She said, 'He is his father's son,' and nothing else, but after that when I was brought to her she would look at me. When I was four or five I asked her why she did not speak to me. 'Because,' she replied, 'I have nothing to say to Donald MacDonald's son,' and after that she was silent once more.

"My grandfather was a quiet, gentle man. It was he who raised me in the early years, along with my nurse. It was he who loved me. He taught me to ride, and the beginnings of swordplay," Nairn said with a smile of remembrance. "Occasionally my father came to see me when he was in the district. It was he who convinced my grandfather to pass over my mother and leave Nairns Craig to me. I loved it when my father came, for he was a big, bluff man with a barrel chest and a laugh that sounded like thunder to a small boy. When I became a man he did not seem so big.

"When I was six he asked me if I should be willing to leave Nairn for a time to live with him on Islay. I would have brothers and sisters to play with, he said. A grandmother who was a princess, who would love me verra much. I went with him gladly, but with one regret. I had to leave my grandfather behind, but each summer I would return from Islay to be with him for three months. We had grand times then! When he died seven years ago, Nairns Craig became mine."

"Yer mam never married?" Fiona asked, curious.

"There was no man who ever suited her, and no man who was willing to have such an unpleasant woman in his house. She could cause chaos among the angels. When I returned for good, she thought to take up our relationship as it had been in my childhood, but I quickly disabused her of the notion. I told her that as master of Nairn, I would brook no foolishness. She would come to my board each day, and we would speak together. To my surprise, she agreed."

"Ye don't fill me with confidence regarding yer mam," Fiona said, sounding concerned. "Will she welcome ye with a wife, my lord?"

"She doesn't have any choice," he answered her. "Ye are now mistress of Nairns Craig Castle. My mother must accept ye, or I will turn her out. Ye carry my bairn, Fiona mine. *My heir*. I will not have her distressing ye, and should she attempt it, she will find herself placed in a convent to live out her days in prayer, sustained by salted fish and brown bread. Be warned. She will be jealous of ye, for ye are young and beautiful, and I wed ye."

When they stopped for the night, Fiona told Nelly what The MacDonald of Nairn had said about his mother. "I will have to behave as mistress of the castle for as long as we are there, Nelly. We canna allow this woman to frighten us or to discover our true purpose."

"It would seem, my lady, that for now yer only purpose is to have yer bairn in comfort and safety. It is unlikely that any information of importance will pass into yer hands or hearing once the winter sets in here in the highlands. The bairn will come in the spring, and after that perhaps we will be free to go home," Nelly said hopefully.

"What do ye two whisper on?" Nairn said, coming upon them.

Fiona laughed. "Roderick Dhu would court my Nelly, and the lass seeks my advice, my lord."

"And what advice do ye give her, sweeting?"

"She says I am to box his ears and tell him to mind his manners," Nelly told her master pertly.

Colin MacDonald chuckled. "Ye will have him before a priest before the poor man knows what has happened to him," he teased her. "Now run along and give the poor laddie a kind word while I tuck my sweet wifie into our bed." Tugging one of her braids playfully, he turned the pretty maidservant about and sent her off giggling.

"Ye'll have her eating out of the palm of yer hand soon, my lord," Fiona told him, a small smile touching her lips.

He had made her a bed of pine boughs and put a large fur throw over it. When she lay down in her chemise and cloak, he gently laid another fur over her. "I don't want ye catching cold, sweeting, not in yer condition. And no swims in the lochs, for they're too cold now. Ye'll not die if ye don't have a bath until we get to Nairn."

"Yes, my lord," she answered him meekly as he lay

by her side atop the fur robe, wrapped in his own cloak. "Are ye not to join me?"

"Not while we're traveling, Fiona mine. I would not injure ye. When we have a bed to cushion us, then we will dally for a bit until yer belly is too big for comfort's sake." Turning his back to her, he soon fell into an easy sleep.

She was astounded, and not just a bit guilty. He truly wanted a child. Pray God the bairn was not his father's spit, but she wondered, would Colin MacDonald even see it if it were? It was comforting to know that her child would be safe with this man. Nelly was right. It was unlikely that she would obtain any further information of use to the king in the next few months. Best she settle into her new home and have her child. If The MacDonald would make peace with James Stewart, then all would be well. She would face that future when it came. Until the autumn of the next year she did not have to worry. Only when the handfast was past would she face trouble on the horizon.

It took them a bit over two weeks, traveling overland from Islay, to reach Nairns Craig Castle, which was in the vicinity of Inverness. It sat atop a steep, high cliff, and had two rectangular towers and a Great Hall, connected by high, dark stone walls. Its only access was a slender track of roadway up the face of the cliff. A narrow strip of land on the far side of the castle offered a view of high walls with absolutely no outlooks at all, and the forest below.

"It has never been taken," Colin MacDonald said proudly.

"I can certainly see why, my lord," Fiona replied dryly.

He pulled his stallion to a stop for a moment. "Ye are about to enter my home, *yer home,*" he said to her.

"Ye are my wife, Fiona mine. Do ye not think ye can call me by my name? It is but a small boon, lady."

"Aye, Colly, I will call ye by yer name in the privacy of our home, but in public I would not dishonor ye by addressing ye as anything but 'my lord.' Will that suit ye, Colly?"

He took her hand in his and kissed it. "Aye," was all he said, but his smile went all the way to his eyes.

She smiled back, cursing James Stewart in her heart as she did so. Did he realize the havoc his passion to rule Scotland was causing? And what of Angus Gordon? What had he thought when told of her disappearance? Did he miss her? Did he truly care, or had that English girl already captured his heart? She breathed deeply, resolutely shaking off her questions and her sadness.

The castle gates were open to receive its lord. Fiona noted the two doors were bound in iron and, looking up, she saw the iron yett ready to be drawn down in the event of danger. Within the court they stopped, and Nairn lifted her from her gelding, gently setting her upon her feet for a moment, then softly kissing her mouth.

"Welcome to Nairns Craig," he said. Sweeping her up in his arms, he turned to carry her up the steps into the building.

Before he had progressed more than a few steps, however, a woman appeared at the top of the stairs. She was petite, but her look was commanding. "So, Colin MacDonald, ye are back," she said in cold tones, "and ye have brought yer latest whore with ye, I see. She'll not enter into *my* house. Why do ye not house the wench in the stables with the rest of the animals?" Her arms were crossed over her spare bosom.

Fiona saw a small muscle near Nairn's eye twitch

several times, but for a moment he said nothing. Instead he carried her up the steps, pushing past his antagonist and setting Fiona upon her feet once more within the entrance hall of the castle. When the petite woman whirled about, her mouth opening to protest, Nairn roared, "Don't say another word, madam! *This is my wife*. When did I ever bring my whores into this place or shame ye with lewd public behavior?"

"Yer wife?" The lady, obviously his mother, Moire Rose, was astounded. "Who is this wench? Where did ye meet her? Where were ye wed? I demand that ye tell me this instant, Colin MacDonald!"

"My wife is Fiona Hay, chieftain of the Hays of the Ben," he began. "We met at court. We were wed on Islay in my brother's hall. As my wife, Fiona is now the lady of Nairn, madam. Ye will render her the respect due her as such."

"I suppose she is with bairn," his mother said scathingly.

"Aye," Nairn said proudly. "Did ye doubt I would not get a bairn on her immediately, madam?"

"No, I didn't doubt it," she said bitterly. "But for yer coloring ye are all MacDonald, yer father's son, from yer great height to yer randy and fertile cock." She turned her gaze to Fiona, saying caustically, "Ye know yer not the first wench to give him a bairn."

"But I am the first one to give him a legitimate heir," Fiona said quietly. She felt a sudden desire to protect her temporary husband from this vicious harridan and her poisonous tongue. She stared directly at the older woman, her gaze icy and unwavering.

Moire Rose opened her mouth but no words came out.

"God's bones," Nairn said, "I can't believe my eyes! Not in all my lifetime have I seen anyone render

ye speechless, madam." He held out his hand. "Now
give me the keys to the household, for they are Fiona's
from this time onward."

Yanking them from her girdle, Moire Rose flung
the keys at his feet and stormed from the entranceway.
Colin MacDonald picked up the keys and handed them
to Fiona. "I'll have the servants assembled so they may
meet their new mistress," he said. He took her arm and
led her into the small family hall, where a cheerful fire
burned.

"The priest was right," Fiona said slowly. "Father
Ninian observed that yer mam is sustained by her own
venom and has a wicked tongue and evil mind. 'Twas
harsh, I thought, but now that I have met her, I can see
he spoke the absolute truth. I am sorry he left us to go
farther south. I would value his counsel right now."

"Don't ever let that woman suspect any weakness
in ye, sweeting," he warned her. "Remember yer husband is the Lord of Nairns Craig, and yer its mistress.
'Tis yer word and not hers that will rule this household." Then he asked, "Ye do know how to manage a
household, do ye not, Fiona mine?"

Fiona laughed as she settled herself in a chair by
the fire. "Ye've waited until late, my lord, to inquire,
have ye not? Aye, put yer mind at rest. I know well how
to manage a household. Don't forget 'twas I who raised
my sisters. Although Brae had a housekeeper, I always
observed Mistress Una for the day when the responsibility would be mine."

"I am relieved to know that Angus Gordon's
household will not be discommoded by yer absence."

"Don't taunt me, Colly," she said low. "Angus Gordon loved me, and I loved him. One day he may come
knocking at yer gates seeking my return. I could go
with him."

"Over my dead body," he answered her fiercely.

She laughed. "Don't tempt me. Ye owe me much for yer mistreatment of me, Colin MacDonald, but I may forgive ye yet, my lord." Then she said, "I think it best we not tell yer mother the full truth of our courtship. She would as like to send to Braē to rid herself of me. Angus, most likely, would not have me back, but the situation would create a feud for both yer honor's sake. I should not like that."

"Nor I," he responded honestly. "But if I were he, I should want ye back—and that, too, would make a dangerous situation, Fiona mine."

"So we are agreed then, Colly, that we will make our peace for everyone's sake."

He nodded. "I don't want to fight with ye, sweeting."

Again Fiona laughed. "I know," she told him drolly, "yer objective has always been verra clear, my lord."

"I've missed ye these past nights," he murmured, kneeling by her side, taking her hand in his, and kissing the upturned palm.

"Oh, fie, my lord," she scolded. "Ye'll not get me in yer bed before ye feed me. I am ravenous from our ride today!"

"Then, lady, by God, you shall be well fed, first by my kitchens, then by my passions!" he cried, leaping up and shouting loudly for his servants.

Chapter 10

After a bit more than a month's absence, the laird of Loch Brae returned to the court in the last days of October, having escorted the queen's young cousin from York. They had traveled slowly, for Mistress Williams was a delicate creature and could bear the shaking of her transport cart only a few hours a day. Although she rode, she rode badly and preferred not to mount the gentle palfrey that was hers. They did not leave each day until midmorning. They ceased their travels in midafternoon. It made for a tiresome journey, and Angus Gordon was happy to be back at Scone. In the morning, he determined, he would depart for Brae, and his brazen wench. He loved Fiona. He was going to tell her so. The sooner their marriage was celebrated, the happier he would be.

The royal household steward greeted their party as they dismounted in the courtyard. "I will escort Mistress Williams to her majesty," he said. "The king has asked to see ye as soon as ye arrive, my lord. Here is his personal page, who will escort ye to his presence."

Angus bid a polite farewell to the young girl who had been his companion for the past few weeks. "I hope ye will be content with the queen, yer cousin, Mistress Beth," he told her.

"Thank ye, my lord. Ye made the trip a pleasant and easy one for me. I do not like traveling particularly. Will I see ye again?"

"It is unlikely, Mistress Beth. I am for Brae in the morning." He kissed her hand.

Elizabeth Williams followed the royal household steward. "Farewell, then, my lord," she replied.

"Lead on, laddie," the laird said to the page. Angus followed the boy, who brought him to the king's privy chamber, ushering him inside and closing the door behind Angus Gordon. "My lord!" Angus said, bowing to James Stewart, who sat before the fire.

"Pour yerself some wine, Angus," the king said jovially, "and then come and tell me about the trip."

The laird followed his instructions, and when he had settled himself opposite the king he said, " 'Twas an uneventful journey, my liege. The lass was waiting at the Convent of Saint Frideswide in York. The only difficulty was that she is not a good traveler, and it was necessary that we proceed slowly. She's with the queen now."

"Good, good," the king said. "I knew her dislike of travel, which is why I sent ye, Angus. I knew ye would not be impatient with Beth. She's a sweet lass, is she not?"

"Aye," the laird answered shortly.

"She'll make a man a good wife," the king persisted.

"Aye," came the dutiful response. Then the laird smiled at the king. "Now, my liege, I have done yer bidding, and on the morrow I will depart for Brae. My lass will be waiting. I plan to fetch the priest from Glenkirk Abbey, and marry her. A wedding feast will be set. I'll not admit it to my sister Jan, for 'twould give her too much power over me, but she was right in that I should have wed my lass when we first came together instead of waiting these two years."

A moment of guilt overwhelmed the king, but he

manfully swallowed it back. "Angus, my old friend," he began, "there has been a terrible happening. Fiona has been abducted on her way home to Brae. We can find no trace of her. We don't even know who took her." He went on to explain to the stunned laird. When he had finished he said, his voice rich with sympathy, "I am so sorry, Angus Gordon, but I will give ye the queen's cousin to wife if ye will have her. I know first ye will want time to recover from this tragedy."

Angus Gordon was numb with shock, but not so numb that he did not quickly refuse the king's apparently generous offer. "My liege, if the truth be known, Mistress Williams is pretty, and she is certainly sweet-natured and obedient, but as God is my witness, my liege, she is the dullest female I have ever met. I thank ye, but I will not wed her. I must go home to Brae, and I must search for my lass, for if I can't have her to wife, I will have no woman to wife. 'Twas not to be a marriage of convenience or one in which lands were exchanged. I love my lass. There is no other for me." He quaffed down the rest of his wine, then arose.

The king stood, too. He put a hand on the laird's shoulder. "Go and take yer rest, Angus. My page will take ye to a comfortable chamber, for the apartment ye shared with Fiona is stripped bare. Come to me in the morning before ye depart."

When the laird had departed, the king poured himself another goblet of red wine and sat down again before the fire. Slowly he rotated the goblet back and forth between his palms. Angus Gordon must absolutely not mount a search for Fiona Hay. There was always the danger he might stumble upon something. There was also a chance that he might remember The MacDonald of Nairn's interest in Fiona and then go to Nairn, where she was undoubtedly now in residence. There would certainly be an altercation. No matter who won it, James Stewart would lose. No. Angus Gordon could not look for his beloved. She was proving invaluable, as he had thought she would. Only the day before he had received her first communication, reassuring him that the Lord of the Isles did not mean to pledge him fealty yet, but neither would he provoke a confrontation. There would be peace in the winter months. James Stewart would have to find another mission for Angus Gordon in order to keep him from the highlands, if he was to keep Fiona Hay there, too. The king put his mind to the problem.

In the morning, after Prime, the laird of Loch Brae returned to the king's privy chamber to bid him farewell, but the king said, "I can't let ye go yet, Angus. I need someone I can absolutely trust to go to England to see that the hostages are being treated well. I am sending Atholl, and he wants ye with him. Ye will also arrange for the English to wait a wee bit longer for their first payment for my maintenance."

"My lord! I have been away from home for too long. My lass is missing, and I must find her! I have done yer bidding, and in doing so Fiona has been lost to me. Don't ask anything else of me, I beg ye!" He had not slept the whole night through thinking of Fiona. Who had taken her and why? Was she yet alive? *He had to know!*

"*Angus, I need ye,*" the king said again. "I will mount another search for Mistress Hay, I swear it! But if ye don't go with Atholl, I will not get the truth. One of his sons volunteered to go as a hostage. 'Twas done, I know, to prove his family's loyalty to me. Atholl will surely return and complain to me in order to get better treatment for the hostages, whom I know from my own experience are being well treated by the English. If ye are there to testify to this, then I will not have to bother them about Atholl's complaints. It is also important that the English wait for their payment. It is proving difficult to collect the moneys needed and to maintain my government. If ye do this for me, I will create ye Earl of Brae," the king said slyly.

"I must find my lass," the laird said stubbornly.

"We'll find her, Angus," the king said soothingly, "but are ye truly certain ye'll want her back? She was taken over a month ago, and if she is alive, who knows what may have befallen her, poor lass. Her captors were obviously the worst of highland bandits and may not have treated her gently. It is a harsh world, I fear."

"I want my lass back," the laird said once again, "and I will find her, my liege. Somewhere, someone saw something."

"Angus, Angus, don't make me do this," the king said. "If ye will not go to England willingly, then I must command ye to go."

The laird was surprised. "Ye would do that?"

"Aye," the king told him. "I must rule all of Scotland, or I canna rule at all, Angus. We will seek for Fiona Hay again, but while we do, ye will go to England in my service. Atholl leaves in a week. That will give ye time to go home to Brae and tell yer family of what has transpired. Then ye must return, Angus. If ye attempt to defy me I will put ye and yer whole family to the horn. Even my cousin, Hamish Stewart. While ye were gone, I executed Duke Murdoch and his ilk. They were my own kin, but a danger to Scotland for their unbridled ambition. They lie in their graves now, Angus

Gordon, because I will be king in fact and not just in title. Can ye understand?"

The laird nodded. Strangely he did understand, but it did not make it any easier to accept the disappearance of his Fiona. "I'll leave for Brae now," he said, "and be back in five days' time, my liege. I will accept yer pledge to seek after Fiona Hay, for if she is not dead, then whatever has happened, she will be my wife. I love my lass." Standing, he bowed, and departed the king's privy chamber.

James Stewart felt his shoulders beginning to relax even as the door closed behind the laird of Loch Brae. It had been a near thing. He hadn't been certain that his friend would not defy him, risking a charge of treason for the love of Fiona Hay. The king was glad he had not.

The laird of Loch Brae sensed he was being spied upon, but he did not look up. Instead he mounted his horse and rode through the gates of the palace at Scone onto the road that would eventually lead him to Brae. Fiona would have taken this very road a little over a month ago. Who had taken his brazen wench and why? He had no enemies that he could recall who would do such a thing. Perhaps it had just been, as everyone seemed to think, a crime of opportunity, but if it was, why had no trace of Fiona, Nelly, and the baggage cart been found?

What a great stubborn fool he had been! Not once, even after Fiona had showed him she loved him, had he told her that he loved her. How that must have hurt her, and he hadn't meant to hurt her. His sister Janet had always said he was spoiled and wanted his own way all the time. He had always denied it, believing those qualities to be hers, not his. Now he realized that perhaps she had been right.

He did not regret taking Fiona Hay as his mistress in exchange for the cattle she had stolen from him. But after a few months he should have married the lass. He suspected he had been in love with her all along, from the moment she had ushered him into her tumbling-down tower house with such dignity and grace. She was every bit his equal, and he had always known it.

But he had never told her. Instead he had played a cruel game with her—taunting her, embarrassing her before all of Scotland, and pretending that he didn't care when the truth of the matter was he damned well cared. Now she was lost to him, and she didn't know that he loved her. Loved her above all women. Had always loved her, even if he hadn't admitted it. Had she, perhaps, known the feelings he couldn't, or wouldn't, express? Women were intuitive that way. Perhaps that was why she had been so patient with him.

He had to find her, tell her he loved her and wanted only her for his wife. He realized that the king was sending him off because he thought the situation hopeless and wanted to distract him. But it wasn't hopeless! Fiona was out there. She was alive, and whatever had happened, he wanted her back! And in this matter above all others, Angus Gordon meant to have his own way.

He reached Brae with a day-and-a-half's hard riding and immediately sent to Greymoor for his sister and brother-in-law. Jeannie Hay was at the castle when he arrived, and he was surprised to find Jamie-boy not so aggravated by her presence any longer, but then Jeannie was almost demure in her behavior, which was a decided change. When Janet and Hamish arrived, he gathered them all together and told them what had happened.

"There is no evidence of her anywhere," he concluded.

"But who would steal Fiona?" Janet asked.

"I think 'twas the cart that they were after. If the king's men had guided her away from Glen Gorm, she might have been safe and home at Brae, but they ran like cowards and left her to the brigands."

"But they didn't kill her," Hamish Stewart said thoughtfully. "They did not find her body or Nelly's, or evidence of graves, did they? There is more to this than meets the eye, Angus," his brother-in-law decided.

"Aye, I agree with ye," Angus Gordon said, "but I canna for the life of me figure out what it is. The king offered me the queen's young cousin, a sweet lass, in exchange for my loss, but of course I turned him down. Beth is sweet, but Jesu, a boring little wench!"

"We'll mount our own search," Hamish Stewart said.

"I must return to Scone," the laird said. "I am to go to England with Atholl on the king's business. I did not want to do it, but the king insisted, even commanding me and threatening to put us all to the horn if I did not cooperate. I believe he thinks to take my mind off my troubles. I am to be made Earl of Brae upon my return."

"Are ye, now?" Hamish Stewart said thoughtfully. "I would say that the king is attempting to purchase yer cooperation, Angus. I know that ye served him in England as a lad, but he has made none of those others who were with him the offer of a title. I find it all most curious," Hamish Stewart concluded.

"Don't look askance at an earldom," Janet Gordon Stewart said tartly. "Angus Gordon, the Earl of Brae. My! Does it not sound grand?"

"It sounds verra grand," her husband replied. "Too grand for Angus's role in the matter, Jan. Tell me again, Angus, about Fiona's abduction. She was taken in the Glen of Gorm, ye say."

Carefully the laird went back over the story that the king had told him, thinking carefully, repeating it almost word for word.

"It seems to me that despite their inexperience the king's men were too quick to flee," Hamish Stewart noted. "Why was that, do ye imagine? Why did not one think to turn Fiona's horse so she might go with them? A most curious incident, Angus."

"What are ye saying, Hamish Stewart?" his wife demanded.

"Perhaps it was meant that Fiona Hay be abducted," he replied.

"Hamish, yer a fool seeing shadows where none exist!" Janet returned. "Are ye saying that the king was in on some kind of plot? What possible reason could the king of Scotland have for such a thing? Neither Fiona nor Angus is important to him. I don't know where ye get such ideas." She turned to her brother. "The king has rewarded ye because of yer loyalty and friendship. Think no more on it, my lord earl. Oh, I am so proud of ye, Angus Gordon, and I know that Father would be, too. An earldom for Brae! Who would have thought such a thing would ever happen?" She kissed his cheek and sniffled noisily, her eyes misty.

"But where is my sister?" Jeannie Hay demanded, suddenly her old self again. "Ye love her, Angus. Will ye be content to simply let her disappear?"

"The king has promised to send another search party out to seek my lass," the laird said. "If she is alive, I will not desert her no matter what, Jeannie. I do indeed love her."

"We'll look ourselves, lassie, while Angus is in England," Hamish Stewart said. He was not satisfied with the simplistic answer his wife had given her eldest brother. He was a Stewart, and he knew how complicated the Stewart mind could be. For the life of him, however, he could not figure out why the king had separated Angus and Fiona. What reason could there possibly be for such a thing?

Angus Gordon was uncomfortable being back at Brae. Everywhere he went evoked a memory of Fiona Hay. In desperation he took his horse one day and rode up Ben Hay. The tower house was bleak and deserted, his men having withdrawn months ago. Fiona's brothers-in-law had been made to understand that Ben Hay and its tower belonged to her. Stepping into the hall of the tower house, he recalled the wedding that had taken place there that morning so long ago. He could almost see Fiona standing haughtily, a length of Hay tartan across her then skinny chest, the chieftain's badge gleaming from her shoulder. How proud she had been, successfully marrying off Elsbeth and Margery, knowing that she had secured the futures of her five siblings, that she had done her duty as she had promised her dying mother she would when she was just a child herself.

"Yer alive, lass," he said softly. "I can feel it. Yer too strong to have disappeared off the face of the earth. We'll find ye, Fiona Hay. I found ye once. I'll find ye again. I don't intend losing ye forever."

Angus Gordon then rode back down the ben to Brae. He called to Hamish to join him in a goblet of wine. "Ye'll seek for her, will ye not?" he asked him.

Hamish nodded. "I will. Jan's explanation may

well be the truth, but I'm a cautious man and a wee bit distrustful, particularly of another Stewart. We're a canny family, Angus."

"I appreciate yer help, Hamish. She is out there somewhere. I know it!"

"I think ye may well be right," Hamish agreed. "I am curious, however, as to why this happened, but I suppose we'll not ever know that unless the king knows and is willing to tell."

Angus Gordon left Brae the following day and returned to Scone. If he could not look for Fiona himself, he knew that Hamish would seek after her, for Hamish loved nothing better than a conundrum except solving one, and this matter was indeed a puzzle. And two days after his return to Scone, he departed it, riding south with the Earl of Atholl and a small party of men for England.

Atholl was a changed man, and the laird had the oddest thought that perhaps Atholl was truly afraid of the king. He remembered the king saying Walter Stewart was so fearful of him that Atholl had given his own son to be a hostage so the king might believe his loyalty. He listened to the men who were riding with him. They all spoke in hushed tones of how the king had brought his cousin, Duke Murdoch, and two of Murdoch's sons, plus his father-in-law, the old Earl of Lennox, all to trial. That other Walter Stewart, Duke Murdoch's son, was the first arrested. Next, during a session of parliament at Perth, Duke Murdoch and his next-born son, Alexander; the Earls of Angus, Douglas, and March; Lindsay of Glenesk, the Hepburn of Hailes, and a number of other high-ranking lords, including the constables of Scotland and Dundee, Lord Stewart of Rosyth, and the Red Stewart of Dundonald, all found themselves imprisoned. They were considered to have been allies of Duke Murdoch's family.

The youngest of Duke Murdoch's sons had escaped to the west. He returned with a party of supporters to burn Dumbarton and slay the Red Stewart, who had been released from prison by his nephew. The king's men gave chase, and the young man was forced to flee to Ireland. Murdoch and his other sons, along with his father-in-law, the eighty-year-old Earl of Lennox, were tried and convicted of charges that amounted to high treason. Duke Robert was beyond his nephew's grasp, and so the king took his revenge upon his cousins and executed them. The rest of the noble criminals were tried. Most were fined or had their estates forfeited to the king. Some remained imprisoned for the time being. The king meant to terrify those who would attempt to thwart his efforts at reigning, but his vengeance had a mean-spirited quality to it. While the nobility were frightened, they were also resentful of this fierce young king.

"He has to be strong after the anarchy that has overrun the country," Angus Gordon said to his companions, defending the king.

"Strong, aye," Atholl agreed, "but it is not a crime to show mercy, my lord of Brae. James has no pity in his heart. He means to rule even if he must kill us all. While ye were away, a Stewart cousin struck a page in the king's hall within the king's sight. James Stewart ordered the miscreant brought before him. He had the man's hand extended out upon the high board, and the injured page stood at the king's command with a sharp knife upon the very wrist of this unfortunate. There they stood for an hour while our sweet queen, her ladies, and the clergy present pleaded for mercy for this Stewart cousin. Even the young page forgave the blow.

Finally the king relented, but he banished his cousin from court and from his presence. This is a man who will be king at any cost, my lord of Brae. Ye would be well advised to be wary of him."

"Ye know the nature of the Scots well, my lord," the laird answered him. "Ye know that the king must be stronger than any other man if he is to retain control over his own kingdom. We are not an easy people, and in past memory too many of our rulers have been weak-willed, feebleminded, unscrupulous, unprincipled, or corrupt. This king is not like that. His love of justice is greater than any man's I have ever known, my lord of Atholl. In time, when things are more easily managed, James Stewart will be less stern with us. For now, I would trust in him."

"My nephew is fortunate in yer friendship, Angus Gordon," the Earl of Atholl said, "but ye would still do well to heed my advice and be wary of him. Put not yer trust in any princeling, my lord. Power changes men from what they once were into something quite different."

"I thank ye for yer good thoughts, my lord," the laird told him, "but I will put my faith in the king. He has never disappointed me yet, and unless he does, I would be a poor liege man not to believe in him."

Walter Stewart, Earl of Atholl, offered no further words on the subject to the laird of Loch Brae. Perhaps James Stewart would never turn on his old childhood friend. And then again, perhaps he would. The king was a man who had no trouble when it came to attaining his goals for Scotland. Atholl looked ahead over the hills beyond which lay England. They had important business to consider, and he would see his son again. It was all he could concentrate on now. Scotland was in good hands, even if his nephew was proving a stronger and harder man than any of them had anticipated. Scotland would survive, possibly even thrive, under James Stewart's rule.

PART III

SCOTLAND

Winter 1425-Summer 1430

Chapter 11

Celtic tradition was ingrained in the highlands. On February second the fires blazed on the hillside in the midst of a snowstorm. It was Imbolc—a time when the ewes lactated, indicating the lambing season was upon them—a tradition in the Celtic world celebrating the days growing brighter and longer, the spring that would eventually come despite the cold, the snow, and the general gloom surrounding them now.

Nairns Craig stood tall and dark upon its cliff. Icicles hung precariously from the eaves of the castle. Snow had to be shoveled daily from the roofs to prevent collapse. The two wells serving the castle were frozen. They were broken open every new day. Fiona was kept busy in her capacity as lady of the castle, treating chilblains on the servants and the men-at-arms, dosing coughs and runny noses. It was a bitter winter. The worst in memory.

Bed, it seemed, was the only place she could get warm. She looked forward to day's end, cheerfully making the rounds to be certain that all the fires were safe and banked, then hurrying to the master's chamber that she shared with Colin MacDonald. The great oaken bedstead, with its heavy homespun hangings that could be drawn about to keep the draft out, was her refuge. It was made with a large feather bed, lavender-scented sheets, and a fine down comforter. There was also a magnificent red fox throw that she was extremely grateful for on these snowy nights. And, of course, there was Nairn.

None of this was really his fault. He never would have thought to steal her himself. Had not the king said that he had been deliberately taunted into doing the deed? In the months she had been with him, she had learned a great deal about Colin MacDonald. There was no meanness in him. He was a big, kind, charming man, and, dear heaven, he loved her. She greatly admired the deep loyalty he had for his clan, for his eldest brother, the Lord of the Isles. There was an honesty about him that touched some chord within her. And she was softening in her attitude toward him. She could not help it.

The same could not be said of his mother, Moire Rose. This was not a woman jealous of her son's new bride. Moire Rose appeared to dislike her son almost as much as he seemed to dislike her. No. The old woman simply did not want to share the authority she had held over Nairns Craig for most of her life.

As for the servants, they were not unhappy to have a new and cheerful mistress. Fiona quickly made it plain she would not tolerate disobedience or thievery, but her tongue did not lash the servants to tears, nor were honest mistakes met with a beating upon bare buttocks until the poor unfortunate bled and begged for mercy. She was kind and patient.

"If ye are not hard," Moire Rose warned Fiona, "they'll steal from ye. Spare the whip and ye'll not get the best from them."

"Whatever they did for ye, lady, it was from fear," Fiona said calmly. "I have always treated my servants fairly and have not been disappointed in their behavior or their performance. Kindness is not a bad quality. I am not above turning out a bad servant."

Moire Rose retired to her apartment with her personal servant, a wizened old crone called Beathag, who had once been the lady's nurse. On the occasions she ventured out, the servants gave her a wide berth, and Beathag, too, for the crone was as difficult as her mistress.

"They say Beathag has the evil eye," Nelly confided to her mistress. "It is known she practices the black arts, my lady."

"She had best not practice them in my house," Fiona said sternly.

On Imbolc night Fiona bathed quickly in her oaken tub, shivering as she stepped forth to be briskly rubbed dry by Nelly. Nairn came in and dismissed the girl with a kind word. Then, taking up his wife's hairbrush, he began to work it through her thick black hair. When he had finished, Fiona braided the length into a single plait and climbed into bed. It had become habit with them to do this each night. Stripping himself, Nairn bathed in her tub, then dried himself swiftly, for the night was bitter. He joined her, drawing the side curtains about them but leaving the curtain at the bed's foot open so they might view the fire and enjoy its warmth.

"For the first time in my memory Nairns Craig seems like a home," he told her. "The servants are happier and work better, it seems. The meals the cook is preparing these days are far better than those which we ate before. Why is that, Fiona mine?" He half sat, the plump pillows behind his broad back, Fiona between his legs, where he might fondle her at his leisure.

"Everyone is content," she told him, "and that contentment makes for a pleasanter household. The servants are no longer frightened. As for yer meals, I tell the cook what to prepare. I have even showed him

some new dishes, and how to use the spices he had
hidden away. There is no magic to it, my lord. I am
pleased ye have noticed these changes and are satisfied
with them."

He kissed the top of her dark head while his big
hands caressed her belly, which had begun to burgeon
with the bairn she was carrying. Her white breasts were
showing faint blue veins. He rested his hands upon her
rounding flesh and felt the child within her stirring beneath his touch. "He's going to be a braw laddie," Colin
said in a pleased tone. "I'll teach him to ride and use the
claymore myself. And ye, sweeting, must teach him
manners so he will not shame himself or the clan when
he visits in his uncle's hall."

Fiona laughed softly. She had mellowed, she
thought, over the past few months. She was glad Colin
had no doubt that the child she carried was his. He
would be good to that child, and until she could return south with her bairn, he would have a fine father
in this man. "So yer certain it's a son, my lord," she
teased him.

"Aye!" he responded enthusiastically. "We'll call him
Alastair after my brother, the lord. I will ask Alexander
to stand as the lad's godfather, Fiona mine. It canna
hurt my laddie to have a powerful patron."

Alastair. It was the Celtic for Alexander. She hadn't
considered what she would name this child. Certainly
she could not name him after his true father, Angus
Gordon, nor would she name him for her own father.
"Alastair James MacDonald," she told Nairn. "For your
brother, but for the king as well. One day the Lord of
the Isles will have to give his fealty to James Stewart
whether he wills it or not. I'd have our laddie named
for both of these great men, Colly. Agreed?"

"Aye, sweeting! 'Tis a good name, Alastair James. I

hope he will have yer black hair, for I love it so. I would not wish him my flaming top." He chuckled. His hands moved up to cup her breasts.

"And he may have yer blue eyes, Colly," she said, joining in the game that really was no game. "Oh, my nipples are so sensitive."

"And yer so damnably seductive, like one of our ancient fertility goddesses," he murmured in her ear, the tip of his tongue teasing it and then blowing softly on the wet surface. Turning her on her side, he moved behind her. "Soon we'll not be able to play," he whispered, fitting her leg in the proper position, then slowly sheathing himself in her warm, welcoming body.

"Ah." She sighed, feeling the hard, throbbing length of him within her. "Then," she said low, "ye'll have to take one of the serving wenches in the stables, Colly. Ahhh, my lord, 'tis good!"

His hands steadying one of her hips, he pumped himself gently within her until he felt her love juices dousing his manhood, and he then released his own pent-up passions. "No, sweeting," he told her when he had withdrawn from her and they were cuddled together beneath the warmth of the down and the fox fur. "I'll take no other for my pleasure when ye can no longer service me. Ye've spoiled me for any other woman, Fiona mine. The thought of even a meaningless tumble is distasteful to me now. I love ye, Fiona mine. *I love ye!*"

She turned so she might face him, seeing the love he offered her so unconditionally shining forth from his blue eyes. "Don't ask it of me yet, Colly," she pleaded with him. "I am not ready yet to give ye any more than I have already given ye. Ye canna expect it of me." She could feel the tears welling.

He gently stroked the curve of her jawline with a

single finger. "But yer softening toward me, sweeting. I can see it."

"Aye," she admitted, "but it doesn't mean that I will ever love ye, Colly. The bairn within me makes me feel differently. Once he is born, I may become what I was before, and hate ye for stealing me away from the laird of Loch Brae."

"Brae had his chance with ye, Fiona mine. He would not honor ye with his name," Colin said in a hard voice. "Ye know that I didn't hesitate to make ye my wife, even if handfast is only a year's time. When Father Ninian returns to Nairns Craig, we will have him give us the church's blessing, *and ye will love me.*"

"I will make ye no promises, Colly," Fiona warned him once again, but she knew he was not listening to her. He was absolutely determined that she be his wife, not just for a year but for always.

Spring came, and the king ignored the highlands. A messenger arrived from the Lord of the Isles bearing the news that he was coming to visit his brother, that others would be joining him, too, and that the castle should prepare for the arrival of at least a dozen or more chieftains.

"Why do they come here?" Fiona asked.

"They come here because it is the one place no one will think a gathering would be held," Nairn told her. "They come to discuss what to do about James Stewart. Will they give fealty or will they not? Will they wait for him to call them to Inverness, or will they go south to Perth or Scone to pledge loyalty?"

Later, Fiona and Nelly stood atop the castle walls of Nairns Craig watching as the invited guests arrived. To their surprise they were joined by Moire Rose, a wine-and-dark-green length of Rose family tartan clutched about her narrow shoulders.

"Ye canna possibly know the tartans of the north," she said dourly, by way of opening the conversation. "I'll instruct ye so ye don't embarrass yerself. There! The red and green with the yellow-and-white stripe is MacFie. The yellow and black with the red stripe is a MacLeod of Lewis. Ye knew the shameless daughter of that clan, Margaret, did ye not? Ah, there are the Chisholms with the red-and-green plaid with a white stripe, and the Camerons with their red and green with the yellow stripe. The Campbells are the blue and green with the yellow stripe, and the MacIntyres are the green and blue with red-and-white stripes."

"I do recognize some of the tartans," Fiona said quietly. "The red and green is Matheson, the green with the black-and-white stripes is MacLean, and the red, green, and blue plaid is MacIntosh."

"How do ye know them?" Moire Rose asked, curious in spite of herself. "Ye grew up in the eastern highlands."

"Those plaids were represented in The MacDonald's hall when we were there last autumn," Fiona explained.

Below them a man in red-and-green plaid with a white stripe, followed by one in a green-and-blue tartan with light blue, red, and yellow stripes, rode up the castle hill.

"A MacGregor, and a Malcom," the older woman noted. "Ahh, and here's as fine a pair of troublemakers as Scotland has ever known." She pointed a bony finger at the two men, one in a red, black, and green plaid whom she identified as Alexander MacRurie, and his companion in his green-and-black tartan with the yellow stripe, one Ian MacArthur.

Fiona made a mental note to ask Nairn's opinion about the two men his mother had spoken so scathingly upon. "Who is the gentleman riding up the hill with the pretty woman, my lady Moire?" she asked her mother-in-law.

"Well, well, well, this is an important meeting," that lady replied. " 'Tis Angus MacKay, and his wife, Elizabeth, who is The MacDonald's sister. And see, behind them. That fat fellow in his green-and-navy plaid with the yellow stripe? 'Tis the Late MacNeill, so called because he is always one of the last to arrive at any gathering."

Fiona giggled, unable to help herself, and to her great surprise, a faint smile touched Moire Rose's lips, but it was gone before she might really be certain. "I had best prepare a chamber for The MacKay and his wife," Fiona told her companions. "I was not expecting a lady, and thought to let the men sleep in the hall, but for The MacDonald."

"Wait," Moire Rose said, excited. "Listen! Do ye not hear the pipes, lassie? 'Tis The MacDonald, Lord of the Isles himself."

Sure enough, up the hill came the Lord of the Isles, mounted upon a fine white stallion, led by his four pipers and followed by a large troupe of his men. The first line of the men carried pennants of bright scarlet silk upon which had been embroidered in gold thread the lord's motto, Per Mare Per Terras (By Sea, by Land). The lord and his men all wore a bit of heath, the clan's plant badge, in their caps. The pipers were playing the MacDonald march.

" 'Tis how his father came first to Nairns Craig," Moire Rose said softly, her tone almost tender.

" 'Tis verra grand," Fiona answered her. "Colly says the lords of the Isles are kings, and certainly this lord makes his entrance like one. James Stewart doesn't like such pomp and show."

"The MacDonalds have more pride than the Stewarts," Moire Rose said proudly. "They have more pride than any other clan in Scotland."

The two younger women left Nairn's mother standing upon the tower walls.

In the upper hall Fiona spied a serving maid and sent her for linens for the second-best bedchamber. The Lord of the Isles would be sleeping in their best. The serving girl returned laden down with the necessary sheets and coverlets. Fiona took them from her and sent the girl for firewood for the bedchamber's fireplace. Then she and Nelly quickly made up the big bed and opened the windows to air the room. The maid returned once more and, kneeling, laid a fire, leaving the extra wood in a basket by the fireplace.

"Fill a bowl with flowers, lassie," Fiona ordered the girl, "and set them here upon the table. Quickly! I must go down to the hall to greet our guests. This room must be ready to receive The MacKay and his wife, who is yer master's half-sister. Come along, Nelly, and help me change my gown so I don't disgrace my husband." She hurried out and down the hall to their own apartments, Nelly in her wake.

Nelly chose a simple dark blue undergown for her mistress, over which she added the deep blue and silver brocade surcoat. Fiona's dark hair was gathered up into her silver caul. "Ye'll do," Nelly said.

Fiona hurried from the chamber and down into the hall, reaching it just as The MacKay and his wife entered from the courtyard. Nairn gave her a quick smile and, taking her by the hand, brought her forth to introduce her to his half-sister and her husband.

Elizabeth MacKay was a big-boned handsome

woman with dark chestnut hair and the family's blue eyes. She looked Fiona over boldly and then pronounced, "Alex did not lie, Nairn. Ye have taken a beauty for a wife, and I see she is already full to bursting with a bairn. The MacDonalds do not waste time."

"It is delightful to see ye again also, sister," Nairn said drolly. "May I present my wife, Fiona, to ye?"

Fiona curtsied politely, but her sister-in-law said, "Oh, don't be so formal with me, Fiona Hay. Come and give me a kiss on the cheek. When is my nephew due to be born? 'Tis yer first, I know, but have ye figured it out yet?"

Fiona kissed Elizabeth MacKay upon her soft cheek, saying as she did so, "I would think the bairn is due shortly, my lady. 'Twas conceived almost immediately after yer brother stole me last autumn."

Her newfound sister-in-law chuckled richly at the remark. " 'Tis not really like Nairn to be quite that bold," she noted. "I have known him to take what he wants in past times, but never have I known him to be quite so verra audacious. Alex says he loves ye. He must."

"So he tells me, lady," Fiona answered.

"Ah," Elizabeth MacKay observed, "yer still not won over entirely by yer insolent husband, are ye?"

"I am reconciled to my fate for now, and perhaps a wee bit softer in my attitude to Nairn than I was several months ago, lady," Fiona told her, "but ye canna expect me to be mad with love for a man who stole me from a man I did love. I am many things, lady, but I am not a liar where the heart is concerned."

" 'Tis better yer not," Elizabeth MacKay replied. "Men are not verra practical, nor are they as clever as we women are. 'Tis better one of ye has a cool head.

Poor Nairn with his fiery locks is not suited to it at all, is he?" She laughed, patting Fiona's hand.

Fiona liked Elizabeth MacKay. That was becoming a problem. She liked all of the MacDonalds she had met. How coldhearted James Stewart was to believe she could distance herself from Nairn so completely that she could betray him and his family. She understood the king's desire to have complete control of all of Scotland, but she also comprehended the attitude of the MacDonalds, who had always been their own masters, answering to no one but God and the Lord of the Isles, who answered only to God. Change, she realized, was difficult for everyone. She wondered if there was a way in which everyone's objective could be gained without going to war, but then she grimaced at her own folly. This was Scotland, where nothing important, or for that matter unimportant, was settled without a fight. For now her function was to listen to the gathering of chieftains in the hall as she went about her duties as their gracious hostess. Then she must find a way to pass along any information to the king. Why had he not called a gathering of the northern clans yet? In a few months' time she would have been with Nairn a year.

"Yer looking much too serious for such a pretty lass, my bonnie," the Lord of the Isles said as he came up to greet her.

"I am considering if I have enough food for all these men," Fiona told him ingenuously. "I don't want my hospitality lacking, my lord. I've never provided for such a large group before." She smiled up at him.

"Do not fear," he told her. "I will wager that virago, his mother, has been in yer kitchens behind yer back making certain that the honor and the hospitality of Nairns Craig is not shabby."

"She gave me the keys to the household the day I arrived," Fiona said, not bothering to say the keys were thrown at Nairn's feet.

"This is different. Is she pleasant to ye, or is her tongue as foul as ever?"

"She has kept to her rooms mostly," Fiona said, "for I showed strength with her that first day. Today, however, she joined my Nelly and me upon the walls watching everyone's arrival. She was almost friendly."

"Then ye have seen a side of her that few have, my bonnie." He chuckled, then left her to continue overseeing the preparations for the evening meal.

Made curious by his words, Fiona made her way to the kitchens. "Matthew," she said to her head cook, "has the lady Moire been here to give ye additional instructions this day or previously?"

"Aye, my lady," the cook answered. "She came early this morning to inquire what I had planned, and then said that ye had decided we needed additional fare. At her order I have roasted an additional roe deer and done another six geese, as well as added a ham to the menu. There is always plenty of bread, butter, and cheese."

"Verra good, Matthew," Fiona said. She didn't know whether to be angry, offended, or amused by her mother-in-law's actions. Then she realized that Moire Rose had probably saved her a great deal of embarrassment by her timely actions, even if she hadn't spoken with Fiona first. Back in the hall she did not see Moire Rose. Realizing suddenly that the woman would not come into the hall unless invited, she called to a servant, saying, "Go to the lady Moire's apartments, and bid her join us in the hall this night."

The servant bowed, clearly surprised by the request, but he hurried off.

Fiona walked slowly about the hall, picking up snatches of conversation here and there. She knew the serious talking would not begin until after the meal. Making certain that the men all had wine, or ale cups in their hands, she joined Elizabeth MacKay as she sat before the fire in a comfortable high-backed chair.

"I hope ye found yer chamber to yer liking. 'Tis only the second-best, I fear, for I had to put yer brother in the best," she explained with a small smile. "I didn't know ye were coming until I saw ye riding up the castle hill with yer lord."

" 'Tis a fine room for any guest, expected or not," her sister-in-law said, smiling back. "The bowl of primroses is a pretty touch." She sipped at a silver cup of wine. Then suddenly she said, "God's boots! There is herself entering the hall. We're all in for it now."

Fiona arose heavily, making her way as quickly as she could across the room, greeting Moire Rose politely. "Welcome, lady. I am happy ye have joined us this night." Then she lowered her voice. "I thank ye for yer aid in the kitchen. We should have been embarrassed without yer timely intervention. I didn't realize the Lord of the Isles would arrive with so large a troupe of men. Should ye see me about to make a mistake like that again, will ye not come and tell me? I canna learn without yer help. My tower house was small compared to Nairns Craig."

"Yer a clever lass," Moire Rose said quietly, and again there was that ghost of a smile upon her lips. Then she said, "Ah, there is my old friend, William MacFie. I shall go and greet him. 'Twill frighten him to death, for he was always fearful of me when we were children."

"Why?" Fiona asked her, very curious.

"Why?" Her mother-in-law laughed harshly. "I

was bigger than he was, for he is a verra little man. The Wee MacFie, they call him. I gave him the name, and it stuck. I am a small woman, but I could beat him in foot races every time. He didn't like me for it at all."

"Yet he is yer friend?" Fiona was surprised.

Moire Rose chortled, and without another word she made her way across the hall to greet the Wee Mac-Fie, who actually blanched at the sight of her approach, looking desperately for an escape and finding none.

Now here was something she would not have thought. Moire Rose had a sense of humor. A dark one, but nevertheless it was there. She wondered if Nairn realized it. There was more to this woman than she or anyone else had thought. Her tongue was sharp, her heart was bitter, but perhaps she was not quite as bad as they had all believed.

Nairn came to her side, chuckling as he attempted to put an arm about her now nonexistent waist. "There have been many comments on how truly pleasant the hall looks, and how fine our ale and wine are, sweeting. I know the dinner will be as good."

"It will, and thanks to yer mother, my lord, for I had not ordered enough, never having entertained so large an assembly. She suspected it and discreetly advised Matthew to prepare more, saying I had thought better on it. It was a kind thing she did."

"Is that why ye tendered her an invitation into the hall this night?"

Fiona nodded absently, looking about and deciding it was time to serve the meal. "Let me go, Nairn," she told him. "I must be about my duties before the men are too drunk on our ale and wine to eat the fine meal Matthew has prepared for them." She hurried off to instruct the castle steward, and within minutes the servers were coming into the hall with plates and bowls, platters and pitchers. The high board was restricted to the family members to prevent insult to any of the chieftains by implying that one was more important than another. Only The MacKay and his wife were, understandably, at the high board. Below the dais the other chieftains scrambled for places.

The meal, consisting of a roast pig, two roe deer, a dozen geese, six capons, a ham, a large eel stew, a great pie filled with small game birds, several broiled trout from the swiftly flowing streams belonging to Nairns Craig, bowls of new peas, and lettuces braised in white wine, was much appreciated by the men. With gusto they ate and drank, tearing great hunks from the loaves of bread, spreading them lavishly with sweet butter using their thumbs, slicing wedges of sharp cheese with their dirks, washing it all down with wine or brown ale. The servants ran back and forth refilling pitchers and platters until the appetites of all the guests had been satisfied. When all the dishes had been cleared away, a servant brought bowls of tiny strawberries to the three ladies at the high board.

Colin MacDonald stood up. "Now that ye have eaten, my lords, I welcome ye again to Nairns Craig and ask that ye listen to what my brother, the Lord of the Isles, has to say to ye."

The hall grew very quiet, even the servants ceasing their labors, as Alexander MacDonald arose to speak to the gathering of the chieftains. The torches and the candles spread mysterious shadows across the room as he spoke.

"My lords," he began, "I must thank my brother of Nairn and his bonnie wife for offering us their hospitality. May I remind ye that this meeting among us is to remain secret. Today is the last day of May, in the year of our lord fourteen hundred and twenty-five. None of us has yet been called to Inverness to pledge fealty to James Stewart. It is verra possible that the days of our autonomy are coming to an end."

Here and there were shouts of disapproval, but the Lord of the Isles held up his hand, and silence once more settled upon the hall.

"I don't like it either, and I will resist it, but we must face facts. In the eastern highlands and south of the Tay this king has united the clans. There has even been talk here in the north and in the west among some of the clans of pledging fealty. I will stop no man from doing so, nor will I count him my enemy unless he chooses to make himself such. I have called ye here to tell ye that each must do what he decides is best for his clan. Some of ye are small, no more than a few hundred men, and others of ye can command a thousand or more to yer banner. Be warned, however, that any who pledge fealty to James Stewart with the idea of then gaining his help to attack me and mine, will suffer in the worst possible ways. I will come down on ye like a wolf upon a hapless sheep. I will spare none of yer people, men, women, the aged, babes suckling at their mam's tit. I am the Lord of the Isles, and I will remain so."

Duncan Campbell stood up, saying, "And if we swear fealty to this Stewart king, and he asks our aid in overcoming yer power, my lord, what then? Our loyalties will be divided. Honor bound, we must obey the king, our overlord. Yet like ye, we are highlanders."

"Yer strong enough to stand by me until the last moment, Duncan Campbell," the Lord of the Isles said. "Yer family is not small or weak."

The Late MacNeill rose up. "I am here for my brother, Gilleonan, who is ill with running bowels and could not come. We are a small family, my lord, and pledged to ye as yer vassals. There is no doubt as to the course we will take. We will follow ye as we always have. We will not pledge ourselves to this Stewart until ye do." He sat back down.

"Discuss this among yerselves," the Lord of the Isles said, "but keep a rein on yer tempers. There will be no fighting or killing in my brother of Nairn's hall. Remember there are women here."

The chieftains began to discuss the matter in reasonable tones at first, but slowly their voices escalated as their deliberations deepened and views were frankly exchanged. The smaller families were concerned about their ability to defend themselves, not just from James Stewart, but from the larger families who would prey on them no matter the course they chose, as they had always preyed on them. The larger clans considered the wisdom of deserting their alliance with Alexander MacDonald to join with Scotland's king. Yet there was the distinct possibility that the new king would reward those who quickly came to his side rather than waiting for a gathering to be called in Inverness.

Robert Cameron muttered, " 'Tis like tossing the dice. One canna be certain if they will win."

"Are ye thinking of deserting our ancient confederacy, then, Robbie Cameron?" said William MacIntyre heatedly.

Those at the high board listened with interest to the exchanges going on about them.

"Duncan Campbell is not to be trusted," Nairn said to his elder brother. "The Campbells have always been jealous of our power."

"But not strong enough to defy us until now," Alexander MacDonald replied. "I can see he is considering the advantage of kneeling before James Stewart, but should he do so before I do, he will make an enemy of the MacDonalds for all time. The smaller families

I canna blame for attempting to protect their own, for I will acknowledge to ye, and ye alone, brother, that I know in the end I will yield, too."

"James Stewart said to me when he reconfirmed my title and lands that I should kneel before him immediately after ye, Alex, and so I shall, but not before then, I swear it."

The Lord of the Isles clapped his younger sibling upon the shoulder and said, "I love ye, Nairn. I'm glad for the day our father brought ye to Islay to raise up with the rest of us."

Suddenly all eyes in the hall swung to Ian MacArthur, who said loudly, "Why do we not kill this Stewart king, my lords? 'Twould save a great deal of trouble for us in the end. He has no heir yet. The queen, I am told, delivered of a daughter. Old Atholl is the nearest male relation to the throne. Kill James Stewart, and the lands south of the Tay would erupt in chaos with the struggle to gain his throne. We might seek for Duke Murdoch's surviving son, the other James, who I am told is in Ireland." Ian MacArthur looked about him for support.

Alexander MacRurie leapt up, saying, " 'Tis a fine idea Ian has put forth. If we kill James Stewart, the matter is settled for us. And if we put his nephew to do the deed, who can blame us?"

"Are ye so stupid," said Fiona, standing up behind the high board, "that ye think Duke Murdoch's Jamie Stewart would be willing to avenge his father and brothers for naught? And dare ye offer him coin to do the murder? He could not take it for shame, and would be called a Judas. So what would he want, my good lords?" she demanded scathingly of them, and then as quickly answered her own question. "I will tell ye what he would want, ye fine pair of fools. *He would want yer support!* And ye would have no choice but to give it him lest he make yer part in the murder of an anointed and rightful king public knowledge. Do ye think the church would let stand such wickedness without becoming involved? So ye would trade a just, though hard, Stewart for a cowardly and guileful Stewart? Ye would never be able to trust him. 'Tis surely no bargain." Fiona sat back down in her seat to let them digest her words. Highland women were outspoken, and none thought it odd that she had taken part in the discussion. Indeed, many of the chieftains were impressed, and considered her words thoughtfully, for they had been told of her intimate acquaintance with the king and his queen.

"Such an act would surely bring fire and sword to the highlands," Elizabeth McKay said quietly to those at the high boards. "Fiona speaks wisdom, and I hope ye will listen well, my brother." She looked directly at the Lord of the Isles. "What think ye of Lord MacArthur's suggestion?"

"I think he is a fool, as our bonnie Fiona so wisely observed," Alexander MacDonald said. " 'Twould be unworthy of a MacDonald to be part of such a plot. I will espouse no such thing, sister, and ye know it well without asking," he finished.

"Yet," his sister said, "MacArthur's close adherent is The MacRurie, who is a part of the MacDonald family, brother. How will ye keep him under control?"

Alexander MacDonald smiled wolfishly. "When the day comes that we must go to Inverness, and the king desires a member of our family to make an example of, do ye nae think MacRurie will do, sister?"

"Ah, Alex, our da would be proud of ye," she said, smiling at him. " 'Tis a plan worthy of Donald of Harlaw."

Fiona listened to them as well as to the continued discussions in her hall. This proposed assassination by Ian MacArthur and Alexander MacRurie was something she would pass on, for although it would undoubtedly come to nothing, the king should be warned. She was worried as to how her information could be transmitted, for she was in no condition to go to Inverness to visit the cloth-and-ribbon merchant and none of the other agents had come to Nairns Craig this spring. She turned to her brother-in-law and asked, "Have ye seen Father Ninian, my lord? I would have him here to baptize the bairn after it is born."

"I have heard he was somewhere north of Nairns Craig, my bonnie," the lord answered her, "but do not fear. He came to Islay earlier this spring, and told me then he planned to be with ye and Nairn come June."

"June comes in tomorrow, my lord," Fiona said.

" 'Tis a fine month for a bairn to be born in," the lord told her with a broad smile.

Fiona laughed. "Any moment would suit me for this bairn to be born. I am as swollen as an overripe grape."

"Is my nephew an active wee fellow?" Elizabeth MacKay asked.

"He is never still," Fiona responded, "yet in the last day or two he has quieted, it seems."

Elizabeth MacKay gave Moire Rose an arch look. "The bairn will be born soon," she said with certainty.

Nairn did not come to bed that night, and Fiona slept badly. In the morning, however, she was up, dressed in a loose-fitting dark green gown, and in the hall to supervise the servants seeing to the early meal. Oat porridge, fresh bread, two hams, several bowls of hard-boiled eggs, stone crocks of butter, and a new wheel of hard, sharp cheese were set out, along with pitchers of foaming brown ale. The chieftains, most bleary-eyed, were nonetheless awake, and had attended to their personal needs. They sat down at the trestles, eating hungrily as if they had not eaten in a month, swiftly emptying the pitchers of ale.

Then, one by one, they began to take their leave of Nairns Craig. Fiona stood with her husband at the entry to the hall, bidding each man a polite farewell. She knew each man's name and spoke it as he came abreast of her. The chieftains were pleased by her womanly manners, and many complimented Nairn on his good fortune in his wife. When they had all departed but for The MacDonald and his relations, Fiona returned to the hall again to make certain the trestles were cleared off and set to one side of the room. Then the morning meal for the rest of her guests was brought out.

The Lord of the Isles, who had been in the hall earlier to bid his vassals and allies farewell, was already seated at the high board with his sister and his brother-in-law, The MacKay. "Yer wife is a great asset to us, Nairn," he said. "She spoke well, and with much common sense last night. Many commented upon it. I am verra pleased with ye, my bonnie," he told Fiona, a smile lighting his whole face.

"I don't wish to raise my children amid the din of constant war, my lord," Fiona told him. "No woman does, be she of high or low station. 'Tis ye men who cry war and then send our sons into battle. I but sought to keep the peace for as long a time as possible."

"But if our autonomy is threatened, we must defend ourselves," the Lord of the Isles said sternly.

"All James Stewart asks of ye is loyalty," Fiona said. "He has a mighty task to bring Scotland under control.

He wants the towns to become great commercial centers like the English have because that is what makes them prosperous, but how can the towns grow when the clans are always burning them in retaliation for one thing or another? If he knows ye will keep the peace here in the north and west, then ye will undoubtedly be left in peace. Why does a man like Alexander MacDonald, Lord of the Isles, a man known for his honor, find it so difficult to swear fealty? If ye were but one man, it would not be so hard, but ye are the key to peace in these highlands. Without yer support most of the others will not swear, and they remain a thorn in the king's side. Eventually he must pluck that thorn or be called craven and weak-willed, as his father was. He will not allow his own honor to be compromised thusly, my lord."

"Let us see if the king calls us all to Inverness," the Lord of the Isles said. "I don't have to make a decision before then, do I?"

Fiona shook her head in despair. How could she tell this great and powerful chieftain that he was making a terrible mistake? By not swearing to James Stewart now, he was but antagonizing the king. James Stewart had a long memory and a single goal: to unite Scotland. He would do whatever he had to to attain that goal, as Fiona well knew. Suddenly a sharp pain caused her to stagger, and a pool of water puddled around her feet. Shocked, she looked down at it.

Her attention engaged, Elizabeth MacKay's eyes went to where Fiona's were. She saw the water and, standing up, announced, "I knew it! The bairn is to be born this day. Did I not say it last night? Did I not say the bairn would come soon? Well, don't stand there, ye great fools! Fiona must be taken to her chamber, and the birthing table brought. Hurry now!"

Chapter 12

Colin MacDonald almost knocked his brother over as he rushed to reach his wife. "Do ye have pain, sweeting?" he asked her, picking her up and walking quickly across the hall to the staircase leading to their chambers. "Ah, Fiona mine, I canna bear to see ye hurting."

"Then ye should not have gotten a bairn upon me, Nairn," she said with a small attempt at humor. She winced. "Ohhhhh!"

The castle servants had been galvanized into action. A serving wench had dashed ahead of Nairn to alert Nelly. Another ran off to find the birthing table.

Elizabeth McKay turned before going up the stairs, saying to her husband and brother, "Keep Colin's spirits up as best ye can when he returns to the hall. And that does not mean getting him drunk, my laddies. Ye'll both answer to me if ye do!" Then she was gone.

"She did not say *we* could not get drunk," the Lord of the Isles said to his brother-in-law. "Is it too early for ye?"

" 'Tis never too early, Alex," came the reply, "but I suspect she'd be verra angry with us. She has a fierce temper, yer sister, my wife. I retain a potter in the keep to replace all the crockery she throws at me and anyone else who runs afoul of her ire."

Alexander MacDonald laughed aloud at this revelation.

In her chamber Fiona struggled to bring forth the

life she had been nurturing within her womb. At first she would not cry out when the pains wracked her greatly, but Elizabeth encouraged her, saying, "A woman is expected to shout aloud when her babe is being born, Fiona. Don't hold back!"

"My mother never shouted," Fiona said through gritted teeth. "I was the eldest, and I never heard her shout when my five sisters were born alive and my wee brothers were born dead. My father did all the shouting, screaming at her to give him his son each time, cursing her when the lassies came into the world alive and the laddies were birthed dead and cold as stone."

"Yer not yer mother. My brother cares not a whit if it is a son or a daughter, do ye, Nairn? We want a healthy baby, lass. That is all. Now, cry out with yer pain, and help the bairn to come."

She was rewarded when Fiona shrieked and cried out, "I am being torn apart, lady!"

"Nay, nay, lassie, 'tis an easy birth yer having. Another wee push, and I will see the bairn's head," Elizabeth MacKay promised. "When the next pain comes, bear down with all yer might."

"It's coming!" Fiona shouted, letting out a shrill cry.

"Oh, verra good, dearie, verra good," Elizabeth MacKay praised her sister-in-law.

Colin MacDonald was visibly white as he let Fiona clutch his hand until he thought she would render it bloodless. Seeing his condition, Fiona said, "Get out, Nairn! I don't want ye swooning on the floor. There is no time to attend to ye if this child is to be born. Oh! Oh! Oh!" she gasped.

"I'll not leave ye, sweeting, nor will I swoon like a maiden," he promised her, although he wasn't certain he could keep the latter promise. Seeing her in such obvious pain, realizing he was the cause of it, was almost more than he could bear. He swallowed hard.

"I have no more time for ye, Colly," Fiona told him. "Blessed Mother! Ahhhhhhhhhhh! Lady, what is happening?"

"One, perhaps two more pushes, Fiona, and yer bairn is born," Elizabeth MacKay said. "The head and shoulders are already out." She opened the baby's mouth and yanked out a clot of mucus. The child coughed slightly and began to cry.

"Is it a lad?" Fiona asked her.

"That's the part usually born last," Elizabeth MacKay laughed. "Ye'll have to give me another push if we're to know. It's got black hair like yers, though."

Another fierce pain wracked Fiona, and she pushed with what she thought was her absolute last bit of strength. Suddenly she no longer felt as if she were being torn asunder. Indeed, she could actually feel something sliding out of her body. Then the child was howling in earnest.

" 'Tis a wee laddie, though not so wee," Elizabeth MacKay said with a wide smile. "Well, Nairn, ye have a son." She held the bloody infant up for her brother to see. "Take yer knife, Colin, and cut the cord as I tell ye," Elizabeth MacKay said, laying the squalling child upon its mother's belly as she directed her brother, then knotted the remaining cord expertly. She handed the baby to Nelly. "Clean him up, lassie, and wrap him well so he may go into the hall with his da to meet his overlord and his uncles."

Tears of joy pouring down her face, Nelly cleansed the birthing blood from the baby boy. How very much like Angus Gordon he looked, but Colin MacDonald would not realize it, for he had not known the laird particularly well. He would assume the dark hair was an inheritance from Fiona, and no one ever could really decide who babies looked like. Nelly swaddled the baby in fresh soft cloth. Then, without waiting for further instructions, she placed him in Fiona's arms.

Looking into the face so like Angus Gordon's, Fiona felt her heart break again. His father's son, but he was unlikely ever to know his real father. Kissing the damp, downy dark head, she handed the baby to Colin. "Here is yer son, my lord," she said quietly. "I hope he pleases ye."

Colin MacDonald accepted the tiny bundle she offered him. He was delighted, and amazed at how sturdy his laddie was. Blue eyes looked up at him. He felt as if he were being scrutinized carefully, and hoped he would not be found wanting. "Welcome to Nairns Craig, Alastair James MacDonald," he said. Looking down at Fiona, he smiled. "Thank ye, Fiona mine. Yer a fine breeder." Turning, he left his wife's chamber with the baby.

Alexander MacDonald watched his brother cross the hall cradling the swaddled bundle. From the grin on Colin's face he knew without asking that the child was a lad. "Congratulations, brother!" he exclaimed, and peering down at the infant he said, "The babe looks strong. He'll survive."

"Let me see him! Let me see my grandson!" Moire Rose pushed past the Lord of the Isles and The MacKay. "Give him to me, Colin." When her son had placed the baby in her outstretched arms, an almost beatific smile lit Moire Rose's face. "Ah, he's a braw laddie," she crooned down at the child. "A verra braw laddie, he is!"

"They say ye would not look upon me when I was born," Colin said, struggling to keep the bitterness from his voice.

His mother gazed directly at him. "I looked at ye,"

she told him. "When they were not there watching me, I looked at ye. I saw yer father in yer face, Colin MacDonald. For all my red hair and blue eyes ye were a MacDonald. I hated him then, for he had deserted me. But I loved him, too. Ye were a reminder of what I had lost. I believe this bairn looks like my father," she said, "and he is my grandson." She handed the baby back to him.

"He is also a MacDonald and my son," he said to his mother.

"Aye," she answered softly, "but he is not my MacDonald." Then she left the hall without another word.

"I have never seen her like this," Nairn said. "It's as if she has become a different woman. I don't understand it at all."

He took his son back to Fiona, telling her of what had transpired in the hall with his mother.

Strangely Fiona understood, for in an odd way she was in a similar position to Moire Rose all those long years ago. "Perhaps the bairn has brought out the good in yer mother, Colly," she told him. "Don't question it; just accept it. She is an old woman now."

The Lord of the Isles and the MacKays had decided to remain at Nairns Craig in hopes that Father Ninian would arrive. Nairn sent Roderick Dhu in search of the priest so the baby might be baptized immediately, since his godparents were there. When Alastair MacDonald was three days old, Roderick Dhu returned with the tall, ageless cleric in tow. The baby was baptized in the hall of Nairns Craig, sanctified for the occasion. The Lord of the Isles and Elizabeth MacKay stood as his godparents. Fiona was brought into the hall upon a litter so she might partake in her son's christening.

The day after the baptism, when the guests had

departed, Father Ninian said, "I will hear confessions of any who would come to me."

As priests were few and far between in remote sections of Scotland, the priest knew he would stay for a week to ten days hearing confessions, marrying, and baptizing, as well as praying over the graves of those who had died since his last visit. Each morning he held a mass in the hall, and it was well attended by the inhabitants of the castle.

When Fiona went to make her confession to him, she passed along the information to Father Ninian that she wanted him to have, telling him in careful detail of the talked-of plot to kill the king. "They will not do it, of course, for both are cowards, but the king should be warned nonetheless, I believe."

The priest nodded. "Aye, lady, I agree."

"In the autumn," Fiona said, "the year will be up that the king asked of me. I want to know when I may take my leave of Nairns Craig and return to my own home. If I don't leave then, Nairn will badger me into speaking my vows with him before ye, Father, and ye know I canna wed him. Tell the king I have learned all I can here. And ask why has he not called a gathering of the clans in Inverness so these highlanders may swear loyalty to him and be done with it."

"I will come myself in the autumn before the term of the handfast is up so I may carry the king's answer to ye, lady, and help ye to extricate yerself from this benign captivity. But will Nairn let the bairn go?"

"When I tell him the truth, he will have no choice," Fiona said with assurance. "He is every bit as proud as Black Angus."

"I understand," the priest replied, his amber eyes sympathetic.

Fiona insisted upon nursing her son, for she treasured the minutes spent with the baby at her breast suckling strongly. And the infant grew quickly, his small limbs rounding and fattening, his cheeks smooth and rosy. His bright eyes missed nothing. His little dark head swiveled at the sound of his mother's voice and Nairn's. They had to get away soon, Fiona thought, for Nairn was positively mad for the child he believed was his son. Fiona felt truly guilty—and angrier than ever before at the king.

What was worse, the baby loved Nairn, who could bring an infantile giggle from the child when no one else could. "Ah, there's my laddie," he would croon upon spying the baby cooing in his cradle each morning. "There's his da's little mankin."

And if Nairn loved Alastair, Moire Rose was even worse, pouring all the love she had denied her son out upon her grandson. She would sit in the hall for hours on end rocking the infant's cradle and singing him lullabies in her high, reedy voice.

Alastair James MacDonald was the darling of the household. No servant passed without stopping a moment to speak a word, smile a smile, chuck his chin. And the child responded to it all.

"He's going to be verra spoiled," Fiona said ominously.

The baby had been born on June first. In mid-September the priest appeared once more at Nairn's Craig. "I've come to see how the bairn is doing," he told Nairn. "I'll soon be going south, for winter in the highlands is hard for a man on the road."

"Would ye think of sheltering here for those months?" Colin asked him. "God knows we have use for ye. I'd build ye a church of yer own if ye would but remain, Father Ninian. 'Twould not be a rich living, but ye'd have plenty to eat and plenty of souls to save, I guarantee ye. Ye could go traveling in the summer months as ye do now, but ye'd have a home to come back to in the cold times."

" 'Tis a generous offer, my lord," the priest said, "but how could I accept ye when I have refused the lord himself a half a dozen times? 'Tis better I return to my abbey as I am accustomed to doing, but I thank ye."

Nairn shook his head ruefully. "I want a priest for the castle," he said. "Now that we have begun a family, Fiona and me, I would be more civilized. There was once a priest at Nairns Craig, but he was as old as my grandsire and died several years before him."

"I will inquire of my abbot for ye, my lord," Father Ninian said. Then he smiled. "Tell yer steward to send out the word that I am here for marriages, baptisms, and my other usual duties. I will hear the confessions of the castle folk, for my penances must last ye all until I come again in the springtime," he finished with a chuckle.

Fiona could barely wait to speak privately with the priest, but as was her custom she made certain that everyone else in the castle saw him first. Only in the evening of the second day he was with them was it her turn to closet herself with Father Ninian in the tiny room off the hall that was set aside for his privacy. She knelt before him, hurrying through a list of minor sins, asking him to shrive her.

Before he did, however, he spoke to her in low tones. "Ye will want to know, my daughter, of the king's answer to yer questions of several months ago. He sends word that he needs ye to remain here at Nairns Craig for the present. He says he is pleased by the information ye have sent him, for it has been invaluable in helping him to decide just how to deal with the Lord of the Isles and the highlands. The Campbells have sworn their fealty to James Stewart, not waiting for a gathering of the clans at Inverness but going to Perth in midsummer. The final thing I am to impart to ye is that the queen's cousin, Elizabeth Williams, has married a gentleman of her royal guardians' choosing, and is already with child. The king wanted ye to know this. Now, my daughter, I will administer yer penance." He placed his hands upon her head.

Fiona, however, felt nothing. It was as if the blood in her veins had frozen solid. She was numb with shock. Deep within her heart and soul she had dared to hope that Angus Gordon would not marry Elizabeth Williams. That one day, perhaps, they might meet once more and together begin anew. It had been, she knew even as she thought it, a childish dream, but still, she had hoped. Now her silly, secret little wish was naught but cold ashes. Angus had not died from pining away for her. She had disappeared from his heart as surely as she had disappeared on the road to Brae. The laird of Loch Brae had done his royal master's bidding and wed the English girl. He had even gotten a child upon her. That child would be the heir to Brae, not her son, Alastair, who would now never know his real father.

Fiona felt close to weeping, but she stiffened her spine instead. She mutely accepted the mild penance that Father Ninian gave her, but her outward appearance of meekness belied the anger that was boiling inside her. Had there ever been a man in her life who had not betrayed her? Her father had little use for her, and had used her as a servant to raise her sisters. The king had used her, threatening her sisters, taking Angus Gordon away from her in order that she do his bidding. *And Angus!* Her beloved Black Angus! His was the greatest betrayal of all. Why had he not sought after her when he returned from York? Why indeed! He had obviously been too busy dancing attendance upon Elizabeth Williams, toadying to the king and queen. No man shall ever use me again, she thought to herself. *No man!* Then she arose from her knees, leaving the priest.

In the hall that night Fiona looked particularly beautiful. She wore a gold-and-copper surcoat over her orange tawny undergown. When the meal was over, she said, "Nairn, do ye still fancy to keep me as yer wife, or have ye changed yer mind?" She smiled seductively at him, her emerald eyes glittering in the candlelight.

"Ye know I will never let ye go, Fiona mine," he said seriously.

"Then we had best let Father Ninian bless our union while he is here. Our handfast time will be up in another few weeks, but the priest will long be gone by then. If ye would wed me in God's eyes, then let us do it and be done with it so we may get on with our lives."

"Ye have but to name the day!" Nairn said enthusiastically.

"On the morrow, love, before the mass, with all the castle folk as our witnesses," Fiona told him boldly.

"Agreed!" he cried, his eyes overflowing with his happiness. "Then ye do love me, Fiona mine! I knew ye would one day."

"I must love ye," she lied to him, "or I should not wed ye properly within the sanctity of the church. Now, Nairn, I would be alone tonight. Take a bath before the ceremony, and don't come drunk to yer marriage, my lord. 'Twould not please me at all." She then stood up and departed the hall.

To her surprise Moire Rose came to her chambers shortly afterward. "Why are ye doing this?" she asked Fiona in a quiet voice.

"Because it is time," Fiona said. "Ye know that sooner than later he'll get another bairn on me, and without a marriage the poor wee mite will be bastard-born. Did ye like bearing a bastard?"

The older woman looked directly at Fiona, her blue eyes serious. "Be warned, Fiona Hay, that if ye should ever shame him—"

"Madam, I will not shame him, nor bring shame upon Nairn. On that ye have my word. The word of the Hay of the Ben."

Moire Rose nodded. "I believe ye," she said, and left.

"Why?" Nelly asked her, near to weeping.

Fiona told her of the priest's words and then said, "Do ye want to go home to Brae, Nelly? It makes no difference now if he knows where I am. I will send ye back if ye truly desire it."

Nelly shook her head. "No, my lady. My place is with ye."

The two women embraced, and Fiona instructed her serving woman, "Go and fetch the priest to me. If my lord or his mother asks why, say I wish to speak to him about the wedding."

When Nelly returned with Father Ninian, they crowded into the servant's little chamber, where they might speak in privacy. Nelly remained outside the door to guard them.

The priest wasted no time demanding an explanation. "Why have ye instigated this marriage, lady? Is it wise?"

"Today," Fiona said, "part of the king's message, a part that seemed innocent to ye but that ye did not understand, although the words were straightforward enough, told me something I did not want to hear. The queen's cousin has been wed to the man I love. The true father of my bairn. There is no going back now for me, good Father. I must therefore do what is best for me and for my son. Colin MacDonald loves me, and he adores his son, Alastair.

"The king has used me like a common whore with not a thought for my heart. He claims that my sacrifice is for Scotland. Well, I will sacrifice no more. Why should I? If I canna wed the man I love, then I will wed the man who loves me, and who loves *our* son. Tell James Stewart that I will spy no more for him. He thinks to make the clans quail or crawl to him by not calling a gathering at Inverness. Well, some like the Campbells may do his bidding, but the Lord of the Isles will not give the Stewart king loyalty until he is ready to do so—and the majority of the clans will wait for the MacDonalds before going on their knees before James Stewart.

"Ye may tell the king that he can frighten me no longer with threats against my kin. I no longer care. Am I not entitled to some happiness, too? Besides, what excuse could he possibly use now for persecuting innocent young women and two little girls? I have done his bidding, and I will tell the world I have done it if he presses me further. Does he think Brae will remain loyal knowing what he has done to us? Knowing that *his* son bears the name MacDonald and not Gordon? I will be used no more by this Stewart king. Tell him I do not break my oath of fealty to him, but that I am a woman and can bear no more."

The priest could hear the raw pain in Fiona's voice. There was nothing he could say that would comfort her. Her assessment of the situation was correct. She had been used. He could not blame her for washing her hands of the situation and marrying Nairn. She was a softhearted female. The king should have realized that she could take only so much. The poor lass had reached her limit, and so he would say when he saw the

king in Perth this winter. Fiona was no threat to James
Stewart. She was simply a woman.

"I believe ye have chosen the right road, my daughter," he told her. "Marriage or the church is the best route
for a woman to take. Ye have a fine son and the hope of
other children. This difficulty between the king and the
MacDonalds will eventually sort itself out. As the king
gains firmer control of the rest of Scotland, Alexander
MacDonald and his ilk will seem less important and will
rub less against James Stewart's pride. Time is a great
healer of all wounds."

"Is it, good Father?" Fiona's voice cracked slightly.
"I pray God and his Blessed Mother that ye are right."

Then, giving her his blessing, Father Ninian left her.

"I have not gathered enough of yer special seeds,
my lady," Nelly fretted. "The summer has been wet, and
the flowers are slow to bloom, and many of the flower
heads have rotted before going to seed. I have barely
enough for two months' use."

"Don't fret yerself, Nelly," Fiona told the girl. "I
owe Nairn a child, do I not?"

Poor Nelly's eyes threatened to spill over again
with her misery. If the laird of Loch Brae had repudiated her, she could not have felt worse than she did.
Her kindly heart ached for Fiona.

Fiona put her arms about her servant, comforting
her. "Ohh, Nelly, I was a bairn to believe that it would
all work out as I wanted it to despite everything that
has happened. I must try to be more practical from now
on, Nelly. We are hardly in a wretched situation, are
we? Nairn loves me even if I don't love him. I will be a
good wife to him, Nelly, for he is good to me. I owe him
that much, do I not? He has been hoodwinked by the
Stewart king every bit as much as I have been. I will not
tell him, though. Let him believe that he has won me

over." She laughed ruefully, but then, looking at her companion, she said, "Ye, too, have a reason for remaining, do ye not, my little Nelly? Roderick Dhu would court ye in earnest, I believe."

Nelly's tears had quickly passed with her mistress's comforting words. She actually blushed at the mention of Roderick Dhu.

"Aye," she admitted. "The skinny creature seems to have honorable intentions toward me now, my lady. Do ye disapprove?"

"Nay," said Fiona. "If ye love him, then ye will not want to go back to Brae. I am selfish and want ye happy, too."

"I have always been happy to be in yer service, my lady," Nelly replied sweetly. "Now," she said briskly, "what will ye wear on the morrow for yer wedding? I will need to see the gown is fresh."

Fiona thought a moment, then said, "I will wear the dark green velvet houppelande with my husband's plaid across the front and my own clan badge holding it. I would do Colin MacDonald honor."

In the morning while Fiona was dressing, Moire Rose came again to Fiona's chamber.

"I have seen to a wee feast this morning," she said.

Fiona thanked her. "Today we all begin anew with each other. There is dissension in the world all about us, but here at Nairns Craig, ye and I will make a place of peace for our family, for when my sons must go to war, they will understand how truly valuable peace is, and fight all the more for it."

"I was verra bitter when my Donald left me," Moire Rose told Fiona frankly. "I knew he was wed to another. I knew he would not leave her, and yet I foolishly thought I might hold him with his son. But he had other sons." She sighed deeply. "I was a verra foolish lassie. I would not listen to my father, and I rejected my own son until finally my Donald took the boy from me, allowing him to visit only my father each summer. Seeing my own bairn return from Islay so happy and thriving only compounded my bitterness. And after my father died, I continued my intemperate behavior."

"But since Alastair was born ye have changed, Moire Rose," Fiona said.

"Aye, yer coming at first angered me, and then my wee grandson came into this world. I looked at him, Fiona, and realized then that I could not waste any more time in anger. I let myself lose my only child even before he was born. I have no one to blame but myself. Donald MacDonald was honest with me. I accept yer proposal that we all begin anew today. Ye have brought happiness into this house, although I realize it has not been easy for ye. Ye loved another once, I believe, but I will ask ye no questions. I already have yer word that ye will not bring shame to my son, and I believe ye."

To Fiona's surprise her mother-in-law enfolded her in a bony embrace. "Thank ye, my child, for what ye have done for all of us and for the gift of love ye have brought us all."

Fiona gently hugged Moire Rose back, kissing her on the cheek before breaking off the embrace. "I had best finish dressing," she said softly.

The older woman nodded. "Aye. They're already waiting on ye in the hall. Nairn is so nervous, ye'd think this was the first time he was marrying ye." She chuckled. "I offered him a wee dram of wine, but he refused me, saying that ye had bid him come sober to his marriage."

Fiona could not help but smile at the woman's

words. "I also bid him bathe himself," she said mischievously.

"He smells like a bouquet of flowers," Moire Rose assured her. Then with a nod she left.

Fiona pulled on her clean white stockings and a pair of soft leather ankle boots. Nelly tipped a soft cotton chemise over her mistress, followed by the forest-green velvet houppelande. Next the servant brushed her mistress's long black hair, fitting it into the silver caul. She affixed over it a silver brocade and green velvet fillet with a single green stone in its center that rested in the middle of Fiona's forehead. Lastly, Nelly carefully draped the length of plaid called Hunting MacDonald, which Colin MacDonald favored. It was a leaf green with both narrow and wide white stripes, and here and there within the pattern were woven blocks of a darker green. At her mistress's shoulder Nelly pinned the silver brooch of the Hay chieftain. The badge was circular with a falcon rising out of a crest coronet. Engraved upon the badge was the clan motto: Serva Lugum, Keep the Yoke. Fiona smiled. She had, it seemed, been yoked since birth. There was little chance she would ever be unyoked.

She descended into the hall with Nelly by her side, Nairn's piper leading them as he played. To her surprise the sun was shining through the high windows. It was a good portent, she thought. There were branches of colored leaves decorating the room, and all the castle folk were assembled. She heard Alastair whimper from the arms of the girl chosen to watch over him. Upon the high board were Father Ninian's traveling crucifix and a pair of silver candlesticks, and in them burned good beeswax tapers. The piper ceased.

"Are ye ready to proceed, my daughter?" the priest asked her.

Fiona nodded, reached out to take Colin's hand, and drew him before Father Ninian. The priest began, but Fiona heard little of what he said. The man by her side should have been Angus Gordon, but Angus Gordon had so easily given her up for dead, or lost, and taken a milk-and-water English wife to please his king. *Damn him for it! No,* she told herself fiercely, she had to put her anger behind her. She could not, would not, start this real marriage to Nairn with a heart filled with bitterness. Colin was a good man, and he loved her. He deserved a wife who was faithful not only in body but also in mind.

Farewell, my Black Angus. She would think of him no more.

They were wed. Nairn kissed her heartily, then turned about and declared a holiday for the castle folk and all his clansmen.

"What will ye have of me, Fiona mine? For this day I will give ye anything it is in my power to give ye. I love ye that much," he declared loudly before everyone in the entire hall. "Ye have but to name yer gift, and it is yers!"

"Make peace with yer mam," Fiona said quietly, but everyone heard her and looked in surprise from the bride to Moire Rose. Fiona beckoned her mother-in-law to them. "I will have peace in my house, Colin MacDonald. Yer mam and I have made our peace, but we will have no true peace until ye make it, too. That is the gift I would have of ye, my lord and husband."

Mother and son looked at each other, neither certain of what to say, but then Moire Rose said softly, "Fiona had said this would be a new beginning for us all, Nairn." Tears filled her blue eyes. "Ye look so much like *him,* my son."

"Now there is something we already have in common, madam," Nairn told her gently. "We both loved Donald MacDonald." He enfolded her in his big embrace while those in the hall erupted into cheers.

"Ye have performed a miracle, my lady," the priest told Fiona sincerely. "God will bless ye for it. It was surely fated that ye come to Nairns Craig."

"Be certain ye tell the king that when ye see him," Fiona whispered. Hearing her son howling, she started to leave the high board to go and feed him. "I will be back after I have let yer son drink his fill," she told her bridegroom, who, she had to admit, looked very handsome in his kilt and white shirt.

He grinned, calling after her, "He will need a playmate shortly, sweeting. We must think on it."

Fiona turned, saying, "A puppy, perhaps, Colly?" Then, laughing, she hurried to fetch the child.

"Ye are a fortunate young man, Colin MacDonald," the priest said. "Many cases of handfast, or bride-stealing, don't end as happily as yers has. Remember the tragedy of yer wife's parents. Don't forget to thank our good Lord when ye pray this night. I shall say compline before ye seek yer beds. And tomorrow after the mass I shall be on my way. I will not return until the spring."

"Are ye certain," Nairn asked Father Ninian, "that ye will not stay with us, good Father? Ye would be more than welcome."

"Nay, my son," the priest replied. "I will renew myself at Glenkirk Abbey this winter, immersing myself once more in the religious life of my house. But come the first wind from the south, the sight of the snow melting on the bens, a violet beneath my foot, and I shall be on my way once more to bring what Christian comfort I can to these highlands. Perhaps when I am older I will settle in one place, but not now, my lord, although I thank ye for the offer."

The remainder of the day was spent in feasting and dancing. When the afternoon came, they went outside into the castle's big grassy courtyard, where the men stripped their shirts off and hurled javelins and heavy round stone balls to see who could gain the greatest distance. Kegs of ale were set up, and shortly the men's aim was less than accurate. The piper began to play, following them back into the hall as the day waned. Fiona once again danced the bridal dance with her husband, after which the men began to dance, and Roderick Dhu was suddenly prancing boldly before Nelly, holding out his hand to her.

For a long moment Nelly hesitated, but finally she accepted his invitation, and they danced together. Everyone in the hall knew what it meant. In his invitation to the dance Roderick Dhu had made plain his intentions to court Nelly formally. Until she either accepted him or rejected him, no other man would seriously seek the girl's company. The look upon Nelly's face made clear there was no happier lass in the hall that night.

"Do ye approve?" Nairn asked Fiona.

Fiona nodded. " 'Tis her choice. I offered to return her to Brae, but she insisted upon staying with me, and not alone for yon laddie. She is my servant, but she is also my friend, Colly. Nelly will have her own will in this matter."

"As ye didn't," he said softly.

"Oh, in the end I have gotten my own way, Colin MacDonald. I would not have wed ye in the church if I didn't want to. Now, let me go, for the bairn needs his nourishment before he is put to bed."

"We must find a wet nurse for the laddie."

"Not yet."

"Soon," he said through gritted teeth. "My son encroaches upon our time together. I find I am growing jealous."

"In a few months we will choose a healthy lass to nurture our laddie. By then I will undoubtedly be with bairn again, my lord, if ye can but do yer duty by me." With a mischievous wink she rushed off.

He watched her go to their son, her sudden change in attitude making him intensely curious. Turning to the priest, he said, "Since yer arrival she has turned about. What did ye say to her, Father?"

The priest looked up reluctantly, for his plate was filled with the sort of fine foods he would not see once he had reentered his abbey for the winter, contemplating how he should answer.

"From the beginning I have counseled marriage within the precincts of the holy church, my lord. Yer wife was angered at ye when we first met almost a year ago, for she was newly stolen. But in that time the bairn has come and suckled at her breast. She is content at last. She has made her peace with herself. Do not question yer good fortune. She is a fine woman and has brought calm to yer house."

"I suppose ye are right, Father," Nairn replied, thinking that the priestly counsel was good. Fiona's heart seemed to be turning toward him, as he had wanted all along. Yet, suddenly, in the midst of his happiness, a tiny worm of doubt began to writhe within him.

"In yer regular travels ye pass near Brae," he said. "What news of the laird? Did he seek after Fiona?"

"Aye, he did," Father Ninian replied, "but you covered your tracks well, my lord, and he found no trace of her."

"So he simply gave up? I'd not have thought it of him."

"The king gave him a wife," the priest said, remembering what Fiona had told him—and wishing to turn Nairn's thoughts. "The laird's wife is with child."

"Is she? Then may she have a son as fine as mine."

Colin remained in the hall after it emptied, watching his wife go about her evening duties. The trestles had been cleared and put back against the walls. She went from candle to lamp, snuffing them out. She banked the fires in the fireplaces neatly, then called to him. Colin rose and accompanied his wife up the stairs to their bedchamber.

"I have sent Nelly to bed," she said softly as he barred the door behind them. "We can help each other to undress, can we not?" She sat down and, holding out her foot, said, "Unboot me, my lord."

He drew the boots off and followed with her knitted stockings. He sat down so that she might do the same for him.

"Stand up," he said.

Fiona obeyed the command, facing him and unlacing his shirt as he unlaced her gown. Her hands smoothed across and up his chest, pushing the garment off his shoulders. He pulled the houppelande from her, letting it puddle about her ankles. Swiftly Fiona stripped her chemise off, then unbuckled the wide leather belt he wore. His kilt fell to the ground. His fingers were clumsy as they undid her fillet, then her caul, which he put aside upon a table.

"Tell me, Nairn," she said in a low, seductive voice, "have ye ever made love to a woman slowly?" She drew the word out so that it sounded like *slooowly*.

"Aye," he told her, fascinated by this new woman she had suddenly become.

"Ye have not made love to me slowly," she told him. "It has always been a battle between us. Ye were always quick."

"I feared if I didn't take what I could of ye quickly," he said honestly, "I would not get anything of ye, Fiona mine."

She slid her arms up about his neck, pressing her nakedness into his nakedness. "I told yer mam that we would all make a new beginning, Nairn." She pulled his head down so that their lips were almost touching. "Wouldn't ye like to have a new beginning with me?" The tip of her tongue ran across his mouth as she reached around him and squeezed his buttock.

"Jesu, yer brazen!" He groaned, feeling the heat of her thighs pushing against him. "I want ye, Fiona mine!"

"Slowly, Nairn, go slowly with me." Her lips brushed teasingly against his lips. "I would spend the night in pure pleasure within yer strong arms. 'Tis our wedding night."

She was driving him wild with her seductive bedevilment. He drew a long, deep breath to clear his head, to regain control of this situation. Her faint smile mocked him. "I didn't know ye could be such a witch," he finally said with a chuckle. "Ye have been most restrained until now, sweeting. If ye loose the beast in me, ye must pay the consequences. Are ye prepared to do so, Fiona mine?"

She laughed low. It was a smoky sound. "I will tame the beast in ye, Colin MacDonald," she told him boldly. "But can ye truly tame the beast in me is more to the point." Arms about his neck, she vaulted herself lightly, wrapping her slender, strong legs about his waist.

He met the challenge, his mouth fusing against hers with a fierce passion. Tongues intertwined sensuously. Her flesh against his was afire. Fiona threw her head back, and, bending, he plunged his tongue between her breasts, drawing it slowly upward between the twin hillocks, across the flat of her chest, sliding over the pulsing flesh of her straining throat to the tip of her chin. She vibrated beneath his touch, and he mocked her, "Yer already hot to be sheathed, sweeting, but we shall go slowly, as ye have requested of me." Then, walking across the floor with her, he set her upon the edge of the bed, drawing her legs up and over his broad shoulders, spreading her to his view.

Fiona was shocked, but she did not protest. She would meet his every desire openly and honestly. Still, she was hardly prepared when his fiery head disappeared between her thighs. She felt just the very tip of his tongue touch her little sugar button and begin to flick voluptuously back and forth over it. So acutely foreign yet thrilling was the sensation, that for a moment she lost her breath. To her surprise she felt a small flame of excitement beginning to lick at her awareness. She gasped, and the feeling spread until she was engulfed, almost suffocating with the pleasure he was giving her.

"Colin! Oh, holy Mother, yer killing me!" She tried to writhe away from him, for it was becoming too much to bear, but his big hands gripped her hips in an iron grasp, holding her firmly.

"Give yerself to me, Fiona mine." He groaned, then his mouth and tongue were working upon her sentient flesh again.

She had never really allowed herself to trust so

completely. She had never truly given up total control of herself. But now he tempted her, dared her, enticed her to entrust herself to him completely, as she had never before trusted anyone, even Angus Gordon. For a moment her body stiffened with guilt, but then she relaxed once again. Colin MacDonald was her husband. Fiona inhaled, and when she exhaled she gave herself over totally to this passionate man. Almost instantly she was rewarded as wave after wave of delight poured over her until she was mindless with pure, unadulterated enjoyment.

Raising his head, Colin saw upon her lovely face the satisfaction that he had given her. His manhood was hard as iron and quite ready to be equally satisfied. Drawing her up upon their bed, he lay next to her, pulling her into his arms and kissing her deeply, his tongue pushing into her mouth so that she might taste herself on it. Fiona shuddered, and her eyes fluttered open. He moved to fondle her breasts. The twin orbs were firm, the nipples thrusting forth defiantly. His mouth closed over one of those nipples, drawing hard upon it, his mouth filling with her milk, which he swallowed eagerly.

"Colly!" Her tone was half shocked.

Slowly he lifted up his head, saying, "Why should our son have one of the best parts of ye, and I be denied, Fiona mine? By morning yer breasts will be full enough again for the bairn." He moved to her other breast.

Her fingers entwined themselves within his red-gold hair. His actions somehow made them more a part of each other than they had ever been. She caressed the nape of his neck.

Once again he raised his head, his blue eyes meeting her green ones. "I canna go slowly any longer, sweeting," he said in a thick voice. Then he covered her body with his, entering her with great restraint.

"Ah, my lord, I want ye deep within me, Colly. Fill me full with yer loving!"

Pushing her legs up and back, he plunged further within her than she could ever remember taking a man inside her. Finding a rhythm, he moved upon her until both of them were almost demented with their passion, and at its pinnacle both cried aloud with release.

Afterward he cradled her within the circle of his arms, stroking her dark hair, crooning aimlessly to her. "Never have I known such a lass as ye, Fiona MacDonald," he said admiringly.

She chuckled weakly, exhausted by their bout of eros. "In the battle of love," she told him, "I think we are more than well matched, my lord husband. I have never been loved before as ye loved me tonight." She sighed happily and nestled against his chest.

Colin smiled in the darkness of the room. He had, he firmly believed, finally eradicated the ghost of Black Angus Gordon. "I love ye, sweeting."

"I know."

He waited for the words he so longed to hear from her. Would she finally say them tonight? Or did he have to wait?

Fiona debated with herself. Did she love him? She didn't know. He was certainly a magnificent lover, but he was also a romantic at heart. He needed to hear her declare herself. "I feel differently about ye than I have in the past," she said. "I think I could love ye, Colin MacDonald. Mayhap I already do, but when I finally have the courage to speak those words, my lord, ye will have no doubt that I mean them with all my heart and with all my soul."

"Then I will wait, sweeting, for I know ye to be an

honest woman who would not deceive me." He kissed the top of her head.

For the briefest moment Fiona was flooded with guilt, but she overcame it. She had done nothing to harm the MacDonalds. She had told Father Ninian before she spoke her church vows that she was through spying for James Stewart. In the morning she would return to the priest the king's coin. She was the lady of Nairn now, and would have no further use for it.

Chapter 13

James Stewart watched the rain drizzling down the window. Outside in the courtyard the day was gray and windy. It was only the beginning of December, but winter was already setting in around them. He watched the horseman who had but recently entered the courtyard dismount, handing the animal over to a stableboy. There was something familiar in the rider's stature, and then the king smiled. He shouted for his page, and when the boy came said, "A priest, one Father Ninian, has just arrived. He is but newly dismounted and coming through the north door from the courtyard. Fetch him to me, and then bring mulled wine."

The page bowed and ran off quickly.

The king rubbed his hands together and hummed a little tune. He had known that Ninian would come soon, but with Ninian one never could be quite certain of exactly when he would arrive. Ninian Stewart, humble priest, only son of Euphemia Ross's elder son, David, the Duke and Earl of Strathearn. He was illegitimate and was born five months after his father's death. His mother had lived only six years following the lad's birth. At her death James Stewart's father, King Robert III, had placed the boy in the abbey at Scone to protect him. He would become a priest, thus removing him from the Stewart family's internecine warfare over who would rule Scotland. Few, if any, of James Stewart's relations would remember David Stewart's bastard. Perhaps Atholl, but he would never connect him with Father Ninian, having seen his brother's son perhaps a few times in his infancy and childhood, but not since.

The door opened. Father Ninian Stewart was ushered into the room. The two men embraced, and then James Stewart said, "Go and fetch the mulled wine, Andrew. The good father will be well chilled from his ride on this dank day."

The youngster hurried from the room to do his master's bidding.

"Andrew who?" the priest inquired, seating himself by the fire.

"Leslie," the king replied.

"What happened to the Douglas page?"

"The Douglases are not in favor right now, Ninian," the king told his cousin. "I sent the lad home. I have a daughter, Margaret," he added, "and another bairn coming, hopefully a prince."

"I will pray for the queen's continued good health."

The two men sat speaking on small matters until after the Leslie page had returned with their hot mulled wine and departed once more, closing the door behind him. The king sipped his wine.

"Ye will want news of the north, of course," Ninian Stewart said quietly.

"The Lord of the Isles?"

"He is determined to hold off giving you his pledge of fealty until he absolutely must."

"The Campbells have given me their loyalty," the king said.

"They are generally at odds with the MacDonalds, as you know, and don't have much influence among the clans, cousin."

"So until the MacDonalds give me their faith, I canna expect the other highlands clans to do so. Why is Alexander MacDonald so stubborn?"

"Because the MacDonalds have been kings in the highlands since time immemorial. It is difficult for them to give their authority over to a Stewart king, south of the Tay." Why didn't James understand, Ninian wondered. They had been over this ground a hundred times before. The king called the Lord of the Isles stubborn, but James was just as stubborn. Worse, he refused to accept that the Lord of the Isles thought of himself as the king's equal, possibly his superior. "Call a gathering of the clans next summer in Inverness," the priest advised. "They all waited for it this summer, cousin, and were disappointed that ye did not ask them to come. The longer ye wait, the more ye offend the Lord of the Isles and his allies. I knew ye would be a strong king, but there is no shame in showing a wee bit of understanding."

"I didn't call them to Inverness this summer because I wished to test the mettle of the clans," the king said. "And what was the result, cousin? The Campbells and their allies came on their knees to me. I will divide and conquer these overproud men of the north! Another summer or two, and they will certainly be frightened enough to come to me and pledge their fealty."

"Ye must understand that the Lord of the Isles does not believe he needs ye, and he is correct. He knows that ye need him far more if ye are to gather the clans in the north to yer banner. Invite the clans to Inverness, and let them all make their peace with ye with honor."

"In time," James Stewart said, "but not yet."

"I have brought something for ye." Holding out his hand, Ninian displayed the king's coin in his upturned palm.

The king took the coin, recognizing it, and asked, "Where did ye get this? It is surely not yers, cousin."

"Fiona Hay returns it to ye," the priest told the king. *"Why?"*

"Because she will no longer spy for ye, cousin," was the simple reply. "Ye have driven her too far."

"Did she fall in love with Nairn?" the king asked, irritated.

"She is fond of him, but love him? Nay, I do not think so. However, she has wed him. She says she will not spy on him and his kin for ye. 'Tis dishonorable."

"If she does not love him, why on earth did she wed him, Ninian?" the king demanded of the priest. "When I sent her north, I truly believed her passion for Angus Gordon would keep her from any foolish involvement with Colin MacDonald. What happened, or is she merely fickle?"

"Fiona was *enceinte* with Angus Gordon's child when ye sent her into the highlands, cousin. She was not certain of her condition, and so she was afraid to refuse ye lest she later discover she was not with child and ye accuse her of perfidy."

"Jesu!" the king whispered. "Ninian, I didn't know! I swear it by the Blessed Mother and my own sweet Joan. I didn't know!"

"MacDonald handfasted her in his brother's hall on Islay. He truly believes the son she bore to be his own. The child is named Alastair James for his brother and for ye. When I visited Nairns Craig in early autumn of this year and passed along yer latest message to Fiona, she was devastated to learn that the queen's cousin had wed her former lover.

"As the term of the handfast was coming to an end, Fiona asked me to marry her to Colin MacDonald before I returned south for the winter. She believed that there was nothing else for her to do. Now that she is Nairn's true wife, she will not spy for ye. Ye canna blame her, and besides, the information she passed along was not of such great a value that ye will miss her. Let her go, James Stewart."

"Ye have grown fond of her, have ye not?"

Ninian nodded. "I have. She is a fine woman who has faced facts and made the most of her life that she could. She protected her bairn as best she might, and now, married to Nairn, she will give him her complete loyalty. She told me to tell ye her fealty to ye stands. She is yet yer liege woman, but she will not spy for ye."

" 'Tis a strange sort of loyalty she offers me," the king grumbled.

"Give over, James Stewart, and let the lass go. She can bear no more than she has. 'Twas a cruel thing ye did, cousin, when ye forced Fiona Hay into yer service. And ye have robbed Angus Gordon of his son and heir, although I suppose Mistress Elizabeth will give him a houseful of bairns."

The king looked decidedly uncomfortable, but then, knowing whatever he told the priest was confidential, he said, "Elizabeth is not wed to Angus Gordon. She wed Ian Ogilvy. Angus is yet in England with our uncle Atholl negotiating better terms for my maintenance payments."

"Then why," the priest said, an angry edge to his voice, "did ye send word to Fiona Hay that Mistress Elizabeth Williams had wed with a husband of her guardians' choice? It was yer message delivered by me that precipitated her decision to marry The MacDonald of Nairn."

"I only meant for it to keep her in the north with Nairn," the king said. "I knew she would assume I meant the bridegroom was Angus. I thought it would

further anger her and make her more determined to remain rather than come sneaking back to her tower on
the ben. I did not know there was a child, or that she
would wed Nairn. I thought her pride would keep her
where I wanted her rather than returning in shame."

"Cousin," the priest said disapprovingly, "ye have
meddled in lives with an abandon that belongs only to
God, and stolen Angus Gordon's son from him. I do
not know what will happen to the laird of Loch Brae,
but I thank God that Fiona Hay will be safe in Colin
MacDonald's love, for, cousin, love her he does. Have
ye confessed all this mischief to yer confessor?"

" 'Tis state business," the king said by way of explanation. "Ye have heard it. These decisions I made for
the good of Scotland, ye choose to believe are my sins.
Give me a penance, Ninian, and I will perform it."

The priest shook his head in the negative. "Nay,
cousin, I will not shrive ye, for ye are not sorry at all for
what ye have done. Ye know that a penitent must be
penitent." He smiled slightly to take the edge from his
decision, for he did not want to offend his cousin.

The king shrugged. "I canna be sorry for doing
what I believe is best for Scotland. I do not know what
else to do but what I have done. Ye will, I hope, continue to be of service to me."

"Aye," the priest said, "but not just for ye. For all
the clansmen and clanswomen who have become my
friends over the years I have traveled the north bringing
God and His sacraments to those good peoples. They
are not yer enemies, cousin. They are a remnant of our
past as a proud and free people. In time they will come
to ye if ye will but treat them with respect and kindness.
Do not listen to the counsel of greedy and ambitious
men, cousin."

"I canna show weakness, Ninian."

"To show respect for another, cousin, is not weakness," was the calm reply. The priest drank down the last of his mulled wine, then stood. "Unless ye need me further, I would pay my respects to the abbot and bathe before vespers."

"Go," James Stewart said, "but come and see me often until ye decide to return to the north."

The priest bowed respectfully, then departed.

The king sat back down, swirling the remaining wine and spices in his cup around and around. He was irritated at himself for having misread Fiona Hay. Certainly the information she had sent him had been valuable to a point, but hardly earth-shattering. He had placed her with Nairn because one day, he instinctively knew, she would have something of real value to pass on to him. But now she would not, and all because he had been too heavy-handed in his handling of her. He must accept his loss. Fiona Hay was as gone from his life as she was from Angus Gordon's life.

And here James Stewart felt a twinge of guilt, for he was basically a decent man. Pray God Angus never learn of his part in separating the lovers. Pray God and His Blessed Mother that Angus never learn that he had a son who would grow up known as Alastair MacDonald. The king envied his friend that unknown son, for he wanted a son, too. The queen had already birthed a daughter, whom they had named Margaret. She was a lovely, fat baby with her mother's auburn hair. James Stewart had great plans for his daughter. He dreamed of a marriage that would one day make his daughter queen of France. In the interim the king prayed for a son.

The following spring, the queen bore a second daughter, who was called Isabella. The year after,

Queen Joan finally gave Scotland its long-awaited heir, a small prince who was called Alexander, but the baby was weak. It was feared he would not reach manhood, and so it was necessary that the queen continue in her efforts to give Scotland more princes.

The little prince had been born at year's end. Even in the snowy highlands the word had spread that the king at last had a son, and the good-natured highlanders celebrated the child's birth.

At Nairns Craig, Fiona sat at her loom in her hall watching her children playing upon the floor. Alastair would be three in late spring. Mary was sixteen months old, and a new baby would be born before the snows were off the bens in earliest spring. Mary was her father's image, and had been named for both her grandmothers, whose Celtic names were variations on the more Anglicized version.

"Times are changing," Fiona had said after her daughter was born. "Eventually we will make our peace with the king. Our daughter may even go to court to serve the queen. Better her name be understood by all, particularly those who don't speak our Gaelic language."

Moire Rose agreed with her daughter-in-law.

The MacDonald of Nairn laughed. "I cannot win between the two of ye. Is it natural that a wife and a mother-in-law be such good friends?" he teased them.

"If they live in the same house, it certainly is!" Fiona said, and Moire Rose laughed her odd harsh laugh.

The king had not called a gathering of the clans in either 1426 or 1427. The highlands remained relatively calm, but the Lord of the Isles and the majority of the clan chieftains had not yet sworn their fealty to James

Stewart. He finally had no choice but to call a gathering of the clans in Inverness or admit to not being in full control of his entire land. The assemblage was set for mid-July. The tower of Inverness Castle was repaired for James Stewart's arrival that summer.

The Lord of the Isles sent out messengers to all the clans ordering them to Inverness in answer to James Stewart's command. In the four years the king had been back in Scotland he had left the highlands to themselves, and The MacDonald had seen that the peace was kept. The Lord of the Isles had almost decided to give this king his fealty. Before he made his final decision, however, he wanted to gain a full measure of the man.

Fiona knew that her brother-in-law would stop at Nairns Craig before reaching Inverness. His messenger said he would be traveling with his mother, the old Countess of Ross, who would also swear her fealty to the king if her son did. The lord's wife, a shy woman, preferred to remain on Islay. As Fiona had not been back to Islay since her initial visit, she had yet to meet either of these women. The old countess was said to be by far the more interesting.

They arrived at Nairns Craig in the company of Father Ninian. Fiona was delighted to see the priest, for she had birthed her second daughter three months prior. The infant, who was to be called Johanna, in honor of the queen, stood in need of baptism. Euphemia MacDonald, Countess of Ross, offered to be the baby's godmother, a great honor for the MacDonalds of Nairn. And afterward when Alastair and Mary had also been admired, and Johanna fed, the family gathered in the hall for the evening meal.

Father Ninian brought news. The infant prince, Alexander Stewart, had not lived through the winter, but the queen was with child again, and it was hoped she would provide the needed heir. "Ye are fortunate in yer bairns, Colin MacDonald," he said. "Yer son, praise God, is a healthy laddie, and yer daughters likewise."

"I'd like another lad," Nairn said, looking to Fiona.

"Ye'll wait for the next one, Colly," she told him boldly. "I'm worn out bearing yer bairns so quickly. If we're to have another son, then ye must let me rest a bit. When Johanna is weaned, we will discuss it again, my lord."

The Countess of Ross, a big handsome woman, chuckled. "The lassie is right, Nairn. If ye love her, ye'll not kill her with yer bairns." She turned to Fiona. "Don't let him bully ye, lassie!"

Nairn burst out laughing. "Bully her? It is not possible for me to bully Fiona. Rather, she bullies me."

"She but keeps him in line a wee bit," Moire Rose said in defense of her daughter-in-law. "Nairns Craig is a happier place because of Fiona Hay. I bless the day she came here."

"My mother-in-law attributes to me more than I am deserving of, I think," Fiona said, embarrassed, signaling her servants with a raised eyebrow to begin bringing the meal.

"Will ye come to Inverness then, sister?" the lord asked her.

"Indeed. I would not miss it for the world. 'Twill be a grand day when ye and James Stewart make yer peace together."

"I have not yet decided," Alexander MacDonald said, toying with his cup.

"Then why do ye go, and why did ye call the clans to obey the king's summons?" Fiona asked cleverly.

"I merely wish to see the man, and then I will decide." The lord speared a haunch of venison off a platter held out to him by an attentive servant.

Fiona laughed. "Ye lie, Alexander MacDonald. 'Tis yer pride that will not let ye admit that this king is different."

"We shall go and see, my bonnie," the Lord of the Isles replied, but his eyes were twinkling at her boldness. From the moment he had first met Fiona Hay he had loved her for her courage. Of all his sisters-in-law, and he had several, she was his favorite.

They set out from Nairns Craig on a bright summer morning. Once they reached the main road to Inverness, which ran through the town of Nairn and past Cawdor, the road was crowded with the clansmen headed for the gathering. Fiona rode her gelding while the Countess of Ross and Moire Rose shared a comfortable padded cart with Nelly and the children. The countryside about them was beautiful, the blue hills reflected in the blue waters of the lochs. Outside of Inverness the Lord of the Isles left them to join his own troupe of four thousand men, his ranks swollen by those of his sons: Ian, his heir; Celestine of Lochalsh; and Hugh of Sleate.

The town would not have enough room to house the clansmen, especially with the king and court there. It had been decided that they would camp outside Inverness. Great pavilions for the Lord of the Isles were set up in the center of the encampment, with smaller tents surrounding them.

In order to make a great show both to honor James Stewart and to intimidate him just a little, it had been planned that the clans would all come down from the hills surrounding the city at the same time. James Stewart watched, fascinated, from Inverness tower as the highlanders arrived, arrayed in their many colorful plaids, silken banners flying in the wind, their pipes screeching but one tune, the MacDonald march. They covered the hillsides, their feet thumping as they entered the city, led by Alexander MacDonald, Lord of the Isles, and his powerful family. It was a great display.

"He is not shy about his position here, is he?" the king said to his uncle of Atholl.

"Ye must force him to yer will, my liege," Atholl said grimly. "These MacDonalds always have been difficult. If ye can break them for good and all, so much the better for Scotland."

"We will see," the king said with a small smile. He already knew what he would do, but he had shared it with no one lest his plans be revealed to others.

Having displayed their might parading through Inverness, the clans marched to their encampment outside the town. Their servants and women were already there. The fires were blazing, the meat roasting. The Lord of the Isles had invited his younger brother of Nairn and his family to share his accommodations. They had been assigned a large tent that was divided into three rooms. Charcoal braziers were scattered about the space and would take the chill off the evening air. It had been a long day. The children were fed and put to bed with a nursemaid in one of the two sleeping spaces. Moire Rose would also share their quarters. Johanna was in her cradle in the master suite.

Roderick Dhu and Nelly, still courting, had brought food into the tent's living space from the cook fires. There was salmon, just caught that afternoon in the river Ness, which flowed outside their tents and through the town. It was broiled and served with wild cress that had been gathered from the shallows of a nearby stream along their route. And there was also beef that had been packed in salt and roasted over the fires. Bread, butter, and cheese completed the meal for the two women, who ate together, Nairn having joined his brothers and nephews in the Lord of the Isles' pavilion.

"What will happen tomorrow, Fiona?" her mother-in-law asked. "What is this Stewart king really like? Will he be vengeful?"

Fiona shook her head. "I don't know," she said honestly. "I can tell ye that he is determined to rule *all* of Scotland. He will settle for no less. If he has left us alone these past few years, it was because he was busy in the lowlands, or perhaps he thought to intimidate us, or possibly both. He is a determined man."

Moire Rose nodded. "I would see him, for I have never before seen a king of Scotland."

"I hope ye will not be disappointed," Fiona said. "He is not handsome. The lord and Nairn both tower over him in height but, to be fair, not in stature."

Outside, the encampment began to quiet down. The two women sought their beds. After lifting Johanna from her cradle, Fiona nursed the sleepy child, changed her napkin, and set her back down in her cradle. Then, bathing in a small basin that Nelly had brought her, she asked her servant, "Did ye see the old woman? Is she comfortable?"

"Aye, I helped her to undress and settled her down," Nelly said. "She ought to take a young woman in service, for she needs one. Her poor old Beathag can barely walk now, let alone come on such a trip."

"Beathag has been with Moire Rose her entire life. I think she lives on simply because her mistress needs her," Fiona said. "Go to bed now, Nelly. Tomorrow we'll get to see the king."

"I have seen him," Nelly said sourly. "I do not think much of James Stewart. I think the clans foolish to trust him. Ye trusted him, and look what he did to ye, my lady."

"Hush, Nelly, do not be angry anymore. I am content with Nairn, and we have fine bairns. What more can a woman want but a good man and children?" Fiona patted her servant comfortingly.

"Ye do not really love him, and ye have a right to love," Nelly said.

"I do not love him like Black Angus, 'tis true," Fiona admitted, "but I love him in another way, and he loves me. Oh, Nelly, what if Colin MacDonald had been a brute and not the kind of man he is? Neither of us could have borne it these last three years. I have more than I ever expected to have, and ye do, too. When will ye marry Roderick Dhu? He is desperate for ye to become his wife. Ye've courted for two years."

Nelly sighed. "I love the great gawk," she said, "but what if one day we could go back to Brae, my lady? I could not go with ye if I were wed to my highlander. Better I remain a maid."

"Nelly, we will not be going back to Brae. Black Angus has wed with the queen's cousin. I would not be welcome there. I have my own husband, and ye have a chance of a good husband, too. Take it, lassie!"

Nelly bid her mistress good night and went out into the living space, where her pallet was located by a charcoal brazier.

Fiona lay down upon the bed that had been made up of fir boughs covered with a feather bed. Pulling up the fox coverlet, she fell asleep. She awoke to hear her husband swearing softly as he stumbled about in the darkness. "Colin! Ye'll waken the bairn," she cautioned him.

The sound of her voice drew him to the bedding.

He yanked his boots off and almost fell upon her. "Ah, sweeting, there ye are," he said, his hands fumbling to find her breasts.

"Yer drunk!" she accused him, but she couldn't help laughing softly. She had never seen him this way.

"Just a wee bit drunk," he assured her. "My brothers could not walk to their beds, and had to be carried," he bragged, placing a wet kiss on her lips. "Jesu, yer sweet," he muttered against her soft hair. "Do ye not love me a little bit, Fiona mine?"

"Aye," she told him. "A wee bit, Colin MacDonald." She shifted to find a more comfortable spot, for he was lying half across her.

He nuzzled her neck. "Ye know what I want, sweeting," he said suggestively. His hands were caressing her gently.

"Colin," she chided him, "ye have to go before the king in the morning. If ye don't get some sleep, yer head will ache ye something fearful, I guarantee ye. Ye'll shame us all."

His knee was levering her thighs apart as he attempted to slip between her legs. "I'll sleep all the better and awake happier if ye'll love me, Fiona mine," he wheedled tenderly.

"Yer worse than Alastair when he wants a shortbread," she scolded him, but the hardness probing against the insides of her thighs was exciting. She slid her arms about his neck and drew him down. His breath was pungent with wine. "If ye fall asleep on me before 'tis finished, Colin MacDonald," she warned him ominously, "I swear I'll do to ye what we did to that bull calf born last year."

His laughter was low and smoky. "When, Fiona mine," he asked her, "when did I ever not finish what I began?" Then he thrust into her warm body, pleasuring them until both were near unconscious with a mixture of exhaustion and contentment.

When she awoke in the early hours just before dawn, he was snoring softly by her side, his red head against her round shoulder. Fiona crept from the bed, making a great effort not to awaken him. Slipping out into the living space of the tent, she saw Roderick Dhu and Nelly curled together for warmth and companionship. Gently she shook them both.

"Wake yer master," she told the clansman, "and get him down to the river to bathe. I will not have him before James Stewart smelling of stale wine and passion. Then bring me some hot water so I may make my own ablutions and yer master can scrape the fur from his face."

Roderick Dhu was on his feet, nodding at her. "Aye, my lady."

"Fetch Johanna, and I'll feed her," she instructed Nelly.

The encampment was beginning to stir. Nairn returned from the river, bleary-eyed but clean, to find his wife still nursing their daughter. For a moment he stopped to watch her, enjoying the scene. "She's got a head like mine," he noted proudly.

"So does Mary," Fiona reminded him, and handed the infant to Nelly to return to her cradle. "Put on a clean shirt," she instructed her husband. "I'll fetch ye some mulled wine and bread."

The king had called the gathering for ten in the morning. The Lord of the Isles and the other chieftains of the highland clans were invited into the king's hall along with the Countess of Ross. They came to the monarch's castle, flags flying, pipes playing. The castle was set by the edge of the river Ness, a broad blue waterway that flowed into Beauly Loch, and finally Moray Firth. Only the lord, his mother, the clan chieftains, and their women were invited into the king's hall. The clansmen were asked politely to remain outside as neither the castle nor its hall was big enough to contain them all.

Led by the Lord of the Isles, the men entered the hall. It was a good-sized room of gray stone but had no windows. At its far end was a dais with a gilded wooden canopy, beneath which the king sat upon a throne. He watched through narrowed eyes as the highlanders made their way toward him. Although he had never met the Lord of the Isles, he recognized him immediately, not simply because he preceded all the others but because he looked like a dark-haired version of The MacDonald of Nairn, who strode behind him.

Alexander MacDonald bowed before King James. "My lord," he said, "I welcome ye to the highlands. May yer stay be a pleasant one, and may ye return often here." It was a gracious speech, graciously spoken.

The king stood, looking down on all of them. "Ye are late in coming to render me yer obedience, my lords."

"We but awaited yer call to this gathering, my lord," the Lord of the Isles replied. "Ye were slow in issuing it."

"I am told there are some among ye who would have my life," the king answered. "It was necessary that I decide what course of action I would take in the face of such perfidy." Raising his hand, he signaled his guards. Alexander MacRurie and Ian MacArthur were hauled forth from the ranks of their companions and flung at the foot of the dais. "Ye two spoke on my murder. I canna trust ye. Yer deaths will provide an example to yer companions." Again the king signaled, and before anyone realized what was happening, the two unfortunates were pinioned and swiftly beheaded with well-sharpened swords that had been prepared for just this occasion. The heads hardly rolled, but blood gushed from the severed necks of the two men, spilling across the floor, sending the women assembled within the room shrieking and seeking a place where the blood would not reach.

"Seize them all!" the king's voice thundered as he pointed to the Lord of the Isles and his companions. "Throw them in the dungeon prepared for their arrival!" Stepping over the river of blood, he held out his hand to a now stony-faced Countess of Ross. "Come, madam, for ye are to be my guest for the interim."

Fiona stepped forward and cried, " 'Tis dishonorably done, James Stewart! The lord and the chieftains have come unarmed into yer hall this day to make their peace with ye. Is this how ye treat those who would pledge loyalty and friendship to ye? *Shame! Shame!*"

The king looked across the hall at the woman who had spoken. She was tall for a woman, and he was sure he knew her. She was certainly very fair. A chieftain's wife by the look of her. Then he recognized her. "Once, madam, ye pledged yer loyalty to me," he said meaningfully.

"I have kept my pledge, even to speaking on yer behalf, my liege, in The MacDonald's hall. If he is here today, it is partly because of me. How dare ye break the laws of hospitality to unjustly imprison these men? Ye who love justice above all things. Is this yer justice?"

"She is as brave as she is bonnie," Alexander MacDonald whispered to his brother, Colin MacDonald. "If she weren't yer wife, and if I did not have a wife myself, I would wed her this day!"

"Leave my hall, madam, and don't come back!" the king roared. "Do ye dare to instruct me? A little cattle thief and a whore?"

The Lord of the Isles gripped his brother of Nairn's arm in a tight grasp. "Don't move, Colly, or the bonnie Fiona will be a widow. He only insults her because she has pricked at his conscience."

"Better an honest whore, *my liege,* than a dishonorable king!" Fiona said with devastating impact, then turned and walked from the hall, the chieftains' wives following behind her.

The king opened his mouth with the full intent to order Fiona's arrest, but in the shadow of his throne his cousin, Ninian Stewart, said softly, "She is a woman with three bairns, one new and at her breast. She would make a magnificent martyr, cousin. The highlands would be aflame for years to come. Let her go."

The king's mouth snapped shut audibly.

There was another within the room who, shocked, had also recognized Fiona. Hamish Stewart in a show of family loyalty had accompanied his cousin north. He had known Fiona instantly. Her skirmish with the king had been more than it seemed to the watching court. Slipping from the hall, he hurried after the retreating clanswomen, catching one by the arm, and asking her, "Who was the woman to beard the king, lady?"

" 'Twas The MacDonald of Nairn's wife, sir," the woman replied, pulling away from his grasp to dash after her companions.

Hamish Stewart was amazed. How had Fiona Hay become The MacDonald of Nairn's wife? He would have sworn she would have moved heaven and earth to return home to Brae and Black Angus. Why had she not? Hamish Stewart followed the clanswomen outside, where a roar of disapproval greeted the news that their chieftains were imprisoned on the king's orders. The highlanders moved back from the castle grounds to their encampment just up the river. Hamish Stewart followed along at a discreet distance. He had to find Fiona. He had to know what had happened.

Chapter 14

Hamish Stewart walked slowly through the highland encampment. Already the men were gathering about the fires, not certain what they should do. Hamish knew the Lord of the Isles' pavilion would be in the very center of the camp and he hoped that the tent housing The MacDonald of Nairn would be nearby. Finally, as he sighted the lord's pavilion, he stopped a young clansman, asking him, "Can ye direct me to the tent of The MacDonald of Nairn, lad?"

"What would ye be wanting with him?" the young man asked. "Have ye not heard? Nairn, the lord himself, and all the others who went into the hall to pledge their good faith to James Stewart, were arrested by that king." He spat scornfully. " 'Twas a craven act!"

"I am kin to Nairn's wife," Hamish told the clansman smoothly. "I wish to offer her my aid should she need it."

"Nairn's wife? A courageous woman," said the young man. "My mother says she spoke out verra bravely and to the king's face in the hall, but he insulted her, calling her a cattle thief and a whore. 'Tis what all those south of the Tay think of us, damn them! They are not true Scots, with their Anglicized speech and their English wives."

Hamish nodded in apparent agreement. He had spoken in the Gaelic language of the highlands to the

clansman, and the plaid he wore was the ancient Stewart plaid, a mix of deep blue, black, and green with a
thin red stripe that was similar to several of the northern clans' colors. "Ye know where my kinswoman is?"
he gently prodded the young man.

"Oh, aye," came the reply. "That tent, next to the
lord's great pavilion, is Nairn's."

Thanking him, Hamish Stewart walked over to it,
lifted the flap, and entered the living space. A tall clansman came forward.

"My lord?"

"Is this the tent of The MacDonald of Nairn?"

"Who would know?" demanded the man.

"I am Hamish Stewart, a friend of his wife's."

"I have never seen ye before," Roderick Dhu said
suspiciously.

"Nor have I seen ye. Tell yer mistress that I wish
to see her, that I saw her in the hall this day and bring
news of her sisters, Jeannie and Morag Hay."

" 'Tis all right, Roddy," Fiona said, stepping forth
from behind a curtain that separated the living space
from the bed space. "How are ye, Hamish? 'Tis been a
long time."

What happened?" was all he could say. The promise she had shown as a young girl had been more than
fulfilled. Fiona was an absolutely beautiful woman with
a calm assurance he never would have imagined she
could possess. When she had spoken out so boldly in
the hall this morning, he had actually felt a swell of
pride.

"Sit down, Hamish," she told him. "Ye look as if
ye have seen a ghostie. Roderick Dhu, fetch some wine
for Lord Stewart. Then tell Nelly to keep Moire Rose
amused. I would speak with my old friend privately."

The tall clansman nodded and went off to do her bidding.

Fiona put a finger to her lips. Then she said in deceptively quiet tones, "Tell me of my sisters, my lord. Are they well?"

"Jeannie has finally wed with Jamie-boy, just last year," he said, trying to keep his voice from betraying his excitement. "She is with bairn. 'Twill be born in early winter."

" 'Tis past time, for Jeannie is sixteen now," Fiona noted. "I am happy for her. I know how much she loves her Jamie-boy. Is he good to her, my lord? It would break my heart if 'twere not so."

"She has him wrapped quite securely about her little finger, Fiona Hay," Hamish Stewart said with a small chuckle.

"And my Morag? Have ye found a husband for her?"

"She and my son have taken to each other," he replied. "Like all the Hay women, she seems to hold a fascination for the gentlemen."

"And Janet? She is well? Ah, Roderick Dhu, here ye are. Set the tray down, then leave us."

The clansman obeyed her, albeit reluctantly, but when he had slipped behind the curtain, Nelly said to him excitedly, " 'Tis Hamish Stewart! What is he doing here?"

"Ye know him?" Roderick Dhu was surprised.

"Of course," Nelly said pertly. "He comes from near the place where I was born, Roddy. How did he know we were here, I wonder."

"He said he had seen our lady in the hall today," Roderick Dhu told the girl. "Be he a good man?"

"Aye!" Nelly averred. "Perhaps he can help our lord. He is distantly related to the king. That is why I think he has come to Inverness. He would want to offer a show of support for his kinsman."

"Where is Moire Rose?" Roderick Dhu asked.

"The old woman is asleep. This morning was too much of a shock for her. She was not a good mother, I know, but she loves our master with all her heart. She is verra frightened for him. 'Tis better she lie in her bed and rest until we know what we are to do."

Fiona popped her head through the curtain. "Lord Stewart and I are going to walk by the river," she said. Then she was gone.

"Let her be," Nelly said, putting a restraining hand on her husband-to-be's strong arm. "There is nothing amiss. Lord Stewart is like a brother to my lady. He is the first of her old friends she has seen since she came north with our lord. She will want to explain to him in private how this all came to be."

Fiona led Hamish Stewart from the encampment to a narrow path that ran along the river Ness. Here and there the river had cut away a tiny portion of the land, making little islands that were connected to the main shore by rustic wooden bridges. It was to one of these small islands that Fiona took her companion. Making certain that there was no one else upon the small spot of land, they sat down upon an outcropping facing the shore.

"Now Hamish," she said to him, "I shall tell ye everything, but listen closely, for I must, of necessity, keep my voice low. 'Twould not do for anyone else to hear this tale. Even Nairn knows nothing at all."

"Nothing?"

"Nothing. I am Colin MacDonald's wife," Fiona told him. "I am a mother three times. My son is three and is called Alastair. We have a daughter, Mary, who will be two in September, and a daughter, Johanna, who

was born in March." Then she went on to explain everything that had happened to her in careful detail since
that morning she had left Scone Palace on the road to
Brae. She spoke calmly, but he could see the vestiges of
pain in her eyes that her soft voice tried to conceal.

Hamish Stewart listened, and when she had finished he took her hands in his. "Ye did what ye had to
do, lassie. I am ashamed that my cousin James is so determined to rule all of Scotland that he would have
forced a woman to his secret service. I realize, however,
that ye dared not refuse him. If only Angus had taken
ye home before he hurried off to England to fetch the
queen's cousin."

"But the king was determined Angus wed with Mistress Williams," Fiona said. "He said he and the queen
wanted to bind Angus closer to them. If I had been at
Brae, he would have found a way for The MacDonald
to steal me away from there, and good Brae people
might have been killed or hurt. It was better this way, I
think. No one was really hurt, and certainly as husband
to the queen's cousin, Angus stands high in the king's
favor. Even more so than before. I did not see him in
the hall this morning, and I will admit to ye that I was
relieved, but where is he, my lord? I would have
thought he would have accompanied the king to the
gathering here in Inverness."

"He is in England on king's business," Hamish Stewart said. Why on earth did Fiona believe Angus was
wed to Mistress Elizabeth? She had no idea that they
had searched high and low for her that autumn and the
following spring when the trees began to bud, even before the snow was off the tops of the bens. Aye, they
had sought for her, but had been unable to find any
trace of her. It was finally decided that she had been
murdered along with Nelly and buried in some

unmarked grave deep in the bens. In his grief Angus Gordon had remained in England as the king's representative. He had not been back to Brae in almost two years.

And now, he, Hamish Stewart, possessed the answer to the riddle that had plagued them all, yet he would be unable to tell anyone. Fiona was married, possibly even happily. She had children. To tell her that Angus Gordon was not wed to Elizabeth Williams, that he lived in self-imposed exile with his broken heart would serve no purpose. Neither would telling Angus that Fiona yet lived, another man's wife and the mother of his three bairns. "Would ye have me tell yer sisters that ye are alive and content, Fiona?" he asked her. "Ye are content?"

"Aye," she said softly. Then, "Do not tell Jeannie and Morag, Hamish. They could not keep the secret that I know ye can. I ask but one thing of ye, though. From time to time will ye send me news of my sisters? Anne, Elsbeth, and Margery, too, if ye hear anything."

"I will, Fiona," he said, and then he turned his head sharply at the sound of a small child's voice calling.

"Mama! *Mama!*" A little lad came into view upon the riverbank.

"Jesu!" Fiona swore, jumping up. "He has gotten away from his nurse, and Nelly, too. Alastair! Stay where ye are, or I will take a birch switch to yer bottom, laddie!"

The child heeded her not, however, and raced across the little wooden bridge to fling himself proudly into her arms. "I found ye, Mama," he said triumphantly.

"Yer a bad bairn," she scolded him, "to run away from nursie and Nelly. They will be frantic looking for ye." She turned to Lord Stewart. "I must get him back quickly else they all have a fit."

Hamish Stewart was staring at the boy. *"Jesu!"* he

said, seeing his brother-in-law, Angus Gordon, in the lad's small face.

Fiona held up a warning hand and spoke to him in the Scots-English dialect she knew her son would not understand. "Ye can say nothing to him, Hamish. When the king forced me to play this game, I was not certain if I was with his bairn. I feared if I was not and cried off with that excuse, he would punish Angus."

"But MacDonald?"

"He believes my son is his son. I will not tell him otherwise for my bairn's sake. Don't look so shocked. Brae's wife will certainly give him an heir if she has not already. He does not need my laddie. Now, I must go. Farewell, Hamish Stewart. 'Twas verra good to see ye again." Then, taking her son by the hand, Fiona departed the small island for the shore, soon disappearing amid the trees along the riverbank.

Hamish Stewart remained sitting upon the outcropping. He needed time to absorb everything she had told him. Had he not heard the story from her own lips, Hamish would not have believed his cousin the king so ruthless. He wondered what would happen to the remaining chieftains the king had imprisoned that day. He did not have long to wait.

The next week the king called for all the clansmen and women who had gathered at Inverness to attend his parliament, where he intended to render his judgment upon their chieftains. The highlanders came fearfully, for a rhyme, attributed to the king, had been making the rounds all the week long regarding the fate of the Lord of the Isles and his allies.

To donjon tower let this rude troop be driven,
For death they merit, by the cross of heaven.

The MacRuries and the MacArthurs had already left the gathering to carry home the decapitated bodies

of their chieftains. So as not to appear to be showing fa-
voritism to any of the clans, for MacRurie had been a
cousin of Alexander MacDonald, the king also hanged
in that week James Campbell, who had been responsible for the murder of the current Lord of the Isles'
cousin, Ian MacDonald.

To everyone's surprise and relief, the king fined the
chieftains and released them. A lecture, as well as a fine,
however, was saved for Alexander MacDonald, Lord of
the Isles. "I canna rule Scotland properly if ye are always
rousing the north for one imagined offense or another,
my lord," the king said severely. "There can be but one
king in this land, *and I am he,* by the grace of God,
anointed with the holy oil, in Holy Mother Church. Ye
will cease yer turbulent lawlessness against me, my
lord, or I will be forced to take arms against ye. I don't
want to do that, for war is expensive and a waste of
good lives. But be warned, Alexander MacDonald, if ye
will not desist in yer proud ways, I will make ye do so.
Now, sir, ye may pledge me yer fealty before this parliament, and then may yer friends and allies do so, too."

Reluctantly the Lord of the Isles obeyed the king,
not wanting to be further publicly embarrassed, but he
was furious over his brief imprisonment. When he
arose from his knees, the king said, "Now, ye, Nairn,
for so I promised ye several years back that ye would
swear second after yer brother."

Colin MacDonald stepped forward, a small smile
upon his lips.

"I feared my lord would not swear," Fiona said afterward. They were safely back in their own tent. She
had her husband ensconced in a wooden barrel Roderick Dhu had confiscated for her. The barrel had been
filled with hot water, and she was now scrubbing her
husband's red-gold head with great vigor.

"Ouch! Go gentle, sweeting," he begged her, and then, "My brother does not consider his oath binding, for the king forced it from him. Had he not sworn, James Stewart would not have let him go."

Secretly, Fiona agreed with her brother-in-law, but she would not say so aloud. "An oath sworn before God and witnesses is an oath to be kept," she said severely. "What harm has been done? All yer brother must do is keep the peace. Can he not do that, Nairn?"

"His pride has been compromised, Fiona mine. He has been publicly shamed and made an example of in the king's hall. How can he forget that? It must be made right, or there are those among the clans who will believe he has become weak. Then he will not be able to keep the peace in the north for James Stewart."

"And how does yer brother propose to salve his pride then, my lord?" she asked scathingly, dumping a bucket of warm water over his head.

Colin MacDonald shook his head free of the droplets. "I don't know yet, for he has not decided what he shall do."

Fiona snorted with impatience and handed her husband the scrubbing cloth and some soap. "Wash yerself, and do a good job of it," she cautioned him. "A week in the king's dungeon, and there is enough dirt on ye to grow cabbages, my lord."

"I wish we were at home," he said, "so we might bathe together."

" 'Tis not bathing together yer thinking about." She laughed. "Jesu, Colin MacDonald, ye have just escaped possible death, and do ye give God a prayer of thanks for it? No! Ye think of coupling with yer wife!"

"Aye," he admitted, not in the least ashamed. "The whole time I was in the king's jail I didn't fight or fret, for I just kept thinking about yer pretty round little titties, and how sweetly ye sheathe me when we join, Fiona mine."

She laughed again. "Well," she told him. "I canna say I am disappointed that ye thought of me, Nairn. I worried a great deal about ye, particularly when they would not let us see any of ye or even bring ye small comforts. Then when the king hanged James Campbell, those of us in the encampment were hard put not to be frightened."

"Campbell deserved hanging," Colin MacDonald said grimly.

"Well, I'm grateful the king did not hang ye."

Nairn rose, pushed himself up and out of the barrel with his strong arms, and attempted to embrace her, but she scolded him, saying, "The living space is not private, and 'tis the middle of the day. What if the children or the servants or, God help us, yer mam, were to come upon us? Behave yerself, Nairn. Now that I have ye safe there will be plenty of time for loving ye, but not here or now, my lord. Did ye sleep well in prison?"

"No," he said, almost purring as she rubbed him dry.

"Then ye will need a good night's sleep, my lord, for unless ye have objection, I would depart for Nairns Craig as early tomorrow as we can go. And when we are home, Colly, ye will not regret controlling yer baser instincts for me now." She drew a clean shirt over his big body, her hand slipping beneath the fabric just a moment to caress his love rod. "If 'tis hungry now, 'twill be even hungrier in two days if I can wait."

He chuckled. "Yer a brazen piece of goods, wife," he told her, but he did not sound displeased with her at all.

Colin MacDonald had no sooner finished dressing

than Roderick Dhu ushered in a royal page. "The lad comes from the king," he said dourly.

"What is it, lad?" Nairn asked the boy.

"The king would speak in private with yer lady, sir," the page told them. "I am to accompany her to the castle."

"Why does he wish to speak with my wife?"

"Is this not the lady who spoke out so boldly in the king's hall the opening day of the parliament?" the page replied.

"I am," Fiona admitted.

"Then ye are the lady the king wishes to speak with," the page said firmly. Then he said confidentially, "I think he means to scold ye, lady. He was verra angry that day."

"Was he indeed, lad?" Fiona said, unable to help the small smile that touched her mouth. "He means me no harm, Colly," she reassured her husband. "I think the lad is right. I will go with him and return soon, I promise."

"Mistress!" Nelly came forward and handed her Johanna. "Take the bairn for safety's sake, my lady." She slipped a sling of warm plaid about Fiona's neck and tucked the baby into it so that it lay cradled against Fiona's bosom. "Aye," she said with a small chuckle. "That will do nicely. No man, even a king, can be harsh to a woman with a tiny bairn clinging to her."

Fiona bit her lip, restraining her laughter, and when she had gone with the page, Nairn said to Nelly, "Yer as clever a lass as yer mistress is, Nelly. When do ye intend wedding poor Roderick?"

"When we return to Nairns Craig," Nelly said calmly. " 'Tis time, I'm thinking, that we settled down properly, my lord."

Roderick Dhu looked stunned at this revelation.

"Yer finally ready?" he asked, amazed, for Nelly had held him off forever, it seemed. "What has happened to change yer mind, Nelly lass?"

"I saw how easily a woman might lose the man she loves," Nelly told him honestly. "And I do love ye, ye great, gangling gawk of a man."

James Stewart looked at Fiona with a sharp eye. In her fine wool skirts and her creamy silk blouse, a length of plaid about her, she was the picture of a highland chieftain's wife.

"What have ye tucked into that shawl?" he demanded of her.

"My youngest daughter, Johanna, named for yer queen," she replied. "She was born a bit over four months ago. I could not leave her, my liege, when ye called me."

"Ye managed to leave her the first day of the parliament," he said dryly. "Why is today different—or are ye attempting to gain my sympathy because of yer recent maternity, lady?"

"On the day ye so shamefully arrested the chieftains," Fiona replied blandly, "my maidservant looked after my bairns. Now she must watch over my husband's mother, who has been made unwell by all the excitement of the gathering, my liege."

"How many bairns?"

"Three, so far. The eldest is a son, Alastair James. The second, a daughter, Mary," Fiona responded. "Ye have two daughters, I am told."

"Margaret and Isabella," he answered. "I do not ask ye here, lady, to discuss our offspring. Ye have disappointed me, Fiona Hay. Why did ye return my coin?"

"I will not inform upon my husband, my liege,"

she said. "Nor will I betray his family. Ye have no right to ask it of me. Besides, I am not privy to the Lord of the Isles' thoughts. Nairns Craig is on the opposite side of Scotland from Islay. As for my husband, he is loyal to his brother, it is true, but he is not an instigator of mischief. In all the time I have been with Nairn, I have been to Islay only once, and that immediately after I was taken. There is naught I can tell ye. Now, let me return to my husband. Ye have forced me to lie to him once more, for I shall have to tell him ye scolded me severely for my outburst in the hall last week. We have no other business, my liege."

"I will release ye for now, Fiona MacDonald," he told her, "but there may come a time when I need ye again. Ye canna refuse me. I am yer king and yer overlord, woman. Will ye break yer fealty to me?"

"As I am pledged to ye, my lord, so were ye pledged to me," Fiona answered him fiercely. "When ye forced me into yer service three years ago, ye broke yer trust with me. As I was pledged to give ye service, ye were bound to protect me and my honor. I have served ye well, James Stewart, but ye have not kept yer part of the bargain between overlord and liege woman. I will promise ye this. I will not rebel against ye as my king, but neither will ye demand service of me again. Ye have not the right to do so any longer." She inclined her head to him then and turned to go, but suddenly she stopped, swiveling her head about. "Be advised, my liege. The Lord of the Isles feels ye have shamed him publicly. He may seek to retaliate simply to balance the scales between ye. He will be a good ally after that, though, and ye can trust him, for his sense of honor and justice is a strong one." With that, Fiona left.

He let her go. The truth was that she was no longer important to him. By challenging her he had closed the book on them. Her warning he accepted as a pledge of her good faith, but he did not give it serious considera- tion. Certainly The MacDonald saw James Stewart's determination. Surely a week in the royal dungeon cooling his heels had reinforced the king's will. It was unlikely that The MacDonald would precipitate any foolish action against the king. No. James Stewart now had the highlands firmly under his control.

"What did he want?" Nairn asked her when she returned to their tent.

Fiona laughed. "It was as the lad said. He scolded me for my bold tongue, but I reminded him that high- land women are outspoken, and then I sent my regards to my former mistress, the queen. I do not think he is pleased with me, Colly, but what have I really done but speak the truth? He knew it, and so he sent me on my way."

Colin MacDonald drew his wife into his arms. "I never want to lose ye, Fiona mine," he said. "Ye must not be so brazen and bold, sweeting." His big hand ca- ressed her dark head.

Fiona laughed again and, pulling away from him, looked into his face. "Telling me to not be brazen or bold is like asking the sun to not rise, please," she teased him. "I am who I am, my lord, and verra unlikely to change, I fear. I think it is a good thing that ye love me for the way I am." Then she drew his head down to hers and kissed him softly. "I have missed ye, Colly. I have missed ye verra, *verra* much."

The smoky hint of passion in her voice was tempt- ing. His grip about her tightened. His eyes narrowed as he contemplated her and the delights they were about to share. She smiled up seductively at him. It was an outrageous and blatant invitation.

Then Roderick Dhu's voice broke the spell. "The

lord is calling for ye to come to his pavilion immediately, my lord."

"Dammit!" Fiona swore softly, and her husband laughed.

"I'll be back as quickly as I can, sweeting," he told her, kissing the tip of her nose.

Fiona smiled, watching him go. She had managed to turn his thoughts from her visit to the king. Pray God she would never be put into such a position again. She wondered what Colin MacDonald would think if he ever learned that his abduction of her had been carefully orchestrated by James Stewart. And what would he do if he learned that Alastair was not his natural born son but the offspring of Angus Gordon? She was fortunate he was such a trusting man with a basically sweet nature. But he could be as determined and strong as she was, Fiona knew. She comforted herself with the knowledge that she was a good wife to him, and always had been. Moreover, she was finally willing to admit she was in love with her big highland husband. Meeting Hamish Stewart had been wonderful, yet frightening. What if Black Angus had been with the king? How could she have faced him? He would have despised her, and she could not have borne it. Angus would have believed the worst, as he had always been wont to do. At least Colin loved her for good or bad.

When Fiona awoke in the morning, Colin was already up and dressing. She stretched herself, enjoying the sensation as she did so.

"Yer awake," he said. "It isn't quite dawn, but we should be under way as quickly as possible."

"How late were ye?" she asked, wondering why he had not wakened her and made love to her as he had earlier intended.

"The chieftains had much talking to do," he answered, but no more.

"Tell me that yer brother will not be foolish," she begged.

"Alexander has been insulted by James Stewart. That insult must be redressed. Ye know that is the way of it, sweeting."

Fiona climbed from their camp bed. "So yer brother, having sworn fealty to the king, breaks that fealty and strikes back at James Stewart. What, pray tell, do ye think the king will do, Colly? Do ye believe that he will let it go? Or will he strike back, too? And then it begins anew. The highlands aflame. Crops and cattle destroyed. Women, bairns, and old folk driven from their homes, hounded to their deaths. For what, my lord? Will this redress either your brother's pride or the equally vast pride of James Stewart? Why must we all suffer the conceit and arrogance of those who rule us?"

Putting his arms about her, he tried to comfort her. "Ye don't understand, Fiona mine," he said gently.

She pulled away from him, outraged. "*Don't understand?* Ye dare to accuse me of not understanding? I understand all too well, my lord. It is verra simple. Men would rather fight. Women would not. There is no more to it, Colin MacDonald. Only that!"

"Hurry and dress, sweeting," he said, ignoring her logic, for it conflicted with his own, and he was certain he was right. "I want to get home to Nairns Craig as quickly as possible. There is much to do to get ready." He cinched a wide leather belt about his waist.

"*Get ready for what?*" she demanded.

Tipping her chin up, he brushed her lips lightly. "Don't be long," he said with infuriating charm, and then he left her.

Fiona shook her head. What mischief were the

MacDonalds up to, and what would the cost to ordinary folk be? Pulling on her skirts and footwear, she called to Nelly to bring Johanna so she might nurse the bairn before they departed. What would be would be. Her main goal was to protect her children and Moire Rose from the chaos that would undoubtedly come.

She thought as they rode that day of how relatively peaceful her childhood had been despite just this sort of squabbling going on about her. She remembered that Black Angus had once told her Hay Tower and Brae escaped the general mayhem because of their relative isolation. Nairns Craig, while inaccessible to direct attack, was near enough to the town of Nairn, the seat of the head of the Rose family, and Cawdor Castle, which had once been home to an evil king called Macbeth, to not be overlooked in any factional fighting between the king's forces and the highlanders, should it come to that. She hoped whatever the Lord of the Isles was planning would not be so dreadful that the king would feel bound to retaliate by setting the highlands aflame. Especially with the autumn coming. She hoped the king would go to Islay to take his revenge should he need to, but she knew he wouldn't. Punishing the highlands would be easier than taking to sea to reach Islay.

She was frightening herself needlessly, Fiona decided. Alexander MacDonald was an honorable man. He had sworn his loyalty to James Stewart. His brief sojourn as the king's "guest" had certainly angered and embarrassed him, but his retaliation would more than likely be a firm protest the king would understand. James Stewart would let it stand, knowing the Lord of the Isles meant nothing more by it than having the last word. Certainly the king would comprehend that, and they would all go on living in peace. Aye! Of course! That was how it would be. No one wanted to rip apart the fragile peace that they had sought for so long between the king and the lord. The king was clever. He would fathom the subtleties of it all.

It was good to be home. The servants had not slacked off in their duties while their mistress was away. The hall was sparkling, a bowl of roses on the high board, the fireplaces clean, the plate shining. Alastair ran happily about, delighted to be free of the confines of the tent, from which he had rarely escaped. His personal nursemaid greeted him joyously, and the two hurried off hand in hand to see the little boy's pony in the stables. Mary would have followed after her brother, but her own personal servant swooped her up for a nap after the long ride. The baby was nursed in the comfort of her own hall, by her own log fire, then turned over to her servant.

Moire Rose sat in her own familiar place opposite her daughter-in-law. "I've done all the traveling I ever hope to do," she said firmly, "and I've seen a Stewart king. Ye were right, Fiona, he was not much to see." She chuckled. " 'Tis good to be back by my own hearth with Nairn safe. I would have died myself had the king executed him like he did MacRurie, MacArthur, and that devil, James Campbell."

"The Lord of the Isles is plotting some revenge on the king for the insult he believes James Stewart visited upon him," Fiona said.

"Aye," Moire Rose answered. "He would, of course."

"It is wrong!" Fiona's voice was near to shouting.

Her mother-in-law looked surprised by the tone. "Why, Fiona lassie, 'tis the way of the highlands to revenge a slight. We have always done so and always will do so. To do less would be weakness."

"If every time someone looks cross-eyed at another someone," Fiona said, trying to master her emotions, "a fight will ensue, how will we ever stop feuds, madam?"

"We will not, Fiona. It is our way." She reached over and patted her daughter-in-law with a bony hand. "Nairns Craig has never had its defenses breached in all the years it has stood here on this spine of rock. It has been here my whole life, my father's life, and long before him. I've waited out a few sieges in my time, lassie."

Nairn made love to his wife. It was a long, sweet bout of tender touches, hot mouth fusing on hot mouth, and skin that tingled in the wake of a thousand kisses. Twice they made each other cry out with pleasure, but afterward, his head upon her breasts, his ragged breathing finally slowing to normal, he sensed her unease.

"What frightens ye so about the normal course of events, Fiona mine?"

"If Alexander is planning something dreadful, don't answer his call, Colly," she begged him.

"He is my brother, sweeting."

Fiona sat up, suddenly forcing him from his comfortable pillow. "I am yer wife," she said quietly. "I am the mother of yer bairns. Do ye not owe me a greater loyalty than ye owe him?"

"Alexander and I are bound by blood, sweeting."

"We are bound by God," she replied. "Would ye place the Lord of the Isles above God, Colin MacDonald? Would ye dare?"

"Aye, I would," he said. He hated it when she spoke to him with such logic. It wasn't womanly. "I would put my brother above God because I shall have to answer to my brother in this life. I shall not have to answer to

God until I die, and I shall make my confession repenting my sins, including my loyalty to Alexander MacDonald, before that event takes place."

"If ye have the good fortune to die in yer bed, and how many of ye highland warriors do?" Fiona asked him with devastating effect.

"Don't speak on it," he gently scolded her. "Ye will bring bad fortune to us all."

"I canna help it," she told him. "I have this great sense of foreboding, Colly. It follows me about like a dark cloud. I canna rid myself of it, though I would. Don't go if the lord calls ye!"

He flung himself from their bed. "Yer being foolish," he told her. "I will not disappoint my brother, for I am pledged to him."

"Yer pledged to the king, too," she said angrily.

"The king is not my blood kin," he shouted at her. "Besides, Nairn has never fallen, Fiona mine. Ye and the bairns will be safe."

"So yer mam has told me," Fiona snapped, arising also.

Their views were too disparate for them to come to agreement on the matter, and so for the time being they avoided it altogether. Nelly and Roderick Dhu handfasted themselves in the hall before their lord and lady as well as the castle folk. When the priest came, they would repeat their vows, but they did not wish to wait any longer. Nelly, her carrot-red hair loose to signify her maiden state, cried happily when her new husband laid a length of his plaid across her chest, fastening it with a fine pewter pin. Fiona had provided a small celebratory feast, and Nairn honored the two valued servants by declaring a half holiday for all his people. It was a happy time.

Outside in the hills about them autumn had come.

The trees blazed with scarlet, gold, tawny orange, and sunny yellow. The loch near them and the lochs they could see in the distance as the leaves fell from the trees, leaving naught but bare branches, were a wonderful shade of bright, deep blue. There seemed to be a peace upon the land. The men hunted deer and boar for the winter store. Fiona and Nelly gathered the seeds of the lacy white flower of the wild carrot that each would ingest to prevent conception.

"I'll bring no more bairns into this world until I am certain Nairn is here to be father to them," Fiona said. "The lord has not deigned his mischief yet, and until it is over and done with, I don't feel safe."

"I know," Nelly agreed. "When I ask him what will happen, my Roddy just pats me like some pretty animal and says, 'Now, then, lassie, such matters are not for the likes of ye.' The great gawk! Does he not think I can understand that a feud with a king can bring naught but trouble to the highlands? What is the matter with men, lady?"

Fiona shook her head. "I do not understand them myself, Nelly," she told her servant. "Ohhh, look over there! 'Tis a great patch of white flowers for us to harvest. We just have time before dark."

The two young women worked diligently, garnering the seeds they needed. When they had finished, the sun was close to setting, a half circle of fiery orange showing just above a bank of dark purple clouds edged in gold. Already the evening star gleamed in the darkening blue above them. As they walked the distance to the castle gate, Nelly suddenly cried out and pointed. Fiona stared, seeing a flame spring up on a distant hill. Was it a woodland fire? she wondered nervously. Then her heart almost rose in her throat to choke her as she saw another fire on another hill, and another, and yet another.

" 'Tis a signal of some sort," Nelly said. "Look! Before our gates the men are lighting one, too."

"God help us!" Fiona whispered. Picking up her skirts, she began to run toward Nairns Craig while all about her the hills blossomed with fires.

Nelly, close on her mistress's heels, did not drop her precious basket of flower heads. They were going to need then, she suspected.

At the gates Fiona demanded of the man-at-arms on duty, "What is this fire being lit for—and the others as well?"

"Why, my lady, 'tis a call to arms from the Lord of the Isles," he replied. "We have been waiting for weeks for it to come. There is another signal fire behind the castle so those in that direction may know the time has come, too."

Fiona hurried past him, making directly for the castle's hall. There she found her husband, a large goblet of wine in his hand. "Why is the Lord of the Isles calling ye to arms?" she demanded. "What is he going to do to avenge his honor?" The last word was uttered scathingly. "Tell me, Colin MacDonald, or as God is my witness, I will cut out yer black heart, and ye'll not go anywhere!" Her dark hair had fallen loose from her caul, and her green eyes flashed angrily.

"Why, sweeting, there is nothing to fret about. We but go to burn Inverness, scene of our disgrace. That is all."

Chapter 15

The words slammed into her brain like a brand. *Burn Inverness.* For a moment she couldn't speak, and then a rage such as Fiona had never known overwhelmed her. "Ye would raze Inverness? Have ye lost what few wits ye have, Colin MacDonald?" she screamed at him. "I will not let ye go off blindly to be killed!" She stamped her foot angrily at him.

The MacDonald of Nairn burst out laughing. His poor sweeting had never known such a situation, and she was, of course, frightened. He stepped forward to put his arms about her, but Fiona jumped back, almost hissing at him like a feral beast. "Fiona mine," he said, pleading. "Don't distress yerself. I will leave on the morrow and be back in a few days' time at the most. There is naught to be fearful of, my darling."

"Do ye not understand, Colly?" she demanded of him. "Are ye so thickheaded that ye don't understand? *The king will retaliate!*"

"James Stewart is not in Inverness any longer, sweeting. We waited until he was south of the Tay, returned safely to Perth." He smiled at her. "There is no danger. We mean the king no harm, but the insult done to the Lord of the Isles must be avenged or he will be thought weak by the clans."

Fiona shook her head wearily. His loyalty to his brother was so deep and so blind that he could not see the terrible peril they would all be in when the king learned that Inverness had been burned by the Lord of the Isles and the highland clans. "Why would ye burn Inverness?" she asked him. "What have the people of that fair town done to ye that yer brother would destroy all they have? 'Twill not hurt the king. 'Twill only displace the poor townsfolk—and with winter coming on, too!"

"They hosted the king, sweeting. The people of Inverness rebuilt the hall where our disgrace was publicly displayed. We have sworn our fealty to James Stewart, but not to the people of Inverness," Colin MacDonald explained to his disbelieving wife.

"The king believed it necessary to make an example of yer brother," Fiona said to her husband. "I do not agree with him, but then I know Alexander MacDonald a wee bit better than James Stewart did. If he had known yer brother, he would have taken his hand in friendship two years ago instead of attempting to force the clans to his royal will and embarrassing them when he finally called a gathering. But yer brother, who has ruled here in the north, should know that the king believed he must be publicly harsh in order to convince ye that he means to rule *all* of Scotland and not just south of the Tay. He has executed two bad chieftains and a murdering Campbell for causing the wrongful death of a MacDonald kin. James Stewart favored neither one side nor the other, instead being impartial. Why can Alexander not simply accept what has happened? It is past. Let us have peace."

"Not without the honor of the MacDonalds being restored," Nairn said stubbornly. "This king must surely understand that."

"James Stewart will take the burning of Inverness as an insult upon *his* honor, Colly," she told him. "He will come north to punish us. Remember, he has learned all he knows from the English, and they are mean fighters, tacticians, and rulers. Yer brother, in his arrogance, is about to poke a stick into a bees' nest. When this is over, we shall all be badly stung, but The MacDonald on Islay less so than those of us here in the highlands. I don't call that just. Yer brother commands us to war, and then we suffer for it."

"Yer a woman, Fiona mine," he said. "Ye canna possibly understand," he told her, but he found that her words discomfited him greatly.

"Yer a man, Colin MacDonald, and canna help yer childish behavior that would put a brother ahead of yer bairns."

He held out his arms to her. "Come and kiss me, sweeting, and let us quarrel no longer."

Fiona shook her head. "I'll not kiss ye, or cuddle ye, or couple with ye until ye are safe home to me again," she told him. "Sleep in the hall tonight, my lord, with yer men. I will not share my bed with ye."

"What if I am killed, sweeting? Will ye not regret yer harsh decision then?"

"Yer hide is too thick for an arrow to pierce, and besides, what danger do ye face from poor frightened townspeople, my lord?" she mocked him. Then she left him.

Eventually, he knew, she would understand the ways of a highland chief. His duties not just to his own people, but to his overlord. He had indeed sworn fealty to the king, but he knew in his heart that his first loyalty would lie, as it had always lain, with the MacDonalds. They were his family, his clan, and he regretted that Fiona could not comprehend it. He would teach Alastair the same loyalty soon, and the sons that would come afterward, too.

Fiona knew her duty. In the morning she stood,

her two eldest children clinging to her skirts, her infant daughter in her arms, watching as her husband and his retainers marched off down the castle hill to the road leading to Inverness. Unlike many of the chieftains who could muster two thousand or more men, The MacDonald of Nairn had but two hundred, and they were Rose family clansmen—his mother's people, for although he was a MacDonald by birth and acknowledged by his father, his inheritance had belonged to a lesser branch of the Rose family.

"They are like little boys playing," Fiona said grimly as the piper led the troop off, banners flying bravely.

"Will they all come back, I wonder?" Nelly asked.

"I believe so," Fiona said. "This is not a war they go to fight. They go to burn, pillage, and loot a hapless town of women, bairns, and shopkeepers. They should be ashamed of themselves, but they are not. They will all return to their homes boasting of their victory."

"Yer hard on him," Moire Rose said, coming up next to Fiona, smiling down at Alastair and Mary.

"Do ye agree with yer son then, lady?"

"No, I don't. I always thought the warfare foolish, but unlike ye, I didn't dare to say it aloud. It is our way and will not change."

"Ye must say it aloud now," Fiona told her. "James Stewart will not take this act of terror lightly. He will retaliate, lady. When he does, I would have Nairn align himself with the king, and not the Lord of the Isles. If both of us nag at yer son, my husband, then perhaps we may turn him from his path of self-destruction."

"He'll not listen," Moire Rose said fatalistically. "When Colin went to live with his father on Islay, he was taught the first rule of life was total loyalty to the Lord of the Isles. All Donald's children were taught that. Not one of them would break that rule, Fiona. *Not one.* Ye have no hope of changing a lifetime's habit, I fear."

"Then it is unlikely Colly will live to see his bairns grown," Fiona replied sadly. "They will burn Inverness, and the king will strike back at them. He will bring fire and death to the highlands."

Alexander MacDonald carried out his purpose and burned Inverness to the ground. His highland army of ten thousand strong slaughtered the inhabitants of the town and looted everything they could. The MacDonald of Nairn returned home laden down with booty on a cold, rainy day. It had been raining for three days straight, and the barren branches of the trees were black against the gray sky as the men rode up the castle hill.

Fiona had grown calm with her purpose over the short time her husband had been away. By the time the king learned of the carnage in Inverness and could prepare a force to come north again, the winter would have set in. It was unlikely the king would strike during the winter months. He would wait until spring. And in those intervening months she intended to convince Colin MacDonald that his first loyalty must be to the king to whom he had sworn fealty. She would use whatever means she had to, attain her goal. Fiona greeted her husband warmly.

Pleased, he grinned boyishly, certain she finally understood his reasoning. He flung his booty at her feet; two bolts of fine soft wool—one the gray-blue color of a winter sky, the other a soft purple heathery tone. There was a forest-green-and-gold-brocade surcoat and several gowns. A length of sheer lawn for making veils. Several gold chains and a jeweled rosary. For his mother he had fetched back a bolt of wool in beige and cream tones to flatter her hair, several strands of agate, and a gold ring. For Alastair there was a miniature claymore, and for Mary, a pretty blue gown. This last sent a shiver through Fiona. What little lass had the dress belonged to, and had she been slaughtered?

He read her thoughts. "I took it from the shop of a cloth merchant," he told her. "It had been newly made, probably by his wife, who is a seamstress and earned a living sewing."

She nodded, not wanting to know any more. "Come, my lord," she said softly, "ye will be hungry, and I have the meal ready. Then ye must bathe, for I will wager ye have not done so since ye left me."

He flashed her a quick smile. "There is not usually time to bathe when a man is pillaging and looting, Fiona mine." He was pleased when she laughed aloud at his sally.

They sat down to table, and he ate heartily of the game pie, the capon with the lemon ginger sauce, the freshly caught trout, and the ham. He had grown used to the greens she insisted be served, and actually felt better for eating them. Tonight she served him braised lettuce and cress, small beets, and onions in a dilled cream sauce. The bread was soft and fresh, the butter sweet, the cheese sharp. And best of all, his meal was hot. He hadn't eaten any hot food in the time he had been away. He had missed it, although he had chided himself for growing soft. Nodding at the hovering servant wanting to know if he wished his goblet refilled, he savored the sweet wine. His mother and his wife smiled at each other over his appetite. His piper began to play softly, and Colin MacDonald sat back, content and mellow, glad to be safely home again after his sortie to Inverness.

"Is the whole town gone?" his mother finally ventured.

He nodded. "We burned the king's hall first. 'Twas a fine sight, and now the memories of the Lord of the Isles' shame are no more."

"Come, my lord," Fiona said before the conversation could become more detailed. "Ye will want to get out of those stinking garments and bathe yerself before ye go to bed."

"I'll not bathe if I am to be confined to the hall again," he threatened her mischievously.

"Oh, Colly," she told him, "I was angry with ye then, but not now. Indeed, I am relieved to have ye safely home again." She smiled softly at him. "I have missed ye in our bed." She held out her hand to him. "Come along, my lord."

"Good night, madam," Nairn said to his mother, who nodded pleasantly in his direction at his words and smiled as they departed the hall, knowing full well her daughter-in-law's intentions. Alas, Moire Rose thought, she would not be successful.

They lay, bathed and aroused, on a sheepskin before the fire. Fiona touched his manhood, and Colin groaned.

"Ye like it when I use my tongue on yer little love button, do ye not, sweeting?" he asked. When she nodded slowly, he said, "Give me the same kind of pleasure, Fiona mine. Take me in yer mouth." His voice was almost strangled with the request.

The truth was, she had wondered about doing such a thing, but had not dared for fear he would be shocked. She was curious and had been for some time. Slowly she began to absorb him, sweetly sucking upon him with slow deep strokes. He moaned, but she did not cease, for the sound was one of utter pleasure. Fiona was fascinated that she was able to render him so helpless by her actions. Inquisitively she ran her tongue around the ruby head of his member, and again, and yet again. Holding him in one hand, she let her other hand wander to fondle his twin pouch. A single finger strayed innocently beneath him and touched the flesh beneath the pouch. He cried out softly. She pressed the spot again. He cautioned her in a tight voice that he was near to spilling his seed, and she must cease.

Fiona's head was spinning with the erotic sensations she had received by using him in this fashion. He came over her, his big body covering her, and he was like iron as he entered her. She opened to him, taking in his love rod, closing her flesh around him, wrapping her legs about him so he might delve his deepest into the soft hot swamp of her welcoming sex. Fiona sighed deeply, feeling her breasts give way beneath the muscle of his chest. "Oh, Colly!" she whispered. It had never been quite so good between them. Not like this. "Oh! Ohhhhh!"

She was magnificent. She was incredible. He had never known her so totally unsparing of her passions with him. He began to move upon her, his buttocks tightening and releasing, tightening and releasing as he built to a crescendo of passion.

Beneath him Fiona writhed as he plunged within her, arousing her to a fever pitch of excitement such as she had never before experienced. She could feel him throbbing, and she ached for release. Her nails raked down his back. "Please! *Please!*" she whimpered. His body thrust harder and harder. She could feel the approaching maelstrom. She gasped, struggling desperately for air. Her whole body, her very brain was afire, and in a moment she would explode into a thousand fragments of pure pleasure. She screamed as the wild wave burst over her. His responding cry of utter joy shattered her. They had denied themselves for too long.

Afterward they lay naked before the fire. Smiling, he ran a finger down her length. "Ye have never yielded to me like that before," he said softly. Bending, he kissed her shoulder.

"Ye have never yielded to me like that before," she countered. "It was wonderful, Colin MacDonald." She turned her head so that their eyes met, and kissed his mouth. "Ummmmm."

"Do ye finally love me, Fiona mine?"

Her green eyes twinkled. "Possibly, I am beginning to have a wee bit of a *tendre* for ye, my lord."

"Brazen vixen." He chuckled, pressing her back against the sheepskin rug. The firelight played across their bodies, its heat adding to their own. He licked up the column of her slender throat. "Yer delicious, sweeting," he murmured into the hollow of her neck, nibbling delicately at her sweet flesh. Drawing his tongue over her chest, he lapped at her breasts, his mouth closing over a nipple, drawing her milk into his mouth and swallowing it.

Her fingers threaded themselves through his thick red-gold hair. Fiona smiled. She had forgotten to wash it, and it was dusty with his travels. Tomorrow would be time enough. She abandoned herself to the pleasure of his passion, and it was even better than before. Finally in the middle of the night they managed to leave their place before the fire for the warmth of their bed, cuddling beneath the down coverlet. Something had changed. They both realized it as they slid into a contented sleep.

The winter came, and the news that filtered into Nairns Craig from south of the Tay was ominous. The

king had been furious to learn that the Lord of the Isles
had burned the town of Inverness. Its survivors had
trekked to Scone to plead with the king for revenge and
reparations. Only the snows kept the highlands safe for
the present. In the spring they knew the retaliation
would come. Fiona tried to force it from her mind, but
Nairn would not let her.

"We had a good harvest last year," he said. "Ye
must conserve what is in the granaries and cold storage,
for we may not get to plant a new crop in the spring. If
we do, it may be destroyed before ye can harvest it. Ye
will have to be responsible for Nairns Craig while I am
away, sweeting. My mother will help ye."

"Where will ye go?" Fiona asked him as they sat
together in the hall, the children romping about them.
Johanna was soon to celebrate her first year of life and
was already toddling about on unsteady feet.

"When my brother calls, I must follow him into
battle," Colin MacDonald said quietly. "Ye know it,
sweeting. Don't hide from the truth. If Alexander goes
to war, I must follow him."

"Ye must pledge yerself to the king," she said, working hard to keep the desperate tone from her voice. "If
yer brother chooses to fight with James Stewart, don't
follow him. Ally yerself with yer liege lord. In the end
James Stewart will triumph over the lord. I know it! If
ye fight by the lord's side, the king will punish ye, too.
If ye fight beneath the royal banner, we will all be safe. I
know ye love yer brother and feel a deep loyalty to the
clan as yer father taught ye, but times are changing,
Colly. This world we live in is not yer father's world.
Once the lords of the Isles ruled unchallenged, but now
their authority is in dispute. James Stewart claims all of
Scotland. Even the lord's allies waver in their loyalty.
Unless yer brother will accept the king's authority, he

and all those who follow him will be made to suffer. We have three bairns, my lord. Yer mother is old. Must we suffer for yer misguided sense of devotion? Please, I beg of ye, don't follow yer brother into battle!" Her eyes were filled with tears as she pleaded with him, and The MacDonald of Nairn was moved by her words, yet he refused to yield to her plea.

"I canna refuse the Lord of the Isles' summons when it comes, sweeting. Do not fear. Ye'll be safe within Nairns Craig, and the bairns, too. The king will not take any revenge against ye and my mam."

"James Stewart would take revenge against a saint if that saint stood in his way, Colin MacDonald. Don't say ye were not warned. I know what I must now do. If ye leave us, I will take the children, and yer mam if she will come with us, and go home to Hay Tower. There I know we will be safe from the chaotic games ye men play."

Astounded, he said, "Ye must hold Nairns Craig for me."

"If this castle is as invulnerable as ye claim, my lord, then yer servants can hold Nairns Craig until ye return, or the king's men demand its surrender," Fiona told him. "I will not remain here without ye, nor will I allow our children and that old woman to be in danger. Leave us, and I will depart here. If ye survive, ye know where ye may find us. If the king confiscates this castle, ye may be glad of my small house, Colly. 'Tis not grand, but the roof doesn't leak."

He was amazed by her determination. He did not think her a silly and foolish woman who threatened a man, never meaning to follow through. She meant every word she was saying, and he knew it. The idea, while shocking at first, was not such a bad one. If Nairns Craig stood in danger of imminent attack, perhaps it would be a good thing if she took the children and fled to her own holding. She was not rebelling against the king. If she distanced herself from Nairns Craig and he was killed or captured, she could not be held responsible for his behavior—or used to force him into submission. How many children of Stewart enemies had languished their lives away in custodial confinement. He did not want his daughters bartered into unhappy marriages that benefited James Stewart while making them miserable. He did not want his son brought up to be ashamed of his proud heritage.

"Perhaps, sweeting," he told her, "it might be a good thing if ye and the children hid at Hay Tower if war comes. The troubles will not be anywhere near yer home. It will be fought in the north and in the west predominantly. No one would think to seek ye on yer ben."

Fiona sighed. She had thought to coerce him into renouncing his foolish course, but instead she had given him a means to salve his conscience. "I canna change ye, can I, Colin MacDonald?"

He shook his head, a small smile upon his lips. "No, sweeting, ye canna change me. I love ye with all my heart, Fiona mine, but not even for ye will I betray Alexander MacDonald, Lord of the Isles."

"I can but pray we all survive yer misguided loyalties," she answered him, but then she kissed his lips.

The snows were on the bens and the trees showed no sign of budding when the call to arms came. One icy twilight when a new sliver of moon hung in the western skies, first one, and then another, and yet another signal fire sprang up on the hills. Before dark a messenger arrived at Nairns Craig from the Lord of the Isles. James Stewart and a vast army had crossed the Tay River, bound for the north. The king had struck earlier than any of them had anticipated. It was to be a battle to the death.

They had lost not a man at Inverness, but now, as the two hundred assembled in the castle courtyard, Fiona looked upon them with sad eyes, wondering how many, if any, would return unscathed. As Nairn was preparing to make his departure, his mother, frail with the hard winter they had endured and the loss of her old servant, Beathag, spoke earnestly to her only child.

"I sense what ye are doing is not right, Colin," she told him. "Don't follow the MacDonalds this time. If not for our sake, then for yer own. No good can come of this fighting." Her eyes were filled with tears that began to flow down her weathered, yet beautiful, aged face. "If ye go, I will not see ye again in this life," she told him.

He tried to comfort her, for he had never in all his life seen her so concerned over him. Putting an arm about her, he said, "I am my father's son, mam, and must do my duty by my family."

Moire Rose looked up at him bleakly as he kissed her cheek.

"God bless ye, Colin, my son," she said. Then, pulling from his embrace, she hobbled back into the castle, leaning heavily upon the cane she now used. She would have no servant helping her since Beathag's death in the winter from old age.

"I'll look after her," Fiona said to her husband, "but there is little I can do to calm her fears. We are right, Colly. Ye should not go with the lord. March for the king's camp and align yerself with him. Ye will not suffer for it, and, believe me, ye will not be the only highland chief who arrays himself with James Stewart. I don't approve the burning of Inverness, but I understand now why ye felt ye must join yer brother in razing the town. This is different. That was to avenge an insult, but this is treason, plain and simple, Colly. Will ye mark yer bairns with a traitor's mark? So will they be if the king wins."

"*If,*" The MacDonald of Nairn said with a jaunty smile.

Fiona wanted to shriek at him. Didn't he understand? The Lord of the Isles believed he had ten thousand men beneath his banner, but human nature being what it was, Fiona was certain that a number of the clansmen, seeing the king's might, would switch sides. The messenger last night had stated that the king's troops were equal in size to Alexander MacDonald's. Looking into her husband's eyes, she saw that there was nothing she might say or do that would turn him from the path of his own destruction. It was madness, but she had to admire his sense of loyalty and determination. He was not a complicated man, just a good one. Pulling his head down to hers, she kissed him passionately until both their heads began to spin with the pleasure. He broke the embrace, smiling down at her.

"Farewell, my love," Fiona said. "May God guard you and bring you home safe to us."

"So," he said, his blue eyes suddenly alight, "*you do love me,* Fiona mine." His big hand caressed her rosy cheek.

A quick sally sprang to her lips, but she swallowed it back, saying, "Aye, I love ye, Nairn." Then, before he might see her tears, she turned away from him, walking back into the castle as his voice called after her, "I always knew ye would love me one day, Fiona mine!"

The days took on a sameness. While not isolated, Nairns Craig was off the beaten track. As the ground grew soft again, Fiona oversaw the planting in their few fields that were tillable. Mayhap they would get to harvest them. She carefully rationed every particle of grain in her storage bins, set extra watches on their cattle and sheep. She sent a lad, too young for battle and disappointed that he wasn't allowed to go off with the men, to sit down by the roadside and question any travelers so they might learn what news they could. Fiona knew she should leave, but she could not seem to do so. During the day the yett was drawn down over the entry to Nairns Craig; each night the heavy iron-bound oak doors were shut behind it.

Beathag, whose frail old body had been stored in the cold cellars during the winter months, was now laid to rest in a newly dug grave. This event seemed to make Moire Rose sink even lower. She barely ate anymore, and each day she grew weaker and weaker. One afternoon when the sun shone brightly from a clear blue sky, Fiona had her mother-in-law carried to the roof of one of the towers so she might enjoy the soft air and see the countryside about her. Below, the hills were lush with fresh new greenery, and the lochs about them sparkled, reflecting back the sky's fine color. Together the two women sat for several hours, Fiona sewing a garment for Alastair, who was growing quickly. Finally, as the afternoon waned, Fiona suggested it was time to go inside.

"Let me see the sunset," Moire Rose said in quavery tones.

"If it pleases ye, lady. Ye are not cold, are ye? We have been out here for some time."

"I am all right."

Together they watched as the sun sank below the western hills. The sky was a panorama of blazing colors. Orange melted into a slender length of pale green, which oozed into lavender. Rose-pink clouds edged in violet and gold hung in an aquamarine sky. The horizon was a rich royal purple beneath which the molten red sun slowly sank, while above the castle swallows darted like dark shadows amid the twilight.

Finally Fiona arose and called down to her servants to come and carry Moire Rose back to her bedchamber. The litter was carefully lowered through the trapdoor and carried through the corridor to the old woman's chamber. Once inside, however, as they made to lift Moire Rose back to her bed, Fiona noted how still she was.

"Wait," she said, and fetched the little silver hand mirror Donald MacDonald had once given her mother-in-law. Holding the mirror to Moire Rose's nostrils, she immediately saw that there was no breath of life reflected upon the glass. Her mother-in-law's blue eyes were but half-open. Fiona closed them gently. "The lady is dead," she told the servants. "Put her gently upon the bed. She must be prepared for burial tomorrow." Then she hurried out to find Nelly.

At the gravesite the following morning Fiona wished that Father Ninian had been with them. They had not seen him in well over a year. Moire Rose's delicate body had been washed and dressed in her finest gown. She was then sewn into a cloth sack, for there was no one to fashion a proper wooden coffin. The young boy who watched the road had dug the grave for her, then filled it in.

Several days later came word that clans Chattan and Cameron had deserted the ranks of the Lord of the Isles and allied themselves with King James. It was a terrible blow, for both families were very powerful and had been longtime adherents of the MacDonald lords. He was greatly weakened without them. Fiona prayed that her husband would remember her words and reconsider his position, but in her heart she knew that he would not. If anything, the desertion of longtime former partisans and supporters would but strengthen his resolve to remain by his brother's side until the very end.

One afternoon the boy by the high road came racing up the castle hill, shouting, "Him's been defeated! Him's been defeated!" They brought the lad to Fiona immediately.

"Who has been defeated, Ian?" she asked. "Has the king been defeated, laddie? Tell me what ye heard."

"The Lord of the Isles has been defeated at Lochaber, lady. 'Twere a terrible slaughter, they say. Terrible!"

"Who told ye this?"

"Clansmen of the Rose family returning home. Not our people. The Great Rose's people. They say the lord has asked for peace and forgiveness. The king's troops are pursuing the clansmen into the highlands. They come this way bringing destruction with them. There is not a field left unburned to the south and west of us, lady. So they say."

"Go back down to the high road, Ian," Fiona told him, "and learn whatever else ye can."

"The men on the road could use some water, lady," Ian told her, "and if I can give them some, they will not come up the castle road. They'll be those looking to loot anything, and bitter with their loss to the king. We have really little defense but to close the gates, and if we do, lady, then how can we learn what is happening?"

"I'll send water down to ye," Fiona replied, thinking that the boy was particularly intelligent and loyal.

The next morning Nelly said quietly to her mistress, "Have ye noticed that there are few castle folk about?"

Fiona nodded. "They are fleeing. I canna blame them."

"Should we not take the bairns and go to Hay Tower now, my lady?" Nellie gently asked her. "My Roddy knows where to find us. He has shown me a secret track that goes through the hills south and east toward Brae. We would be safe there. If the king's forces come this way, they will surely destroy Nairns Craig to revenge themselves on yer husband. If we are here, they may kill us and the bairns."

"If Alexander MacDonald has sued the king for peace," Fiona reasoned, "then Nairn should be coming home soon. This castle has never been taken in war. Once the gates are closed, we are safe. Let us gather in all our stores. If the king's forces approach Nairns Craig, we will simply close our gates and wait for them to go away. When Nairn returns home, we will decide what to do. If the king will accept Alexander MacDonald's submission, he will certainly accept Colin MacDonald's submission as well."

The grain in their few fields was not ready for harvest. If they were attacked, they must count the crop a loss. Fiona was glad she had been so chary with last year's harvest. Her bins within the castle walls were more than half full. They could eke those stores out over a winter if necessary. Anything edible, however, was gathered up and brought into the castle. When the time came, they would drive what cattle and sheep they could behind the walls. The poultry already lived there for safekeeping from fox and badger.

One morning Fiona realized that she, Nelly, and the children were virtually alone but for half a dozen elderly retainers and the boy, Ian. She gathered them all in the hall, saying, "If ye have family elsewhere with whom ye would shelter, ye may go. But be certain to return when the troubles are over. Ye will be welcomed." She watched as they all, but for the lad, hurried from the hall. She looked at him. "Do ye not wish to leave, Ian?"

"Where would I go?" he asked her. "Nairns Craig is my home."

"What of yer mother?" Fiona said. "Will she not want ye with her?"

"Me mam's dead," he said.

"And yer father is off with Nairn, I suppose," Fiona replied. "Ye have no grandparents to whom ye might flee?"

"There is only me da," the boy said.

"Do I know him?"

The boy shuffled his feet nervously but said nothing.

Suddenly Nelly gave a little gasp, her hand flying to cover the cry. Then she let her hand drop from before her mouth. "Yer Roderick Dhu's son, are ye not?" she asked, but she already knew the answer. Why had she not seen it before? Though only eleven, the lad was the image of her great, gangling gawk of a husband.

"Me mam died when I was born," Ian said. "They were handfast, and I be legitimate, mistress. Me grandparents raised me, but by last year both were dead. I was brought to serve in the castle. Me da were afraid to tell ye, mistress, lest ye not wed him."

"The big fool," Nelly said.

"Ye'll not be angry at me da, mistress, will ye?"

"Oh, come and give me a kiss, Ian," Nelly said. "Yer the easiest bairn I'll ever have," she concluded with a smile, hugging him.

"Then we are three, and the bairns," Fiona said quietly. "Ian, I think we have learned all we need to know from the men on the road. Go up on the south tower and watch. If ye see any armed party of men approaching, come and warn me. Nelly and I will keep the gates locked today just to be certain we are not taken unawares. Is there any other way into the castle but through the gates, lad?"

"There be a secret passage leading out into the forest behind the castle, lady, but only me da and my lord know of it. Me da told me of it and showed it to me before he left. He gave me orders to help ye and Mistress Nelly escape with the bairns if necessary." He held up a brass key. "This be the key to the door. There be no other, and the entry is so well hidden that even knowing it was there it would be difficult to find. We have a fine rabbit hole to escape through should the fox besiege our den, lady," the boy finished, then went to keep watch upon the roof.

"Wake the bairns," Fiona said to Nelly, "and feed them. See they are dressed warmly. From this moment on we must be ready to leave immediately should we be attacked."

"Why should we leave at all?" Nelly said. "Unless, of course, we wish to go to Hay Tower. For now we are safe here behind these walls, lady. Outside, the countryside is swarming with clansmen, and they do not care whose side we would espouse."

Nelly was probably right, Fiona thought, when she had been left alone. Still, it could not hurt to be prepared to flee if it became necessary. What would she take? It could not be a great deal, for they did not dare to have a cart. A cart would slow them down and make them prey to every returning highlander who came upon them. It could not be easily hidden in the trees if a troop of horsemen rode by. Still, she would find a place for the silver cups the Lord of the Isles had given Alastair as a baptismal gift and for the fine brooch the old Countess of Ross had given her daughter, Johanna. Moire Rose's silver mirror she would save for Mary.

Other than that, they could carry only as much clothing as they could stuff into the saddlebags, and food.

Fiona tried to remember what furnishings were at Hay Tower. They were scant, but she had raised her sisters in that cold heap of stones, and she would raise her children there as well. Eventually, when it was safe, she would find a means of contacting her siblings so that the children might be matched. She sighed. They would never wed with their equals, but at least their futures would all be secure. She owed it to Nairn to provide for the children.

Colin MacDonald. Had he survived, and if he had, why had he not returned home? Had he any idea how worried she was about him? She had been planning for a future without him, she realized. Was it intuition? And what of Nelly's husband? Was he alive, or was it possible that they were both widows now? She realized that she would have to remain at Nairns Craig until she was absolutely certain of exactly what had happened.

The countryside about them was almost unnaturally quiet during the next few days. The stream of returning clansmen on the road below the castle had become nonexistent. It was as if they were the only people left alive in the entire world. They knew they were not, however, for they could see the fires burning in the distance. The fires in fields, cottages, and chieftains' houses burned with an eerie light during the day, and bright red-orange during the night hours. The horizon was hazy blue with smoke. The fires came closer and closer to Nairns Craig, yet still there was no sign of Colin MacDonald.

Then one afternoon Ian scrambled down the ladder from the tower roof and dashed into the hall. "There's a large party of armed men several miles off, lady," he gasped. "They seem to be coming in this direction. Oh, lady, there are so many of them!"

"Alastair!" Fiona called to her son, who was now four years of age. "Go with Ian. He will watch from the roof and, when the men are nearer, will call down to ye. Then ye must come to the hall and tell me immediately, for the enemy will be upon us, I fear. Mary, watch Johanna. Nelly, come with me. We must be certain the gates are fast."

The two women ran out into the courtyard to check that the great wooden beams that they had lifted into place with Ian's help several days before were tightly in place. They were. Beyond it was the iron yett. Together the two women lowered an interior yett that was not used except in case of attack. If the enemy could batter the first yett and the gates down, he would find himself faced with yet another iron barricade to overcome. Content that their preparations were as good as they could be, Fiona and Nelly returned to the hall, bolting the door of the castle behind them. There was plenty of food within the castle, and an interior well for water. They could hold out indefinitely if they chose to do so. They waited.

Finally, Alastair came racing into the hall. "They be on the castle road, Mam," he called to Fiona, who jumped up to hurry to the tower roof.

Ian pulled her up the last step. "They're almost here," he said.

Fiona looked over the edge of the parapet. The sight was a very frightening one. The high road was filled with men on horseback and men-at-arms for as far as the eye could see. The castle road was overflowing with horsemen, and a very impressive host had arrayed itself before the castle gates. Fiona felt the blood draining from her face.

"Dear God!" she whispered. " 'Tis the king himself. The king has come to Nairns Craig, Ian!"

A horseman moved forward, banging his lance hard upon the gates so that a loud noise reverberated like thunder throughout the castle.

"Open in the name of the king!" he shouted.

Fiona stepped up onto the parapet of the walls, steadying herself with a hand on the stonework. "I will not open the gates to any man," she called down to them, "until my husband returns. Why does the king besiege the home of an innocent woman and her bairns?"

"Mistress Fiona," the king called up, "open yer gates! Yer husband, the traitorous MacDonald of Nairn, has come home." James Stewart signaled with his hand, and a horseman came forward leading another beast. The horseman was Roderick Dhu, and the animal he led was Colin MacDonald's great stallion, across which was slung a body.

"I have brought him back, lady," Roderick Dhu called up to her. His dirty face was wet with his unashamed tears.

Fiona thought her heart would break. She felt enormous grief for Colin MacDonald, a man who had loved her so unconditionally and whom she had grown to love. "The family burial ground is there," she said, pointing. "If ye would be so kind, my liege, to have yer men dig my husband's grave, I will allow ye entry to Nairns Craig after he is properly laid to rest. Have ye a priest among that rabble of yer retainers?"

"Aye," the king answered.

"Dig the grave next to his mother, whom we buried but a few weeks back. Yer men will easily find the spot." She stepped down from the parapet and out of their view. "When they are ready, come into the hall, Ian, and we will go out. Thank God yer father has survived."

"What will happen to us, lady?"

"I don't know," Fiona said quietly, and then she climbed down the ladder from the roof and went down into the hall.

"What has happened?" Nelly asked her fearfully.

"The king is outside our gates with yer husband, who has survived, and the body of Nairn. When Nairn's grave is dug we will go out. They have a priest with them. Let us dress the children properly so we may not be ashamed before the king." She hiccuped a sob but swallowed it hard, jamming the cry so fiercely back down her throat that it ached. She had no time now for grief.

When the grave had been dug, Ian came to tell them. From a corner of the hall he picked up his pipes, for he had been apprenticed to the castle's piper. The children were fearful. Fiona took a moment to calm them.

"Yer father is dead," she said quietly. "The king has brought his poor body home to us for burial. It is a kindly act," she lied to them. "He waits outside our gates. Ye will be respectful of the king, for he has the power of life and death over us. Do ye understand me, my bairns?"

"Am I now Nairn?" Alastair asked astutely.

Fiona shook her head. "No," she said. "The king will send us from this place, for yer father rebelled against him. Ye, my son, must not ever rebel against yer liege lord. The king will punish us for yer father's fault, but he is right."

"Is not my uncle Alexander king?" the boy asked, confused.

"There is but one king in Scotland, Alastair," Fiona told her son. "His name is James Stewart. Remember that, laddie."

The boy nodded.

"Now, let us go outside to greet the king and bury yer father," Fiona said, leading them from the castle.

Outside the gates the assembled men heard the sound of an interior yett being raised. It creaked and groaned as its ancient pulley drew it up. Some few minutes elapsed, and the second yett was slowly raised. Then the gates were flung open. Two women and three small children stood in the entry of Nairns Craig. A young lad led them forth, his pipes playing the MacDonald lament as they came. They walked with dignity, ignoring the king and his men as they directed their steps toward the graveyard. Neither James Stewart nor his men moved as the little party of mourners strode past them. They had faced many widows and orphans over the past few weeks, but none quite this close. The king had insisted upon coming to Nairns Craig when they found Roderick Dhu, wounded and protecting his lord's body on the field of battle at Lochaber. Not just a few men wondered why the king had singled out The MacDonald of Nairn and personally escorted his body home.

In the tiny family graveyard Fiona looked down at the shroud-covered body of her husband. "Let me see his face, Roderick Dhu," she said. She knelt by him, clucking in a motherly fashion. Drawing forth a small piece of cloth, she wet it with her own spittle.

"Nairn, Nairn, I'll not let ye go to yer grave with a dirty face," she said, fiercely scrubbing the black and sweat of battle that had dried upon his handsome visage. Then bending her head she kissed his cold, stiff lips.

"Godspeed, my lord. I really did come to love ye."

She rose and brought the children to gaze upon their father for the last time. "He loved ye all, my bairns," she said to the three solemn children.

This done, she ordered Roderick Dhu to draw the shroud back up over her husband's head. The body was laid in its grave. The king's confessor came to their side and prayed over the corpse. The pipes played mournfully as the dirt was shoveled over Colin MacDonald's dead body. Fiona stood stonily silent until the ground was once again filled in. Beside her, Alastair and Mary were weeping softly. Next to them Johanna stood, her fingers in her mouth, uncertain of what was happening.

When the burial had been completed, Fiona thanked the priest and the two clansmen in Stewart plaid who had helped them. Nelly could scarcely take her eyes from her husband. She caught his hand, squeezing it tightly, her other hand drawing Ian between them. She felt almost guilty that her husband had survived when Fiona's had not, but Fiona, seeing them, smiled.

"Better one than none," she said to Nelly. " 'Twas God's choice, not ours, lass. Just remember to pray for Nairn's good soul." She took her children, the others following her, and walked to where the king sat upon his horse. Reaching him, she curtsied low.

A tiny smile touched the king's lips upon seeing the tiniest of the children, a wee lass, struggling to emulate her elder sibling.

When they had made their obeisance, Fiona stood proudly and held out her hand, offering James Stewart the keys to the castle.

Gravely he took them from her. "We will speak later," he told her. "For now I am hungry and long for a good supper."

"Alas, my liege," Fiona said, "I regret I canna oblige ye. The servants departed the castle when they learned of yer victory. Food, I have, in quantity, but no servants to prepare it. There is a rabbit stew, some bread, and cheese Nelly and I have prepared for our supper, but it will not feed this army ye have brought to my gates."

"Were ye not expecting me, then, my lady Fiona?" he asked her, laughing softly at the predicament she found herself in at this moment.

"I did not intend to ask ye to supper, my liege," Fiona replied, and about them those nearest, hearing her retort, chuckled.

"Ye have not changed," the king told her. "I shall share yer meager rations provided the bairns don't suffer hunger."

"Then come into Nairns Craig," Fiona invited him, "although I canna say yer welcome."

Chapter 16

Fiona and Nelly went to the kitchens to see with what, if anything, they might supplement their scanty fare to serve the king and the three lieutenants who had entered the castle with him. To their relief they discovered two fat geese hanging in the larder. The geese were quickly put upon the spit for roasting. Ian took a line and went down to the stream, caught half a dozen small trout in quick order, brought them back, and prepared them so Nelly might broil them.

"Yer a handy laddie," she noted approvingly.

"Me gran and old da were not young. I helped where I could. Old da taught me to fish. 'Tis not difficult if ye know how," Ian said.

At last the meal was ready. Roderick Dhu had kept the king and his men supplied with wine and ale so that they barely noticed the time going by. It was pleasant to sit in a warm hall instead of out in the forest or on a damp hillside.

"Go and put on a clean gown," Nelly said, chasing her mistress from the kitchen. "Yer the lady of Nairn until he says ye ain't, and ye must sit at the high board with him. Ian can look after the bairns. Roddy and me will do the serving."

Fiona hurried through the hall unnoticed and, reaching her own chamber, washed herself in the basin. She put on a clean chemise, her emerald-green undergown, and finally the green-and-gold-brocade surcoat

Colin had brought her from the sack of Inverness. She had never before worn it, but tonight it somehow seemed appropriate. She could almost hear Nairn's laughter at her choice. Digging through her chest, she pulled out a gilded leather girdle and affixed it about her hips. Brushing her long dark hair out, she parted it in the center and gathered it into a gold mesh caul. She peered at herself in her small mirror. Her color was high, but she was surprisingly calm for a woman who had just learned of her husband's demise and buried him that same afternoon. She wanted to cry, but she would not until she could have her privacy. She would not go into her hall tonight with red and puffy eyes. This was the second time James Stewart had taken away the man she loved. She would not give him the satisfaction of knowing that she grieved. He had no right to gloat over her misfortune. After sliding her feet into her house slippers, Fiona went to the hall.

The king, from a comfortable chair, raised a sandy eyebrow. "Ye would join us, madam?"

"With yer permission, my liege. Until ye tell me otherwise, I am still mistress of this castle," Fiona responded quietly with dignity. She signaled to Roderick Dhu. "Tell Nelly we are ready to be served," she told him. "My lords, will ye come to the table, please?"

She gave the king the place of honor, as was his right, seating herself on his left and letting his three men decide for themselves where they would sit. Nelly and her husband hurried forth with the meal. The two geese had been roasted to a turn. The trout lay broiled in butter and wine upon a silver salver. The rabbit stew had gained a flaky pie crust over its top. There was a bowl of small peas and tiny onions, bread, butter, and cheese. The table was set with white linen, and the single silver candelabra glittered with beeswax candles. On the far side of the table were lain fresh ferns and rose petals.

"Since ye needed the time to regain strength," Fiona said sweetly, "we were able to prepare a more substantial meal for ye, my liege."

"Do ye think to cozen me with a good supper then, madam?" he asked, spearing a piece of goose. "Ye might well."

"I seek nothing from ye, my liege, but what ye would give me. My concern is for my bairns. I am a woman, and not concerned with politics. I advised my husband to take his small troop to ye and not to his brother. I can but regret that he did not heed my advice."

The king nodded. "Nairn was a fool!"

"Nay," Fiona contradicted him. "He was loyal to his clan, for that, my liege, is how he was taught. Had ye spent more of yer life in Scotland instead of England, ye would understand that."

The king's three lieutenants looked at one another behind the king's back. The lady was brave, but then they had seen her at Inverness, and knew that.

"Madam," the king said, "ye tread upon thin ice with me."

"I will not allow ye to speak ill of Colin MacDonald," she retorted. "He was a good man for all his foolish choices, and he is now dead while ye sit in his place, in his hall, eating his food."

Suddenly the king laughed. "Fiona Hay, what am I to do with ye?"

"That, my liege, is what I would know."

"I must think upon it," he said. "Ye have my word that no harm will come to ye, yer bairns, or yer servants, however."

"I thank ye," Fiona answered him. "Will ye spend

the night within my walls, sir? I will have the guest chambers made ready for ye and yer men. 'Twill not take long."

"Aye, I will," James Stewart said. "I am tired of the outdoors, and welcome the warmth of yer castle, lady."

"Ye will excuse me, then," Fiona replied, "while my servant and I make ready for ye. Roderick will remain to serve ye, and Ian will play his pipes for yer amusement, my liege." She arose and moved from the hall, Nelly in her wake.

"A spirited mare," one of the king's companions, Duncan Cummings, said. "Have ye decided her fate? Will ye choose her a new husband?"

"As I told the lady," the king responded shrewdly, "I have not decided yet. I know this lady from old, and she is not an easy woman. She has perhaps too independent a spirit. My uncle of Atholl thinks her too clever by far. I believe he may be right."

The morning was gray and chilly as James Stewart descended into the hall of Nairns Craig. A warm meal was ready to be served. The king and his three companions were pleased with the freshly cooked food. Their hostess sat by the fire, her children playing about her. It made a pretty picture, the king thought, and she had deliberately calculated it, it was certain. Finally, when the food had been cleared from the table, the king called to Fiona.

"Come, madam," he said in a stern voice. "I have made my decision as to what to do with ye and yer children."

Fiona rose. She was dressed this morning, he noted, in a most practical fashion: a heavy wool skirt, a fine shirt, and a wool shawl. Bringing her children with her, she came to stand before him, then curtsied. "My

lord, I am ready for yer judgment. I can but pray ye will
be merciful for the sake of my three young bairns." Her
eyes were lowered.

She was a minx, the king thought. Angus was
right about her. "Madam, I have no choice in what I
must do. Yer husband broke his oath of fealty to me
when he took up arms against me. I canna punish him,
for he is dead, but if I don't punish ye, I will appear to
be a weak king. Ye have one hour in which to pack
what belongings ye can, and then ye will leave Nairns
Craig, which I will burn as the MacDonalds burned my
town of Inverness. Ye may take nothing but what ye can
carry yerselves. Do ye understand?"

"I want my horses," Fiona said coldly.

"Ye are in no position to make bargains with me,
lady," he snapped.

"My liege," Fiona said in a firm voice, *"I want my
horses."* She drew in a deep breath to calm her thunder-
ing heart. "Ye canna send me and my servants out upon
the high road totally destitute and without our horses.
Look at my bairns! They are no more than infants. Do
ye expect them to walk all day? They will die before we
reach safety. Colin MacDonald broke his faith with ye,
but I have not done so."

"My lord, ye will not appear weak if ye offer the
lady Fiona her horses," Duncan Cummings said. "Ye
are burning her home and the bulk of her possessions.
She is widowed, her bairns orphaned. A tiny modicum
of mercy would not be taken amiss. Indeed, ye would
be thought a just king for this show of leniency toward
a helpless woman whose ungrateful husband rose in rebellion against ye. The church, I am certain, would approve yer actions." He nodded at James Stewart.

"Aye!" his two companions agreed in unison.

Fiona kept her eyes lowered. She fell to her knees

before the king in a gesture of submission. Would he refuse her? she wondered, truly frightened. She desperately needed those horses; Holy Mother, let him say aye!

"Very well, madam," the king finally agreed. "Ye may have yer horses, but yer cattle and yer sheep are forfeit along with the rest of yer goods and chattel but that which ye can carry."

"Oh, thank ye, my lord!" Fiona cried. Catching his hand, she kissed it gratefully, scrambling to her feet as she did so.

"One hour, madam," he said sternly.

She curtsied, then slowly withdrew from the hall, the children following behind her. The four men watching her go were impressed with her dignity. She had accepted the punishment upon her husband's family honorably. So many wives of the defeated howled and fussed.

Ian was waiting for her outside the hall. With a nod he took Johanna from her and signaled to Alastair and Mary to follow him. Fiona hurried to her own apartment, where Nelly and Roderick awaited her.

"We have the horses!" she said triumphantly.

"I'll ride his lordship's stallion," Roderick Dhu said. "Ian will take my animal; Nelly, the white mare; and ye, the gray gelding. Young Nairn will have his pony. I took the two beasts we will use for pack animals down into the forest behind the castle this morning. They are fully loaded with the items ye and Nelly packed early yesterday."

"I've packed plenty of food from the kitchens," Nelly said briskly. "We'll not have to exist on oatcakes forever. I've cheese, bread, and apples that Ian and I gathered from the orchard, salted meat, and a fat goose I roasted this day!" she finished with a grin.

"I don't know what I would do without ye two," Fiona said gratefully. "I could not do this without ye. When we are safe at Hay Tower, ye are free to leave me for Brae should ye choose. I can ask no more of ye than ye have already given me." Fiona took the hand of each servant and squeezed. "Thank ye."

"We'll not leave ye, lady," Nelly said in a determined voice.

"Ye have not seen my wee tower," Fiona said with a small laugh. "After Brae and Scone and Nairns Craig, it will seem a verra poor place."

Roderick Dhu patted her shoulder. "Lady, we will survive together. I would not leave young Nairn as I did not leave his father."

Fiona felt the first twinge of guilt in many years at Roderick Dhu's words. Like everyone else, he believed Alastair to be Colin MacDonald's son and heir. She wondered if she would ever be able to tell her child the truth, or if, perhaps, it would be better left unsaid.

"We will take the horses through the inner passage that opens out into the forest," Roderick Dhu said.

"Where is the entry?" Fiona asked him, surprised.

"In the stables, lady. When the passage was first excavated, it was thought better that it open into the stables rather than into the castle itself. That way, should an enemy discover it, that enemy could not enter the castle directly. Before I left with my lord, Ian and I inspected the passage carefully and swept it free of debris from creatures. Ian has kept it during my absence. Also, I oiled the lock and the hinges on the door at the end of the passage that will open out into the forest."

Fiona nodded. "Ye have prepared well."

"We canna ride our beasts through the passageway, as the ceiling is but a wee bit above my head,"

Roderick Dhu explained. "Let us go then, for Ian will be waiting for us with the bairns."

The two women donned warm wool cloaks over their garments. Fiona looked about the rooms where she had lived with Colin MacDonald. But for the children, it almost seemed a dream now. She followed Nelly and her husband from the apartment, dry-eyed. She had no time for weeping now. She had to think of the children.

They crossed to the stables. The courtyard was quiet, as the king had not yet allowed his soldiery in to loot Nairns Craig before he fired it. The horses were saddled and waiting, as were Ian and the three little ones. Roderick Dhu went to the back of the stables and opened a door. Lighting a torch, he showed Fiona the passageway, which slanted downward like a ramp.

"It goes beneath the walls and down the hillside," he explained to her. "We will have to carry torches to see the way. I hope the bairns are not fearful, for 'twill be darker than night."

Alastair was mounted upon his pony, and insisted on taking his sister Mary up behind him. The little girl grasped her brother about his middle, hanging on for dear life. Roderick Dhu went first, carrying a large torch to light the passage. Behind him and the stallion came Alastair and Mary, who could ride the pony without fear for their heads in the low passage. Fiona was next, leading the gelding with one hand, holding a torch with the other. She was followed by Nelly, who had Johanna upon her hip and led the white mare. Last was young Ian, who after carefully closing the door behind them and bolting it from the inside, picked up the reins of his father's horse and his torch to bring up the rear.

They moved slowly, carefully down the tunnel. It

was dank and chilly within the passageway, but they
knew the outdoors would be no more welcoming. The
torches flickered eerily along the stone walls; the light
they gave was almost ominous. To Fiona's surprise the
children were very quiet as they traveled the length of
the underground corridor. Finally, to everyone's great
relief, Roderick Dhu said, "Ah, here's the end." They
heard him fit the key in the lock of the dark wooden
door. There was an audible click, and then the door
swung open, revealing a tangle of brambles. Roderick
Dhu sliced through the growth until they were able to
lead their horses through. Free of the blackness of the
stone walls, they all breathed easier.

Roderick Dhu helped his lady and then his wife
into their saddles. Nelly had Johanna before her. He
transferred Mary from her brother's pony to his son's
mount, stilling the children's protest when he said, "We
have a long way to travel today, and the wee pony will
be tired enough at day's end just carrying young Nairn,
Mistress Mary. Ye would not want to kill the poor
beastie, would ye?"

Mary shook her head, her eyes large. "No, Roddy,"
she said, then smiled when he blew her a kiss.

Mounting the big stallion, Roderick Dhu led the
little party onto a barely discernible path and into the
deep forest. Shortly they stopped. The clansman
slipped into the brush on foot to emerge a few minutes
later with the two heavily laden pack horses. "The king
will be surprised to find little of great value at Nairns
Craig," he said with a wicked grin.

They rode on for several hours in the damp
weather, finally stopping to rest the horses and feed the
children. They found themselves upon the crest of a
hill. Looking back, they could see the flames that were

consuming Nairns Craig. The clansman's stare was black.

"How many of Nairn's men survived Lochaber?" Fiona asked him. It was the first time she had actually had the opportunity to discuss the battle with him. "Were there any besides yerself?"

He shook his head. "No, lady. All were killed. I escaped because I was with my lord. He and I stood off those who tried to prevent the Lord of the Isles' escape. When my lord was mortally wounded and died—it was a quick death, lady; he did not suffer—I stayed by his body, defending it from mutilation. The king came, saw us, and forbade that any kill me. Loyalty such as mine, he said, was a rare and valuable quality. Then, lady, he looked at Nairn, and when he recognized him, he said that he would bring his body home for an honorable burial even though Nairn had not acted honorably toward him."

"He understood Nairn no more than Nairn understood him," Fiona said sadly. "I am glad my husband's death was quick, Roderick Dhu. I wish I had the means by which to reward ye for yer fidelity. The king was right when he said it was a rare quality."

"I have my lord's claymore within the luggage," the clansman said. "I have saved it for the young Nairn. I will teach him how to use it when he is old enough, lady."

They traveled farther and farther away from Nairns Craig, going south, then east toward Ben Hay. They stayed off the high road, taking a longer but safer route. At first the children were amused by the journey, but after several days Alastair and Mary began to whine and complain that they wanted to go home to Nairns Craig. They were damp, and they were chilled, and they were tired.

They rode on. Suddenly, the land about them began to take on a familiar look. Through the fog and mist of a September afternoon Fiona saw Ben Hay. Within the hour they were toiling up its steep sides. Reaching the top, Fiona looked about her. She was dismayed. While the tower itself was intact, the few outbuildings were gone. Had the king kept his promise to her to repair the roof? She drew forth the key to the door, which she had carried with her since the day she had left Ben Hay. She fit it into the lock and turned it. The door creaked open, and she breathed a soft sigh of relief. The hall was swept clean, and there was some turf and dry wood by the fireplace. At least they would be warm tonight.

"We'll have to stable the horses inside with us," Roderick Dhu said. "At least until we can get some sort of stable built for them."

Fiona nodded and led her gelding inside, the others following close behind. "There's a cellar beneath the tower," she said. "Go down, Ian, and see if there is any straw there so we may bed the animals." Climbing the stairs to the second floor of the tower, she shook her head. It was dank and full of cobwebs. She climbed to the third-floor attic, where old Tam and Flora had slept, sighing as she saw that the roof had not been repaired and was leaking. She hoped the autumn weather would turn dry and warm, as it often did, so they might make the repairs necessary to Hay Tower. Back downstairs, she found one end of the hall strewn with straw, and the horses being watered and fed with the remaining precious fodder they had brought with them for when their beasts could not browse. There was a fire in the fireplace, and Nelly had several pots hanging over the flames, from which some delicious smells were rising.

The children were playing happily near the warmth of the hearth.

"The roof leaks," she told Roderick Dhu. "The king did not keep a promise he made me long ago to repair it. He thought I should not return, I suppose." She could but hope he deposited the merks as promised. She suspected they would not find the cattle either. During their journey Fiona had told Roderick Dhu the truth of how she had come to be Nairn's wife. He had been somewhat taken aback, but then he had told her he understood. Afterward Nelly had said her husband agreed that the king had badly used Fiona and Nairn.

"The roof is easily fixed when the rain stops, lady," the clansman answered her. "We'll make a shelter for the horses that the wolves canna breach in the winter. We have time before the cold weather."

Along their route that day they had caught several rabbits. Ian had skinned one for his stepmother. Nelly had put it in one of the pots with wild carrots and onions. Now it bubbled enticingly. "I'll make some bread tomorrow," Nelly said. "Praise heaven for the flour we brought along. I don't know where we'll get any more."

"We have wheat, do we not?" Fiona asked.

Nelly nodded. "Aye, several sacks."

"Then we'll grind our own flour. We used to do it when I lived here before. There is not a miller for miles. I'm certain the household implements are exactly where they were left when we departed Hay several years back. We'll look in the morning."

When the rabbit stew had been cooked, they shared it. Afterward they bedded down together in the hall by the fire. When morning came, they reheated what was left of their previous meal and finished it. Then, taking the children, Nelly and her mistress descended to the tower kitchen, which was located in the cellar of the building. Because the structure was atop the hill, the part of the cellar where the kitchen was located was higher than the rest of the level. There was a small door that opened out into an equally small walled kitchen garden.

"It's so overgrown," Fiona said sadly. "My mother began that garden. After her death Flora and I kept it up."

"But there are probably the same herbs ye grew yet there among the weeds," Nelly replied. "We've time to weed it before the winter sets in. We'll harvest what we can, and take seeds for next spring."

Fiona nodded. "Once I went to Brae I never did such humble work as cooking and cleaning, but I well know how, for there were none here but Flora, old Tam, and my sisters and me to do it." She began to search the kitchens, and to her delight found everything as they had left it when they went to Brae. It all needed sweeping and washing and cleaning, but the two women set to work with enthusiasm.

"My lord Alastair," Nelly said to the little boy, "please to watch over yer sisters while yer mam and I set this place to rights. Ye may play outside in the garden, for the day is fair."

The women worked hard while up on the tower roof Roderick Dhu and his son repaired the structure. It took them several days, but shortly Hay Tower was habitable once again. They began to stockpile fuel for the coming winter. Roderick Dhu chopped wood while Ian took Alastair out into the forest to search for fallen branches and kindling. Fiona and Nelly weeded the kitchen garden. To their delight, they found onions and carrots growing along with an abundance of herbs, which they harvested, carefully saving the seeds and putting them in packets which Fiona marked so they would know what they were planting come spring. Father and son hunted deer and were successful. The carcasses were hung in the kitchen larder.

On the second level of the tower were two rooms that had been bedchambers. Fiona and her children slept in the larger of the two, but she insisted that Nelly and Roderick Dhu have the other.

"Yer old servants slept in the attic," he protested. " 'Tis dry up there now that we've repaired the roof, lady."

"Should we be attacked," Fiona said, "the attic is too inconvenient a place for ye to be. Better yer here with us."

He did not argue further with her, for her logic could not be refuted. "Ian can sleep in the hall," Roderick Dhu said. "The lad's got ears like a fox and can hear a feather drop in the forest before the bird even knows it's gone," he said with a smile.

The tower was secure, warm, and dry. It was clean and, if sparsely furnished, at least neat. They were adding to their supply of fuel each day. The larder, while not full, was not bare. Still, they needed more than they had been able to carry with them from Nairns Craig if they were to survive the winter. They found the remains of their old cart, which had been left behind, the laird having supplied his own transportation for them when they left. Together father and son repaired the vehicle so they might take it down the ben to seek what they needed.

"Ten miles past Brae," Fiona told Roderick Dhu, "is a village that has a market every Wednesday. Ye can get what ye need there. See if ye can find a few laying hens, perhaps a milk cow, some flour to supplement what Nelly and I have ground from our wheat supply, a large basket of apples, and whatever else ye think we need to get through the winter. Be discreet, and if any should grow suspicious, claim to be from a village farther north that traitorous clansmen wiped out before the king's men rescued ye." She dug into the pocket of her gown and handed him some coins. "These should pay for what we need."

Roderick Dhu and his son were gone for two days. When they returned there was a brindled cow tied to the back of the cart. Two greyhounds loped alongside the rickety vehicle. "The bitch is past her prime, and her last offspring, a male, is blind in one eye. The owner was willing to take a penny for them." He grinned. "They may not be perfect, but they have ears to hear an intruder, and they can still hunt." He bent down, patting both dogs. He lifted a basket from the cart. "I found this, and her bairns along the road back," he said. "I thought the lasses would like them."

Mary and Johanna squealed in unison at the sight of a black cat with a white spot on her chest, and her two kittens. One was a gray tiger stripe. The other was white with patches of ginger.

"They'll keep the tower vermin free," Fiona noted dryly.

Roderick Dhu had been very resourceful. In addition to the items Fiona had suggested, he had also brought several sacks of onions, a basket of pears, two hams, six small wheels of cheese, a loaf of sugar, and some spices—not to mention half a cart of turf for the fire, atop which were set several barrels of ale and one small barrel of wine. In the next few days they carefully stored the food items while the two dogs and the cat and her kittens made themselves at home.

The clansman had opened a little section of the tower wall beyond the kitchen, and using the stones he

had removed along with wood from the collapsed outbuildings, he built a stable for the milk cow and for the
horses. Together he and Ian thatched the roof. The laying hens he had found would also be housed at night
there, keeping them safe from predators.

"We should survive the winter verra well now,"
Fiona said quietly one night as they finished a simple
supper. "No one will find us here. In the spring, Roderick, ye and Ian will go to Perth to see if the king kept his
promise to deposit my silver merks with Martin the
Goldsmith. The cattle I am owed I don't think we will
get, although I will be bold and ask for them."

"Why would ye think yer silver is in Perth, lady?"
Nelly said. "King James promised ye he would repair
our tower for yer return one day, but he did not do so.
Is it likely that he kept his other promises?"

"We must pray that he did," Fiona said.

The winter was cold but not particularly hard.
Only twice did they hear the wolves howling outside
the tower, but the barking dogs seemed to persuade the
wolves to move on. They did not go hungry, but neither were they ever really full. Fiona and Nelly rationed
the food carefully and nothing was wasted. On March
fifth Johanna was two years of age. Alastair would be
five in June, and Mary four in September. Nairns Craig
was fading from their minds, and they rarely asked now
when Colin MacDonald would join them. They saw no
one, heard no news. It was as if they were the only people left upon the earth.

Then one May morning, up the ben and through
the forest came a familiar figure. He strode along,
whistling, his brown robes swinging about his ankles as
he came. The children saw him first, and, startled, ran
shouting for Roderick Dhu. The big clansman came

forth, his claymore in his hands. Seeing who their visitor was, he handed the weapon to Ian and went forward to greet Father Ninian.

"How did ye know we were here?" he asked the priest.

"The lady Fiona told me her history when we first met."

Fiona stood in the door of the tower, a smile upon her face. "Welcome, good Father," she said. "Come in, and let me give ye a cup of wine to slake yer thirst. Will ye stay with us tonight?"

"Gladly!" the priest said, his eyes taking them all in. They were thin, but certainly not beaten down. He had worried about Fiona when he learned that Nairns Craig had been destroyed. The king had assured him, however, that he had given Fiona, her children, and three servants their freedom, their horses, and whatever they could carry away from the castle. James had thought it generous, but Father Ninian had pointed out that a woman and three small bairns were going to be hard put to survive the winter without shelter.

"Tell us all the news!" Fiona demanded when Ninian had been seated by the fire and a cup of wine pressed into his hand. "Ye are the first outsider I have seen since we left Nairns Craig. At least Roddy and Ian went down the ben to find us supplies last autumn."

Father Ninian looked about the hall. There was a high board with a long bench behind it. His was the only chair in the hall. Upon a narrow side board were set the six cups the Lord of the Isles had sent Alastair for his baptism. It was all very simple. He took a deep breath.

"The rebellion is over," he began. "At least for the time being. On the eve of Saint Augustine in November, Alexander MacDonald came into Holyrood Church in

Edinburgh attired only in his shirt and drawers. The church was full. The Lord of the Isles was forced to come up the aisle upon his knees to the high altar, where he presented his claymore, holding it by its tip, to the king, who took it by the hilt and broke it. The Lord of the Isles then begged the king's forgiveness, admitting his faults and saying aloud for all to hear that he deserved nothing less than death. The king was quite willing to see the Lord of the Isles executed, but the queen publicly begged him to show mercy. And so he did.

"Alexander MacDonald is imprisoned in Tantallon Castle in east Lothian. It is virtually impregnable, lady, protected by the sea on two sides and by earthworks and ditches blocking the other approaches. It is a stronghold of the Douglases, who are again back in favor with the king. Undaunted, however, the lord's people have chosen his first cousin, Donald Ballach, to oversee the lord's power during his captivity. Donald Ballach is a hothead. The clansmen will rise again."

"So Alexander MacDonald has escaped death while Colin MacDonald lies in a cold grave, his castle in ruins, his family reduced to poverty," Fiona said bitterly. "Damn him—and all who war—to hell!"

The priest could not say he disagreed with her. "What can I do to help ye, lady?"

"When the king forced me north, he swore to repair my tower for my return, and he pledged me two dozen cattle and a virile bull—and he promised to deposit five hundred silver merks with Martin the Goldsmith in High Street in Perth. But when I returned to Hay last autumn, the tower was not repaired. Roderick Dhu made the repairs himself with Ian. I don't know if the merks are on deposit, and I don't have my cattle. How can I live, good Father, without the coin and the cattle? The king has taken everything from my children but the little we could carry from Nairns Craig. My son will have no property but mine one day. It is not much, and will not bring him a wife of good family. I will have to settle him with some minor chieftain's daughter, and he deserves better. And what of Nairn's daughters? How will I dower my lasses without my silver? I have endured much for the king, good Father. I ask naught of him but that which he promised me. Can ye help me?"

"I will go to him, lady, and I will plead yer case. There is no guarantee that he will heed my words, but I promise ye I will do my best. I agree that it is unfair of the king to abandon ye now."

"Thank ye, good Father."

"If yer silver is with the goldsmith, what will ye have me do?" the priest asked Fiona. "Will ye have me bring it to ye?"

"Bring me but fifty merks," Fiona told him. "It will be more than enough to support us for some time, and the rest will remain secure in Perth. We are safe upon the ben, for none know that we are here. In my sisters' time we were fairly self-sufficient. I can be so again. As long as we remain upon the ben, not showing ourselves, none will disturb us. As Roddy and Ian are not known hereabouts, it is they who will seek out what we need from the villages. Eventually we will not need to go down the ben at all, and I may raise my bairns in safety."

"We must speak privately, my daughter," the priest said.

Nelly, hearing him, gathered up the three children and took them off as her husband and stepson went outside again to continue their work.

"Yer son deserves to know his father," the priest said, coming directly to the point. "It is not fair ye keep

Alastair from Angus Gordon, my lady Fiona. I know ye
did what ye did to protect the lad, but Colin MacDonald is dead, may God assoil his good soul, and yer son
should know his rightful sire."

"Know his rightful sire, good Father, and then be
known as a bastard? No! Colin MacDonald was my
son's father, if not by blood, then by love and caring. I
will not take that away from either of them." Fiona's
eyes were filled with tears. She had not cried for Nairn.
There had never seemed to be any time to weep, but
now she was close to it.

"Angus Gordon did not know ye were with child
when he went to England to fetch the queen's cousin,"
the priest replied. "Even ye were not certain of yer condition, lady. Do not assign blame to Lord Gordon unfairly, my lady. 'Tis not right."

"I do not blame Angus," Fiona said. "But 'tis not
right that I tell my son the man he loved as his sire is
not his father at all, that he is bastard-born. And what
could Angus Gordon possibly want with my laddie?
No, better Alastair grow up believing he is the legitimate heir of Nairn, rather than the bastard son of the
laird of Loch Brae. What I once told ye was told under
the seal of the confessional. Ye canna divulge any of it,
good Father."

"No, I canna," he agreed with her, "but I still believe ye should make yer peace with the lord of Brae
and let him know his son."

Fiona shook her head. "Ye canna know what it is
to be a mother, but ye must believe what I do is best for
Alastair."

"I must bow to yer maternal instinct, lady," the
priest said. She was a strong woman, he thought. She
would need to be if she intended staying here on her
isolated ben to raise her children. All her efforts must

be directed toward their survival. Somehow it did not seem right. He could not break her confidence, but if Brae should learn of her return, the priest wondered just what he would do. He had not married. Did he love her yet? Could they be reunited? He must pray for guidance.

He had broken the seal of the confessional when he had told James Stewart that Alastair was Angus Gordon's son, and not the son of The MacDonald of Nairn. He had done it to protect the boy, however, and God would surely forgive him for it. His royal cousin was a ruthless man when he chose to be. Executing a child whose father had rebelled against him was not beyond this king. James Stewart had made it very plain from the beginning of his reign: He would have all of Scotland, no matter the cost.

Father Ninian departed Hay Tower the next day, traveling south instead of northward. He found his cousin, James, summering in the hills above Scone. The king was surprised to see him, for Ninian did not usually appear south at this time of year. The queen, who was great with child, was pleased, however, to greet this one Stewart cousin who was totally without ambition, and therefore of no danger to her beloved husband. The royal couple sat alone in their private day room with the priest. Wine and sugar wafers had been served by discreet servants. The windows were open, and a light breeze, scented with early heather and roses, blew through the chamber.

"Why have ye returned, cousin?" the king asked him. "Is there some news ye must bring me that canna wait to come through our usual channels? I don't believe I have ever known ye to come south this early."

"Have ye told the queen of the lady of Nairns

Craig, James? It is of her I would speak to ye," the priest began.

The king looked distinctly uncomfortable. "No," he said curtly. Then he turned to his wife. "Would ye leave us, my love? This matter is not yer concern, and I would not have ye distressed in yer condition."

"Why would *this matter* distress me, James?" the queen asked him shrewdly. "Yer secrecy but intrigues me." She smiled mischievously.

"Joan," he pleaded with her.

"I should be far more *distressed* to have to leave ye, James, than to learn anything Father Ninian might tell ye." She looked to the priest. "Is this furtive matter so terrible that it would cause me to miscarry of my child, Ninian?" She cocked her head at him.

The priest smiled a slow smile. "I do not think so at all, madam. In fact I might use your good offices to aid me with yer husband."

"Oh, verra well," the king snapped. "Tell her all, Ninian, and then tell us why ye are here!" He crunched loudly on a sugar wafer.

Ninian Stewart briefly told the queen of Fiona Hay, and the queen was delighted to learn that Fiona had survived the highland uprising. "But," the priest said, "the king promised the lady in exchange for her valuable services a certain number of cattle and a virile bull. After Nairns Craig was burned, its lady made her way back to her childhood home, where she found the king had not repaired the tower as he had agreed to do when he sent her north with The MacDonald of Nairn. Her only manservant and his son were able to make the repairs so she and her maidservant and the bairns might survive the winter months in safety. It was not easy, cousins, but Fiona is a brave lass, and a good mother to her lad and two wee lassies.

"And, cousin, there is the matter of the silver merks ye promised to deposit for her with Martin the Goldsmith. I visited him before I came to ye, James," and here the priest's voice became severe. "No silver was ever put in Fiona's name. For shame, my lord! Ye must make amends and keep yer word. I would never allow Fiona to learn the truth of this matter. The lack of repairs can be explained away, but the rest canna, I fear."

"My treasury is not without end, Ninian," the king said. "We have the English to pay, and they are not patient."

"Ye gave yer word," the priest said sternly.

"Oh, verra well," the king snapped. "I will deposit the silver."

"No. Ye will give it all to me. I will see it is put safely with the goldsmith. Now, we have the cattle to discuss, cousin."

"A dozen, it was, I believe," the king said.

"Two dozen, and a virile bull," the priest replied firmly.

The queen giggled, unable to help herself. This caused her spouse to look very aggrieved.

"Two dozen, then, and that damned virile bull, too. Now, are ye satisfied, Ninian?"

"I am, and I will escort the cattle myself. They canna go by way of Brae. Fiona has told me the way to bring them, and her man will meet me at an assigned place, where yer people will turn the cattle over to him. That way her location will remain secret to strangers who might consider a woman in an isolated ben fair game."

The king nodded. "As always, she is a canny woman," he said, his tone one of grudging admiration.

"Tell me of her bairns," the queen said eagerly. "She has a son, does she? Ah, she is fortunate!"

"Alastair is a fine lad, and Fiona's daughters, Mary and Johanna—named for ye, my lady—are pretty little lasses," the priest told the queen. "They resemble their father, Nairn, verra much."

"And the lad?"

"He is dark-haired like his mam."

"And this is all that has brought ye back south?" the king demanded of his cousin.

"Like ye, I have a passion for justice to be served. When I return to Hay it will be." Ninian's warm amber eyes twinkled.

"Does Brae know of her return?" James Stewart asked.

"Brae knows naught of Fiona since the day she disappeared," the priest said quietly. "I have spoken to her, but she will have none of it, cousin. She will be independent, she says. I canna force her to reason, though I believe the bairns would be better off. 'Tis a hard life she has chosen, but she will be beholden to none."

The king made all the arrangements for the silver and the cattle, and Ninian left to go north.

At Hay Tower Fiona was delighted by the arrival of her cattle and the virile bull. Now she could survive! They had reclaimed several small fields upon the ben this spring, planting them with grain and hay. What deficiency they had in fodder could be purchased in the autumn. Ninian Stewart had brought Fiona all her silver, explaining that he feared the king might confiscate it at a later date from the goldsmith.

"Ye can hide it here within the tower," he told her. "At least ye need not fear James Stewart will take it back from ye if it is here."

"How can I ever thank ye, Father Ninian?" Fiona asked. "Ye are always welcome upon Ben Hay!"

The priest quickly departed then for the north, satisfied that justice had been served. He would come again in late autumn, he promised, on his way to his abbey.

The summer was surprisingly pleasant. If there were any troubles in Scotland, Fiona and her little family did not know of them, safe in their isolation. The cattle browsed upon the ben, carefully watched over by Ian and the dogs. Alastair, now five and tall for his age, had taken to following Ian into the meadow each day. He was not afraid of the cattle or the bull.

"He should be a little lord, not a cowherd," Nelly fussed.

Fiona laughed. "He is happier with a simple life."

"For now," Nelly answered her mistress. "But what of when he is older, my lady? Do ye have the right to deny him his birthright?"

It was a question Fiona had asked herself since the priest had pricked her conscience, but what else could she do? Even if Angus Gordon were not a married man, would he welcome her back into his life? She did not think so, but it was a moot point. Angus had a wife and no doubt several children, certainly another son, who would be considered the heir to Brae. She had told the priest she would not allow her son to learn that rather than being the true-born son of The MacDonald of Nairn, he was the bastard-born son of the laird of Loch Brae. And she would not. She would keep Alastair, indeed all her bairns, safe from harm of any sort. Safe from the hurtful outside world.

One summer's morning Alastair ran out early into the small meadow where the cattle grazed. He had grown to love the great shaggy beasts with their big horns. He knew them all by sight and, much to his family's amusement, had taken to naming the creatures.

"Good morrow Moibeal. Good morrow Milread," he called to two of them, and the cattle raised their heads to gaze benignly upon the lad. "Good morrow Narsali and Moireach, Giorsal and Sesi." Wandering among the herd, Alastair suddenly realized that Colla, the bull, was missing. "Colla!" he called. Usually the bull, an unusually mild fellow, would bellow softly back at the sound of his name, but this morning there was no reply. Alastair searched back and forth amid the cattle for him, but the bull was simply not there.

Where could he have gotten to? the little boy wondered. Would Ian get into trouble with his father and with Mam for the bull's disappearance? Colla had been there last night, Alastair knew, for he had bid all the beasts of the field a good night before he had gone inside for his supper. Had the bull been stolen? He was, after all, a very fine bull. They needed him. He was a good breeder, Ian said, for already ten of the herd were with calf.

Alastair's small brow furrowed in thought. There was, he remembered hearing his mother say in the hall, a fine meadow below in the glen. He recalled it because his mam and Roderick Dhu had spoken of possibly barricading their own meadow so the cattle would not wander. Was it possible that Colla had wandered down into the glen and found another meadow of good sweet grass? Alastair didn't wait to ask anyone's permission. He slipped into the forest and began to descend the ben. No one else was up yet, and by the time they were, he would be back with Colla.

Eventually the trees began to thin. Alastair forded a pretty little stream, jumping from rock to rock until he reached the other side. After passing through a grove of birch trees, he found himself in a beautiful large open meadow that was filled with fat cattle. "Colla!" Alastair called out, immediately hearing a soft bellow in reply. Laughing, he followed in the direction of the sound, sighting the bull placidly browsing on the thick, sweet grass, surrounded by an admiring group of females. "Colla, 'tis not yer meadow—or yer wives, ye old knave." Alastair picked up a stick and began to herd the bull back to where they had come from. "Come along now, Colla. We must go home before they find us gone, or Mam will be angry."

The bull moved reluctantly, slowly at the lad's insistence, meandering in rambling fashion across the meadow, stopping every now and then to munch another mouthful of grass. They had almost reached the edge of the pastureland when there was the sound of hoofbeats behind them. Surprised, Alastair turned about to see a dark man upon a large black stallion bearing down upon him. The boy stopped dead, afraid.

The horseman came abreast of them, and the rider dismounted. "Have I caught me a cattle thief?" the deep voice demanded as he towered over the child. He seemed very tall and very dark to Alastair, whose small heart thumped nervously.

"No, my lord," the lad finally quavered. "I am not a cattle thief. Colla, our bull, wandered down the ben into yer meadow. I wanted to fetch him back before Ian got into trouble for his loss."

The Earl of Brae looked down into his own face, reflected in miniature. Startled, he could feel the heart he had thought he no longer possessed crack achingly. Struggling to find his voice, he finally said, "What is yer name, lad? Where do ye come from?"

"I am Alastair MacDonald," the little boy replied

stoutly, "and I live upon Ben Hay with my mam, my sisters, Nelly, Roderick Dhu, and Ian."

"What is yer mam's name?" the earl asked, knowing it before the child even spoke it.

"Fiona," Alastair replied.

Angus Gordon shook his dark head slowly. He did not know how he felt, but he certainly was not angry at the little lad. "I'll help ye take yer bull back home, laddie," he said gently. "Would ye like to ride with me upon my horse? Have ye ever seen a beast so fine?"

"Aye," Alastair told him frankly. "My father had a great war horse like yers, but his was as gray as storm clouds. My father was killed at Lochaber."

The earl remounted his horse, reached down, and took the boy up on the saddle before him. The child was light and thin against him. Then, using his mount and the boy's stick, Angus Gordon herded the big bull back up the ben and into its own meadow. His gaze took in the fine cattle grazing there. For a brief moment he wondered if he was missing any of his own beasts.

On the edge of the small upland pasture a boy of about twelve appeared. Seeing Alastair upon the earl's horse, he turned on his heel, racing for the tower house. The earl smiled almost grimly. By the time the lad had reached the tower, its door was wide open. At the top of the steps stood a small group of people. A very tall clansman, the boy, Nelly between them and very much with child, two little girls with red-gold hair, *and Fiona.*

The earl brought his horse to a stop. "Well, madam," he said in a stern voice, "what have ye to say to me?"

"I don't owe ye any explanations, Angus Gordon,"

Fiona said. "Now put my son down. Where did ye get him?"

"Like his mother before him, in my meadow, stealing my cattle, though he says the bull is yers," the earl taunted her.

"The bull is mine, and ye know it, Angus Gordon," Fiona snapped. "Now give me my son, damn ye!"

"Ye mean my son, do ye not, lassie?" he replied. "Am I a fool that I canna see myself in the lad's face?"

"Put Alastair down," Fiona said quietly. "I will not stand upon the step arguing with ye, Angus. We will talk, but not here."

"Aye, we will talk, lassie," he said, "but we will talk at Brae. I am taking the lad with me, and when ye are ready to give me an explanation as to where ye disappeared to, and why *my* son thinks he is a MacDonald, ye will be welcome at Brae."

"My lord!" Her voice was anguished. "Don't shame the lad!"

"What are ye talking about?" he demanded. "This child is my son, and my heir, and ye have kept him from me by deception. I want to know why, and by God, madam, ye will tell me!"

"So," she snarled at him, "yer fine English wife has not been able to give ye an heir, Angus! How unfortunate, but she will not have *my* son to call hers. Set him down, or I will kill ye!"

"My English wife?" He looked absolutely puzzled. "I have no wife, English or otherwise, Fiona Hay."

"No wife?" Fiona looked astounded. "They said ye had a wife. That ye were wed to Elizabeth Williams."

What the hell was going on? "Who said?" he asked her.

"Angus, if ye ever really loved me, get down off that great beast of yers and come into my hall," Fiona pleaded. "We must speak, and it must be now. Please!" She held out her hand to him.

He looked at that hand, once soft and white, now roughened with work, and he felt tears pricking at the back of his dark green eyes. Lifting his son from his saddle, he handed him to the gangling, serious-faced clansman, then dismounted. "Verra well, lassie," he told her, his voice softening, "let us go into yer hall and speak of all of this." Turning to give Nelly a small smile, he said, "Is this fellow yer husband, then, Nelly? Yer aunt and uncle will be glad to know yer alive and safe with a good man."

"Aye, my lord, this is my husband, Roderick Dhu, and my stepson, Ian." Nelly looked at her mistress. "I'll take the lasses to the kitchen, my lady. Alastair, go back out into the meadow with Ian and Roddy, and begin building that barricade. Ye don't want to lose Colla again." Taking the little girls by the hand, she went into the tower while the men went out into the field.

"Come, lassie," Angus Gordon said, and Fiona led him into the tower house. Looking about him, he thought little had changed. It was still a poor place, but it was clean and had an air of contentment about it.

Fiona indicated the single chair by the fire, and she poured him a goblet of wine from the carafe on the high board. "Yer throat will be dry from yer ride," she said quietly, handing him the goblet before sitting on a stool before him.

"What happened?" he asked her, unable to restrain himself any longer. "Where did ye go, and why did ye leave me, lassie?"

"I didn't leave ye, Angus. I was tricked into it . . . told ye were to wed with the queen's cousin as a reward for yer loyalty to James Stewart. Told I was to allow The MacDonald of Nairn to abduct me, then to spy upon the MacDonalds for king and country. I was too afraid to refuse, and I was not certain then I was with bairn."

"Then ye don't deny that the lad is mine?"

"Of course he is yers, but Nairn, bless him, was so in love with me that he believed the lad was his. He thought he took after me with his dark coloring. Then, too, Nairn's sire was dark. He was a good father to him, Angus. He loved Alastair above everything."

"Except ye," the earl observed. "The two wee lasses are his."

"Aye, they are. He was my husband, Angus. After he took me, he brought me to his brother's hall in Islay and handfasted me. I agreed, because by then I knew my condition. I didn't want Alastair bastard-born. And afterward when I was told ye had wed with Mistress Williams, I married Nairn in the bonds of the church."

"Who was responsible for all of this?" Angus Gordon asked her, but he already knew. There was but one person in Scotland powerful enough to have arranged this subterfuge.

"The king," Fiona answered him unhesitatingly.

After a long silence the earl said, "He has always professed to be my friend. He is no friend to me now."

"Don't condemn him too quickly," Fiona said. "Let me tell ye all of it, Angus," and she went on to explain every small detail of her life over the past few years. "I was verra angry and bitter toward James Stewart," she said as she neared the end of her tale, "but now I can see that he had to do what he did in order to maintain control over all of Scotland. A king does not have the luxury of friendship, Angus. He must do what is best for his country. So James Stewart has done, even to executing his own relations."

"Yer more forgiving than I am, lassie."

"I don't say I forgive him, Angus," Fiona said. "I simply understand now what he did better than I understood in the beginning. I will not forgive him for separating us. He betrayed us all. Ye, and me, and poor Nairn, may God assoil his good soul."

"Did ye love him?" he asked her bluntly.

"Not as I loved ye."

"But ye loved him?" he persisted.

"Aye, for it would have taken a hard-hearted woman not to have loved Nairn. He was a bonnie man, if misguided."

Angus Gordon nodded. He wasn't certain he fully understood her. "Come back to Brae with me," he said.

Fiona shook her head. "We canna just pick up where we left off five years ago, Angus."

"Why?"

"Do ye love me?"

"I have always loved ye, lassie. The king offered me Elizabeth Williams, but I would not have her. My family has dragged lass after lass beneath my nose, but none could hold a candle to ye, Fiona Hay. Aye, I love ye, and this time I am not ashamed to say it aloud. Come home to Brae with me, lassie. *I need ye.*"

"I will not deny ye the right to get to know yer son, Angus Gordon," she answered him, "but if ye would make me yer wife, and I will discuss no other arrangement with ye, ye understand, then ye must court me properly, my lord."

"Madam, ye try my patience!"

"I must be certain it is truly me ye still love," she told him, "that it is not just yer son ye want." Her look was direct.

"Brazen as ever," he said, a twinkle suddenly in his eye. Then to her surprise he rose from the chair, pulling her up from the stool. "Where, madam, is yer chamber?"

"Yer . . . yer . . . yer shameless, no, insolent, no, much too bold, my lord!" Fiona cried. But memories, long dormant, memories of lying in his arms were surfacing, and the blood rushed to her cheeks, staining them a bright pink.

"Yer chamber, lassie," he growled, taking a step even closer to her, then sweeping her up in his arms.

Fiona began to struggle in the cradle of his arms, even as he began to mount the stairs. "Put me down, ye great fool!" she said. "Do ye think I can be won over by yer manhood alone? I'm not some innocent and breathless lass." She squirmed. "Put me down!"

Angus Gordon began to laugh. He had missed her. God, how he had missed her! He reached the top of the stairs. "Which door?" he demanded of her.

"That one," she pointed, wishing she were not so weak-willed, but oh, she had missed him! She had never before allowed herself to even think of it. Not since Nairn had stolen her. Particularly when she had been his wife. But her husband was dead, and she was alive. Holy Mother, she was very much alive. Her heart was pounding as he set her on her feet, looking directly at her as he pulled off his garments. Fiona bit her lip in vexation. She had to make a decision. She could either run, or . . . She began removing her own clothing, and then they were both naked, standing before each other, and it was as if the years that they had been separated never existed.

Angus Gordon stepped forward. Taking her heart-shaped face between his hands, he bent his head, his lips brushing tentatively over hers. She was drowning in his dark green eyes, unable to look away, his name sounding over and over again in her head. His mouth closed over hers finally in a long, hard kiss. Fiona didn't know if her own eyes had closed or if she was just lost in his gaze. With a deep sigh she slid her arms up about his neck.

He drew her against him, his head spinning at the touch of her round, full breasts upon his chest. He had never forgotten the wonderful feel of her body against his. Her thighs pressed against him, her soft belly.

"Fiona," he murmured, his fingers swiftly undoing her plait, loosening the night cloud of her hair, which fell like a curtain about them. He caught up a fistful of it and sniffed it. "Heather," he said as the remembrances overcame him. "I can never smell it without thinking of ye, lassie." His mouth foraged over hers once again, their tongues exploring each other, renewing their acquaintance with each other.

His kisses were the headiest she had ever experienced. His lips moved over her face and her throat. His tongue teased within the shell of her ear before his mouth moved onward. He inhaled the very scent of her. Knees weakening, Fiona fell against his arm, exposing her bosom to his eager touch. His tongue licked at her; his teeth nibbled on her; his mouth suckled upon her flesh. Each sweet new assault brought a tiny cry of pleasure from her. She wanted to do naught but rest in his arms being adored.

He laid her upon the bed, and for a moment she regained her equilibrium. "Wait!" she begged him urgently. When he acquiesced, Fiona leaned over him, her dark hair caressing his hip, and she covered him with sweet hot kisses. To his surprise she took his manhood in her mouth, teasing it with her tongue, caressing his pouch with tender fingers, suckling upon him until he thought that he would die of the pure pleasure. She seemed to understand when he had reached the limit of her delicious torture, and rolling upon her back, she drew him down so they might kiss once more.

Fiona let herself melt into his strong, fierce embrace. She spread herself open to him and, with a cry of undiluted happiness, welcomed him into her body. Wrapping her legs about him, she encouraged his appetite until they were both senseless with the hot pleasure that engulfed them. He rode her with a sense of familiarity, and yet she was a different woman. She felt the hardness of him driving into her very depth, and cried aloud when her pleasure blossomed and burgeoned, and engulfed the two of them in a soaring spiral of fiery passion.

And afterward as they lay sated, their bodies relaxed and replete with pleasure, Fiona said, "Don't think ye can win me over so easily, Angus Gordon. I'm not yer mistress any longer, nor will I ever be again. I have been a wife, and a wife is what I will once more be."

"And a countess, too, lassie," he told her. "Ye were given a hard task to complete for the king, but I, his friend, was given an earldom for what I believed was my loyalty. 'Tis ye, my darling, whom I think more deserving of such an honor than I ever was. Now, don't be difficult with me, lassie." Positioning himself upon his elbow, he looked down into her beloved face. "Come home to Brae with me, Fiona. 'Tis where we all belong, and ye know it, even if yer too stubborn to admit it."

She looked up into his face. His dear, dear face. He was the man she loved, although it would be best, she thought, if he were kept just a wee bit in doubt of that. "Oh, verra well, Angus," she said to him. "If ye insist, I suppose we must go home to Brae. But be warned, I'll not go to court even if the king were to beg me upon bended knee. 'Tis too dangerous a place, even for a brazen wench like me."

"Ye'll have no time for the court," he told her firmly.

"And why is that?" she asked, laughing up at him.

"We have a great deal of time to make up, Fiona Hay," he said. "First the priest to marry us. And an earldom needs more than one heir and two wee heiresses. Ye and I have a great deal to do, lassie. I fear there will not be a moment for court or kings or anything else."

"No time but for our love, and for our bairns, and for Brae. 'Tis more than enough for me, my lord. Now," Fiona told him, her hand teasing him in a most sensitive spot, "if we're to service yer earldom with more bairns, my lord, had we best get started?"

"Brazen," he murmured, his lips brushing against her mouth. "Yer the most brazen woman I have ever known."

"And ye would not have me any other way," Fiona declared, kissing him hungrily. "Ye would have me no other way."

Afterword

In October 1430, Queen Joan bore twin sons. One survived and was called James, after his father. There were no other sons, although the queen bore a total of six daughters. As a king, James was respected and loved by the commoners. Sadly the jealousy, rapacity, and ambition that was the hallmark of the Scots nobility did not wane with his leadership. James I was assassinated on the night of February 20, 1437, in a plot devised by members of his own family. He was succeeded by his six-year-old son, James II.

As for Alexander MacDonald, Lord of the Isles, he was finally released from Tantallon. He served the Stewart king as Justiciar of Scotland faithfully and with diligence. Dying in 1448, he was succeeded by his eldest son, Ian, fourth and last Lord of the Isles.

Author's Note

Surnames were not really in use until the sixteenth century, nor were kilts, as we know them today, worn until the sixteenth century. Instead, a length of plaid was wrapped about a man. For clarity's sake, however, I have used surnames and put my men in kilts. As I pride myself on being historically accurate, I did want to be forthcoming with my readers.

If you have enjoyed *BETRAYED*, I hope you will take the time to write me at P.O. Box 765, Southold, NY 11971.

COMING SUMMER 1999

the eagerly anticipated new novel from the *New York Times* bestselling author of BETRAYED.

The Innocent
By Bertrice Small

Deceptively fragile looking, Eleanore of Ashlin had promised her life to God . . . until fate intervened. With her brother's untimely death, Eleanore—known as Elf to those who loved her—becomes the heiress of an estate vital to England's defenses. She is ordered by royal command to wed one of the king's knights rather than take her final vows. With resistant heart, but obedient to King Stephen's will, she complies.

Sir Ranulf de Glandeville is all too aware that his innocent bride wants no man; yet his patience, gentle hand, and growing love for his spirited young wife soon awaken Eleanore to passions she never knew or desired . . . until now.

But their love is not secure from the wicked schemes of an evil woman who hates Eleanore with all her heart—and who will seek to destroy the innocent in a depraved plot that will put Eleanore's life in jeopardy and her faith in love to its greatest test. . . .